HEIRS
OF THE
PROMISE

BOOK 1 OF THE IMMORTAL ARBITER SAGA

HEIRS
OF THE
PROMISE

LANGDON FRANZ

atmosphere press

I want to dedicate this book, first, to my wife, Katie. She supported me every step of the way and never had a problem with telling me when something just wasn't good. This book wouldn't have been made without her.

Second, I want to thank my father-in-law. He's never read a fantasy book in his life but was willing to open mine and stick with it to the end. His input was invaluable. Thanks, Papa!

Third, I want to thank my friend Ryan, who read Heirs of the Promise from front to back in one sitting, pre-edits. That's what true friendship looks like!

And finally, I want to thank my editor, Treena, who took the polished turd I gave her and turned it into gold. She is a true alchemist. *Heirs of the Promise* wouldn't be what it is if it wasn't for Treena. Thank you so much!

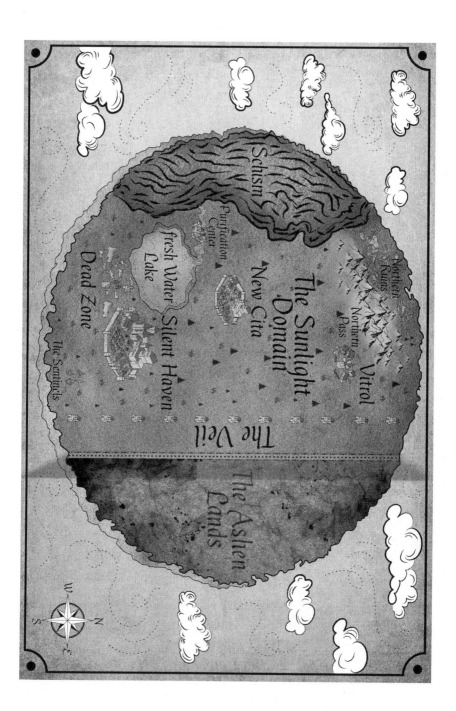

PART ONE

~ CHAPTER 1 ~

Kilal pressed the knife into his wrist, grasping for Immortality. A rusted porcelain sink caught the blood dripping from the open wound as he dragged the sharp blade through his flesh. With a precision gained by decades of practice, Kilal carved a tight circle, two inches in diameter. Next came a straight line from the top of the circle to the bottom. Each end protruded exactly one centimeter past the perimeter.

Every detail had to be perfect. Even a hair's width of inaccuracy would render the Carving obsolete.

Cutting a second path from left to right, the two lines intersected perfectly in the middle of the circle. Kilal paused and wiped sweat from his forehead with the back of his hand.

Bloody business can't keep their air conditioning running or something?

He returned the tip of the knife to his flesh and carved four more lines, enclosing the circle in a diamond. The pounding bass reverberating through the walls was barely more than a buzz. His focus seemed to do a better job than the walls at keeping the music at an acceptable level.

Kilal swapped the carving knife for a smaller blade suited for minute details. With a steady hand and careful attention to detail, he etched a tiny rune, no more than an inch long, in each of the four quarters of the circle. Breath held, Kilal moved the blade through his skin with an efficiency any Arbiter would envy.

Finished, he ran his wrist beneath water from the cracked and rusty faucet and examined the raw, open flesh representing the Carving of Immortality. Satisfied with his work, Kilal walked to the door of the restroom and jiggled the lock. It was secure. It would take more than what an average human was capable of to break through the door. He checked again anyway.

The door vibrated to the rhythm of the bass blasting behind it. Kilal clenched his teeth. His target just had to frequent a bloody club, didn't he?

Confident the door would halt any would-be visitors, Kilal strode into a stall and locked it. Taking a seat on the toilet, he chided himself for being so sloppy. How had he allowed himself to get stuck in a club full of humans hostile towards Arbiters with no active Carvings to defend himself?

"Bloody idiot," he muttered. "Get yourself together!"

Kilal pulled out a third blade—more a pick than a blade—and pierced the center of the Carving. Feet pressed against the stall legs, he locked his knees straight and shoved himself back against the toilet tank. He took a deep breath and rotated the pick one-hundred and eighty degrees clockwise.

The Carving flashed white, and the seizure hit him with the force of a War Plague.

Kilal shook. His body tightened, and his muscles spasmed. The stall vibrated with him. His legs kept him strained against the porcelain. The stall door knocked and rattled, the lock's rhythmic metallic *pinging* mimicking the bass still beating outside the bathroom. The convulsions lasted for what felt like an eternity, but eventually, it was over.

Breathing ragged, eyes half open, Kilal flipped himself over. His knees hit the floor just as the nausea reigned. Bitter bile spewed from his mouth and into the toilet, his already empty stomach twisting like a wrung cloth. Kilal spit, trying futilely to clear the acidic taste from his tongue.

Finished, he flushed the toilet and stumbled out of the stall, back to the sink. He splashed water over his face.

Hunching to fit his large frame into the view of the mirror, Kilal glared at the man staring at him. Pale, clammy skin. Dull, sunken eyes. Oily, dark hair brushing his shoulders. His beard was so thick and unruly, he couldn't remember the last time a razor had kissed his cheeks.

"Bloodshed and Oaths, you look like an Ash Fallen," Kilal said. "Or a man allergic to soap and water."

He ran his left wrist under the faucet again, washing the blood from his skin. When the water ran clear, Kilal stared at the smooth, unblemished skin—as if a blade had never touched him.

He again pulled out the first knife and pressed it against his forefinger. Time to test the Carving. Any good Arbiter worth their oath would. Gritting his teeth, Kilal sliced his finger off with one swift motion. It dropped and rolled into the sink. The finger didn't even reach the drain before white lightning crackled around the severed joint.

It wasn't enough to endure the sharp, throbbing pain of the Carving ritual. He also had to endure the excruciating agony that came with the healing. Instantly regrowing bone, muscles, tendons, skin, and organs was worse than the injury itself. Nerves searing, fibers and flesh regenerated and stitched back together.

Simultaneously numb and oversensitive, Kilal flexed the new finger. The one in the sink disintegrated into a pile of ash.

Immortality was his. For the next forty-eight hours, at least. Then he'd have the joy of Carving everything all over again.

One down, two more to go.

Kilal pressed the blade into his flesh again to work on the Carving of Gravitational Control.

When finished, Kilal returned to the stall. He drove his pick into the center of the Carving and activated it, just as he'd done before, though he wasn't able to flip himself around in time to vomit. Fortunately, there wasn't much left in his stomach. He only spilled a small amount of acidic spit onto his shirt. Unfortunately, any amount of bile still tasted terrible.

Kilal stumbled back to the sink and hovered over it for a moment. He took a few deep breaths before splashing water onto his face and into his mouth, trying to clear the vile tang.

Eyes closed, Kilal pictured the Carving of Gravitational Control as a knob. He 'grabbed' it and twisted it to the right, increasing gravity's effect on him. When dirty bathroom tiles groaned beneath his increased weight, he mentally returned the knob to normal.

Carvings one and two completed, he began his third and final, the Carving of Deific Strength.

The overhead light flickered. Kilal froze. It flickered again. His chest tightened and his breath caught in his throat. The third time the light flickered, ash began falling from the ceiling.

Kilal wrenched the knife from his wrist. It slipped from his fingers and clattered on the floor. He pinched his eyes shut and pressed the heels of his hands into his cheeks until it hurt.

It's not real. It's not real. It's not real. You're not there anymore. You escaped. It's just your bloody mind playing tricks on you.

"You abandoned your daughter."

He opened his eyes and searched for whoever spoke. The hairs on his neck stood on end when his gaze settled on the reflection in the mirror.

"Shut up!" he snapped.

His reflection sneered. "You left her there."

Kilal gripped the edge of the sink, squeezing until it cracked. He held the reflection's stare, glare for glare. "I didn't have a choice."

The reflection rolled its eyes. "That's right. Because you must *save* this floating rock you call home."

8

Ash built up around him, covering the sink, the floor, his shoulders.

"Bloodshed and Oaths, you know that's the truth!" Kilal cursed. "I swore to protect this world. I can't abandon it. For anything."

A nasty smile worked its way onto his reflection's face. "What sort of *father* leaves his daughter in *that* place?"

Kilal growled and slammed his fist into the mirror, shattering it into a hundred pieces. Blood dripped from his knuckles for only a second before white electricity crackled around his fist. The sting accompanying the healing was barely more than a whisper compared to the tightness in his chest and burning in his stomach.

"She's dead," a cacophony of voices said from the broken shards. "That's why you left her there."

"She's *not* dead!" Kilal pressed his eyes shut and leaned over the sink, leveraging the full weight of his two-hundred-seventy-pound frame on it.

The porcelain ripped from its enclosure connecting it to the wall.

"Kill yourself."

"I'll go back for her. I'll go back for her. I'll go back for her," Kilal repeated, rocking in place. He would. He *would!*

The knob of the bathroom door rattled and twisted.

"Hey! Who's in there? Open up. Other people need to piss, too!"

Kilal ignored the would-be visitor, hoping the lock would continue to do its job. His breathing was all he concentrated on.

The tightness in his chest eased, and the hairs on his neck lowered. His grip loosened on the half-dangling sink. Kilal opened his eyes. The ash was gone, and his reflection in the mirror shards scattered around him no longer taunted him.

"Twice in two days," he said, rubbing his face.

Kilal waited for the banging on the door to go away before he retrieved his knife from the floor and returned to his third and final Carving. Though no sooner had he started, the knob rattled again. He ignored it. He guided the knife with keen precision.

Someone pounded on the door again, more urgently than before.

"Get the point and move on," Kilal growled.

He sighed when the door slammed open. It crashed against the wall, and music, fast and rhythmic, flooded the restroom.

A large bald man strode in. His white t-shirt stuck to his sweat-soaked skin, and he wore pants he shouldn't have been able to squeeze into. The newcomer stopped dead at the sight of Kilal, wrist dripping blood and knife in hand. Two other men, dressed similarly, stopped in their tracks as well, one bumping into the bald man. He had a jaw pointy enough to pierce skin, while the other's chin was so flabby he barely had a neck. Three sets of eyes moved as one to Kilal's wrist.

Baldy sneered. "Didn't you see the sign, freak?" he yelled, though his voice barely rose above the beats bumping into the bathroom. "Your kind isn't welcome here!"

"Looks like we caught him before he could finish." No-Neck grinned.

Baldy scrunched his face and pinched his nose. "What's that smell?"

Kilal gritted his teeth. *Forgive me for not consistently caring for my hygiene while I was held captive and tortured in the Ashen Lands.*

The three stepped further into the room, and Pointy-Chin shut the door. The pulsing thrum of the music dampened. The vibration gently wavered through the floor, and the heavy beat could still be counted, but the relative 'silence' in comparison was a blessing.

Baldy cracked his knuckles, but it was his voice that grated on Kilal's nerves. "We oughta teach him what happens to his kind when they go places they aren't wanted."

"Come on, Drig." Pointy-Chin grabbed Baldy's arm. "We

don't know if he's one of those Arbiters who can use more than one Carving. What if he already has one in him?"

"You should really listen to your friend," Kilal said. He returned his knife to the sheath on his belt. The last thing he needed was to accidentally kill the fool.

Baldy smiled. "You can't hurt us. Your oath will only let you hurt Arbiters and Ash Fallen. Not *innocent* folk like us." He shook his arm free of Pointy-Chin and stepped forward.

Kilal sighed, shaking his head. "Technically, you're right. I can't hurt you." Baldy's smile widened. "That is," Kilal continued, "unless I consider you a threat. In which case, I'm free to defend myself. So, what do you think? Should I consider you a threat?"

Baldy faltered and looked at his friends. They gave quick shakes of their heads.

Unfortunately, Baldy was made of dumber stock than most. "Nah." He turned back to Kilal. "I don't believe you. Never heard of such a thing. You're just trying to save yourself."

Bloodshed and Oaths. This bloody idiot is going to make me hurt him.

He unsheathed his carving knife and brandished it at them. "Get out. Now."

Baldy looked from the blade to Kilal, then his friends. He didn't make any gesture to leave. Kilal growled. He didn't have time to deal with fools. He didn't want to hurt them, but what other choice did he have?

Unless...

He held his open hand up and ran the knife across his palm, parting flesh. Blood dripped, and the sting barely registered before white energy crackled around the wound, re-knitting the skin.

The trio paled.

Again, Kilal pointed the blade at Baldy, then at the door. "Get. Out." Baldy wheeled on his friends, shoving them aside as he made for the door—"Wait!" Kilal thundered. His voice bounced off the tiles. The men froze. "Your shirt, Drig. Give it to me."

Bloody idiot. He looked down at his own vomit-stained shirt. *What would you do if Drig wasn't as large as he is? Walk through the club smelling of death and bile? Good thinking.*

Drig didn't argue. He ripped the fabric over his head and threw it at Kilal before charging out the door, his friends on his heels.

Kilal caught the sweaty shirt and groaned. The thing stunk as if it had been dipped in a gallon of cologne. He placed it aside and re-secured the door before returning to his third and final Carving.

When he'd completed the process, Kilal did his best to clean himself up at the sink one last time. He pulled on Drig's shirt and was pleased when a glance into a mirror shard proved he didn't look entirely ridiculous in the small, damp fabric.

Feeling almost like a new man, his three Carvings refueling him with energy and confidence, Kilal exited the bathroom. He ignored the flickering light and the crunch of glass beneath his boots. When he stepped out, he winced. The music assailed him as he headed down the short hall with chipped and peeling black walls.

The hall deposited Kilal into an enormous square room three stories high. Over a hundred bodies, by Kilal's estimation, writhed about on the floor under the probing lights, dancing to the rhythm of the booming bass. Or at least, that's what he assumed they were doing. When had the flailing of limbs and grinding against each other become 'dance'?

Kilal cut across the floor and made his way to the spiraling staircase on the other side of the room. Cologne, perfume, and body odor mingled into a single collage of stink, making Kilal almost as nauseous as activating a Carving.

His wide, muscled frame shoved aside anyone not keen enough to get out of his way on their own, and he quickly freed himself from the knotted mass of moving flesh. He ascended the steps, taking three at a time, and strode onto the third-floor balcony overlooking the club. The clock on a nearby wall flashed bright red numbers. 11:21 p.m.

Just in time. His target supposedly frequented the place every evening at 11:30 p.m. sharp.

Kilal moved to a table at the edge of the balcony. He took a seat and waited.

A young woman approached him, carrying a notebook and a smile. She knelt beside him and placed a hand on his thigh, a brow raised. "What can I get for you, handsome?"

The girl either had *extremely* poor taste in men or was looking for a good tip. Either way, a hundred years ago, Kilal would've reciprocated the flirtatious attitude. Now?

He gently removed her hand from his leg, never taking his gaze from the dance floor beneath them. "Water."

She didn't answer or bother to write his order down. She just stood, turned on her heels, and stormed away. Kilal didn't expect to receive his water any time soon.

He scooted his chair up against the guardrail and rested his arms on it as he scanned the mass of bodies below. The club's name flashed in bright neon colors on the wall across from him.

Forget Everything.

Pressure spiked behind his eyes. The room seemed to warp, the walls bending, flexing outward. What immense power! Frantically, Kilal looked for the source. He found him, stepping through the revolving glass doors and into the club.

Jayden. His target.

Only a few times in Kilal's two hundred years of life had he felt power like that, and it confirmed his decision to hunt Jayden down. Now, he only had to convince the man to help him save the world.

Jayden, chest puffed out, sauntered from the entrance to the dance floor, smiling and pointing at people like he owned the place. He wore a green V-neck t-shirt; the cutout dipping nearly beneath his flat, hairless chest, and his yellow pants were so tight, Kilal wasn't sure if his legs hadn't been painted instead. Although, the six inches or so of skin showing above ankle-high white socks confirmed the man was, indeed, wearing pants. Black leather shoes rounded out his abysmal clothing decisions.

For such a provocative outfit, Kilal would've assumed Jayden had a reason to wear them, but he didn't look like he'd done an honest day's work in his life. The only thing he had going for him was a neatly trimmed haircut over bushy brown eyebrows.

The music stopped, and everything went quiet, but the dancing continued. In fact, the bass still vibrated through the railing and floor. What was going—

Kilal shot to his feet, kicking the chair behind him, and turned about, hands up before him. Three individuals sat at his table. *Arbiters.* And one of them had created a sound pocket around them. Normally, he would've sensed the use of a Carving, but the sensation must have been drowned by the immense power emanating from Jayden.

Kilal eyed the strangers. The one sitting nearest was tall and lean, yet solid with muscle. He sported a black tank top with gray tattoos wrapped around his arms. Carving tattoos! Kilal didn't know whether he should slap him for such foolishness or fear him. If he displayed his knowledge for all to see, surely the man was a threat to be respected, though the lopsided and arrogant grin stuck to his face said otherwise. Probably an Enlightened Arbiter, and a Fighter, at that. Kilal dismissed him without another thought.

The second person, sitting across from Tattoos, was a woman with short blonde hair. Nothing stood out about her. She hunched forward, shoulders folded in, and kept her arms beneath the table. She was trying to display a sheepish personality, which Kilal assumed worked against most people. He almost fell for it until he met her gaze.

He held her gaze just long enough to catch it before she flicked it away. An edge was behind them, a hardness only the most battle-experienced Arbiters obtained. Why had she chosen to partner up with a bloody idiot like Tattoos?

She was the one who'd thrown up the sound bubble. Buzzing in his ears indicated it was a Carving from the Mind branch. And the taste of copper identified the use of a second Carving, one from the Physical branch. A High Arbiter, and more specifically, a Bruiser. Was she prepared for a physical altercation?

Of course, he could've been completely wrong about his estimation of the two. The problem with sensing Carvings was how difficult it was to determine *who* was using them. For all Kilal really knew, he could have switched the two Arbiter's classifications. It was also possible they were both Enlightened instead, each using only one Carving. But Kilal had learned to trust his instincts. After two hundred years of sensing, he found he was usually right with his predictions.

The third and final stranger held Kilal's attention the longest. He wore a long black coat buttoned up to the neck. Matching leather gloves kept his hands concealed. Most ridiculous of all were the dark sunglasses concealing what Kilal knew lay behind them: eyes with veins as stark as the man's skin.

Kilal picked up the chair he'd kicked over. He returned it to the table and sat, carefully putting a few feet between himself and Tattoos. The power he sensed from each of them boosted his confidence. As long as he didn't allow Sunglasses to touch him, he'd walk away from the encounter unscathed. Regardless, an Arbiter always treated another with a healthy dose of respect and fear until they knew what Carvings were in play.

Kilal was the first to breach the silence. He leaned back and crossed his arms. "An Enlightened Arbiter, a High Arbiter, and an Inflictor entered a club. Every table within was theirs to choose from. Which one did they pick?"

They stiffened.

Tattoos sucked at something stuck between his teeth. "I

don't know. Which one?"

Kilal narrowed his eyes. "The wrong one."

The lady leaned forward. She placed her arms on the table and straightened her spine. Good. She wasn't trying to hide who she was anymore. "From where I'm sitting, I think we chose the *right* one. Few Primes remain *un*affiliated with the Heirs of the Promise."

Who? The title meant nothing to him.

"What do you want?" Kilal asked.

"To talk. I'm Issa. This is Iathu." She nodded toward the Inflictor, who gave Kilal a small tilt of his head. "And he's—"

"None of your business," Tattoos said, picking at a dark object between two teeth with his tongue. "What are you doing introducing us like we're all pals?" He leaned back against his chair, propping it up on its rear legs.

Issa's eyes hardened. "*That's* Caz."

Kilal winced at Caz's repulsive lip-smacking. "You gonna ask him to dance next?"

"Are you always this disrespectful to ladies?" Kilal asked.

Caz sneered and leaned forward. His chair slammed onto the floor, and he brought his face so close, the air reeked of stale smoke from his breath. "Ah, I'm sorry. Did I offend you?"

Kilal raised a brow. "Are you really bringing yourself this close to an Arbiter you don't know and whose Carvings you aren't aware of?"

Caz shrugged. "I ain't worried."

Kilal gave him a toothy smile. "You should be."

Whatever Caz saw in his expression made him pause the sucking of his teeth. He leaned back again and crossed his arms. "Ain't here to wipe the floor with you, anyway."

"One moment." Kilal pushed himself away from the table.

He stood and walked to the railing, scanning the dance floor. His head swiveled like a man in charge, but his gaze darted around frantically. The search didn't last long.

A large circle of empty floor had formed around Jayden.

The man flailed about, moving from girl to girl to recruit them as his dance partner. After so many rejections, the guy should have gotten the point, but Jayden wouldn't be dismayed.

Kilal strode back to the table. Caz was rebuking Issa. "Can't believe you're gonna let him talk to us like that."

Issa ignored him.

"Like I asked before," Kilal said, "what do you want?"

Iathu didn't move. His sunglasses remained firmly planted on Kilal and his right hand on the table. Kilal didn't let that hand out of his sight.

"We're representatives of the Heirs of the Promise," Issa said.

Kilal shrugged. "That supposed to mean something to me?"

Caz guffawed.

Issa's eyes widened. "You don't know?" Kilal shook his head. "Bloodshed and Oaths, man! Where have you been?"

Kilal raised a brow. "I've been...busy. Have you not heard of me?"

Issa squinted and studied his face. Finally, she elbowed Iathu. "You know him?"

He gave a slight shake of his head. Caz slapped a knee and spit on the floor. "I knew I recognized you! I saw you earlier this week. You were the guy living in the alley between Westside Boulevard and East Street, right? Nice box house you got yourself."

Interesting. It had been a long time since he'd been around Arbiters who didn't know who he was. Should he be disappointed or relieved? Granted, he'd been missing for the last decade.

Kilal drummed his fingers on the table.

Issa, head cocked, stared at him. "The Heirs of the Promise is an organization operated by Arbiters. We run this city. All new Arbiters to Silent Haven must register themselves, their classification, and the Carvings they use."

Kilal clenched his jaw so hard his grinding teeth could

have competed with the throbbing beat outside the bubble. His fingers stilled.

Iathu inched his hand slowly across the table. Caz smiled and cracked his knuckles.

Kilal pointed at the Inflictor. "If you don't put that hand under the table, I'll rip it off before you can even think to cancel my Carvings." Iathu's lip curled up, showing white teeth. Kilal smirked. "There it is. Not as emotionless as you want to pretend. Now, put your hand away."

Iathu didn't budge. Kilal prepared his Carvings, picturing them as knobs in his mind, ready to 'turn' them and increase his strength and gravity at a moment's notice. Issa nudged her partner. They shared a look, and whatever passed between them encouraged Iathu to finally put his arm beneath the table. The tension eased.

"You two are joking, right?" Caz asked. He gestured at Kilal. "He threatened us! And you're just going to let him *get away with that*?" He turned to Issa and sneered. "I guess that's what happens when a *woman* is in charge."

Issa flinched but didn't say anything.

Kilal, however, snapped his fingers in Caz's face. He'd had enough of the insufferable, big-mouthed Arbiter. "Come here." He beckoned with a finger as if calling a dog. Caz broke into a wide grin and leaned in. When their faces were nearly touching, and Kilal had the pleasure of enjoying his foul, smoky breath again, he said, "You should really treat women better."

A sleazy smile crept its way onto Caz's face. "I do. When they know their place."

"And what place is that?"

"As pretty little trophies meant to be conqu—"

Kilal slapped him. Caz's head ricocheted off the table edge with a sickening crunch. He crashed to the floor, unconscious. With his foot, Kilal shoved him aside.

"Bloodshed and Oaths, thank you," Issa said.

He stood and repositioned his chair, using the motion

to mask looking for Jayden. When he spotted him, Kilal sat down again. He propped his elbows on the table and folded his hands beneath his chin. "Your organization is a mockery to all we stand for. Arbiters are a force of good. We were created to defend the Sunlight Domain and its people from the Ash Fallen. Not band together and lord over those we protect."

"Those days are long behind us. Those values are archaic. They may have worked five hundred years ago, but if you haven't noticed, there aren't many of us left. We can't be the lone wolves we used to be. Things need to change."

Kilal smashed a fist on the table. "What I noticed is an army of Ash Fallen on the other side of the Veil, preparing to sweep through our world again!"

"On the other side of—" Issa frowned. "Where did you say you've been again?"

Kilal cursed himself. He didn't want *anyone* to know what had happened to him, let alone a corrupt group of Arbiters.

"You think the Heirs are the first to do this?" he said, trying to direct the conversation away from his slip-up. "Rally Arbiters together, claiming unity, peace, and a better future? You're all bloody fools! The ones in charge are gathering all the knowledge of Carvings you've each *earned*, and when they have enough, they'll turn on you, using your own powers against you."

Issa sat back and placed her hands under the table. The taste of copper flooded his mouth—she was activating her Physical Carving!

"Three cities," Issa said. "Silent Haven. New Cita. Vitrol. That's all that's left of humanity. We can't keep going on like this. It's time for something new. Join us. It's the only option."

"Where are the Keepers of the Oath? Why have they allowed the Heirs to move into the city?" Issa and Iathu shared another glance. What did they know? Kilal growled, "Where are the *Keepers?*"

"Will you return with us and register yourself, your status, and your Carvings?"

Kilal leaned in slowly. "I would welcome the embrace of a Pestilence Plague before I gave into your demands."

Issa closed her eyes and slumped her head. After taking a deep breath, she stood, and Iathu followed. "You have twenty-four hours to leave the city. This time tomorrow, if you haven't left, you will be black-marked. The first Arbiter to kill you will be handsomely rewarded."

Kilal shot to his feet and shoved the table aside. His hands shook, and the veins in his neck strained against his skin. "You threaten me with my own people? Tell your masters this: their time is short. They should use what remains of it to flee somewhere I won't find them. Elsewise, I won't be trapped in this city with them—they'll be trapped in this city with *me*."

To her credit, Issa didn't even flinch. She just gave a sad shake of her head and walked to the unconscious Caz. With little effort, she hauled him up and threw him over her shoulder. She paused before leaving and glanced at Kilal. "If you change your mind, come to our headquarters. Head to the center of the city and look for...Well, you won't miss it."

Issa headed for the back door of the club, Iathu trailing behind her.

Despite their absence, thankfully, the noise-dampening bubble remained intact for Kilal to brood in. Fingers and glares were thrown his way, but he ignored them and stepped over to the balcony again, chewing on his lower lip.

I could've handled that better. What was I thinking? An empty threat, and for what? If only an army of Ash Fallen weren't looming on the other side of the Veil. He sighed. *One problem at a time.*

Everything had changed while he was gone. The Heirs of the Promise. The Keepers. What had that look between Issa and Iathu meant when he mentioned the Keepers?

If anything happened to them, I'll—

Jayden!

Kilal whipped his head around, but the poorly dressed man was nowhere to be seen. Jayden was gone.

~ CHAPTER 2 ~

Bloody fool! Kilal cursed. *You got distracted.*

He flung himself over the third-story balcony and plummeted to the dance floor. People screamed and dove out of the way. A second before impact, he took control of the gravitational force on him, removing as much of it as he could. His descent slowed to a crawl. In a blink, he returned the effect of gravity on his body back to normal and dropped the final foot to the ground.

A century ago, that maneuver would've had his head spinning. Now, he shook it off as though the changes in force were nothing more than getting out of bed.

Kilal shoved anyone in his way aside as he raced for the exit, ignoring the cries of "freak" thrown his way.

I hope you didn't ruin the only chance you had of finding this guy.

Slamming through the double doors, Kilal bolted onto the sidewalk. Cool air brushed his skin, and the light from the two moons beamed down on him. He was grateful for the cloudless sky. Normally, at least half of the streetlights would've been on, but none were though most looked burnt out. Another sign of the decay he'd seen in the city since returning.

Guided by Ophir and Dampris's glow, Kilal studied the area,

searching for a sign of Jayden. "Couldn't have gone far," he growled.

A woman in a tank top and jeans with more holes than fabric squeaked and jumped out of his way.

Glass shattered over the back of his head. Something warm and wet dripped down, matting his hair to the nape of his neck. The pain of the injury hadn't even pushed through the spike in adrenaline before the gash mended. Kilal ignored the sharp stitching of his scalp and the screams of hate and rage from the people emerging through the double doors behind him. He scanned the streets, looking for any clues of Jayden's departure.

There!

A flash of yellow slipped into an alley three blocks down.

Lowering gravity and giving his strength a small boost, Kilal pushed the balls of his feet off the cement sidewalk, cracking it and propelling himself forward. The three blocks streaked by in four powerful strides. A heartbeat away from the alley mouth, Kilal raised gravity again, increasing his weight, and slowed to a dead stop.

The buildings on both sides of the alley shrouded the path in darkness. For the first time, Kilal was grateful for Jayden's wardrobe choice. He had little difficulty spotting the man sauntering his way through the shadows.

"Jayden!" he called, walking into the alley.

Jayden, nearly at the exit on the other end, halted. "I felt you in there, Arbiter. Watching me." He didn't turn as he spoke, and his voice was devoid of emotion, flat and colorless. "If it's dance lessons you seek, stop by my studio in the morning."

Kilal ignored the ridiculous assumption. He'd sooner endure a Skinflayer's touch. "We need to talk."

Jayden faced him. "That's odd. Because I have nothing to say to you."

"Then listen," Kilal said. "I didn't come all this way to be dismissed without even being heard."

A gust of wind pushed down the alley, carrying trash and the stench of it. The cool air on his skin brought Kilal back to the ten years he'd spent in the Ashen Lands, stuck on the other side of the Veil. There was no refreshing breeze over there, nor a moonlit sky. There was only darkness caused by the descent of gray ash, stagnant air, and the oppressive reek of despair.

That was the reality awaiting his world if he couldn't convince Jayden to help.

"Eldon told me to find you."

The wind faded, and time seemed to stop. Jayden shoved his hands into his pockets and took a step forward. The ground cracked beneath his foot, but Kilal couldn't sense any Carvings.

"Where did you hear that name?"

Kilal tensed, keeping his powers at the ready. "The Ashen Lands. We were prisoners together in the Tower of Eyes."

Jayden's lips quivered and his eyes narrowed. "I don't believe you."

"He said you wouldn't. He also told me to give you a message."

"Receiving a message from a dead man. Impressive."

"Eldon said, 'We failed. Our enemy still lives.'"

Jayden slowly removed his hands from his pockets and clenched them into fists. Pressure spiked behind Kilal's eyes. Just like when Jayden entered the club, the air around him seemed to distort, and the walls of the surrounding buildings appeared to bend outward, almost like Jayden was flexing.

"Liar."

"I am *not* lying," Kilal said, ready to activate his Carvings if attacked. "For the last two years, I've been a prisoner in the Tower of Eyes. I shared a cell wall with Eldon. He told me about you, the Professor, and Aya. He told me—"

"You're using something from the Mind branch, aren't you?" Jayden interrupted. "Is it Mind Reading? Dream Walking?"

"I'm not reading your mind," Kilal said, struck off guard

by the accusation. "I'm telling the truth. An army of Ash Fallen waits just beyond the border of the Veil. A new enemy has risen, Ashen Kane. I need help to—"

"If he isn't using a Carving, then how does he *know*?" Jayden mumbled. He looked at one of his hands, no longer talking to Kilal. "He *has* to be lying." Jayden flicked his gaze back up. His irises were gone—both eyes had turned completely black.

"*I'm not lying,*" Kilal said, consciously keeping his hands from balling into fists. "Why won't you list—"

Jayden launched forward. The ground cracked and broke from the force of the shove, and the bricks from the surrounding buildings tore free and scattered in all directions.

So fast!

Kilal raised his gravity, anchoring himself to the pavement, and increased his strength. He stepped inside Jayden's punch and slammed an elbow up into the man's hairless chin. A *crack* echoed, bouncing off the fractured walls. Jayden's chin split and skin flapped outward. Kilal grabbed the skinny man by the front of his shirt with a grip that would have ripped hair from his chest if Jayden had any, and slammed him into the ground. Pinning him down, Kilal hovered over him.

"I need your help. I'm trying to save our world, and I can't do it on my own. If what Eldon said is true, you and your companions can help. So, please, help me!"

Jayden smiled, ignoring the pain he had to be in as blood seeped from his split chin. His eyes remained black and devoid of emotion. "I don't care about *your* world, Arbiter. Eldon was killed a thousand years ago, and the one who killed him, the one you say Eldon claims is still alive, is also dead. I know because *I* killed him. So...get...off...of...me."

Kilal snarled as Jayden struggled beneath him. He grabbed a fistful of Jayden's hair and rammed his head into the concrete. "Don't care about *my* world? What about your life? Do you care about that? I left my daughter in the Ashen Lands to come find *you*. The sooner you help me, the sooner I can return to my search for her. So, I'll ask you nicely *one* more time. Please, help me." Kilal's chest heaved with each breath.

Please, please don't make returning here mean nothing.

Jayden's eyes narrowed and a small smile touched his lips. Kilal's heart dropped into his stomach. "Some father you are, leaving your daughter in the Ashen Lands."

Kilal roared and grabbed Jayden's neck with one hand, a skinny leg with the other. He stood, wrenching Jayden from the dented pavement and hurled him through the alley. Jayden crashed through a wooden light pole before slamming into the side of a building. He slid to the ground, streaking blood along the bricks.

"I was tortured alongside Eldon." Kilal stormed through the alley toward him. "I didn't read your bloody mind, you fool. I was there!" He pointed east, in the direction of the Veil. "I don't know *what* you are or *where* you come from," he growled. Kilal stopped behind the slowly rising Jayden. "What I do know is there's an army of Ash Fallen of the likes we've never seen waiting to sweep through our land. The land *you* live in. Bloodshed and Oaths, man! If you aren't willing to help me for this world's sake, do it for Eldon! My enemy was his enemy!"

Jayden scrambled to his knees and reached for the remains of the wooden pole beside him. A black, inklike substance... *oozed*...from Jayden's skin, wrapping around the man's out-stretched arm and solidifying. Kilal's eyes widened as a large, taloned hand sprouted from the elongated, obsidian limb. He'd seen a Carving like that before. It let the user reshape body parts into whatever they wanted. But Kilal couldn't sense any use of powers. If Jayden were using a Physical Carving, he'd taste copper. And the blackened eyes...That was something entirely new.

How was he doing it?

Jayden grabbed the pole, the long talons reaching almost

entirely around it. "Leave me *alone!*"

He whipped around in a blur. The top of the pole splintered as it scraped against the blood-smeared brick wall. Kilal rallied his strength, raising it even more. But when the pole slammed into him, he understood the true force of the being before him. And of how badly he'd erred.

Kilal was torn across the open street, smashing through the two-story building. The impact barely slowed him as he tumbled through the air and crashed through the clothing store, scattering racks and fabric everywhere. He barreled through two more walls before being deposited into the parallel street.

His senses blazed. He couldn't comprehend the damage done to his body. Dozens of bones were broken, at least one punctured lung, skull shattered. The pain overwhelmed everything beyond the facts and made him fuzzy and disoriented. But the six-inch splinter protruding from his left eye was what propelled him into unconsciousness.

Or, more precisely, when he yanked the splinter out, taking his eye with it.

~ CHAPTER 3 ~

"Hey." A voice, groggy and barely coherent, pierced through his subconsciousness. Something shook him. "Hey, mister. You alright?"

Kilal snapped his eyes open. He shot to his feet and lifted the stranger off the ground by his throat. The plain-looking man's eyes bulged as he swatted at Kilal's outstretched arm. A woman screamed and swung her purse at him. Kilal caught it in his free hand and wrenched it from her grasp, pulling her off balance. Bright lights shone on him. He squinted and looked away.

Stop this! Another voice pierced the cloud covering his mind. His voice.

He let go. The purse thumped onto the pavement beside the man, who'd dropped onto his butt.

"I'm...sorry," Kilal mumbled, shame warming his cheeks.

The two people cursed him vehemently and skittered back to their car, the source of the beams. They sped off, tires screeching. Burnt rubber filled the air.

Kilal groaned and rubbed his temple. His head felt like it had split in two, and he'd know. It had happened to him once. One of the worst experiences of his life. That hadn't made the wooden stake blasted through his eye more tolerable, though.

Thankfully, the healing seemed to have completed while he'd been unconscious.

His white shirt, drenched red, was tattered and torn, but at least his jeans were mostly intact and his boots whole.

Kilal kicked the ground and growled. "You bloody fool. You stupid bloody fool! Now what are you supposed to do?"

He had no idea where Jayden lived. The information he'd been able to gather, he'd already used. Jayden frequented the club, *Forget Everything*, every night. But after their little rumble, Kilal couldn't imagine he would be back anytime soon.

Kilal walked across the street, picked a direction—north— and kept walking, hands in pockets.

He screwed up. He screwed up *bad*. Jayden was immensely powerful, exactly the sort of person he needed. The sort of person his world needed. But where did Jayden's power come from? If it came from Carvings, Kilal would have sensed them. But, besides raw power, he'd felt nothing.

Even stranger, Jayden had said *Kilal's* world. What was he, and where did he come from?

A figure stumbled out of a small recess of what looked like an abandoned building. Kilal tensed, Carvings ready, but instead of punching the disheveled stranger, Kilal pinched his nose shut. The newcomer stank like a three-day-old rotting corpse. Which probably wasn't much better than how he smelled.

The old man approached him with a limp, grimy palm open. "Any help would be appreciated, good sir." His breath reeked of alcohol.

Kilal held a hand out, halting the man's progress. With his other, he reached into a back pocket and pulled out his wallet. Rifling through it, he pulled out a few coins, each with the number one on it and an imprint of Sha'tum's face.

He grimaced. *As if the people who designed this currency knew what our god looked like.*

Kilal handed the money to the stranger, who took it in kind. "Sha'tum bless you, sir."

"What happened to you?" he asked before the man could stumble back to his pile of rags and paper. He'd only been back two days, and this was the fourth homeless person he'd seen. Ten years ago, there were none.

"Arbiters destroyed my home. Didn't have nowhere else to go."

"Did you claim the Right of Recompense?"

"No one to claim it from."

Dread filled Kilal. "Are the Keepers of the Oath and the Governing Seats not enforcing it anymore?"

The beggar stared up at him as if seeing him for the first time. "You new here? Keepers ain't been around for five or so years. Governing Seats? They're just puppets of the Heirs of the Promise."

The Keepers...gone?

Kilal rocked back on his heels. The news hit harder and more painfully than the physical blows he'd received at the hands of Jayden. It couldn't be. The stranger had to be mistaken.

The look shared between Issa and Iathu flashed in Kilal's mind.

No. Please no.

"What do you mean, gone?"

The homeless man stroked his sorry excuse for a beard. His eyes grew distant. "You know, I remember when the Keepers persuaded the Governing Seats to pass the Right of Recompense twenty years ago. It was a good thing. A great thing. Finally, the normal citizens, the ones hurt by the Arbiter's fights, were gonna get financial help replacing whatever had been destroyed. But I always wondered how the Keepers got the Seats to pass such a law. Those Seats are so greedy they'd sell their own grandmother to a Plague if it made them a buck. So, how'd the Keepers get them to *financially support* those who'd lost something because of the Arbiters?" He chuckled and slapped a knee.

Kilal knew *exactly* how the Keepers had...persuaded them.

I reminded them of their human frailty and explicitly laid out what I'd do to them if they didn't pass the law.

The homeless man returned to the recess where his makeshift bed of dirty blankets blocked the doorway into the building and began smoothing the sheets out. Kilal followed. He grabbed him by the shoulder and spun him about.

"What do you mean the Keepers are gone?"

The stranger's eyes widened, despite his efforts to keep his voice as calm and harmless as possible. He looked everywhere but at Kilal. "Not gone. Dead. Wiped out five years ago. You can thank the bloody Heirs of the Promise for that."

"No." A low moan escaped Kilal's clenched jaw. "That's impossible." His fingers opened of their own accord, and the man dropped and skittered back to his 'home.'

Kilal stared into the dark recess between the buildings where the beggar slept, vision shrouded by memories of his friends. The Keepers were *destroyed*. Alistair, Klea, Braxus... the list went on. Friends. Companions. Brothers and sisters. He squeezed his eyes shut as the last name entered his mind. Requiem Ror.

His wife.

Kilal's chest heaved, and his eyes dampened.

First Lilliana, now Requiem. What else was there to live for? His oath?

He didn't bother wiping the tears from his cheeks. Pride was something he'd given up long ago.

He'd spent many years in times so dark he didn't have a reason to get up from wherever he'd fallen asleep the previous night. He knew what it was to exist but not live. He couldn't go back to those times. If Lilliana and Requiem truly had been ripped from him, he'd have no one to pull him from that pit of despair anymore.

And regardless of his aching heart, Kilal knew the truth: no matter how much he lost, he wouldn't abandon the oath he swore to protect his world.

No, he couldn't think about his daughter and wife like that. He had to believe they were still among the living. Had to! If for no other reason than to make each breath a little easier, a little more bearable. He'd cling to the conviction that they were still alive because that was all he could do. He'd keep moving forward.

He had a job to do, a Jayden to find, and a world to save.

But Jayden had slipped through his fingers, and with him, Kilal's only lead. What was he supposed to do now?

I'm gonna do what I should've done two days ago.

He'd return to the Keepers' headquarters and pay his respects. Then he'd do what he did best. The Heirs of the Promise would soon know he was alive and well.

~ CHAPTER 4 ~

Kilal moved deeper and deeper into Silent Haven, jumping from rooftop to rooftop. He skidded to a stop at the edge of a six-story building and studied his city. Not much had changed in the ten years he'd been gone. Or had it? Undergoing a supposed time of peace, Silent Haven looked...poor, as if it had barely recovered from the last major invasion one hundred and fifty years ago.

He'd barely had a few decades of Carving experience under his belt when the Ash Fallen, led by nearly fifty Plagues, pierced the Veil and ransacked this side of it. River Haven, a city to the east and only a few dozen miles from the Veil had fallen during that attack, and Silent Haven had become the central battleground for the rest of the war. Many good Arbiters lost their lives repelling the invasion. And his beloved city had nearly fallen as well.

Their world took time to rebuild, but little by little, improvements were made. The city certainly hadn't been perfect when he got stuck in the Ashen Lands, but now—somehow—Silent Haven barely looked better than it had ten years after the invasion.

A skyscraper on the western side of the city, standing thirty stories high, pierced the clouds like the blade of a fallen god. It was barely the skeleton of a building. Kilal wracked his brain. Hadn't that been started *before* he'd been teleported to the Ashen Lands? How had it advanced no further? In fact, it looked *forgotten.*

The decrepit skyscraper, the homeless man, the beat-up condition of many of the vehicles Kilal had seen since entering Silent Haven, and the broken and burned-out light posts adorning each street didn't speak of a city advancing technologically or economically.

Kilal's hair stood on end as he thought of *his* city dying slowly. Had it really only happened over the last ten years? Or had it been going on for much longer, and he'd been blind to it?

As if in direct contrast to the abandoned skyscraper, another stood proudly to the north. Lights beamed all about it as if announcing its presence in case anyone failed to notice it. It didn't take much thought for Kilal to guess who the skyscraper belonged to. How many floors would he have to climb before he found the jerks who'd begun the organization?

A car horn blasted in the distance, and another answered. Glass shattered somewhere else, followed by two men screaming curses at each other. Kilal's advanced hearing even picked up on a woman whimpering not too far from him.

He closed his senses off from the world. His chest tightened and guilt pumped through his veins like blood and oxygen. But he couldn't be everywhere at once. He hadn't returned, pausing his search for Lilliana to fix everyone's lives.

I'll save the world, Kilal thought, yearning for all to hear him. *And if I survive, I'll clean the stain this city has become.*

He leapt from the rooftop and soared over the open street below; how he'd missed this. The breeze rushing through his hair. The weightlessness of being hundreds of feet in the air. The freedom of the open sky. He used to spend hours running through the city with Lilliana. Not even a teenager, she'd been able to keep up with him. By the time she was fifteen, it was *him* having to keep up with *her.* She was a prodigy, which is why he'd pushed for her to partake in missions with him.

Requiem had always resisted that decision, and he'd respected her wishes for a while.

His smile faded when he remembered the last time he'd seen his wife. A distress call had come from far to the north, claiming two Plagues and a handful of Mannekins had pierced the Veil and were rampaging unchallenged. With such a small band of Ash Fallen, Kilal had argued it was the perfect mission for Lilliana to get her toes wet. Requiem had disagreed, pleading with Kilal not to take her.

He wished he'd listened.

I'm coming for you, Lil. Just a little while longer, and I'll return. I promise.

Somewhere out there, she still lived. He had to believe that.

He traveled deeper into the city. Kilal didn't take any more breaks. When Lilliana was back, when the Ashen Forces were stopped, then he would rest. Maybe even go on a vacation. Maybe they'd cross the Schism and see what was on the other side.

Kilal came to an abrupt halt high above the city. In the center of Silent Haven, what remained of the Keepers' headquarters stood below him. It was a small, simple building. Three stories high, constructed of brick and mortar. When steel became readily available and technology caught up to begin fabricating buildings with beams and machinery, the Keepers had chosen not to upgrade. They appreciated how the building, just like their oaths, withstood the change of time. It was to be a constant reminder of the humble lives Arbiters were supposed to live.

That reminder was a ruin now, blackened and crumbling. Walls were smashed, the eastern side completely gone, and the top two floors collapsed. All of the windows were shattered. Doors had been torn from their hinges and rested among the rubble. Burn marks scorched the brick exterior, as well as the interior.

The battle had clearly taken place a long time ago, so why

had no one taken care of it? Demolished the building, built a new one? Something, anything other than leaving it as it was?

Bloodshed and Oaths!

It had become an example to any Arbiter who would stand against the Heirs of the Promise.

They continued to dig themselves a deeper grave.

Hate pulsed through his veins, making his neck, shoulders, and spine twitch. His knuckles cracked as he clenched his fists. He'd kill them. Each and every one of the Heirs.

He leapt from the rooftop and plummeted the ten stories into the building below.

~ CHAPTER 5 ~

Kilal landed on the blackened, rotting carpet of the third level. He kept his mass light by reducing the force of gravity on himself by half. From the looks of the interior, he didn't trust the floor to hold his full weight.

A gust of wind blew through the building, and with it, the scent of ash, decay, and mold. Five years later, and the scent remained.

The glow of Ophir and Damphir easily penetrated the crumbling rooftop, and Kilal had no trouble taking in the full extent of the ruins. Scattered chairs and destroyed furniture were strewn about. Everywhere he looked, dark stains covered every surface. There was no mistaking what those marks were.

"They didn't have a chance," Kilal whispered to the open air.

But who was capable of such a thing? The Keepers were the most talented and powerful Arbiters of his time. So who or what could cause the destruction he stood amidst? His confrontation with Jayden gave him a chilling thought. Had the Heirs, too, potentially come from another world? The possibility held too many ramifications for him to dwell on.

Kilal turned in a circle and memories of the room overlayed with the current state of it. He'd built the Keepers from the ground up. The headquarters had been more of a home to him than anywhere else. He squeezed his eyes shut, choking back a sob.

A large square table used to be in the center of the room. The only remnants of it were splintered pieces scattered everywhere. How many times had he sat there, listening to another one of Alistair's terrible jokes? Or weathered the storm of Braxus's barrage of doom and gloom orations? How many looks had he shared with Requiem across it, the voices of everyone else growing dimmer as he lost himself in those beautiful brown eyes?

It was all gone.

A particularly gruesome stain on a wall to his right caught Kilal's attention. He inched closer, each step leaving a boot imprint in the dust and disintegrating carpet.

The mark was a perfect outline of a human.

He ran a finger over it, and the black grime came away. Kilal smudged it around between his thumb and forefinger, sniffing it. The sulfuric stink brought him back to the decade he'd spent in the Ashen Lands.

The name half of the world had adopted was quite literal. A constant fall of ash sprinkled from the sky. The wildlife there had evolved over the millennia to consume the powdery slate, ensuring everything wasn't buried beneath the gray residue.

The outline on the wall wasn't large but of an average build. Which of his friends had been incinerated? The size of the stain was a good match for a few of them. Braxus, perhaps? Kilal could imagine him shoving the others aside, taking the blast himself. Did he think the Elemental Shield he was so widely known for would be enough to block whatever attack had been thrown at him? Kilal almost shivered, phantom fear trickling through him that might have been what Braxus experienced when he realized he was wrong.

He fell to his knees and slumped forward until his forehead rested against the wall.

"Could I have stopped this if I'd been here?" Or would he have only continued living while everyone around him died?

Not that it mattered. Kilal wasn't sure even he could regenerate from a blast that hot. Which begged the question, who could control temperatures like that? The closest person he knew of was Shelah. She was only an Enlightened Arbiter, but she could control fire with a skill demanding admiration, yet she'd never been able to incinerate anything to this magnitude.

Again, the possibility of people from another world gave him pause.

Kilal stood and crossed the room. He made his way through a somewhat intact hallway and descended the dark stairwell at the end to the second floor. It was much the same as the third. Crumbling walls, disintegrating and moldy furniture, dark stains, ripped up tiles and carpet, light fixtures shattered on the floor or hanging by flimsy wires from the ceiling.

He stepped over a door broken in half and into a room. The wall had been blasted out, and he could look out at the city. How many souls slept, comfortable in their beds, while their world slipped closer to destruction?

"Do any of you even care about the lives lost here?" Kilal said.

Cries of "freak" and "you aren't wanted here" seemed to echo around the room. Kilal lifted a hand and rubbed at the back of his head, picking at the blood caked into his hair.

"We die for you, so why do you hate us?"

Poor treatment or not, the oath Kilal and every other Arbiter swore during their Awakening, bound them to protecting the Sunlight Domain and all its citizens.

He slammed his fist into the wall, smashing through the wooden framing.

Sometimes, he *really* wished he could forsake that oath.

Back in the stairwell, the pathway to the first floor was gone; the ceiling, walls, and stairs collapsed into a pile of rubble he couldn't squeeze through. Kilal returned to the second story, to one of the many holes in the floor, and dropped through to the ground level. No longer concerned with his weight affecting the structure, he returned his gravity to normal.

The first floor was much the same as the previous two.

He slowly made his way to the final room, the room he'd been purposefully avoiding. He stopped in the doorway, staring into it. A row of large metal safes lined the other end, most of them still in decent condition. But all were open and empty. The Keepers had used those safes to store dangerous items or ancient relics they could neither destroy nor understand. Kilal sighed. Whatever had been in those safes when the Heirs attacked was now in their possession.

Lips quivering, vision blurring, a knot in his throat, he entered the room. To the left, there was an overturned chair that was still in working condition. A wooden desk stood nearly intact in front of it, an oddity compared to the rest of the building. He turned the chair upright and slumped into it. His body went completely slack, and he leaned back to stare at the ceiling.

And wept.

It was the room in which he'd last spoken to Requiem. She'd begged him to not only send someone else to answer the distress signal, but to not take Lilliana if he were determined to go. A bad feeling, she'd called it. He'd accused her of babying his daughter and worrying too much. It was a simple distress signal. A few Ash Fallen. Nothing he, let alone he and Lilliana, couldn't handle.

Then do it for me, she'd said. *Please. Just...do it for me.*

He'd ignored her. *We'll be back in a few days. You'll barely notice we were even gone.*

When he'd tried to embrace her, she'd shrugged him off and turned away.

Kilal rubbed dusty palms over his cheeks, drying them. "She was right," he said, looking at his hands. "She was RIGHT!"

He slammed his head onto the desk, cracking it.

Ringing silence was his only response.

Why didn't you listen? He slammed his head against the desk again. *Why didn't you respect her intuition, her request?* Again, he slammed his head, splitting the desk further.

It wasn't enough. The pain wasn't punishment enough. He deserved more. He *needed* more. The last ten years had all stemmed from that one decision. That one horrible, naive decision. And everyone he loved paid the price for it.

Except for you, a voice deeper and angrier than Kilal's said in his mind. *You live while they die. Pathetic.*

Kilal scrambled for the knife pouch at his side. He knew what he had to do. A life for a life. It was the only way to make anything right. The voice which spoke before seemed to purr at his resolve.

Ripping the blade from its pouch, Kilal began working on the Carving of Immortality. He would cancel it. Then he would kill himself. It was the only way he could atone for his sins.

Tears staining his cheek, blood covering his forearm, he finished the Carving. And froze. All he had to do was etch an X through it. Then open up his wrist. And fade away into oblivion. No pain. No guilt. No shame or regret. Just...nothing. He deserved to die. So why did his hands shake? Why didn't they answer his command to cancel the Carving?

Kilal stared at his trembling arms.

It's not right. I don't deserve peace. True atonement will come from suffering through this life.

The knife clanged against the floor. He bowed his head until it rested against the cracked desk and cried. He clutched at his chest, wishing he could tear his heart out. Maybe then the pain would stop. He missed her *so much*. Requiem. Every minute of sleep he'd fought for in the Ashen Lands had been filled with memories of her. And he'd failed her. Her and his own daughter. Sobs wracked his body, filling the air with the mournful song of a broken spirit.

They were *all* dead.

Never had he imagined such a fate for the Keepers. They were the best of the best, in both power and morals. Together, they'd kept the land in check and protected. Protected from the rare rogue Arbiter and scarce but ever-increasing raids of Ash Fallen. But no longer.

He couldn't die yet. And he couldn't wallow in self-pity. He had a goal, a job to complete. If not for himself, for those he'd lost.

Kilal left the gravesite of his friends, of Requiem, hollow and in a daze. Mind fogged with sorrow, his feet shuffled him into the city. He had no idea where he was going. And for the moment, he couldn't make himself care.

~ CHAPTER 6 ~

Kilal wandered the streets for a time, lost in memories of the past. Lost in his guilt, accusations thundering in his head. If only he'd listened to Requiem. If only he'd killed Gabriel when he had the chance. If only he hadn't returned to the Sunlight Domain. If only he'd controlled his emotions and handled the encounter with Jayden better. If...if...if.... The list went on. And the voices wouldn't stop.

They never stopped.

You killed them. You killed them. YOU killed them. YOU KILLED them. YOU KILLED THEM!

"Shut up!" Kilal smashed a fist into a wall, pulverizing the few bricks into a cloud of red dust.

He squeezed his eyes shut and mashed his palms into his cheeks, pressing, pressing, pressing until it felt like his bones were on the brink of collapsing. Pain flooded him, and he latched onto it, letting it carry him away from the voices.

When the accusations receded into no more than a background buzz, Kilal removed his hands and wiped the tears from his face.

"Need a bloody Carving to cure my bloody brain," he mumbled. He looked around for the first time and experienced a moment he hadn't experienced in Silent Haven in decades. "Bloodshed and Oaths, where am I?"

He'd wandered into the slums. Except Silent Haven never had slums. The bricks he'd crushed didn't look much different from the rest, but the buildings surrounding him leaned in unkempt ways and crumbled in places he would have immediately repaired had he been the owner. There were no lights on the streets nor any coming from the windows. Cobwebs so thick, he mistook some for white curtains hung in most recesses. Whether doors, cracks and crevices, or holes, the dusty spider silk showed no prejudice. A few cars decorated the street curbs. All three were missing their wheels, most of the windows had been shattered, and their metallic frames had been stripped of most of their parts. Mere skeletons of what they'd once been.

A gust blew through the streets, carrying with it stray trash and the aroma of abandonment. A wrinkled piece of paper attached itself to the side of his head as if that were its destination all along. Another cold howl tore through the lanes, ripping the page from Kilal's skin. As it hurtled by, a word printed on it caught his attention.

He snatched it from the air. Holding it out, Kilal read the text. A mixture of emotions swirled about in his chest, combining into an unpleasant feeling. Anger. Shock. Confusion. Hate. Sorrow. And the one that never left him, like a monster always simmering beneath the surface—guilt.

The paper was a Wanted ad. For a girl, to be precise. Wanted dead or alive by the Heirs of the Promise. And the reward?

"Fifty pounds of aznium!" Kilal nearly shouted. Absurd! Not only were the Heirs placing capture or kill orders on someone who was barely more than a child and likely an Arbiter, but they were also rewarding a fortune to whoever turned her in.

In all his two hundred years, Kilal had only scrounged up around *fifteen* pounds of aznium. And that was a lot!

That was insanity.

Every man, woman, and child with even an ounce of moral

degradation would be after that girl, whoever she was.

"Not if I get to her first."

You didn't return to save a single girl. You returned to save everyone. A low growl rumbled in his throat. He folded the paper into a tidy square and shoved it into his pocket. *We can add her to the list of names belonging to those you've killed, failed, or abandoned.*

Kilal ignored the taunt and looked for any road signs which would help him recognize the area, or at least help orient himself, but there were none.

A particular building caught his eye at the corner of the upcoming intersection.

He jogged across the street, hoping to leave his guilt somewhere behind. The building, if it could even be called that anymore, pulled at him. A memory tickled his mind, but it kept slipping away when he reached for it.

The disheveled structure was one story and made of wood. Much of the exterior was charred black, and the roof had a man-sized hole in it. Like the other buildings, cobwebs dominated much of the recesses and windows. Why did he feel like he knew the place? It was clearly abandoned. The rafters of the cobweb-covered porch overhang sagged and looked a strong gust of wind away from collapse. Rotted wooden pillars held the overhang up. It was a miracle the thing still stood. Yet, as he inched up the front steps, they appeared clean, recently swept.

Looking around, one of the square wooden pillars caused a double-take.

He approached it hesitantly, wracking his brain for the reason it seemed familiar. The wood was dusty, coarse, and brittle beneath his calloused fingers. A simple push would snap the thing in two, even without his enhanced strength.

A strangely shaped cleft caught his attention, and he scrubbed at the dust. He didn't have to brush away much before he stumbled back, eyes wide. The brown stain was old. A cracked hole pierced through the center of the mark, all the way through the pillar.

He knew that hole. Intimately.

Mouth open, eyesight blurry, he glided a finger over the dent and flaky, brown stain.

Thirty years ago, a rogue Arbiter named Impaler made it her sole purpose to kill every religious leader of Sha'tum's holy places. Supposedly, the story went, Impaler was mistreated by a Mother in the name of their God. Kilal never disbelieved her. In fact, he'd found evidence to support Impaler's claim.

The woman who had abused her was Impaler's first victim.

Kilal and Requiem had camped for three days in this holy place, waiting for Impaler to arrive to notch another kill on her belt. Requiem had pleaded with him to try and talk some sense into her, to convince Impaler to stop and turn herself in. And Kilal *had* tried, but the result was in the pillar he now ran a thumb across. Impaler could manipulate her body to take almost any shape. She'd turned a finger into a spear and skewered Kilal's shoulder, pinning him to the mast.

Not all that dissimilar to Jayden, though without the black ooze and equally void-flooded eyes.

It had been his and his future wife's first mission together.

Requiem, I can't do this without you. Kilal leaned his forehead against the wood. His tears mingled with the dust, creating rivulets of chalky mud.

Well, he knew where he was now.

He moved to the door. The hinges creaked in protest as he swung it open.

The sanctuary of the Temple of Sha'tum, Silent Haven's holy place, welcomed him. His heart would have fallen if it hadn't already been at the bottom. Pews broken. Paintings ripped, torn, and scattered. Dust, dirt, mud, and char every-where. The ceiling used to have a beautiful crystal chandelier that now decorated the floor in pieces.

Kilal shook his head and moaned for what was lost. Every

sixth day of the week, this temple had been filled to the brim as the citizens of Silent Haven honored the sacrifice Sha'tum made to gift his people with the power of Carvings. It was the only way to equip them with the ability to defend their world against the Ash Fallen and their leader, Avinoth—and Sha'tum had done it with a smile on his face.

The holy places were instituted to ensure no one would forget what their God had done for them. And now, the temple lay in ruin.

A small table stood at the end of the building where the Mother would give her oration, encouraging all those present to pray and hope for the day Sha'tum would revive and return. Kilal knew the truth: Sha'tum was dead, and he would never return. But who was he to stop the people from having faith?

A pristine, white cloth draped over the table. Four candles decorated it; three of the four were lit. The little light they gave off flickered from the small breeze passing through the room. Despite the condition of the building and the obvious abandonment of Sha'tum, someone still seemed to care to keep his memories alive.

The echo of his footsteps as he passed down the middle of the two aisles of destroyed pews made him wince. Why did he feel like a trespasser? The red velvet carpet which used to cover the floor was gone.

At the altar, instinct took over. He lifted one of the lit candles and used it to light the fourth. With all four glowing, Kilal dropped to one knee and bowed his head, reciting the prayer he'd been taught as a little boy.

"Sha'tum, we thank you for your sacrifice. We thank you for your love. You may be gone, but you will never be forgotten. And when you return, I pray you will find me worthy of your praise."

Peace washed over him. How long had it been since he said those words? Sure, he'd called out to his dead God when he was being sliced, diced, stabbed, peeled, burned, suffocated, and a hundred other torturous things. He'd begged, pleaded, demanded, cursed. But when had he just...prayed? It felt good to do so again, even though he knew no one was listening.

"Hello?" The voice came from the leftmost corner of the sanctuary, through the doorway leading into the innermost recesses.

Where the Mother lived.

Kilal stood and turned. It was dark, and he couldn't make out the person in the corner, only the silhouette. He held his hands up in front of him, palms facing the figure, in a sign of peace. "I'm sorry. I wished only to pay my respects. If I may beg for a minute of your time, what happened here?"

Shuffling footsteps and the *toc* of a cane connecting with the floor grew louder as the person drew closer. The woman emerging from the shadows was old. Ancient. Her skin was closer to wrinkled leather than human flesh. Thinning white hair, easily mistaken for the cobwebs decorating the temple, fell in clumps to her shoulders. She had a stooped back, gnarled and arthritic hands and wore a dirty and creased black robe over disheveled clothes.

The holy place's Mother. Despite her condition, she was the one doing what she could to still care for the Sanctuary.

Dim eyes brightened as she approached. "Kilal?" Her scratchy voice was barely louder than a whisper.

"You have me at a disadvantage, Mother. It seems you recognize me. Forgive me, but my memory hasn't been the best recently."

She chuckled and flipped a wad of hair behind her shoulder in a motion meant for someone much younger. "Age hasn't been kind to me, I know. But you, Ki, barely look a day over two hundred."

The familiarity pulsed, and his heart pumped. "Two hundred?" How did she know? But more than that, "D-did you just ca—" He cleared his throat, blinking rapidly. "Did you just call me...*Ki?*"

The Mother shuffled closer until they were nearly touching. He looked down at the frail woman with furrowed brows. A storm of emotions picked him up and swept him away, and it was all he could do to stay standing.

"I thought I'd never see you again." She lifted a shaking hand to his cheek, but it fell a foot short. All she could do was rest it on his chest. "When Requiem showed up at my doorstep and claimed you were dead.... Well, I always knew that couldn't be true. You are the *Immortal* Arbiter, after all."

Kilal swallowed the lump in his throat and put his own trembling hand over hers. "Claire?" She smiled and light shone through her eyes like the sun peeking through gray clouds on a stormy day. "Is it really you?"

"In the flesh." She grimaced and pulled at some skin on her arm. "If that's even what this stuff still is."

He broke into a wide grin and exploded with laughter. Claire nearly disappeared beneath his large arms as he pulled her closer and wrapped her tiny frame in a great bear hug. His joy threatened to snap her in half.

Claire's happy demeanor broke, and she wept against his chest.

Kilal, still caught in the storm of emotions, rubbed his own wet cheeks against the top of her straw-like hair. "It's so good to see you! What's it been? Thirty years?"

Her response was drowned by another flood of tears. Kilal let her cry until she pulled back from him. Her disposition had shifted from whimsical joy to sorrow.

"I'm so sorry, Kilal," she said. "About Requiem."

He'd convinced himself Requiem had somehow escaped the hands of the Heirs, but Claire's words hammered doubt into his belief. A single tear slowly made its way down his cheek. All he could manage was a nod.

He let go of her and cleared his throat again. "What happened here?"

She looked around at her holy place, her home. "Much."

Kilal crossed his arms and raised a brow. "Claire, I've been gone for *ten* years. I think I need a little more than 'much.'"

His age-old friend hooked her arm around his and led him to the front pew, where she gestured for him to sit on what remained of it. She searched Kilal's eyes, though for what, he couldn't fathom.

A frown wormed its way onto her face. "Where do I even start? The Heirs of the Promise, have you heard of them yet?" He nodded. "Well, they showed up five years ago and turned the Sunlight Domain upside down. The Keepers were destroyed. The Government Seats became their puppets. They banned the worship of Sha'tum. You and Lilliana were gone—everyone thought you were dead. Where *have* you been?"

The weight of the world pressed onto his shoulders. It forced him to curl forward and rest his elbows on his knees, his chin in his hands. "I've been trapped in the Ashen Lands."

Claire gasped and pressed two fingers to her forehead, then to her lips. The sign a Mother made when calling on the protection of Sha'tum. Kilal always found the gesture ridiculous. Sha'tum was dead. But if it helped Claire, the other Mothers, and all those they shepherded feel even the slightest hint of hope and peace, who was he to judge?

His back seemed to buckle, and he slumped forward a little more. "I...I left her back there." A lump formed in his throat, growing to match the pain building in his chest. "Forgive me, Mother. I left her there."

What had moments before been a joyous reunion evaporated into a deluge of tears. He'd held it back as long as he could. Sure, the tears, the emotion, seeped through the wall he'd erected from time to time, but he'd always been able to repair it. Whether it was being back in his sanctuary with a very close friend of nearly sixty years, a friend he'd assumed dead, or the safety and emotional support Claire represented that completely tore down the barriers now, Kilal didn't know. Regardless, they were down, and the tears rushed forth.

"I...I...lost her," he blubbered. "My own daughter!" He barely registered Claire's hand caressing his back. "What sort of father am I? What father leaves his own daughter in a land of monsters?"

"A father who's had a reason more important than him or his daughter," she said. "I know you, Kilal. So, whatever your reason, I know you made that decision because it was what you thought was best, regardless of how hard it was."

"And who would decide something, *anything*, is more important than his own daughter?"

"One who is concerned for *all* daughters. And all fathers. One who is concerned for *everyone*." Claire's response was so quick, it was as if she'd been planning for that very question.

Bloodshed and Oaths, the woman was always right!

No one living knew him better than her. But as comforting as her words should have been, the void in his chest couldn't be filled by sentiments. The tears continued to flow.

Claire pulled his head to her and stroked his hair, cooing and whispering in his ear.

They sat like that for a long time as ten years of pent-up emotion finally found a release. Only when Kilal had nothing left to weep did he pull back.

"Thank you," he said, wiping his cheeks. He took her hands in his. "The end is coming, Claire. An army of Ash Fallen grows. When it invades, it'll be large enough to wipe the remnants of human life from the face of this world. A new leader, a powerful and intelligent Ash Fallen, has risen, and it's determined to kill us all.

"That's why I have returned. I'm here to find...warriors who will cross the Veil with me to that Sha'tum-forsaken place and help me kill this *thing* that holds the army together. That... that's why I abandoned my search for her."

Claire gripped his chin with a firmness he didn't think her frail arms were capable of. "You *did not* abandon her. What good would finding her be if there wasn't a home left to return her to?"

It was a question he challenged himself with daily. It felt good to hear it from someone else, too.

Kilal's mouth filled with the tang of copper. He sat up straight, searching for the source of the Carving.

"Excuse me?" The voice was young, much younger than Claire's. "Mother, is...is everything alright?"

"Of course, child," Claire said. "Come meet a dear friend of mine." To Kilal, she said, "Speaking of finding warriors, I think I may have stumbled upon one."

Kilal's curiosity rose. *A warrior? Here?* And seemingly so young? But he'd learned to never doubt Claire.

Thumped footsteps in the shadowy recesses announced the child's approach. When she emerged from the darkness, Kilal sat frozen. She was much younger than he'd expected.

Sixteen, maybe seventeen. Long, fiery, *greasy* red hair was tied into a ponytail that hung almost to the crook of her back. Red freckles decorated the bridge of her nose. Her eyes were both brown and mistrusting, and her clothes didn't look much better than his. Despite her youth, she was surprisingly tall. The tip of her head would easily graze the bottom of Kilal's chin, which would put her an inch or two over six feet. But what caught his attention more than anything else was the way she held herself. She never let her gaze stay focused on one thing for too long. Her fingers constantly moved, her shoulders hunched, and chest withdrawn.

Everything about her screamed 'victim.'

His heart went out to her. Someone that young shouldn't have such a stance. The copper tingle along his tongue lingered; the girl was the source.

Why did she look so familiar?

His hand shot to his pocket, and he pulled out the Wanted ad. Holding it up, he compared the drawing with the real thing. That *child* was so dangerous to the Heirs of the Promise they would offer fifty pounds of aznium for her, dead or alive?

Upon seeing the paper in Kilal's hand, and the way he

studied it and her, the girl tried to slink away, but Claire held up a hand.

"There's nothing to fear from my friend. Kilal would sooner pluck his own eyes out than turn on an Arbiter for *any* amount of riches."

"I don't know, Mother." She squared up to him and raised her chin, as if challenging him to even think about turning her in. "I've been betrayed for far less."

Kilal stood and walked to the altar with the four burning candles. He held the Wanted ad above the closest flame, and it ate away at the paper. When there was nothing left to consume, Kilal returned to the pew.

"What are we talking about? What bounty?" he asked.

The tension visibly drained from the young girl.

"Allyria, this is Kilal. He's a dear friend I've known for a long time."

"He doesn't look old enough for that to be true."

Claire snickered. "Trust me, child. He ages well."

Kilal approached Allyria and held his hand out. She shrank away from the invitation, and he let it drop. "It's a pleasure to meet you, young lady." He flourished a bow.

"I'm not *young*," she snapped. "I'm seventeen!"

Kilal widened his eyes, and he curled forward in a mock bow. "My deepest apologies, eldest one. If I'd known the depths of your wisdom and maturity, I never would have insulted you in such a way."

He glanced up at her, and the familiar quiver of her lips as she tried to maintain her serious composure was a welcome reprieve to the desolation around them. How often had Lilliana attempted to feign hurt or insult just so he would shower her with more attention?

"So 'not young,' how did you end up in these humble accommodations with the revered Mother?"

"Come." Claire shuffled back into the dark recess both she and Allyria had come from. Kilal followed beside her and took her arm in his. "Let's discuss this over some warm tea."

He smiled. *Some things never change.*

How many cups of tea had they consumed together beside a cozy fire? The answer had to be in the thousands. Memories of better times flooded him as he followed Claire.

~ CHAPTER 7 ~

Inside Claire's living chamber, Kilal nearly stopped cold in his tracks. Those were the conditions she lived in? It was worse than some places he'd occupied in the Ashen Lands. He had to let go of her arm before his rising anger and flexing muscles crushed her brittle bones.

A soft glow came from three lit candles, one in each corner of the room opposite the one they stood in. Hanging from the ceiling were some electrical wires that had, at one time, powered lights. The bulbs were nowhere to be seen. Furnishings consisted of a small bed with the mattress bleeding straw stuffing and a few blankets not much thicker than the pillowcase, a water-damaged dresser with two of its five drawers missing, a small desk covered with clutter, and a stained red carpet that had once been a beautiful crimson silk. A small black pot rested over a wood fire, and a toilet sat in one of the corners with a candle. The walls, once covered in expertly painted murals of Sha'tum, were nothing more than barely recognizable images of chipped and peeling paint. And it was cold. Really cold.

The sanctuary was entirely without heat, aside from what little the candles gave off. Kilal had tossed the chill up to the hole in the ceiling, but now he knew the truth: the radiator, like the lights, didn't work.

It shouldn't be this way! How had a Mother of Silent Haven's holy place been forced to live in such squalor? No one should have to live in conditions like that. Especially when the rest of the city around them enjoyed basic commodities every citizen had the right to.

"Allyria. Would you pour three glasses of hot water and place a tea bag in each one?" Claire asked.

"Yes, Mother," she said, but not before giving Kilal a sidelong glare, as if daring him to do something while her back was turned.

As Allyria prepared the tea, Kilal reattached himself to Claire's elbow. "When did you come to Silent Haven?" he asked. "And why are you living like this?" So many questions, so little time.

She laid a hand on his and patted it fondly. "When I heard you'd disappeared, I transferred from New Cita. When did you return?"

"Three days ago."

"Tell me what you already know of the Heirs of the Promise."

"Not much," Kilal admitted, though he divulged the little information he had. As he spoke, he helped Claire to the bed and sat her down. She probably didn't need his assistance; she looked frailer than she felt while he held on to her, but neither of them pointed that out.

"No one knows where they came from," Claire said. "There are four of them. Fazin, Tor'et, Sienna, and their leader, Wolfe. They first showed up in New Cita. Their arrival was marked by the murder of New Cita's Governing Seats and over a dozen Arbiters. Two weeks later, they'd taken Vitrol. Then they came for Silent Haven.

"Everywhere they went, they spread their lies. Sha'tum was a tyrant. The Arbiters are his way of maintaining fear over the Sunlight Domain. The oath an Arbiter swears is forced upon them to oppress and entrap them to do the will of the Keepers.

"When they arrived in Silent Haven, dozens of Arbiters

stood by them. For three long days, war filled the streets. Keepers against the Heirs and their Oathbreakers. I'm assuming you can guess how that ended."

Kilal gave a curt nod, his heart sinking lower and lower with every new detail.

"With the Keepers either dead or in hiding, the bloody Oathbreakers and their Heirs turned Silent Haven against the worship of Sha'tum. It's now illegal to worship him in any way. Citizens are encouraged to report any neighbors, friends, families, or coworkers suspected of still holding to their beliefs. Trespassing in a holy place has become grounds for execution."

The bed creaked and groaned as Kilal sat beside her. He leaned back to the serenading of more protests from the mattress until he was staring at the ill-kept ceiling. "Why did they leave you here?" He turned his gaze to the back of the hunched woman he hadn't seen in thirty years.

"As a punishment. I'm to be a living and spiritual reminder of what awaits any who think to follow Sha'tum."

That's why you live in such squalor. Kilal groaned and placed a hand over his face. "How do you survive? Mothers rely on the generosity of the citizens. If that isn't coming in, then how?"

A tingle raced down his leg when she placed a hand on it. His body still remembered the good times they'd had many decades ago, before Requiem. "There are still those who haven't given in to the new laws. They do what they can. But most importantly, I've learned to be content with the little I have."

Kilal sat up. "I had a reason for returning." He stroked his beard, somewhat disgusted by its oiliness. A film of red covered his vision, and he longed for nothing more than to get his hands on Wolfe. "But I don't know if I can continue knowing the atrocities and rampant murders the Heirs are guilty of. Someone needs to stop them."

Allyria handed him a warm cup of tea. "And that someone is you?"

He took a sip. It tasted like memories of better times. He

allowed himself a few seconds to revel in the long-forgotten comfort of Claire's homemade recipe. He'd earned that much, hadn't he? "I don't see much way around it."

"Good." Allyria planted herself in front of him with both hands on her hips. "I can help."

A burst of laughter almost escaped him. Almost.

"I think you'd be better off taking care of Mother," he said between sips.

Honey, sugar, Kilal thought, trying to remember Claire's recipe. What gave it its spice? Each taste enveloped his lips and tongue with a subtle tang that only enhanced the sweetness.

"You don't think I can help?" Allyria drew her lips into a flat line.

"To be honest," another sip, "I don't know anything about you. And what I know of the Heirs worries me. Not even the Keepers could stand up to them. And they were some of the most powerful Arbiters of our time."

"I'm an Arbiter, too." She said it as if it had been some well-kept secret.

Kilal let some of the warm liquid roll around in his mouth before swallowing it. "I didn't think anyone would order a hit on a seventeen-year-old girl because she annoyed them. What classification are you? Enlightened? High?"

He only sensed her using one Carving from the Physical branch. But that didn't mean she was an Enlightened. She could be a High and just not be using her second Carving.

Allyria narrowed her eyes and somewhat folded in on herself, as if coiling her muscles and preparing to spring away if he presented any threat. "You're not supposed to ask questions like that."

"On normal occasions, I'd agree. But like I said before, I don't know you. And if there was even a hint of a chance I'd take you with me; knowing who you are would go a long way to improving those odds. Besides, we have a common enemy, which makes us allies."

She pursed her lips and seemed to mull it over. Kilal took advantage of the silence and enjoyed more of his tea.

"Well, I guess it's not like I can get into any more trouble than I'm already in. I'm neither of those. I'm a Prime."

Kilal choked on his fresh sip. It spewed from his mouth, spraying his legs and Allyria's dirt-caked shoes. She yelped and hopped backward. Coughing, he couldn't keep his brows from nearly climbing off his face. "A Prime Arbiter?" he sputtered. "That's not what I expected."

"Yeah," she said, kicking at a stain on the carpet. "What of it?" Her boastful demeanor became ripe with suspicion.

Kilal shook his head and ran a hand through his hair and over his beard. "It's just been a really long time since a Prime was born."

Allyria—like him—could use three Carvings, one from each of the branches: Mind, Physical, and Elemental. Kilal wasn't exaggerating when he'd said it had been a really long time. The last Prime Arbiter he'd heard of must have been over fifty years ago. Yet there stood a brand new one.

"Did you know?" he asked Claire.

"Yes."

Kilal returned his attention to Allyria. "When did you undergo the Awakening?"

She paused her assault on the mark on the floor and tapped her chin. "About two months ago?"

"Two months?" he whispered. That was unheard of! He'd been considered old when he underwent the Awakening, and he'd been thirteen. "Who administered it?"

The stain on the carpet no longer held her attention. Allyria's gaze moved to the wall, and she shuffled her feet in its direction. "What does that matter?"

"The Keepers of the Oath were killed five years ago," he said. "So, I'd like to know if the one who administered the Awakening was someone I knew."

She picked at a piece of peeling paint. "He called himself Healer."

The name meant nothing to Kilal.

"It was horrible," she continued, wrapping her arms around herself. "I...I...wanted to die."

Kilal didn't need to ask why. The Awakening—he remembered his thirteenth birthday well. He'd woken up with the Sign of Sha'tum on his wrist. His parents and brother had lamented the finding. His mother and father debated hiding him. No one needed to know. But any family found hiding an individual with the Sign would be executed. So, saying goodbye to his mother and brother, he and his father had ventured out to the nearest Arbiter establishment.

An Arbiter was required by law to activate the Sign and, once Awakened, the individual would...evolve. It was not a physical transformation. It was an evolution of the spirit. It awoke the ability to use Carvings. And it was absolute torture. Kilal spent three days writhing and wriggling in his own excrement and vomit, wishing someone would kill him. Lilliana's had been much milder. A few hours was all it took for her.

He hoped Allyria's Awakening had been closer to Lilliana's than his.

"It was," Kilal said. "And you never forget the pain."

"Wonderful."

"So, Prime Arbiter," he pressed, "how did you end up here?"

Allyria shrugged and walked to the small fire in the middle of the room. The slight breeze kept the shadows dancing. For a moment, they landed on the girl, obstructing much of her face. The wood crackled and popped as the flames had their way with the few remaining logs.

"That bloody Wanted ad." She spit on the fire. "Heard some folks talking about this place, how the Mother gave safe haven to Arbiters trying to come and go in the city in secret. Came here two days ago. Been here since."

It was surely only a fraction of the story, but Kilal didn't push further. There would be a time for that soon enough.

One thing, however, did bother him.

"You help Arbiters get into and out of the city?" Kilal placed a palm on Claire's back.

She nodded. "But the last one I helped was over a year ago. My contacts and methods are long gone now."

Kilal moved his hand in a circular motion on her back. "Thank you," he said.

Her eyes brimmed with tears, and she gave him a mischievous smile. "For what? I only helped those in need. I believe a man I used to know said such things when thanked for his efforts."

"Sounds like a pretty great guy." He winked.

"Oh, he is." A tear fell to her cheek. "The best."

"Seriously, thank you. Those were my brothers and sisters you helped when I could not. There aren't enough words to express my gratitude."

As a non-Arbiter, Claire didn't have any devotion to his kind. And yet, she still cared for them in their time of need.

Claire wrapped one of his thick, muscular arms with one of her own. Her slender skin and boney limb almost looked like a child's in comparison. Her head rested on his shoulder, and a tightness gripped his chest—a longing for a different past.

Allyria faced them with arms crossed. "Were you guys married or something?"

Kilal cleared his throat.

Claire chuckled. "Once, *long* ago."

"So much for marriage being a *life*long thing," Allyria muttered.

"When did you hear about what the Mother did for Arbiters?" Kilal asked, wanting to change the subject.

Allyria furrowed her brow and tapped her chin. "A week ago?"

That wasn't good.

Claire must have felt him tense. "Is that a problem?"

"Possibly. It means if the Heirs don't know about you yet,

they will soon." His mind leapt into action, analyzing the best course of action.

"How would they know?" Allyria asked. "I wasn't followed. I promise."

Kilal chewed his lower lip. If they *had* followed Allyria, she wouldn't know. Of that, he was certain. "If you haven't trafficked anyone out or into the city in at least a year, and you managed to do so *without* the Heir's intervention, then why are people on the street talking about it *now*? Or at all? My guess is they've figured it out, and whoever you heard it from works for the Oathbreakers. Whatever they said, they've probably said dozens of times in random places all over the city."

"Why?"

"So Arbiters on the run, like you, would hear about it and think this is a safe place to hide out in. Sooner or later, someone will either catch you leaving or they'll send someone in looking for stowaways."

The color drained from the two ladies' faces.

"What...I...where shou—" Allyria stammered while pacing back and forth, unable to get a complete thought out. "What are we sitting around here for, then? We need to leave!"

"We have some time," Kilal reassured.

"How can you know that?"

He held up a finger. "You've been here for two days, and no one's shown up." A second finger joined the first. "Claire, you said even taking a step into a holy place was punishable by death. I've been here for at least an hour, and no one has arrived. Maybe they used to have someone stationed to watch this place, but I bet that stopped a long time ago. If there were someone watching, we'd already have had guests."

Allyria began nodding along as he explained, as if he were echoing her thoughts.

"But we can't stay here for much longer," he confirmed. "Not without testing fate, and in my experience, fate has never looked kindly upon me. If we stay, we increase the risk to Mother."

"We can't—*won't* do that."

Kilal was surprised by the vehemence and determination in Allyria's voice. She was a strong Arbiter, even if judging based on her classification alone, but there was something else she'd just revealed, if only for a moment. Something familiar. It was the primary trait he'd looked for when recruiting the Keepers.

A genuine desire to protect others.

"Why can I only sense one Carving active in you?" Kilal asked.

Allyria's face reddened. Her hands suddenly needed her attention. "I only know one."

He rubbed his temple with a hand and furrowed his brow. "You're a *Prime* Arbiter." The bed groaned as he repositioned himself. "And you only have *one* Carving ready?"

Kilal thought her blush couldn't have deepened. He was wrong. "Well, it's not like I've had anyone teaching me or anything!"

"What about the one who initiated the Awakening?"

"Dead."

He shook his head and stared up at the ceiling. It wasn't in much better repair than the sanctuary itself, but at least the pitiful bed chamber ceiling didn't have a giant hole in it. "There was a time when the Awakening of a Prime Arbiter would have been celebrated throughout the land." Now? Apparently, they lived on the streets, the only notoriety being from a group hunting them down.

"Must have been nice," she muttered.

"So, what Carving do you have active, and when did you etch it last?" He already sensed it was from the Physical branch, but he didn't know what specific type it was.

"Just basic strength. And...two mornings ago. I think."

Kilal groaned loud enough to wake a hibernating bear. The Carving itself he could understand, but the lapse of time? "That was almost forty-eight hours ago."

"I know that!" she snapped. "I lost my knife, okay? I can't

exactly carve anything without it."

"You can carve with anything that cuts flesh," Kilal corrected, shaking his head. "Those blades just make it easier." And
an Arbiter worth their oath carved as necessary—and *never* let
more than forty hours expire if it could be avoided.

Allyria's knowledge and training were woefully lacking.
Worse than Kilal expected, and he hadn't expected much.
There was no way he was setting foot outside of the holy place
and into a possible war zone with her so unprepared.

"Tell me what you know about the three tiers of Arbiters."

As Allyria shuffled from side to side, the heels of her shoes
scraped against the rough carpet. "Is now *really* the right time
for this? Shouldn't we be getting out of here?"

"It's definitely *not* a good time for this," he said. "However,
the moment we leave the temple, we must be prepared to be
attacked. And you need to be able to protect yourself when
that happens. As I explained, I'm confident the Heirs aren't
going to come barging in here in the next hour, but I can't
guarantee anything beyond that. So yes, we do this *now*."

While the girl focused on forming her face into the scariest
scowl he'd ever seen, Claire got up and fetched two small logs,
which she placed on the fire beneath the black pot Allyria used
to boil the water and poked them with an iron rod.

"Well," Allyria finally said, "Enlightened Arbiters can use
one Carving from one of the three branches."

"Which are?"

"Mind, Elemental, and Physical."

"Okay," Kilal said. "And can they use a Carving from any
branch they wish?"

She flashed him a look of irritation, as if to say *I was
getting to that.* "No. The branch they wield is predetermined
during their Awakening."

Kilal nodded.

Hands behind her back, Allyria circled the fire, kicking at
invisible debris.

Claire returned to his side.

"Enlightened Arbiters are the most common type. Second is the High Arbiter, who can use two Carvings, one from each of two branches. Those branches, like an Enlightened Arbiter, are predetermined during their Awakening." She paused, presumably to allow Kilal a chance to ask questions, but he kept silent. "And the last and rarest form is the Prime Arbiter. *We* can use three Carvings, one from each branch."

Kilal didn't miss the inflection she placed on 'we.' Was she trying to insinuate her self-worth was greater than his because she presumed him to be either of the other two classifications? There was a time in his life when Kilal would've gladly shown her how childish she was being. But that time had long since passed.

"What about Inflictors?"

Allyria stopped in front of the crackling fire and brought her hands up before the flames. "Never seen one before. Supposedly, they can cancel all Carvings an Arbiter has prepared by simply touching them. I was told they were Sha'tum's way of maintaining balance. A sort of checks and balances. Or something like that."

"Something like that," Kilal mumbled. "Mother?" He stood and turned to Claire. Her eyes drooped, and she was more hunched than before. Had she looked that tired when he'd first arrived? "We're going to need your desk. Do you have any rags, an extra bucket or two, and more candles?"

"Of course."

"Allyria, help her, please. I'll clean off the desk. Gather as many rags as you can. Preferably clean, but any will do."

Allyria helped Claire to her feet. Together they stepped out of the room, leaving Kilal alone.

~ CHAPTER 8 ~

Next, he dumped some water from the pot into one of the buckets, which—fortunately—contained the liquid. With the amount of rust coating the bottom, Kilal hadn't gotten his hopes up. Three more rags were dropped into the warm water, wrung out, and placed on a corner of the desk. They would be necessary to clean Allyria's arm and examine it.

Lastly, Kilal pulled out the knife kit attached to his belt and tossed it to her.

"Take a seat," he instructed. The chair wobbled and creaked under her weight. It would've crumbled to pieces if Kilal had sat in it. "Start with your strength Carving. When you finish activating it, I'll give you a Mind and Elemental Carving."

"Why don't I just carve all three at once, then activate them at the same time? Get it all over with as quickly as possible?"

"Doesn't work like that. One at a time."

"Why?"

"Because."

When she accepted he wasn't going to elaborate, Allyria turned her eyes to the kit in her hand before hesitantly pulling the biggest blade of the trio out. Kilal knew the turmoil raging through her. The desire for the power granted by Carvings warring against the pain one must endure to obtain it.

She slowly dragged the edge of the knife along her wrist.

Whimpers and grimaces filled the room. A tear trickled from her cheek. It dropped amongst the blood oozing from her arm. The rune was barely a quarter finished before her hand began shaking.

"Take a break," Kilal said. "And wipe the blood away with the wet rag."

As she did so, he searched for any words of encouragement and comfort he could give her. He found none. So, he just stood there, a silent statue looming in the shadows.

Despite her trembling hand and lack of pain tolerance, Allyria still finished the Carving in under ten minutes. And it was perfect. Kilal didn't know how many times she'd etched that particular Carving, but he couldn't imagine it wasn't many. Definitely not enough to warrant the skill she'd just demonstrated.

She was good. *Real* good.

What sort of Arbiter could she become under his guidance?

Doesn't matter, he chastised. *I won't be taking any more mentees, remember? After I find Jayden, I'm out of here.*

So, you'll abandon her just like you did your daughter?

Kilal shoved his shaking hands into his pockets.

Finished with the Carving, Allyria swapped out the large knife for the pick. She took a deep breath and shoved the point into the center of the design. One clockwise rotation and she seized, but the effect was far milder than what Kilal had endured in the bathroom of *Forget Everything.*

The stronger the Carving, the worse the convulsions.

"I'm ready for the other ones," she said once the spasms eased, rubbing tears from her cheeks.

"No, you're not. Test it. Make sure it works."

"I know it works."

"Doesn't matter. You *always* verify. Always. Someday, it could be the difference between life and death."

"Okay, okay," she muttered. "Um..." She swiveled her head around. "How do I test it?"

She had a point. Normally, Kilal would've had something a mentee could crush, break, or snap. But he wasn't going to do that to Claire or the temple. The sanctuary was already destroyed enough.

"Punch me." He pointed at his gut. "If you can make me grunt...the Carving is active."

Allyria appeared thoughtful. "Really?"

Kilal smiled. "Trust me, I'll be fine." He meant to soothe any fear or trepidation she may have about hitting him, but it didn't look like she took it that way.

"Have it your way." She stood, faced him—and punched him in the sternum.

The crack echoed through the quiet room. So did Kilal's grunt.

White energy sparked and buzzed around his chest, and fire spread from the healing wound through his body. Allyria gasped and stepped back.

"Congratulations," Kilal said after the wind returned to his lungs. With the back of a hand, he wiped a trickle of blood from his mouth. "Not only did you strip precious time off your Carving, but if I weren't me, I'd be dead."

Allyria looked to the Mother for support. She received none. "*You* told me to punch you!"

He pursed his lips. "I meant in the gut. And you used the max strength of your Carving. Bloodshed and Oaths, that was foolish!" His tone was harsh, and he instantly regretted it. The timbre, not what he said.

She flinched and recoiled, clearly not expecting the rebuke. "I-I'm sorry."

Kilal sighed. The fault really lay on him. The girl knew *nothing*. He shouldn't have expected her to have even the most basic foundational understanding. "You didn't know you could throttle the output, did you?"

Allyria shook her head.

"Okay." He gestured to her seat and continued. "Your basic

strength Carving gives you access to up to ten times the power of the strongest human. But can you operate at that level for the full forty-eight hours?"

She scratched her head and tried to focus on anything but him. "No?"

Kilal raised a brow. "Good guess. But you're right. Each of the branches works differently. Physical runes have minimum and maximum values. A basic strength's minimal value is ten percent of its maximum output."

"So, one times the power of the strongest human?"

Kilal nodded. "The more strength you tap into, the quicker the Carving will decay." The confusion on her face was evident. "You don't know about that either, do you?"

She scrunched her brow. "If I said yes, would you believe me?"

"If I said yes, would you believe me?" Kilal echoed.

She didn't respond.

"A Carving can last up to forty-eight hours," he continued. "But the more you use it, and the higher power thresholds you access, the quicker it'll decay." Her confusion remained. "Okay, think of a glass of water where the water turns to poison when time is up. No matter what, every forty-eight hours, you'll need to get a new glass. But as you drink the water, the glass could become empty before the time is up."

She clapped her hands and held one up. "So, if I use the maximum output of my Carving, ten times the strength of the strongest human, that would be like gulping the glass of water. It'll be used up far quicker than if I sip it instead."

"Exactly." Kilal was impressed; she caught on quickly.

"So, how do I throttle?"

"Every Arbiter has a different technique that fits them. I like to picture a knob with a range of zero to one hundred. When I want to raise my strength to fifty percent of the max output, I rotate the knob clockwise to that number. That's the method I tend to teach new Arbiters, too. As you mature in your abilities, you may develop new techniques, but for now, I recommend this."

"Okay. A knob." She narrowed her eyes and scrunched her face in concentration. "So...how do I *grab* it?"

That was always the hardest part for a novice to understand. And for him to explain.

"Carving use is misunderstood as being a physical phenomenon. But it's not. It's a spiritual phenomenon. From the moment of our Awakening, we evolve *spiritually,* as well as physically, but those evolutions are seeded from different things.

"The physical evolution comes with the use of our new body, which correlates to our Arbiter classification. Our new bodies naturally make us stronger, faster, and more resilient to damage, grant us quicker healing, and reduce our need for sleep, food, and water—and all of these differ for each body. The higher the classification, the stronger the body.

"But Carvings themselves correlate to a spiritual evolution. And as such, you need to focus on your center, and within it, the source of your power. Like a bright sphere in the surrounding darkness.

"Close your eyes. Search for that source. You know you've found it when warmth fills you and you suddenly feel perfectly relaxed."

Allyria, doubt all over her face, closed her eyes.

Minutes passed in silence. Kilal took the time to turn his own attention inward, delving into his spirit, finding the glowing sphere representing his evolution as an Arbiter. It was warm and welcoming, and for a brief moment, as he let the heat radiate through his body, he felt *good.*

But all good things come to an end.

Kilal withdrew from the globe and opened his eyes. He waited for Allyria to find her source. Eventually, the tension eased from her shoulders, the stress melting from the muscles in her face.

She'd found it.

Eyes still closed, she smiled. "It's so...beautiful."

Kilal smiled, too. "Eventually, this will become instinctual, and you won't have to do it this way anymore. But for now, picture the knob *within* the glowing sphere and rotate it to whatever percent you want."

Eventually, Allyria—still smiling—looked at him again. "I think I've got it. So how long can I use max power for? Or minimum power? Or fifty percent?"

Kilal shrugged. "There isn't a definite equation or easy answer to that. Each Carving is different. It's up to the Arbiter to be aware of their usage, know the feeling of decay, and gauge how much more they have left."

Allyria pursed her lips and rolled her eyes. "So, what you're saying is, I need a hundred years of experience to be a good Arbiter?"

Kilal mimicked her eye roll and pouty demeanor. "I know, right. Working hard is the *worst*."

She narrowed her gaze and gritted her teeth. He'd forgotten how easy it was to get under a teenager's skin. "Have you ever used a healing rune?"

She shook her head.

Kilal gestured for her to stand and took her seat. Brushing aside the bloody rags on the desk, Kilal grabbed a piece of paper and a pen. Dozens of healing Carvings came to mind, and he sifted through them until he settled on one he was comfortable teaching her.

Most of the ones he'd stowed away in his memories were too powerful for her to handle. The price of activation alone would probably be more than she could bear. The seizures accompanying them would damn near consume her. It's better to step her up slowly.

The Carving of Advanced Healing would do the trick. It was strong, more so than a beginner's Carving of Healing, and the activation wouldn't be enjoyable, but it would enlighten her to the steep cost that came with power.

Sketch finished, he stood and let her take the chair again. "Alright. Here's your access to Advanced Healing."

Claire coughed, and Kilal nearly jumped. He'd forgotten she was still in the room. Sometime during his lecture, she'd moved to the bed again and was resting on it.

She gave him a small wave and a mischievous smile. He knew what that smile meant: *I know you're enjoying this, so stop pretending otherwise.* Kilal rolled his eyes and returned his attention to Allyria.

The Carving knife was in her hand, but it still hadn't tasted her blood again. Based on her expression, the all too familiar conflict was back at the forefront of her mind.

In the beginning, when he'd first started carving, the suffering had almost not been worth the benefit. With how wet her cheeks already were and the shaking of her hand, Kilal wasn't sure the advantages would outweigh the pain in her eyes.

When she took a deep breath and wiped her face with the back of her hand, a surge of pride warmed Kilal's chest before she'd even pressed the blade into her wrist.

Attagirl.

Her hand moved with impressive skill. For someone who hadn't carved anything other than a basic strength rune, Allyria was quick to pick up on the small details of the new design.

But even child prodigies made mistakes eventually.

"Stop."

She was halfway through when she looked up, brows furrowed.

Kilal pointed at the Carving he'd sketched on the paper, to a rune in the top left quadrant of a circle enclosed in a diamond. "You see these three rings intertwined together?" Allyria nodded. "What's different about yours?"

She looked from the three she'd etched to the ones Kilal had drawn. "My middle ring is smaller than the other two. But yours is larger."

"Exactly," he said. "The Carving is ruined."

"But it's barely different!" Allyria whined. She slouched back in her seat.

"*Barely* is the difference between life and death."

"What isn't the difference between life and death?" Allyria muttered.

"The more powerful the Carving, the more intricate and elaborate the four runes are. And the more precisely each must be drawn. Perfection is the only standard."

"So, what am I supposed to do?"

"Cancel it."

"Umm...how do I do that?"

Kilal repressed a sigh. *It's not her fault.* "Carve an X through the whole thing."

She let out a low moan and went to work. By the time she was done striking it out, the first rag he'd given her was completely saturated with blood and replaced with another.

"Grab the pick," he instructed. "And activate the Carving like you normally would. It will cancel and heal the flesh back to normal. Then, you'll have to start over."

She flopped her head against the desk, but did as he told her. When she rotated the pick one hundred and eighty degrees, the Carving flashed white and receded into her skin. Thankfully, there were no additional consequences to canceling like there were for activating, aside from an uncomfortable sting as the flesh stitched closed.

"Great," she said. "Now I get to start again."

"Do it right this time, and you won't have to do it again."

She leveled a glare at him he was fairly certain she hoped would kill him. Claire snickered from behind them.

A few minutes later, Allyria looked up expectantly. Kilal analyzed her work. It was perfect.

Impressive. That was an advanced Carving, and it normally took a dozen or so attempts to get it right, but she'd accomplished it on her second try.

If Kilal had the time, and they had a normal mentorship, he'd tell her to cancel it again and re-carve. A hundred times. To get her so familiarized with the design, the margin of error would be near zero.

Without that luxury, Kilal gave her an approving nod. "Good job."

Allyria beamed.

"Now, activate it." He handed her the second bucket. "And if I were you, I'd lay on the floor. This isn't going to be enjoyable."

She paled.

The seizure was a bad one; she threw up in the rusty bucket when it was over.

"This will...happen," she panted, on all fours, "every...time?"

"Welcome to being an Arbiter."

Allyria groaned and returned to her chair, slouching into it.

"Now, test it."

"And how am I supposed to do that?"

Kilal nodded toward the knife on the desk. She squeezed her eyes shut and groaned again.

Blade back in hand, the edge pressed against the flat of her palm, she took a deep breath and calmed her quivering before sliding the knife over it. She stared at the open wound—and yelped when it began mending itself. The yelp turned into a squeal when she inspected her fully healed hand a heartbeat later.

"Amazing!" She looked at him with furrowed brows. "But why does the healing hurt more than the cut?"

"The greater the power, the greater the cost."

She ran a finger through the dust on the desktop, creating some sort of doodle. "It shouldn't be that way. It's stupid."

Kilal took the knife from her hand. "It is what it is. You'll get used to it."

"Is this like the strength one?" she asked. "Does it decay too?"

"Yes, but not in the same way. Healing Carvings will give

you a finite amount of mending power, and once it's used up, it's done. You can't dictate how much of it you use. But that's the beauty of Carvings. Now that you have the design down, you can experiment with the four runes that create it to customize it and make it your own.

"I've seen Arbiters who couldn't heal serious wounds, but they could heal minor wounds and injuries constantly for the full forty-eight hours. Whereas, on the opposite spectrum, I've known an Arbiter who customized his to only activate when he was on the brink of death. His head was nearly severed, but he was restored to perfect health in an instant. Imagine the surprise of his enemies!" Kilal laughed as he recalled the event. "The possibilities are infinite. All you need is time, the will to endure, and the drive to discover.

"When I became an Arbiter, I spent weeks locked in my room with a mountain of rags, multiple buckets, and my knife kit. I tested every Carving I knew, modifying them hundreds of times. I recorded every failure, every success, and what those successes entailed. I even discovered a few new Carvings. You should have seen...."

He trailed off. Allyria was biting her nails and staring at the floor.

"... How little you were paying attention?"

She didn't respond. His monologue must have sent her into the world of daydreams.

Kilal sighed. "The last one," he continued, raising his voice a little; it seemed to grab her attention. "Elemental won't be as bad. I'm going to give you a mild Stoneskin Carving. It'll help with some protection if we get into trouble." He sketched the runes encompassed in it onto a second page.

Allyria studied the design and got to work. After the first line, she paused and ran a rag over the bleeding wound. She stared at it, her brow furrowed and lips pursed.

Good job, Kilal thought, anticipating Allyria's confusion. It was the same confusion every Arbiter with healing active for the first time had when they etched their second Carving.

She finally looked up at him. "Why isn't it mending?"

He gave her a proud smile. "Great question. The answer?" He shrugged.

"That's it? No explanation?"

Kilal shrugged again. "Sorry, but that's the best I can do. No one knows why other Carvings aren't healed like normal injuries. The only thing I can guess is that's just the way Sha'tum designed it."

Allyria frowned again and stared at the cut. "I guess it makes sense. This way gives some freedom in the order I carve."

Exactly.

Question answered, she returned to her work.

Despite being a mild Carving, she still lay on the ground before activating it, though the seizure was barely more than a muscle spasm and only lasted a few seconds.

"So, how do I test this one?" she asked after completing the process.

"Just like with strength," Kilal said. "Pretend it's a button. Except this time, you're going to 'press' that button, and as you do, think of a body part."

Allyria pinched her brow in concentration and stared at her hand. There was a moment of relaxation in her face before the skin shimmered and hardened into stone. "Ha!" she said, waving her transformed hand in front of him triumphantly. She wiggled her fingers and made a fist, her joints softly scraping as though they were made of sandpaper. "This is awesome!"

"Just repeat the process to return the hand to normal."

Instead, Allyria turned her whole arm into stone. Then the other. Kilal allowed her a few moments to revel in the newfound power. After what she'd been through, she deserved at least that much.

"How long will this last?"

"The Elemental branch is the easiest," he said. "It's almost impossible to overuse."

"Almost?"

"It would take an extreme investment into that Carving."

After turning her hand to stone and back again, Allyria turned innocent eyes to him. "But what would happen if I did overuse it?"

"It's called burnout. Basically, your brain melts."

She grinned. "Right." When he continued staring, expression flat, the smile quickly faded, and the blood drained from her face. "Mental note," she whispered. "Don't use this Carving too much."

Kilal knew she wasn't at risk of such a fate. He'd only experienced burnout once, and that had been an—*No.* He shook his head. No need to go back there.

He wiped the blades and packed up his knives, then crumbled the two pieces of paper to toss in the smoldering fire beneath the cooking pot. Allyria helped gather the rags when she paused, staring at her own crimson-soaked clothes.

"I've seen people pass out from less blood loss than this," she said. "How come I didn't? I don't even feel dizzy."

Ashes, she asks good questions.

"It has to do with the new bodies I told you about. As a Prime Arbiter, you have the best natural healing factor. From minor cuts, like carving, even if etched on a place like your wrist, it would be hard to lose more blood than you regenerate."

She frowned. "Is that how you knew I had a Physical Carving active? Because of our Prime body? Can like bodies sense one another?"

"No, but close. Like *Carvings* can sense one another. An Enlightened Arbiter using the Physical branch could sense when a High or even a Prime is using a Physical Carving too. They can't tell what it does or if they can use other branches, but they can sense at least that much."

"But what does it feel like? How do I know someone is using a certain kind?"

"The Physical branch floods your mouth with the taste of

copper. Elemental feels like a warm gust of wind against your skin. And Mind Carvings are like low, unintelligible whispers in your ears."

Allyria's eyes widened, and she took a long breath. "There's a lot more to being an Arbiter than I thought."

"Don't worry," Kilal said with a hint of mischief. "Give it a few years, and it'll all become second nature."

She rolled her eyes. "If I live that long," she mumbled.

~ CHAPTER 9 ~

When they'd finally cleaned their mess, Kilal turned to Claire. "Now that Allyria is ready, we can be off. I'll take you both to my place." He mentally crossed his fingers, hoping his apartment was still his.

It had been ten years since he'd been there last. His rent should still be getting paid by an automatic payment system, but in his experience, if something could go wrong, it probably would. And in this case, if his apartment was no longer his, he wasn't really sure what he'd do with Allyria and Claire.

"Kilal." Claire's bony fingers stopped him from grabbing another armful of rags. "I'm not going with you."

He dismissed her with a wave of a hand. "That's ridiculous. Of course you are."

Her grip on his arm tightened. The look on her face made Kilal's stomach clench. He'd seen it before, and he already knew how things were going to end.

"I'm not going with you," Claire repeated.

He pulled his arm free and squared up with her. He wasn't going to just let it go. Not after everything they'd both been through. Together and apart. Heat rose in his cheeks, and his chest strained. "Why? Please. Let me take care of you. Like you once did for me."

If he thought she looked old earlier, her current state made that look young. "Ki, I'm ninety-eight years old. I'm weak. Tired. Do you really think I'll be able to traipse around the city with you two?"

"I'll carry you."

"And if the Heirs attack, what then?"

"I...I..." He looked for something to punch, but found nothing. "I DON'T CARE! You don't deserve to live like this—or be treated like this. You've done so much for me, for Req, for all Arbiters. More than I can ever repay you for. Please don't make me leave you here." His words caught in his throat, and when they squeezed out, they were barely recognizable. "Please. I've lost enough. Don't add to that list."

"Allyria, my child, why don't you wait for Kilal in the sanctuary?" Claire said, her gaze to the side.

Kilal didn't hear or see the girl's response, though the room grew a little emptier from one frantic heartbeat to the next.

The silence rang in his ears as Claire approached and took his hands into hers. "My time among the living is coming to an end. But while I'm here, I'll do what I can for Silent Haven. There are still citizens in this city that need me. They need hope. They need the memories of Sha'tum. I cannot abandon them."

"Then what was the point?" Kilal asked. "Why did we have to meet again just to—"

"So we could say goodbye." Claire grimaced. "Promise you won't remember me as the worn-out leather husk, but as the young, silken-skinned woman you met all those years ago."

"What 'leather husk' are you talking about? I see only beauty and strength before me." Kilal lifted her tiny frame and settled her feet on top of his own. "Do you remember the first time we danced?"

Claire giggled, and for a moment he was swept eighty years into the past. The room melted around him, and a cozy space lit only by the flames of their fireplace replaced it. "You were so awful, you nearly broke my toes."

Kilal chuckled. "If that wasn't a sign to toss me back onto the streets, I don't know what was."

"I was only protecting all the other ladies who would've fallen for you only to have their feet broken." They shared a chuckle. "But, you were an excellent student," Claire continued. "Do you remember the dance contest we went to in New Cita?"

"The one where everyone nearly laughed us out of the place because they just knew our size difference would make it impossible for us to win?"

Claire made a noise more akin to a purr than anything else. "We proved them wrong, didn't we?"

"Ha! Like we were going to let some pompous jerks show us up."

They were swaying, the two of them. Back and forth, dancing to a tune only they could hear. And it felt good. Comfortable silence lingered, and Kilal would give anything to be frozen in time, in that moment. Just him and Claire. Together. Enjoying a slow dance, the first she'd taught him.

He broke the quiet first. "Thank you."

"For what?"

Still moving to a silent tune, Kilal placed a finger beneath her chin and tilted her head up. "You found me in my darkest time, and without you, I wouldn't be here today. You saved me. You showed me how I could live with myself, how I could atone for the sins of my past.

"For so, so long, I was nothing more than a monster. Something incapable of being loved. You showed me that I wasn't be—that I wasn't beyo—" He paused and took a deep breath, hoping to calm the waver in his voice and the emotion balling in his throat. It didn't work. "You showed me that I wasn't beyond forgiveness. I'm the man I am today because of you. Thank you."

Claire shuddered in his arms and wept.

Kilal led them around the room, shadowing the dance

steps he'd learned all those years ago. They were ingrained in him now, and he'd never forget them. Their partnership as husband and wife may have ended what seemed like a lifetime ago, and he may have found his soulmate in Requiem, but some bonds couldn't be broken. Claire would always live in his heart.

They indulged in a few more circles around the room, and they would have taken many more if Claire left it up to him—but she didn't.

"It's time, Kilal."

"Please. Just a little longer."

She stepped off his boots and pulled away. "Allyria's bored to tears by now, I'm sure."

He rolled his eyes. "She's a teenager. She's always bored."

"That may be, but it doesn't change that it's time for you to take her and go. I'm sorry, but I've reached the end of my endurance. I'm..." She placed a hand over her mouth and yawned. "I'm so tired. Always so tired."

Kilal's legs and arms took over, and he helped her to the bed, all the while mentally screaming at his limbs to obey him. To stop making their parting harder than necessary. He peeled back the sheets and eased her onto the lumpy mattress.

With a strength he didn't think she had anymore, Claire lurched up and grabbed hold of his shirt. "Take care of Allyria. Please. Promise me you'll treat her like she's your own."

"I..." He barely managed to wrestle his shirt away, but when he did, she exhaled loudly and slumped onto her pillow. How could he promise such a thing? He would leave sooner or later, and where he would go, he wouldn't take Allyria with him. He wouldn't do that to another child. But Claire's eyes were so wide and pleading; how could he say no? "I'll take care of her. I promise."

Claire sighed and smiled, her eyes slowly closing. "Thank you...I'm glad we got to see each other again."

She was asleep before Kilal could respond.

He leaned down, pressing their foreheads together, and whispered, "May we meet again someday, in this life or the next. Sha'tum, if you are able, welcome her into whatever waits for us when we pass."

The fire was dim and emitted little heat. Kilal scooped up a few more logs and placed them on the ashes. It didn't feel right leaving her, but he couldn't dispute any of the arguments she gave for staying.

Before he left, he placed the rest of the money he had in his wallet on the desk. He didn't know if she'd even be able to spend it, but it was the least he could do.

Claire's breathing became light and rhythmic.

"I'll never forget you," he murmured from the doorway.

Though every emotion and desire demanded he stay, and the voices in his head accused him of abandoning her, Kilal mustered the will to endure and stepped out of the room.

Allyria sat on the front pew, humming a tune he didn't recognize. When he approached, she jerked upright. Their gazes met for a moment before her eyes darted elsewhere.

"Um, is...everything alright?"

"No." The honest answer. "She's asleep, but she wanted you to know she's glad to have met you and that you have a good heart. She's sorry about whatever happened to cause you two to cross paths, but she's glad she got to be a part of your life, if only for a little bit."

Sure, he improvised all of it, but Claire wouldn't disagree. And based on Allyria's glimmering eyes, reddening cheeks, and blossoming smile, it was something she needed to hear.

She picked at a splinter in the pew. "Claire's a good woman. Probably the only person to ever care about me. And I only knew her for a few days." The splinter lost its appeal, and she looked at him. "Is that sad?"

Kilal sat on the pew next to her. The poor thing groaned from the added weight. Allyria shifted away from him, sliding to put a few feet between them.

The candles on the altar were out. The city was quiet, and the wind calm. Behind the altar on the wall, a painted glass mural of Sha'tum hovering in the sky was smashed. It had once depicted The Bloodshed, when their God rained his essence upon the land to bless them. Now it was nothing but a bare wall with chunks of glass skewered into it.

"She found me in a similar state," Kilal said. "I would've killed myself, but Claire showed me life is worth living." Why was he speaking of this again? Especially to a stranger? "She treated me better than I deserved. So, if it's sad, then I guess we're in the same boat."

Allyria lifted her feet onto the pew and hugged her legs to her chest. "I guess we're both pretty sad."

"Come on." He stood and stretched, releasing a long, loud yawn. To say he was tired would be like saying the Veil had only tickled his skin when he'd crossed through. And the encounter with Claire had done little to ease his mental exhaustion. When was the last time he'd had more than a few minutes of shut-eye? Days? Weeks? Months? "Let's get you out of here."

"Hey, you never told me what you are," Allyria said. Kilal raised a brow. "You know, about your classification of Arbiter."

Oh. That.

Kilal tried for an innocent smile. "Hasn't anyone told you, you aren't supposed to ask questions like that?"

She balled her fists at her side. "That's not fair!" Kilal chuckled. "Shouldn't I be able to sense which Carvings you have active?"

It was a common question and a common misconception.

"No. Because I'm not actively using any at the moment. Just because I have *three* Carvings ready to be used, doesn't mean I'm tapping into them. When I increase my strength or manipulate my gravity, then you'll encounter sensory experiences."

She nodded along as if every word made sense. Explanation over, he strode out of the holy place.

Back in the fresh night air under the illumination provided by Ophir and Dampir, Kilal took a moment of silent introspection. He wasn't well. He wasn't anywhere close to it and hadn't been for a long time. And picking up another stray to add to his self-imposed list of responsibilities didn't bode well. But what choice did he have? Leave Allyria? If he did, she'd be as good as dead. That wasn't an option.

Ten years ago, he would have happily scooped her up, trained her and cared for her. So why the hesitancy now? Did his mission really trump the life of another Arbiter? And which mission was he even thinking of? Finding Jayden and saving his world? Or returning to his search for Lilliana?

A gust whipped at his clothes, and Allyria braced herself against the strength of it. When it died down, leaving Kilal in silence again, Allyria's humming broke through the quiet.

A thought stuck out to him, one he didn't particularly care for. Instead of considering how he could maintain his goals while also taking care of Allyria, couldn't he consider how she could help him?

Allyria was a powerful Prime who had already exhibited a skill for Carving most Arbiters took years to achieve. What if he wasn't placed in her path to save her, but she was placed in his path to help him? And why pick one over the other? Perhaps fate brought them together for that exact purpose.

Kilal recognized the validity of it, but that didn't mean he had to like it. Allyria was a child. Yes, one with great potential, though a child nonetheless. But as he stared at Ophir, a privilege he'd always taken for granted, he thought of Lilliana in the Ashen Lands.

She couldn't see Ophir or Dampir, and it had been ten years since she'd seen anything but gray, ash-filled skies. And if he didn't stop the force of growing Ash Fallen, Kilal's world would be plunged into a darkness where the twin moons would be lost to memories of a time long past.

He had few options left. His lead was gone. His friends and

companions were too. He was alone except for Allyria. Would recruiting a Prime Arbiter, even one as young as her, really be a bad thing? If it meant the possible difference between saving his world and daughter, shouldn't he take it? No matter what that entailed for either of their futures?

Allyria's scream ripped him from his reverie. Pressure spiked behind his eyes, a warm gust of wind tickled his arms, and a streak of pink tore toward him from the shadowy recess of the alley across from them.

What the—

The pink coalesced air ripped through his arm, slicing it from his shoulder.

~ CHAPTER 10 ~

Allyria screamed.

Kilal grunted. The searing agony nearly drove him to his knees. No sooner had the arm flown free, flipping violently into the air and collapsing into a pile of dust when it hit the ground; white electricity engulfed his shoulder. Bone grew, protruding from the severed joint. Each inch brought a heightened level of misery.

Ligaments sprouted around the bone and muscle. Sinew stretched from the exposed flesh. Kilal's knees shook, and his eyes threatened to roll into the back of his head. Skin extended from the shoulder and along the arm. When it was completely covered, in one motion, it expanded with additional muscle to match the one it had replaced.

It was done.

The pain faded, and Kilal cleared his throat and wiped a tear from his cheek. He rotated the new arm, wiggled his fingers and gave the limb a good flex. Good as new. The despair clamoring to replace the void left behind by the pain was shoved aside until it was merely a light buzz in the background. It was the best he could hope for.

Allyria sat on her butt, staring at him, mouth open. Her entire body was covered in stone.

Impressive. The last person he'd taught that to took weeks to be able to fully cover his body.

A trio of Arbiters—two male, one female—exited the alley across from them. The man on the left was as tall as Kilal. His long, dark hair was slicked back and draped over the popped collar of a black trench coat. The long coat was buttoned from his neck to his laced black boots.

The other man was short where Trench Coat was tall and stocky where Trench Coat was slender. He had wide, muscled shoulders and a chest that would put most men to shame. He wore a black tank top tucked into blue baggy pants and a pair of heavyset boots. Spiked bracelets adorned each wrist, and the bandana around his forehead was no different. Pointy, greasy hair protruded from his scalp, neatly styled between the bandana.

The lone female stood between Trench Coat and Spike. Blonde hair streaked with pink brushed her shoulders. A container's worth of coral makeup covered her cheeks. Pink jewelry decorated her ears, nose, fingers, and toes. She wore a pink dress that had to have taken most of the morning to get into and open-toed rose high heels. It was easily the most ridiculous outfit Kilal had seen. Ever. And he'd seen some gaudy getups.

Kilal raised a brow. Is this what had become of Arbiters since he'd been gone? Were they more concerned with their reputation and 'costume' than defending the citizens of the Sunlight Domain and keeping their oath?

"Told you the ash-eating old woman was harboring runaways again," Spike said.

Blondie rolled her eyes. "And I'm sure we won't hear the end of it."

"I'll let him brag me to sleep every night with a smile on my face," Tench Coat said. "Look who it was she was hiding. That one's worth *fifty pounds of aznium*."

Keeping an eye on the Arbiters, Kilal held a hand out to Allyria. She glanced at it but didn't take it and helped herself up instead. Stone skin scraped against stone skin as she stood.

Spike pulled a piece of paper from his pocket. He unfolded it and showed it to the others. "It's her, alright," he said, voice as deep as his chest was wide.

Blondie snatched the paper from Spike's hand. She gave the Wanted ad a good look before turning to Allyria. "Never seen the Heirs offer so much for an Arbiter's life. Especially one so young."

"I don't care how old they are," Trench Coat said. "For fifty pounds of aznium, I'd kill my own mother."

"What about your own life? Is that worth fifty pounds?" Kilal interrupted.

Blondie snorted. "Far, *far* less."

"Then you should leave. There's no need for us to kill each other. We've all sworn the oath. We're all on the same side. The only side that wins by us killing each other is the army on the other side of the Veil."

The three Arbiters stared at him blankly. Then burst into laughter.

Trench Coat wiped a tear from his cheek. "The other side of the Veil? You hear this guy? No, the side that wins is the side that gets paid."

Kilal ground his teeth. He unclenched his fists and gave it another shot. "What is fifty pounds of aznium going to get you when Ash Fallen sweep across our land? You think they'll take your spoils and leave you alone? Or the Heirs of the Promise? When they turn on you, what will your aznium be worth then?"

"A bloody lot!" Spike said, to which the other two chuckled and echoed their agreement.

Kilal growled. Those idiots were so blinded by their greed, he feared there was only one way the confrontation would end. But he wasn't ready to give up on them. Killing Arbiters wasn't something he took lightly. At least, not anymore.

"Look," Kilal said. "I just want to give you a fair opportunity to leave this confrontation alive. So please, take it. For the sake of the oath we've sworn and the land we protect, don't make me kill you." Though he hoped they would, he had the sinking suspicion the trio wouldn't take him up on his offer.

"What about him?" Trench Coat said, ignoring Kilal's plea. "How much you think he's worth? You took his arm clean off, and he regrew it in seconds. Never seen a healing Carving like that. Gotta be worth a lot."

Blondie and Spike shook their heads.

"Don't remember seeing anything about him," Spike said.

"Whether there's a bounty on his head or not," Blondie added, "I bet the boss would pay nicely for removing a threat like him from the streets."

"Uh-huh," Trench Coat agreed.

Kilal sighed as a plan formed in his head. He hated it, and it might put Allyria and him in more danger, but if he could avoid killing fellow Arbiters, it was worth the risk. "I'll tell you what. I'll give you fifteen pounds of aznium if the three of you quit working for the Heirs and leave the city."

It was every ounce of aznium he owned, but he valued an Arbiter's life as more than fifteen pounds of the metal.

Trench Coat smirked. "You're about thirty-five pounds short there. And that's just for the girl. Not much of a deal, is it, Crave?"

Spike—Crave—cracked a few knuckles. The pops echoed through the empty streets. "Not much of a deal at all."

"Consider the other thirty-five pounds and whatever you would get for me as the price for your life." *Just take the deal.*

"In case you weren't aware, there are three of us and only two of you, one of which is a *child*," Blondie said. "I think we'll take your fifteen pounds and then your lives."

Trench Coat dropped into a crouch and ran a palm over the pavement. "You see, fifty pounds is just a *lot* of aznium. And like I said, I'd kill my own mother for that amount. So don't take it personally."

Kilal raised his gravity and strength and stomped on the

street. Spiraling cracks webbed outward. "Bloodshed and Oaths! Has every Arbiter in this city lost their bloody mind? I've only been gone for ten years. Ten! How has everything and everyone become so...so ...rotten?" Blondie rolled her eyes while Trench Coat embellished a loud yawn. "I've met Ash Fallen with more common *decency* than half the people I've been in contact with here! How can you be so cavalier about taking a brother and sister's life? What about our oath? What about our land? What about just *doing the right thing?*"

Only when he paused his tirade did he realize he'd made more than one small crack in the street's infrastructure. But it wasn't like anyone would notice. The whole sector had been abandoned, and it was probably because of men and women like the three before him. Arbiters like them who'd so quickly turned against their oath and their God in favor of the Heirs and the monetary value the corrupt organization represented. Kilal was tired of it. He hadn't returned to the Sunlight Domain to clean it up. But he also hadn't realized it needed such a thorough scrubbing.

Unfortunately for those three, they would become the beginning of what was to come next for Silent Haven. But first, "Last chance," Kilal said. "Turn around. Leave us alone. *Please.*"

His tirade and destruction of the street had put them on their heels. But it wasn't enough to bring them to their senses.

"I don't think so," Crave said.

Their eyes grew hungry. Trench Coat licked his lips. All they saw was the financial riches he and Allyria represented.

So be it.

"Allyria," Kilal said. "Why don't you go back into the temple and wait for me?"

She didn't argue or even hesitate. She scrambled into the building, the inhuman scraping of her stone legs rubbing together trailing her.

Attagirl. The fact that she could maintain her stoneskin

for so long was astonishing. It had been a while since he'd encountered a newly awakened Arbiter with her capacity to use Carvings. If they both lived through the next few months, she would make a powerful Prime.

Kilal returned his attention to the trio. Their postures, their wary eyes, and the pressure rising behind his eyes told him all he needed to know. They were preparing to attack.

He didn't want to kill them. He'd prefer to never have to kill a fellow Arbiter again. But a rabid dog can't be saved. It can only be put down. A fight was what they wanted, so a fight was what Kilal would give them. And by the end of it, they'd realize just how foolish they were. Fifteen pounds of aznium and a still-beating heart was a mighty fine fortune compared to the reality they'd traded it for.

He couldn't deny the adrenaline pumping through his veins. With all the pain he'd endured in the last twelve hours, he needed a release. A release from reality. If only for a few minutes—because it would only take a few minutes to finish off the trio, and in the process, forget...everything.

~ CHAPTER 11 ~

Kilal shot forward. His gravity was as low as he could take it, and his strength was increased by a factor of twenty-five. Trench Coat and Blondie were quick in their response. They split up, moving to flank him.

Let them.

Crave wasn't so quick—he slammed his fist into the short man's face. It exploded into a mist of blood and gore.

Kilal leapt, soaring high into the air. He barely cleared the streak of pink air aimed at his neck. He raised his gravity, lurching in the air, and slammed back down to the ground. The street shook and cracked. He charged Blondie, who was preparing to launch more condensed air.

The pavement rippled like the surface of a pond disrupted by a falling rock. Trench Coat's hand shot out of the pavement and grabbed Kilal's leg, holding him in place. The sudden stop lurched him forward, snapping his ankle. As he fell forward, he twisted and kicked at the grappling hand, ignoring the pain, but Trench Coat's fist had become glistening black metal.

Bloodshed and Oaths! Whatever that guy had turned his skin into, it was strong.

Victory gleamed in Blondie's eyes. She arced her arm forward, and Kilal prepared himself to rip his own foot off to escape the iron grip.

A junked car with no tires tumbled through the air. Blondie cursed and leaped aside. The car screeched as steel met pavement. The front window shattered, and shards of glass cut her skin as she rolled.

Allyria ran up the sidewalk to parallel him.

"Get inside!" Kilal said, his tone leaving no room for argument. He was grateful when the girl only nodded and ran back to the dark recess of the holy place.

Kilal stood. He increased his gravity *and* strength to fifty percent and slammed his free foot on the pavement. A large chunk of the road crumbled and collapsed as if it were made from rotted wood. He and Trench Coat fell into the sewer below. The stench of feces, rats, and rotten eggs assaulted him.

Trench Coat smashed into the brown and green water, splashing Kilal. His sternum cracked and caved beneath the impact of Kilal's foot. The stone grip fell away, and Kilal shook himself free.

He returned his strength to normal and lowered gravity to leap out of the sewer. Kilal barely landed back on the street when his instincts screamed a warning. He twisted just as a bolt of pink condensed air whipped by.

Blondie's chest heaved, and her eyes widened. Minor cuts decorated her arms and cheeks, and little streaks of blood darkened and smeared her makeup, giving her a hysterical look.

Kilal stalked her, walking a circle. She threw another bolt at him, which he dodged easily. She gathered more of the pink air in her hand, but Kilal struck like a viper. He lunged and smacked her hand up just as she released the bolt. It streaked into the night sky, leaving a haze of fuchsia behind until it dissipated far above them. He locked both of her wrists in an iron grip and raised them above her head. With his other hand, he grabbed her throat.

"Maybe I'll take you up on that offer to leave?" she gasped.

Kilal gave her a sad smile. "I'm sorry, I can't do that." But something about her kept him from squeezing.

A tear joined the streaked, bloodied makeup. "Please. I'm only twenty-five. I...I...I'll leave the city. I'll stop working for t-them. I promise."

His chest tightened. "I've let Arbiter's like you go before. They always ended up hurting more people. Why should I believe you'll be any different?" Gabriel Sunsetter had been the most recent natural consequence of letting someone live.

She licked her lips, and another fresh tear joined the first. "Please. I don't want to die."

Everything Kilal knew of Arbiters, of people, of life, told him to snap her neck. She would kill again. She'd gotten the taste for it and the lavish lifestyle it afforded her. Maybe not today, maybe not this week. But she *would* kill again. And that blood would be on his hands.

Twenty-five.

Just like Lilliana would be now...

He let go of her. "Get out of here."

Eyes wide, Blondie didn't waste a second. She turned on her heels and ran. Probably faster than she'd ever run before.

How many lives did I just doom?

"Why would you do that?" Allyria nearly shouted as she sprinted up to him.

Kilal scratched his chin and watched as Blondie took a corner and disappeared. "Because I'm a fool."

Allyria started, and her jaw clicked shut. "What type of answer is that?"

Kilal sighed. "The only answer I can give." She glared at him but didn't say anything. "Are you alright?" he asked.

She bristled, as if offended. "Why wouldn't I be? I didn't get hurt. Remember, I had to *hide*."

"Physical injuries aren't the only type a person can endure. Most people, let alone teenagers, don't witness bloodshed." He stood in the way of her seeing what remained of Crave's splattered head. "That can have an impact on someone's psyche. So, I'll ask again. Are you alright?"

The hardness from moments ago was nowhere to be found as she kicked a pebble and wrung her hands. "I've seen worse," she said quietly.

Kilal hated that he believed her.

Wherever that girl had been, whatever she'd been through, no child should have to suffer.

"I'm sorry," was all he could say. The sun peeked over the horizon, and the first rays of dawn tickled his cheek. "Come on. We need to get off the streets before the city wakes up."

"What about..." Allyria gestured to the destroyed road.

Normally, Kilal would have filed paperwork with the city and ensured the taxes were used to repair the damage, but he glanced around at the disheveled homes and buildings and shrugged.

"I don't think anyone is going to care."

~ CHAPTER 12 ~

Silent Haven woke. Vehicles droned by. Salesmen motivated enough to wake early hawked their wares on the street corners. And those not financially stable enough to own a vehicle were already making their way down sidewalks to whatever destination they were headed to.

Kilal winced at the screeching tires one or two blocks over, and Allyria nearly jumped out of her skin.

Shoulders hunched, head lowered, he guided them north, taking as many side streets and alleys as possible. Even scrunched up the way he was, he was still taller than most people they passed. The odds that he wouldn't be remembered by at least one person were becoming slimmer and slimmer with every minute.

A particularly dirty man bumped into him.

"Bloody fool," the man cursed. His eyes were wild, and he tried to grab Kilal's forearm, but still slick from sweat and sewage water, Kilal easily slipped the grip and kept walking.

They darted into the next shadowy alleyway they crossed.

"This is taking too long," Kilal said. "We need to scale the roofs."

"The...roofs?"

"Yeah. Look at me. I've already attracted too many wandering eyes. But now, prancing about wearing bloody, ripped clothing and stinking of sewage? I'll be remembered. And you aren't much better."

Allyria put her hands in her pockets and kicked a metal can. It clattered down the alley. "I wouldn't say we're *prancing*." Kilal raised a brow and pursed his lips. She blushed. "I...I..." she kicked another can. It ricocheted off the brick wall before skidding to a stop. "I can't jump these buildings, alright."

Kilal had expected as much, and he already had a plan. One she wouldn't be happy about. "I'm going to have to carry you."

Allyria froze mid-kick of another can. "No..." she took a step back, towards the entrance of the alley. "No, we're not going to do that."

"I'm really sorry. I can't imagine what you've been through, and maybe someday you'll share it with me. But right now, we have a mission, and Arbiters accomplish their mission even if it costs them their lives. You don't want to do this. I understand. But you have to. We have to."

Her nostrils flared, and her lips quivered. A tear dripped from her chin.

Kilal smiled. "Or is this about me smelling like sewage?"

"What? No! That's not it."

He lifted an arm and sniffed his armpit. "Well, that's good. I was getting a little self-conscious." She placed her hands on her hips and tapped a foot, shaking her head. He kept the smile as he crouched and presented his back. "Come on. The quicker we get this over with, the quicker you can get some food in your belly. And I can have a shower."

He turned his head so he could face her. She stared at his back for a moment before finally nodding. Reaching for him, she paused, her hand shaking.

I will find out who did this to you, Kilal thought. *And I'll kill them.*

Allyria closed her trembling hand into a fist. She took a deep breath and climbed onto his back, wrapping her arms around his neck.

"Hold on."

Her grip tightened. Much to her credit, she didn't scream when he jumped. Tense arms clamped around his throat, Allyria hid her face in the nape of his neck.

The first roof landing was smooth. How many times had he done that with Lilliana? Dozens, at least. She, too, had been initially hesitant about the prospect of soaring hundreds of feet in the air. Eventually, Kilal had to force her to take that first leap. At that time, he'd had the sinking suspicion she was pretending to be scared. The longer she was scared, the longer he would continue carrying her instead of expecting her to jump on her own. When he made her take that first vault, though, she'd cleared the distance with ease.

But Allyria wasn't his daughter, and he was sure a fear of heights wasn't her issue.

***

In record time, Kilal landed on the roof of his apartment building and eased Allyria down. She wouldn't meet his eyes. What sort of thoughts pounded through her head?

"You did good," he said. "Thank you."

The gloom over her face seemed to fall away like scales, and she smiled.

Kilal walked to the stairwell door leading down to the seventh floor. The gravel covering the rooftop crunched with each step.

"Why aren't we going through the front door?" Allyria asked.

"There's a guard at the desk who checks you in and out. I haven't been here for a while, so I'm sure whoever the guard is, they won't recognize me. And I'd rather not explain to anyone where I've been."

"And where is that, exactly?"

He rolled his eyes. "Ophir. Then Damphir."

Allyria's eyes widened. "You went to the moons?" He drew his lips into a flat line and narrowed his eyes. "Oh." She huffed and crossed her arms. "You could have just said you weren't going to tell me."

Kilal checked the doorknob. Locked. "I could have. But this was more fun." He ripped the metallic handle from the wooden door and entered the dark stairwell.

They descended three floors until, on the seventh, Kilal stepped into the dimly lit hallway of his apartment level. The ceiling lights flickered.

Can't believe they're still like that. He'd had them specially designed to blink and produce low light. Since they were still like that, he could only assume he still owned the floor.

"Jeeze," Allyria said. "This place can't afford to take care of itself any better? Ashes, it's creepy in here!"

"If you broke into this building to rob it, and you stopped here, what would you do?"

"I definitely wouldn't stay on this floor."

"Exactly."

The flickering lights illuminated the peeling and cracked yellow wallpaper. The carpet was brown and dingy with a faint musky smell.

Everything was still exactly as he wanted it.

Kilal passed two doors on his right and one on his left. At the corner, he went left. When he'd purchased every apartment on the seventh floor, he'd had the doors professionally painted to appear as if they'd suffered water damage. Why would a door inside a building have water stains? He had no idea. Fortunately, management never asked that question. Because he paid them not to. And the stains added to the overall personification of *rundown* and *leave me alone.*

After the second door on the right, Kilal took three more steps and then turned abruptly to the left. He smashed his fist through the wall at eye level. His punch broke clean through. A puff of white dust ejected from the impact, coating Kilal's arm in powder. He fished around until he felt what he had come for: a clear plastic bag with a key in it.

"Come on," Kilal said. "It's right around the corner."

The door to apartment 707 loomed. Kilal hesitated. Once he opened that door, he'd unlock ten years of lost time and memories.

A knot formed in his throat, and his heart quickened. He'd bought the apartment the day he brought Lilliana home. The lump grew bigger. Every time he came home, she would be waiting for him with a smile as bright as the sunrise. He had a sudden urge to slam the door open, race in, and call her name. She would wrap his waist in a hug and squeeze until his ribs were close to breaking.

It's okay, she would tell him.

And everything would be right.

The knot in his throat seemed to have grown to the size of an apple. Kilal struggled to swallow. A low moan escaped. He turned it into a cough, though he was sure it didn't fool Allyria, and wiped a single tear from his cheek while covering his mouth.

"Everything alright?" she asked.

"I didn't think I'd ever come back here." His voice was quiet, as if his volume could impact the reality he wished to be waiting for him behind the door. "I gave up on the possibility ages ago."

"Well, you're here now, so that's good, right?"

Kilal's answer was a long time coming. "I don't know."

He unlocked the door and opened it, but didn't enter.

You left her back there. She's still in that nightmarish land, and here you are, playing house with her replacement.

"No, I'm not," he whispered.

"What was that?"

"Nothing."

Kilal drowned the accusatory voices in his head and stepped into his home.

It was simple, modest. The living room greeted them. A gray L-shaped couch faced a TV mounted on the wall. Kilal smiled. He and Lilliana had struggled to get the bloody thing perfectly level. He didn't care one bit if it was off by a few degrees, but she had to have it just right. A few plants, now long shriveled and dead, adorned the room. A pang of guilt twinged in his chest. Those plants had been Requiem's babies. She'd cared for them nearly as fervently as he'd cared for Lilliana. And now, they were dead. Just like—

NO!

"It's so dusty in here," Allyria said. She walked past him and ran a finger over the top of an end table. It came away coated in thick, gray soot.

The lights flickered. Ash began falling. Everything...everything was coated in it! The bulbs flickered again, and when they turned back on, Lilliana lay on the couch. She was covered in blood, her body torn open. She stared at him with eyes full of hate.

Kilal blinked rapidly. *It's just a hallucination. It's just a hallucination.*

When Lilliana's arm began rising, he'd had enough.

"Shower's that way," he blurted, brushing past Allyria and hoisting a thumb towards the hall in the opposite direction. "Use whatever you find."

"*You left me.*" Lilliana's voice, scratchy and lifeless, pierced his ears.

"But what about—"

Kilal raced past the kitchen and slammed his shin against a step stool. The crack of bone against wood was surprising, and the pain racing up his leg would have brought a shiver down his spine if he hadn't been so desperate to get away. He entered his room and threw the door closed behind him. Back pressed against it, he brushed frantically at the ash on his shoulders, but for every pass he made, more soot fell.

"*You left me.*" It wasn't Lilliana who stood before him, accusing him. Requiem Ror, battered and broken, hovered in the air. Her eyes were black sockets, and her jaw hung uselessly. *"Your...fault."* The jaw managed to move in a not-quite-right sort of way.

Kilal pressed harder against the door until the hinges protested. "No...It wasn't..." he choked out. "Please. I didn't want to leave you. I tried getting back."

Ash began swirling about the floating apparition with violent turbulence. As her arm was torn off, followed by a leg, she raised her remaining arm and pointed a finger of tendon and bone at him. *"Dead. All dead. Because of you."*

The lights flickered again, and Lilliana stood beside Requiem, caught in the ash storm. She, too, began being torn apart.

"Because of you," they echoed together.

Kilal collapsed on his butt.

"Do you know what I regret?" Claire said. She stood before the ash storm with gaunt skin and hollow eyes.

"Please," he sobbed, pulling his knees to his chest. "Don't say it."

"I regret not letting you kill yourself."

"No. You don't mean that." He covered his ears and rocked back and forth, knocking his head against the door. "You don't. You don't. You don't." Each repetition felt hollower and hollower.

Sometime later, Allyria forced her way into his room. She found him curled in a ball, crying and repeating "I'm sorry" over and over again.

~ CHAPTER 13 ~

The next two hours dragged by. Kilal cut his hair, trimmed his beard, showered, and changed. His movements were slow and lethargic. His brain demanded he remember his time in the Ashen Lands running, hiding, fighting, getting captured, killed more times than he could remember, and finally, fleeing. But he resisted. He couldn't think about it. He would be back in that Sha'tum-forsaken place soon enough. Until then, he needed to focus on his current task.

When he exited his room, Allyria lay on the couch.

"Glad to see you've made yourself comfortable," he said.

She was in a pair of Lilliana's old black jeans and a blue shirt. When she met his eyes, she blushed and turned away.

It's not every day you see a grown man weep like a baby.

"Come on," he said. "Let's get some food in us."

"Not that I don't want that," Allyria said, still not meeting his gaze. "But I've already checked, and you don't have anything to eat."

"That's because you were looking in all the wrong places."

"You gonna punch a hole in the wall again, except this time to pull out food?"

"Nothing so dramatic."

He walked into the kitchen. It shared a wall with the living room, half of which had been knocked out. From the waist up, it was open to the living room. Allyria turned around on the couch. She rested her elbows on the backrest and placed her chin in her hands. He could feel her eyes following him as he rummaged through the kitchen.

He checked the fridge and, despite already being told it was the case, was somewhat surprised to see it empty. That was not his doing. Which could only mean Requiem had cleared it out when he went missing. Did that mean she'd known what was going to happen to her? Or, after he'd been gone for too long, had she given up on him? Cleared everything out of the apartment and left, thinking she'd never return?

Streaks in the dust layer covering everything indicated to Kilal which cabinets and drawers Allyria had already checked. He opened them anyway. What he was looking for wouldn't be something she would've thought was food. The clack of a cabinet door shutting followed each Kilal tried.

Eventually, in the cupboard beneath the sink, he found what he was looking for.

"Have you ever had combat rations?" He pulled two square plastic containers out from beneath the sink.

"No. They don't sound very tasty."

"Oh, they're not." Kilal smiled and nodded for her to join him at the kitchen table.

"Then why are we eating them?" Allyria pulled out one of the deep brown oak chairs and poked at the package in front of her.

Kilal tapped the top of his box. "They're easily stored. They're designed to last a lifetime if they stay sealed. And they provide all the nutrients a body needs."

"What about the enjoyment of eating? Do they provide that?"

With a quick jerk of his wrist and the protest of plastic ripping, he snapped the seal and removed the top of the container. "Absolutely not."

Allryia pushed the box around with her fork. "And delivery isn't an option?"

Kilal didn't warrant the question worth a response.

The four-inch by four-inch package held a block of brown food that was nearly as hard as the plastic it was held in. He wedged his fork in the space between the block and the container and, using it as a lever, pried the block out and picked it up. It was dry and smooth, a consistency not normally found in food.

He clamped down on a corner with his teeth, and with a crack that could have been his teeth or the block breaking, snapped off a piece. It was as satisfying to chew as it was to look at. His saliva dissolved it into a muddy paste that he forced down his throat.

It truly was a horrible experience. Regardless, warmth filled him, both from the special chemicals added to the food to energize and the memories of all those he'd eaten with.

Allyria bit into hers. She immediately scrunched her face into a visage of pain and misery. She chewed slowly, coughing intermittently. When she finished swallowing, she rushed to the sink, put her mouth under the faucet and turned on the water.

"That's the worst thing I've *ever* eaten!" She wiped drops of water from her chin with the back of a hand as she sat back down. "It's what I imagine eating mud to be like, except this is somehow *worse*."

Kilal took another bite and smiled as he worked at the hard material. He waved the block of food in front of himself and spoke with a mouth full of brown paste. "This is an Arbiter's best friend. You'll get used to it."

She rolled her eyes and sank her teeth into it. She grabbed the edge of the table and shook it, mimicking the effects of a seizure as she ate it. One of the legs rattled against a loose screw.

"Blah!" she gasped once she'd swallowed. "I don't think I will."

Kilal laughed.

She met his eyes, blushed, then turned away. "So, are we gonna talk about...about...how I found you?"

Kilal finished off the chunk in his mouth. "No," he said, returning the square of food back to its container. That was the beauty of the creation. It had all the nutrients a human needed to survive, and it expanded in the stomach, filling the consumer after only a few bites.

"Why?"

"Because."

"Really? That's it?"

"Yep."

"That's not very mature."

Kilal leaned back on his chair, propping it up on its back two legs, and crossed his arms. "Tell me what you know of the Heirs. I'm extra keen to know where they came from?"

"Tell me what happened to you to cause you to be in such a...state."

"No."

Allyria leaned in her chair too, also propping it up on its rear legs, and crossed her arms, mimicking him. "Then I guess we've reached an impasse."

Kilal exhaled a long, drawn-out breath and returned his chair to normal. She stared at him with a stubbornness a statue would be proud of. He didn't really see a way around telling her. At least, not if he wanted any information from her.

"Fine," he said through a clenched jaw. "I lost my daughter ten years ago. During that time, I also lost the woman I loved. I was just reunited with a woman I haven't seen in decades, and I'll probably lose her very soon as well. And I was...reminded of all that in a very...painful manner."

"I'm sorry," Allyria said. "How did you lose your daughter?"

"By being careless."

"I'm sure there's more to it than that."

Kilal grunted. "A distress call came in from the Northern Pass stating two War Plagues and a handful of Mannekins were rampaging in the area. Nothing I couldn't handle."

"Two War Plagues is nothing you couldn't handle?" she asked, clearly not believing him.

"I took Lilliana with me. She was fifteen, and I figured it was the right time to get her hands dirty," he continued, ignoring her question. "Some didn't agree with my decision."

Kilal rapped his knuckles against the tabletop. Why hadn't he just listened?

"When we arrived, we didn't find any Ash Fallen. It was an ambush set by...a man I let live when I shouldn't have. We fought for a while. Eventually, they backed us into the ruins of an underground shelter. The place was full of dusty, broken machines I'd never seen before. Somehow, Lilliana managed to activate one of them.

"It came to life and covered the entire room in white light. She screamed my name once before everything was taken from me. Sight. Hearing. Physical sensations.

"Then, the next thing I knew, I was lying on the cold ground. The sky was above me, and it was gray. Ash descended in a steady fall. Two other Arbiters were teleported to my location with me. I convinced them not to fight me. It didn't matter; they didn't last long." He paused and looked at his hands, flipping them back and forth, clenching and unclenching them. "At least their blood isn't on my hands," he mumbled.

"Where were you teleported to?" Allyria asked.

"Across the Veil and into the Ashen Lands. And Lilliana wasn't with me."

"I'm...so sorry," she whispered, picking at a stain on the table with her thumb. "What was it like over there?"

"Gray."

"Is it really covered in ash?"

"It would be if everything hadn't evolved to eat the soot."

Allyria scrunched up her face. "Eat it?"

Kilal nodded. "Plant life, animals, even the Ash Fallen consume the ash. Among other things. At least, when they aren't trying to eat you."

She stopped picking at a stain and shivered. "What happened to Lilliana's mother?"

He shrugged. "She didn't have a mother."

Allyria pursed her lips and raised a brow. "Everyone has a mother."

Kilal shot to his feet, knocking his chair back with a loud clatter. He put both hands on top of his head, lacing his fingers together as he did so. "*Everyone* has a mother? How is that possible? Why has nobody told me?"

She threw her block of food at him, which he caught, chuckling. Clearly not amused, Allyria said, "You know what I meant."

Kilal retook his seat and tried to pass back her food square. She shook her head and held up a hand, warding it off. He quirked a brow again and kept the food outstretched to her. Huffing, she finally took it and broke off a small piece with her teeth.

"I found Lilliana wandering in a snowstorm far to the south. She was near the unfinished wall the Governing Seats thought would be smart to build to block off the edge of the world. As if that would stop people from throwing themselves into the unknown. She was five, malnourished, beaten and bloody. She had no memory of the events that led her to that moment. I took her with me, gave her a home, and treated her as my daughter. So that's why I say she didn't have a mother."

Kilal stood and walked to the sink. He cleared his throat, breaking up the knot building there, and filled a cup with water. The memory of that fateful day flashed before him.

He'd been tracking a War Plague which had destroyed a farm and killed the inhabitants. It was a terrible snowstorm, one of the worst Kilal had experienced in his long life. It made tracking difficult. For two days, he'd stalked the Plague south, where the trail led him to the wall overlooking the edge of the world.

There, Kilal found a young child stumbling through the

snowbanks. She was barefoot and her clothes were ripped and tattered. Long black strands of her hair were coated in ice, and her skin had been colder than some corpses he'd touched. The storm only worsened, and he was faced with two choices: leave the child to die and continue his hunt or bring her someplace warm. He chose the latter.

The War Plague escaped, but he never regretted his decision.

He filled a second glass of water and brought both back to the table, handing one to Allyria. She snatched it from his hand and loudly gulped the liquid down.

"I'm sorry," she said, wiping water from her chin with her shirt sleeve. "About pressing you. That was insensitive."

The crunch of food in Kilal's mouth answered her. "Your turn," he said.

"I really don't know much," she admitted. "My parents were...not the best." She wrapped her arms around herself and shivered.

I'm sure that's a gross understatement.

"I ran away when I was twelve. When my mom wasn't on some drug or another, she was trying to find some. My dad... well...he..." She clenched her hands into fists and sneered. "I wish I could meet him now. Things would be different this time."

Kilal's heart ached.

"Not long after I ran away, rumors spread about four unknown Arbiters appearing in New Cita. They killed a lot of our kind and some of the Governing Seats. Afterwards, they recruited Arbiters, local officials, what remained of the Governing Seats, and the wealthy. When they'd taken over New Cita, they moved onto Vitrol then south to Silent Haven."

"Sienna, Fazin, Tor'et and Wolfe," Kilal said, repeating the names Claire had told him.

Something about it didn't sit well with him. Four Arbiters alone shouldn't be able to do that much damage. How had he never heard of them? If they were that powerful, he would've known about them.

And yet, he couldn't dispute what seemed to be the facts. They'd appeared out of nowhere and took over the Sunlight Domain.

He couldn't help but think of Jayden. Were those four from another world too? Did they know each other? An idea presented itself. A very bad idea. What if they *did* know Jayden? Hope surged through him. He had no idea where Jayden was, but maybe the Heirs did. And he knew exactly where they were.

"What about Vitrol? Any word about what's happening there?"

"I don't know. Word from the north is pretty sparse. I barely hear anything about New Cita, and no news comes from Vitrol."

That wasn't good. The Sunlight Domain was withering at a frightening pace. The last thing it needed was for the three remaining cities to stop communicating, especially when an army of Ash Fallen was gathering on the other side of the Veil.

The last great invasion had reduced the Sunlight Domain from six cities to three. And the newest force of Ash Fallen was even larger. A shiver ran up Kilal's spine. Was the end of his world only weeks, maybe months away?

Something about Allyria's tale didn't sit right with him. Like a missing puzzle piece. One of many.

"If all the Arbiters were either killed or recruited, how did you find one for your Awakening?"

Allyria picked at a strand of red hair, twirling it around a finger. "When I woke with the Sign on my wrist, I showed the others I ran with. There were five of them, three guys, two girls. I thought they'd be excited." Her face lit up like a nighttime bonfire. "Imagine what we could have done with an Arbiter with us. The coin we could have stolen, the influence we could've had. We could have owned the Undercity!" The light in her eyes faded, and she returned to twirling her hair.

The Undercity. That explains a lot.

It was the name given to the abandoned ruins *beneath* the sewer system. They were discovered accidentally a few hundred years ago, and no one knew what their purpose was. Not a single document existed which talked of the strange labyrinth. Kilal could never understand why anyone would build an area the size of a city beneath the sewer system.

The Undercity remained empty for many decades, but over the last two centuries, the poor, orphans and runaways, criminals and men and women on the run had made the Undercity their home. He'd fought to clean out the ruins and help those who sought refuge there, but the Governing Seats wouldn't budge on their position: out of sight, out of mind. So, nothing was done about them.

"They didn't share your vision, did they?"

"No. They saw the Sign as a payout. They turned on me, hoping the ash-eating Heirs would give them a tidy sum for my capture."

"I'm sorry," Kilal said. "It's not easy being betrayed by those you trust. And no matter how many times it happens, it always hurts."

A teardrop splashed on the tabletop. "Yeah. I knew them for a long time. It still hurts, thinking about them." Her jaw clenched, and she sneered. "But why should it? They betrayed me! Why should I care about them anymore?" She slammed a fist on the table.

Kilal reached a hand out to take hers, but stopped himself. No physical contact. "It just shows you aren't like them. You care about people. And that's a good thing. The moment you stop caring, that's when you should be concerned."

She brushed another tear from her eyes before it could roll down her cheek. "What about you? You've been around for a while. Have you found a way to stop the pain?"

He gave her a sad smile. "I gave up trying to find that answer a long time ago."

She pursed her lips and nodded.

"What about the Awakening?" Kilal asked again. "How did you find an Arbiter while running?"

"There were rumors of a man in the Undercity who could heal people."

Kilal whistled. "A healing Carving that heals *others*? That's incredibly rare. What was he doing living down there?"

"I don't know. But I found him. He activated the Sign, and I underwent the Awakening. But when he found out I was a Prime, he..." She put her hands beneath the table and bowed her head, slumping forward slightly.

Kilal sighed. "He tried turning you into the Heirs of the Promise, too. Probably hoped for a handsome sum in return for a living Prime."

Silently, she nodded.

This poor girl. Again, he reached out his hand to comfort her, but halted halfway. *First her parents, then her friends, then the man she trusted to help her. No one, especially not a child, should have to experience betrayal like that. No wonder she doesn't like to be touched. She's put up a wall tougher than a War Plague's skin.*

"I'm sorry about pressing you, but I need to know everything," Kilal said, feeling like an emotionless tyrant. "How did you get away from that man?"

"The Shadow," she said simply as if that should mean anything to him.

"The...Shadow?"

"I don't know who or what it is. But everyone in the Undercity whispers of it. It always attacks in the dark, and it only targets...bad people. I was bound by a Carving and thrown over his shoulder. We hadn't gotten out of the Undercity before the Shadow attacked. Whatever it was, it made quick, bloody work of the healer. It didn't say anything to me. One minute I couldn't move; the next, Healer was scattered about the sewer in pieces, and the Shadow was gone."

Kilal scratched his chin. *Interesting.* He knew of some Carvings which could shroud a person in darkness. Maybe the Shadow was simply another Arbiter who did what they could to punish the wicked. Jayden's black-skinned and taloned hand shot to the forefront of his mind.

Could it have been him? Or one of the others like him?

Another surge of hope warmed his chest. Just a few hours ago, he'd entered his apartment defeated. Now he had two possible leads: the Shadow and the founders of the Heirs of the Promise. Maybe he'd be able to find Jayden and continue the mission he'd abandoned his search for Lilliana for. And avenge the Keepers and all the other Arbiters killed by the Heirs.

A smile wormed its way onto Kilal's face. *This may turn out well after all.*

"I hid for a while," Allyria said, continuing her tale. "Ran. Never could quite leave the city. There just isn't anything between here and New Cita I could live on. So, I moved about. Healer showed me a basic strength Carving, so I tried to always have that active. I'm not sure why he taught it to me if he was just going to give me to the Heirs, but I'm happy he did. That's about the only reason I survived.

"Eventually, I heard whispers of Mother Claire and her ability to hide and help Arbiters out of the city. And you know the rest." She said it so flippantly she might as well have been telling him the recipe for an apple pie.

"Well, despite everything you've gone through," Kilal said, "you've done well by yourself. Surviving on the streets isn't easy. And you held your own during the fight against Blondie and her henchmen. Your control over Stoneskin is already impressive. And listening to orders is always something I place high value on, and knowing when to disobey those orders, even higher. You should be proud of yourself. We may have just met, and I'm sure it doesn't mean much, but I'm proud of you."

Her cheeks turned a shade of red that would put her hair

to shame. An invisible spot on the table caught Allyria's attention again, and she began scratching at it with a thumbnail. "Thank you," she mumbled. She stopped and cocked her head. "Blondie?"

Kilal nibbled on his food, thinking about his next steps. "Huh?"

"You said, 'Blondie and her henchmen.' Are you talking about—?"

"Yeah. The Arbiter I let go. The one in all pink. It's how I remember people. I name them after a distinguishing characteristic."

Allyria frowned. "She was *covered* in pink. Wouldn't Pinkie or even Pink have been a better nickname?"

He shrugged. "She had blonde hair."

She opened her mouth but snapped it shut. "Whatever," she muttered.

Kilal pushed his chair back, trying his best to not scrape the feet across the tiled floor. "I'm going to get some sleep."

She started. "Sleep? Now?"

"I haven't slept since I made it back this way. That was a few days ago. So yeah. Sleep. Now."

"How *did* you make it back this way? Crossing the Veil, I mean?" she asked between chewing on her lower lip.

"By placing one foot in front of the other." He held up a hand, silencing the protest building on her tongue. "For another time. I sleep now."

"And after that?"

"When the sun goes down, I'll pay a visit to our mutual friend."

"That doesn't sound like a good plan."

"It's my only plan. Make yourself at home while I sleep." The chair squeaked as he stood.

He didn't feel the need to warn her against leaving the apartment. She, more than most seventeen-year-olds, understood the dangers awaiting her outside.

His eyelids felt like a ton of bricks. Immortal or not, Arbiter or not, he still had his limitations. And he'd pushed them to the max. Leaving Allyria stunned and wide-eyed, he went to his room and collapsed onto his mattress. When was the last time he'd slept on a bed?

Kilal was asleep before he could find the answer.

~ CHAPTER 14 ~

When Kilal woke, the sun had long since receded beneath the horizon, and Ophir and Damphir were high in the sky.

He'd slept for ten hours.

He re-carved in the bathroom, got changed, checked on the sleeping Allyria—who had passed out on the couch—and made his way to the skyscraper in the center of the city.

***

Kilal approached the tall building that *buzzed* with the massive amount of electricity it used to keep the place lit. What hypocrisy! The rest of the city was struggling, and the enormous headquarters was sucking power as if there was no end to it.

Giant lights, nearly as big as he was, jutted from the building at specified intervals of about twenty feet. They swiveled left to right, up and down, utilizing a mechanical contraption Kilal had never seen.

As he looked up at the sky-piercing building, he had a sensation of déjà vu and was thrust back into the Ashen Lands, to the day he'd been captured and brought to the Tower of Eyes. Standing before the monolithic tower, shackled and surrounded by Plagues, the enormous black tower loomed over him. Eyes, as big as the lights, moved all about, but that day, they'd stopped and focused on him. All of them.

Kilal had never felt so insignificant.

He shuddered as a beam washed over him, ripping him back to the present. His lungs burned. How long had he been standing there, holding his breath? He sighed and breathed, calming his heart and mind.

"You're not back there anymore," he whispered.

His hands itched and tingled, and for a moment, he saw them as they truly were: covered in blood. The newest addition to his torment, Crave and Trench Coat, weighed heavily upon his soul. As he looked up at the building once again, flexing his hands, he couldn't help but wonder how many more people would join the long list of names of those he'd killed.

"Please, no more."

He squeezed his eyes shut until his face hurt, forcing the emotion to subside. He was on a mission. And it didn't include pitying himself.

The glass tower doors seemed to widen as Kilal approached, as if inviting him in. Barely more than a shove, and they swung open, slamming against their break. Thankfully, they didn't shatter.

Two men in black uniforms stared wide-eyed as he strode through the second door and down the guided pathway with waist-high barriers on both sides. The room he entered was large enough to contain apartment 707 and easily two stories tall. White marble ricocheted the echoes of each step, shattering the silence. The walls on all sides alternated four feet wide by twenty feet high chunks of black granite with white streaks, followed by the same-sized chunks of glass. Behind the guards and to their right, a young woman sat behind a large desk with a computer and lamp. Directly behind the guards was a lone elevator.

The whole floor was a gaudy display of wealth and power if Kilal had ever seen one.

Both guards gripped silver rods with bronze spots in their

gloved hands. Aznium was especially dangerous to Arbiters. One touch to his skin, and he'd be writhing on the floor.

Striding up to the duo, Kilal tasted copper.

Arbiters? The realization was followed by disgust. *Arbiters standing guard for a corrupt organization? How far we have fallen.*

To think Arbiters would swear themselves to a *company* and become their typical employees. They were better than that!

The one on the right—Chuck, his red nametag read—regained his composure quicker than the man on the left, Bron. So Kilal addressed Bron.

"I'm here to speak with your *masters*," he said, referring to them as if they were nothing more than guard dogs. He kept his tone soft but serious. Neither of them would misunderstand the reason he was there.

Bron swallowed and blinked rapidly. "Do you have an appointment?"

"No." Kilal crossed his arms and loomed over them. "Is that going to be a problem?"

"Yes, it is," Chuck said, giving Bron an annoyed shake of his head. "They don't meet just any vagabond off the street. And especially not at this time of night."

"I'm sure they'll make an exception for me."

Chuck sneered. "And why is that?"

"Because, if they don't," Kilal smiled wickedly, "I'll tear their precious building down around them."

Chuck swallowed, too.

He turned to look at the young lady at the desk. She watched them with an attentiveness Kilal didn't normally see in the younger generation. Chuck gave her a nod, and as the woman leaned, Kilal raised a hand.

"If you push that button under your desk, I'll kill Chuck and Bron, then you. Please don't make me do that."

The woman paled but eased back.

Thank you.

"Fine," Chuck said, spitting on the gleaming marble floor. "We'll do this the old-fashioned way." He snapped the rod forward, and pressure swelled behind Kilal's eyes.

"Chuck, Bron," he said, looking from one to the next. "You're both Enlightened Arbiters, with only a basic strength Carving activated." They both paled. "You've abandoned your oath, forsaking the land and people you swore to protect, to enslave yourselves to a corrupt corporation."

Bron at least had the decency to blush at the accusation.

Kilal crossed his arms and gave the two a withering glare. "Things are about to change in Silent Haven, and siding with the Heirs means siding against *me*." He slammed a thumb against his own chest. "So, which master would you like to serve? Sha'tum and the oath he made us all swear? Or the Heirs? You have three seconds to decide."

He held three fingers in the air. When the first dropped, Chuck's eyes nearly bulged over crimson cheeks. When the second finger dropped, he leveled the silver rod at Kilal's chest, forcing him to take a step back.

"To the edge of the world with you, you bloody son-of-a-Plague! I'll have you crying on the floor before you—"

Kilal lurched forward. He reached past the aznium rod and grappled Chuck's arm, wrenching it and breaking the man's wrist. The rod clattering on the floor could barely be heard over the guard's pain-tinged squeal.

"And you think this gives you power over me?" He leveled a glare so full of vehemence and *impatience* Chuck's squealing stopped, and he seemed to forget about the pain of his broken wrist. "You're wasting my time," Kilal pressed through gritted teeth. "And my time is *very* precious to me."

Bron took a step back and lifted his rod in both hands.

Kilal turned to him. "Go home."

The untouched guard's hand shook with such violence Kilal was surprised he hadn't dropped his weapon. "I-I c-can't,"

Bron stuttered. "They w-will k-kill me."

"Fair enough."

Still holding onto Chuck's wrist, Kilal stepped forward and kicked Bron in the chest, narrowly avoiding being touched by the aznium rod. The air escaped Bron's lungs in a loud "*ooofff*" as he flew into the air and crashed hard on the ground. His skid was stopped by the granite wall.

The guard didn't get up. He wasn't dead, Kilal was sure of that, but he'd wake up wishing he'd taken the offer. Though at least that way, the man would have plausible deniability as to why the Heirs shouldn't kill him.

"You're dead," Chuck said, gasping between each word. His eyes were wide, his face pale, and spittle covered his lips and chin. "No one crosses...Wolfe."

Kilal rolled his eyes. He let go of Chuck and backhanded him across the jaw. He tumbled across the floor and came to a stop only a few feet from Bron.

The already abandoned rod rolled a short distance in front of Kilal.

The base was wrapped in black leather. A handhold. Further proof Bron and Chuck were Arbiters; a regular human could have held the rod without a wrapping.

Leaving the lethal weapon there was about the worst option Kilal could take, but he hadn't ventured there to figure out Silent Haven's aznium problem. He was there for the leaders and what they could tell him of Jayden, if anything. He'd deal with everything else...afterward. Plus, if he brought it with him, there was always the chance it would be used against him.

"If there even is an afterward," Kilal mumbled as he strolled up to the receptionist. *Afterward* insinuated he'd defeat the Ashen army and its leader and find Lilliana.

The young woman with brown hair and matching wide-brimmed glasses stared up at him. Poor girl probably never imagined this would be how her day would end up.

Kilal didn't sense Carving manipulations from her. Not an Arbiter, then. Or just really scared. Though likely she was just an innocent citizen looking for a paycheck.

He tried his best to give her a reassuring smile. She grimaced and leaned away.

"I don't suppose you'll give me the locations of those in charge of this corrupt organization?"

A tear trickled down her cheek. She shook her head.

"And I don't suppose you'll take me up on the offer I gave Bron. To go home? Maybe you came down with a stomach bug and needed some bed rest?"

"I-I-can't," she said, not taking her eyes from Kilal.

"Cameras?"

Her silence was all the answer he needed.

"Alright," he whispered, "then I guess we're going to have to do some acting. When I count to three, I need you to yell 'no' and shoot forward as if you're going for the button beneath the desk. I'm going to hit you. I'm sorry, but it's the only way for you to look blameless on camera. I promise you won't feel a thing. Well, tomorrow you will, but not tonight. Cough if you agree to follow along."

Her hands shook, and her mouth remained shut.

Come on. Work with me.

Finally, she coughed. Well, it was more a squeak than a cough, but he understood what she was going for.

Thank you.

"One. Two. Three."

"No!" She lunged from her seat. Kilal slapped her, and the impact echoed through the large room. He was ready and caught her head with his other hand before it bounced off the desk and laid her gently on the wooden top.

"I'm sorry," he whispered.

A sign-in sheet on the desk caught his attention. He picked it up.

The most recent arrival was a Tor'et Delmount at 10:13

p.m. His destination was Floor 23. Kilal looked at the clock hanging on the wall behind the desk. 11:03 p.m.

Less than an hour ago. And he still hasn't signed out.

Finally, something fortunate had turned in his favor.

"Time for a little visit to Floor 23."

He crossed the room to the elevator door and pushed the call button. The bell rang, and the elevator door opened immediately.

Entering the confined space, Kilal looked at the numbered buttons on a panel on the wall and hit the one marked '23.' As the door closed, he hoped whatever cameras were recording the first floor weren't actively manned and were just used to look back upon. The Heirs would be aware soon enough of his arrival, but he wanted that to be on his terms.

Either way, as the elevator ascended toward Floor 23, he prepared himself for the confrontation ahead.

~ CHAPTER 15 ~

The elevator announced Kilal's arrival with a *ding* and a feminine voice. He readied himself as the door slid open.

An empty nondescript hall awaited him. White-tiled floor. Bare ivory walls. The lights in the ceiling gave off an eerie, pale glow.

Exiting the elevator, he swiveled his head left to right. The hall stretched in both directions before cutting a ninety-degree angle and continuing around the corner. Two doors were down the hall in both directions. One door was directly in front of him.

Kilal felt for anything—a tingle of power, a noise, a scent. Nothing. So he picked the left hall, for no specific reason, and strode down it.

His footfalls echoed as if the floor was designed to amplify sound. He lowered his gravity until his steps were silent.

What's my plan here? Open each door? That's not the worst *idea, but I don't see another way around it.*

An unwarranted memory of an Arbiter he knew a hundred years ago cropped up. Sight was his name, and he'd discovered a Carving that would let him see through any substance made of metal or wood. Kilal had never understood the purpose of such a power. Who needed to see through a wall when he could just tear it down?

When Sight died at the tentacles of a Pestilence Plague, the knowledge of that Carving went to the grave with him.

Kilal sighed.

That would have been an extremely useful ability right now.

But there was no point worrying about what he didn't have. That wouldn't change anything. He had no means of knowing where Tor'et was on the floor. So, he did the only thing he could.

Standing at the first door with a 1 on the front of it, he readied himself and cracked it open. When he didn't feel or hear anything, he pushed it open just enough to peek inside. The room was just as bland as the hallway. The only difference was a cluttered desk with a computer and a stiff-backed chair behind it.

Continuing to the next door, Kilal repeated the events of the first. The same room greeted him, except that the desk was tidy and meticulously arranged.

Two more rooms passed quickly with nothing inside. The fifth door Kilal came across looked no different from the rest, but he paused when he closed his hand around the bronze doorknob. He didn't sense anything. No activation of Carvings, no pressure behind his eyes. So why were the hairs on his neck raised?

Something is behind this door.

He'd learned to trust his instincts a long time ago, whether they seemed irrational or not. Strength Carving at the ready, Kilal cracked the door open.

Power wafted through the small opening, slamming into him. His eyes felt like they were going to burst, and goose-bumps sprung up over his skin. A blood-curdling scream cut through his ears, and what felt like, into his soul.

So...much...pain.

Casting all care and stealth aside, Kilal threw the door open and leaped into the room.

He froze, eyes wide. An all-too-familiar smell assaulted his nose. Urine, death, sweat, and tears. Blood was *everywhere*. His feet slipped on the slick surface, and only the quick reaction of lowering his gravity kept him from falling on his butt.

The interior of the room was different from the previous four. This one had a few walls knocked out, as it was at least double the size of the others, and the remaining walls had been replaced with gray stone. The only similar thing was the tiled floor. Well, if it weren't covered with blood, some wet and fresh, some dried and cracking.

A man sat strapped to a stone chair, half-naked, in the center of the room.

Kilal lurched backward as the door slammed shut behind him. His back hit the wall, and he slid to the floor. Not too long ago he was locked in a similar room. For two years, his torture had been never-ending. He squeezed his head between his hands.

The room twisted and warped, mutating into the cell he'd once inhabited. The lone light in the ceiling flickered and ash descended.

Kilal's breaths came quick and shallow. He was back. *He was back!* It was all a lie. He never escaped. A game. It was all a game to his captors, and he was their pawn.

"No!" he wailed.

The figure standing next to the prisoner turned to Kilal. Fear paralyzed him, and even the shallow breaths he'd been able to take stopped. His wail caught in his throat, and it was all he could do to not close his eyes and curl into a ball.

Shaved head. Hairless face. Eyes and mouth stitched shut. Long, pale torso with too-long arms ending in hands with nails that had never been trimmed. A black sackcloth rag wrapped around its nether regions. Bare feet with toenails as long as the fingernails. In each hand, it held curved knives with jagged and rusted hooks all along the blade. They were dripping blood.

His blood.

Kilal found his breath again.

Bloodshed and Oaths, fight!

He would stand. He would activate his Carvings and tear his torturer limb from limb. They may have played him for a fool, but they'd made a mistake. They'd removed his shackles, and he would make them pay!

His will broke. "Please, no more," he managed to croak.

"Who are you?" the torturer said.

Said? The torturer never spoke.

The creature held up a pale hand, and a ring on its forefinger glinted yellow in the dim moonlight. That was never there before. Neither were the earrings with yellow gemstones protruding from each ear.

What the—

His torturer snapped his fingers, and Kilal erupted in flames.

Everything snapped back to reality, to the room he'd entered. The real room. The one before his mind had trapped him in the past.

He saw the torturer for what it really was: a man wearing black pants with suspenders hooked over a white button-up shirt with rolled sleeves. An attractive face, in a rugged sort of way, was covered in stubble with only the neck shaved. His yellow eyes matched the gemstones of his jewelry.

Kilal's eyes burst. The stench of his own burning flesh and hair overwhelmed him before his sensory system ceased working. He screamed as his skin melted and dripped like wax from a lit candle.

Despite the excruciating agony, he managed to picture the Carving of Gravitational Control in his mind and turn it into a dial. He rotated it clockwise, throwing his gravity to the max. The floor groaned, then gave way, and Kilal crashed to the level below. He didn't stop there, though.

Three stories down, he finally returned gravity to normal. He smacked against the new floor, shattering both legs. Out of view of the finger-snapper, the fire began going out. Flames receding, crackling white energy encompassed his body, and as Kilal rolled out of view of the hole above, his Carving of Immortality worked on healing his wounds.

He took three long breaths, enduring the wave of seizure-inducing pain as his broken legs, destroyed eyes, and ruined skin repaired. In the fourth breath, his sight returned. He forced himself onto his side and pushed to his feet, his bloody hands leaving a perfect outline on the white tiles.

On his fifth breath, black shoes descended from the hole in the ceiling.

Kilal rushed to the large wooden desk that had been common in each room except for the torture room above. With hands still growing flesh, he grabbed both edges of it and raised his strength. He wheeled toward Tor'et and threw the desk at him before he'd lowered through the ceiling enough to spot him or defend himself. It hit him in the torso, flinging Tor'et across the room. He smashed into the wall with the desk on top of him.

Barely a heartbeat after the collision, Kilal lunged. He kicked the desk pinning Tor'et, and both crashed through the wall with a loud crack, wooden joists giving way. The desk slammed Tor'et into the next wall and once again collapsed on top of him.

Kilal trailed him, not giving the Heir a second to recover. He smashed the sole of a boot into the Heir's face before rearing back and stomping on Tor'et's visible hand. The crunch echoed, and Tor'et howled through broken teeth.

"Who are you? Where are you from?" Kilal yelled. He grabbed Tor'et by the throat, ready to snap his neck at a moment's notice.

The Heir glared at him, and despite the damage Kilal had done, his disdainful gaze maintained a glimmer of...confidence?

A slight shift in the desk was all the warning he needed. Kilal smacked Tor'et's head back into the wall and snatched the newly revealed hand, which he'd loosened from beneath the desk. Kilal intertwined their fingers, preventing him from being able to snap his. Twisting his wrist and yanking it upward, the Heir's bone fractured, and with a powerful squeeze, Kilal mangled Tor'et's hand into a broken mess.

"Who. Are. You?" he growled, adrenaline pulsing through him.

Pinned beneath the desk and the weight of triple gravity with two broken hands and a smashed face, a normal foe would be beaten. But Tor'et pursed his lips and gurgled. Blood leaked from the corners of his mouth.

Kilal leaned in, anticipating words to come next.

He was wrong.

A whirlwind whipped from Tor'et's body, tossing the desk and Kilal. They tumbled and twirled head over heels. The vision of his gravity control dial had no sooner formed in Kilal's mind than he crashed through the ceiling and into the room above. He hit the floor and skidded to a stop against a white wall, denting it.

Son of a Plague! What was that?

Elemental Carvings gave the user the power of *one* element. Kilal's gravity control didn't let him manipulate *anything* else. Tor'et shouldn't have been able to use both fire *and* wind.

If Tor'et could somehow pull that off, how quickly could he also heal?

Kilal was on his feet and at the edge of the hole, spurred on by the unknown, but the Heir was gone.

Whirling about, he lowered his gravity and leaped through the fresh openings in the ceiling to the man still strapped to the stone chair. His skin was already beginning to regain its color, and his eyes were more alert, less clouded by pain. Had Tor'et let that man retain his healing Carving so he could be tortured longer?

Kilal quickly broke the manacles keeping his arms bent behind his back and the ones keeping his feet locked together.

When Kilal tried to lift him, the guy shoved his arms away.

"Leave me," he groaned.

"Not gonna happen, friend." Kilal easily slapped the refusal aside and hoisted him to his feet.

"Ahnk."

Kilal started. "Ahnk Silver-Tongue?"

He managed a smile. "The only."

Ahnk was a mentalist capable of...*convincing*...most people to heed his words. Kilal and the other Keepers were fortunate he'd been born with a heart desiring to help others. His Carving, if it were to fall into the wrong hands, would make for a *very* dangerous Arbiter.

"This is...good news," Kilal said. Ahnk was a member of the Keeper sect stationed in New Cita. If he was still alive, then... who else was?

"I'm Kilal."

Ahnk started and nearly slipped from his arms. "The Immortal Arbiter?" he whispered, staring. He shook his head and winced. "But...but you're dead!"

Kilal smirked. "Wouldn't be very immortal if that were the truth."

"Then...where?"

He sighed, the weight of ten missed years upon his shoulders. "Later. Let's get you out of here before Tor'et attacks again."

He could confront the Heirs another time. Saving even one good Arbiter was worth postponing his quest. No matter how much it hurt to do so. He'd already abandoned his daughter. And he'd abandoned the Keepers. It didn't matter that it wasn't his fault. He still took the responsibility for it and wouldn't add Ahnk to that list as well.

"No," he said, trying to push Kilal away again. "Tor'et is a coward. He stays and fights only when the odds are in his favor, and you showed him they aren't. He won't be back anytime soon. Lend me your knife, and I'll be able to make my way out of here."

Kilal handed over the pouch of blades still hanging on his belt. Ahnk turned his back and made quick work of the Carving. Kilal turned away too, giving the Keeper the privacy he knew Ahnk wanted.

Arbiters were...protective...of their Carvings.

"I've never seen someone able to control *two* elements," Kilal said. "How does he do that?"

A grunt and hiss of pain answered him.

Oh, the joys of carving.

"He's not an Arbiter," Ahnk said. "Nor are the other three."

Kilal frowned and rubbed his chin. "Then what are they?"

"We don't know. We've been trying to figure that out for a long time. But if you think Tor'et is powerful, wait until you meet the others."

I don't care about your world, Arbiter.

Jayden's words sounded in his head like a piercing gong. He needed to meet the other three heads of the Heirs, and next time he'd be prepared for their power.

When the Carving was activated and the seizure finished—and Kilal was surprised by the intensity of it—Ahnk handed back his knives.

"Do *not* test it," Kilal said as he reattached the pouch to his belt.

Ahnk raised his arms out to his sides and shrugged. "Then how do I know it's active?"

Despite how vital testing a freshly active Carving was, Kilal would rather go a second round against Tor'et than let someone influence his mind.

He shrugged too. "Better hope you did it right." Ahnk lowered his arms, but didn't make any kind of command. "Carving or not, I'm not leaving you," Kilal continued. "This whole building is going to be on alert now. There's no way you'll be able to get out alone."

The Keeper gave him a sly smile. "Give me more credit than that. I'm the Silver-Tongue. I don't think there will be an issue."

Kilal couldn't hide his skepticism. "Where was that tongue of yours when you were captured?"

Ahnk scratched the back of his head and had the good sense to blush. "My Carving wasn't activated."

Kilal groaned, to which his blush turned a shade darker. "How does th—" But not more than twenty-four hours ago, he'd cut into his own wrist in a rundown bathroom because his Carvings had run out. "Nevermind."

"Besides, no one has *invaded* the Heir's headquarters since...ever. Their security is much like their compassion. As in, it's very lacking. Now, since that's settled, I guess we'll part ways."

Kilal approached the Keeper and mustered the most no-nonsense look he could. "We leave. Together. Now."

Ahnk took a step back, his eyes hardened and his jaw set. "You know, I can make yo—"

Kilal had his hand over Ahnk's mouth before he could finish his sentence. He squeezed, making sure the mentalist couldn't speak. "If I get even a hint of a Carving being used, I'll break your jaw. Nod if you understand."

Ahnk nodded.

Kilal released him and turned his back, heading for the door. When footsteps didn't follow, he stopped and glanced back. Ahnk had that same look as he did before: hard eyes and a set jaw. Was he really going to make him break his jaw?

"I'm leaving. Alone," Ahnk said. "And you're not coming after me. I wasn't the only one captured, and she's probably in far more danger than me."

Kilal's heart skipped a beat. "She?"

The Keeper smirked and shook his head. "She always told me about your cold-hearted stubbornness and resolution to do what you thought necessary. Like breaking an ally's bones. But being the focus of it sure is different than hearing about it."

Kilal's heart felt like it was going to beat out of his chest. Could it really be?

The next word caught in his throat before working its way out. "Who?"

"Tor'et said they took her to Floor 27," he said, rolling his eyes. "Bloody idiot talks too much when he thinks he's won. Guess I should be thankful for that."

The wooden doorframe in Kilal's left hand splintered and cracked beneath his grip. "Who?" he growled.

"Requiem Ror."

Kilal lowered his gravity and raised his strength to the max, one-hundred times that of the strongest man. He jumped straight up, blasting through the floor and into the next level.

Requiem, I'm coming for you.

And anyone who would dare get in his way, whether from this world or another, would rue the day Sha'tum had sacrificed his life and created Arbiters.

~ CHAPTER 16 ~

Four levels higher, and Kilal landed lightly on his feet, having returned gravity to normal. White energy crackled quietly around him, healing the knicks and cuts he'd received from breaking through wooden beams and supports.

He surveyed the destroyed floor behind him and the trail of destruction left on the other three. No alarms had yet gone off. Kilal was beginning to believe what Ahnk said about the security. The Heirs were so arrogant that besides a few guards and a receptionist in the lobby, it really did seem like they had no protection.

He tried to sense Carvings in use, but felt nothing. And why would he? Ahnk said they weren't Arbiters. They didn't use Carvings.

Ready for anything, Kilal headed down the barren white hallway. The echo of his footsteps seemed more haunting than before. Which of the rooms he passed contained another tortured Arbiter? How many had been brought here and killed? How many had turned and joined Wolfe and his Heirs just to stop the pain?

The first door he opened revealed an empty room. The next four were the same. The sixth door opened into a space near the center of the floor. And it wasn't empty.

"Tell me what you found, and I will stop your suffering," a

calm voice said from within.

Kilal stood in a wide room nearly triple the size of the others. Computers and other gadgets with blinking lights and humming electronics lined the walls. The space was dark save for the second half, which could be seen through a glass barrier. That area was bare except for a light beaming from above and a single chair with a woman tied to it. Her head was slumped forward, but Kilal could see the metal of a collar through parted black hair. Tattered, ripped, and blood-soaked black clothing clung to her. Even though he couldn't see her face, he knew it was her.

Requiem.

Instincts screamed at him to dodge.

Kilal threw himself backwards into the hallway, narrowly avoiding aznium rods swung at his head. Two guards, dressed similarly to Chuck and Bron, charged through the door, silver sticks above their heads.

With a roar, he loosened the control he had on his simmering rage and charged.

He met the first with a heavy boot to the chest. The guard grunted and sailed backward, slamming into the glass wall. It didn't even crack.

The other guard swung at him. Kilal stepped back, letting the rod pass before his face, then landed a crushing kick with his shin to the outside of the man's forward-leading knee. It snapped, and the man howled. As he crumbled, Kilal swiftly brought his leg back, shifted his stance, and rammed his other shin into the side of the guard's head. It tore from his neck and splattered blood all over the glass. The dismembered head landed with a sickening *thunk*.

Kilal stepped over the body and back into the room. There were only two minions left inside. One appeared fairly normal. Brown hair, wide-rimmed glasses nearly slipping from his nose, white lab coat. The other man was just like the previous four guards, except...

This one has seen real battle.

The guard's face was hardened and scarred, his eyes sunken deep into the sockets. He was wide of shoulder and tall, almost as tall as Kilal.

Neither of the two men moved when Kilal entered the room, and he didn't know whether that was out of arrogance or apathy. Was he really so insignificant to them they need not even acknowledge his presence?

He growled and sunk a fist into a machine to his right. Metal screeched and crunched beneath the strength-enhanced blow. Maybe that would get their attention.

"Let her go," Kilal said. "And maybe I won't find out who your loved ones are and treat them as you've treated mine."

The guard narrowed his eyes. His hand went to the leather-wrapped aznium rod at his belt, but he didn't grab it.

The scientist stopped drumming away at the computer and turned an irritated look upon him. "What a bother," he said, his voice so calm Kilal wondered if the man realized his predicament. "Who are you, and how did you get in here?"

"I punched my way through Tor'et to get here." He ignored the first question.

The scientist raised a brow. "You got past him? Well, I'm sure you didn't kill him. He certainly fled. The insufferable man is more concerned about his life than anything else. Do me a favor, next time you cross paths with the bloody fool... finish the job."

Interesting. Do all top members of the Heirs hold such animosity for each other? If so, that was a weak spot he'd have to take advantage of.

"I'd worry more about yourself right now," Kilal said. "Let her go. *Now.*"

His barely bridled rage demanded to be let free. Requiem's unmoving form, only a few yards away, stoked the flames of his white-hot hate. Claire's accusing eyes and tone blaming him for Requiem's death only fueled it more. It wasn't really

Claire who'd said those things, just the horrifying apparition, but it didn't lessen the pain. Or the truth. But he had a chance to prove himself wrong.

He hadn't killed her. In fact, he could save her. And despite the calmer, more sensible Kilal reminding himself of Jayden and the questions he needed answered, he'd do just about anything to stop at least one of the voices.

The ground cracked beneath his feet as he increased his gravity and took a step into the room. His lip curled and his temper darkened. "I don't see you *letting her* go."

The scientist and guard shared a look. When the scientist returned his eyes to Kilal, light ricocheted off the glasses, and for a moment the man looked like a white-eyed Ash Fallen.

"Do you believe you're even an ounce of a threat to me? That we're on equal terms?" the scientist said in his disappointingly calm voice. "I don't recognize cockroaches. Kill him."

He turned back to his machine, and as he did, he held out his left hand to the guard. There was a ring with a large blue gemstone wrapped around his forefinger. He placed his hand on the guard's shoulder, and sapphire lightning crackled around him.

What the Plague is that?

The guard went rigid, and his eyes rolled into the back of his sockets. Spasms took over, and his body twitched and contorted in ways human forms weren't supposed to. Muscles expanded, splitting seams on his uniform and bursting forth from them. The guy's face broadened, and the features too, until Kilal didn't recognize the thing before him. It held more similarities to a War Plague than the human it had transformed from.

The abomination stood nearly a foot taller than Kilal and easily twice as wide. Its knuckles brushed the ground. The howl it let loose shook the tower.

Kilal curled his lips and matched it, howl for howl.

~ CHAPTER 17 ~

Kilal slammed through a wall, the abomination's hand around his throat. The impact destroyed at least one machine. Adrenaline surged through him in a way he hadn't experienced since returning through the Veil.

The fight wasn't a battle of wits. He didn't have to calculate every move in anticipation of what Carving his opponent was using. It was a battle of pure strength and will, and there wasn't much in his life Kilal was better at.

The abomination smashed him into the wall of the hallway opposite the room, and his head broke through the sheetrock. The mutated guard locked his elbow and ran down the hall, dragging Kilal with him, ramming his head through support beam after support beam. White energy crackled, healing each injury between every impact.

The constant agony fueled his determination further.

Kilal increased his gravity, and the pair came to a screeching halt. The force pushed him down with such momentum he was ripped out of the monster's grip. On the floor, he lowered his gravity again and kicked the wall, propelling himself across the tiled hall and out of reach of the surprised mutant. He leaped to his feet and dove forward, ducking beneath a wild punch.

Its right side was open, unprotected. Kilal punished it by

planting his feet and sinking a fist into its abdomen, precisely where the liver was, with as much force as he could muster. The abomination made a strange gurgling noise and stumbled.

Kilal twisted and moved around the beast as it collapsed to its knees, clutching its side. He pressed himself tightly against the thing's broad back, wrapped his arms around its neck, and squeezed. The monster bucked and tried to stand, but Kilal raised his gravity and maxed out his strength, keeping the thing on its knees.

Holding tight, Kilal shifted his hips and shoulders in one powerful movement and ripped the beast's head off. He leaped back in time to avoid most of the blood spatter.

Most.

Chest heaving, adrenaline still pounding through his veins, Kilal held the abomination's hair in an iron grip and strode back into the room. The scientist kept punching away at the keyboard, oblivious to his presence.

Until Kilal tossed the head in.

It smacked against the machine the scientist worked at, covering it in blood. Though it made him stop typing, the man didn't even have the decency to act surprised.

"You had your chance," Kilal growled. "Now you'll end up like him."

No! Remember Jayden! We need answers!

And if something happens to Requiem? Ashes take your answers!

Kilal stalked a tight circle around the scientist. Unlike the creature he'd fought, that man demanded careful attention. Who knew what would happen if the scientist touched him, and becoming a mindless monster wasn't something he had planned.

The man turned and pushed his glasses up the bridge of his nose. "You killed my mutant." Kilal got the impression he was talking more to himself. "And so quickly. Fascinating." He started as if a brilliant idea had just come upon him. "A deal.

Yes, let's make a deal."

What nonsense was this? Did this guy really think Kilal would be so foolish? "The only agreement we'll make is the one where I kill you painlessly in return for letting Requiem go. Or painfully, if you don't."

The scientist *tsked*. "Stronger than my mutant, yes. Smarter? No. Disappointing."

Kilal growled and approached. "Painfully it is."

The man lurched backward and pulled a device out of his pocket. It was small, no more than four inches in length and three in width. It contained two buttons, one small and white, the other large and red. The man smiled; victory danced in his eyes as he held the device up between them.

"One push of this button, and she dies." His thumb hovered over the big red one.

Kilal stopped mere feet from him. Was he bluffing? Kilal couldn't afford to find out. "Hmm...are you fast enough, you wonder, to get to it before I can press it?" the scientist said as if reading his mind. "Possibly. You are *fast*. But if you aren't... then what? Yes, you will kill me, of that I'm certain. But is trading my life for hers worth it?"

Kilal growled. His muscles tightened and the veins on his neck strained. The bloody son-of-a-Plague was right—and he knew that Kilal knew.

With a growl of frustration, Kilal smashed a machine to his right. The man jumped, and blood rushed to his cheeks. No, it wouldn't do anything for Requiem, but...but...

Hands shaking, vision nearly crimson, Kilal forced a deep breath.

Tear him to pieces. Break him! End him!

A second and third deep breath followed.

"What's your trade?" he said, each word an exercise of control.

"Yes, of course," babbled the scientist. "This woman is clearly someone important to you. If you tell me who you are *and* let me leave—*alive and unharmed*—I'll let her go."

Kilal had already anticipated the latter half of the deal, but the former? His *name*? It seemed like a fair trade on the surface, but it couldn't be that easy. What did the guy have up his sleeve?

A low whimper came from Requiem. Kilal could only imagine her fear and pain.

She was a weak High Arbiter, a user of Mind and Elemental Carvings, but she'd always refused to hurt anyone. Some said it was because she was too weak to do so. He'd been convinced it was because she was too kind, too loving. Now she sat here, guilty of nothing, bound by ropes with a collar around her neck. She was bloody and beaten.

It didn't matter what had been asked for in exchange for her freedom. Avinoth himself could have been standing there, the father of the Ash Fallen, the invader of his world and destroyer of half of it, and Kilal would give him whatever he demanded if it meant saving Requiem.

"Kilal."

The scientist furrowed his brow and stroked his hairless chin. "Kilal. Kilal? Kilal," he repeated in a whisper. "That name..." He snapped his head back, eyes wide. Kilal felt the urge to squirm beneath that gaze, as if he was nothing more than a lab rat who'd just been discovered to have two hearts or a lizard's tail. "The Immortal Arbiter?"

Kilal didn't respond. He'd promised to give his name, nothing more.

"That's im—no, nothing is impossible." He peered at Kilal with an inquisitive expression. "But where have you been?"

Should he be pleased his reputation was known by even the oathbreakers?

Bloody child, Kilal cursed. *Why wouldn't they know of you?*

"Yes," the man purred more than spoke. "It really *is* you. *Delightful.*"

"The deal," Kilal pressed before the guy could get any more

excited. "Let her go. And leave."

He considered following up with the typical threat of, 'If I see you again, I'll kill you,' but the scientist was far above simple threats. That didn't change the validity of it, though. Kilal *would* see him again, and he *would* kill him.

"Of course."

The man hit a button on the control panel he stood before. A beep answered from the device, and a line appeared in the middle of the glass wall. In near silence, the two doors split and slid into a recess on their corresponding wall.

He and Kilal seemed to do a little not-dance, Kilal moving side-to-side to the right and the other guy mimicking him until he stood at the doorway.

"I believe it goes without saying, but don't press the big red button. And good luck." He gestured with his head towards Requiem. "I really hope she doesn't kill you. I'd hate to lose an opportunity to dissect the Immortal Arbiter."

With that, he ducked out of the room and was gone.

Kilal scrunched his face in confusion and an ounce of trepidation. *Kill him?* Why would she do that? As unbelievable as the claim was, there was something about the way he'd said it that made the hairs on Kilal's neck raise.

There was sincerity in his voice, but why?

Kilal shook himself. No, Requiem wouldn't kill him. The scientist was only trying to get under his skin, maybe even cause him to cast suspicion upon her, ruining their reunion before it even occurred. Would Kilal really let the man have that?

Haunting silence settled upon the room like a cold blanket. Kilal was alone with the woman he hadn't stopped thinking about for ten years.

He took a hesitant step forward. Where was it? Where was the ash fall indicating a dream state or delusion? Had the time he feared more than any finally arrived? Was he going to wake only to find it had all been a fabricated reality created by his torturer back in the Tower of Eyes?

Kilal slammed a fist into an open palm. "No," he growled. "I'm here. I escaped."

Feigning confidence, he strode closer—but his hand froze, outstretched, inches from her shoulder. She was a small lady, barely reaching a few inches over five feet. Slumped over as she was, she looked barely more than a child.

"I'm here," Kilal whispered. "And I'll never leave you again."

He broke the shackles around her feet and the ones keeping her arms bent behind her and locked to the chair. She fell forward, but he caught her. And by the blood of Sha'tum, did it feel good to hold her again. He breathed her in, not minding the scent of musty copper and sweat. It was Requiem Ror, the woman he loved, his *wife*, and he was finally united with her.

Kilal swallowed the knot in his throat and brushed a tear from his cheek.

He pressed the small button on the device that would unlock the collar. It lit up, turning from red to green, and split in two. Both halves of the collar fell to the ground with a thunderous clatter.

Requiem shuddered and took a deep breath. He put a finger beneath her chin and lifted her head, moving her hair out of the way with his other hand.

"It's me, Req. Kilal. I'm ba—" The words caught in his throat. His hand shook, and a hot rage flooded through him. Her face became blurry, and he had to blink away the tears.

The left side of her face was nothing more than a mass of twisting and crossing scars. The corner of her lip was pulled down, and her eye was half closed from the scar tissue around it.

"Wha...wha..." he gasped, trying to get the words out. "I'm...I'm so sorry."

Recognition filled her eyes as they finally focused on him. She lifted a hand and rested it on his cheek. He couldn't help but lean into her palm, but if she hadn't been sitting before him, he wouldn't have recognized her touch. Her skin was rough and calloused. What had she been through to make her that way? Kilal didn't know, but when he found out, he would cross the Veil a hundred times if necessary, enduring being disintegrated and remade repeatedly, to reach the one who did this to her.

"Kilal?" Her voice was deeper, rougher, like her hands.

He placed his palm over hers—hers a dwarf in comparison—and smiled. "Yes. It's me."

The right side of her mouth curved upward a little, the left side unresponsive. Tears built in her eyes. "I missed you so—"

The smile vanished and was replaced by a sneer. The shadows in the room flickered like inverted candlelight, and the darkness behind him seemed to *simmer*. Black pooled in around her eyes until they were nothing but void-filled orbs. Her hand moved from his cheek to clamp around his throat.

And squeezed.

Kilal grabbed her wrist. "Req, it's me, Kilal!"

The flicker of the shadows increased as if a gust howled through the room.

"Kilal died ten years ago," she hissed through clenched teeth. Her grip on his throat tightened, and he had to grapple her wrist with his other hand to help the first pull her arm away.

"No," he gasped. When had she gotten so strong? "It's me. I've been...in the...Ashen...Lands."

Her eyes grew distant. She no longer stared at him, but at something beside him. "He's lying," she whispered.

Was she speaking...to him? Or something else.

Requiem's eyes narrowed, focusing on him once more, and her grip became even *tighter*. Kilal, confounded by the raw power she displayed, increased his strength to keep her hand at bay.

"Lies." She held her other hand out, and the darkness around the room seemed to converge onto her outstretched palm, coalescing into a blade dripping shadows.

That isn't good.

"Remember..." he said, trying a different avenue of approach, "Lilliana?"

"Lies!" she screeched.

And thrust the sword through his chest.

~ CHAPTER 18 ~

Kilal increased his strength but was still barely able to pry her grip from his throat. Hand removed, he lowered his gravity and shoved her. They both flew backwards. Requiem released the sword. It puffed into shadow and dispersed before it could even hit the floor.

White energy crackled around the wound, hot pain searing his chest as it was stitched closed. He coughed up blood, spilling it onto his chin, and eyed Requiem warily. How was he going to convince her it was really him?

And Bloodshed and Oaths, what happened to her?

The scarred face. The strength. The shadows. She hadn't been capable of those things ten years ago, and he'd never heard of such a drastic change in an Arbiter. The darkness weaving, maybe. She could use Carvings from the Elemental branch. All she'd have to do was learn a Carving that gave her that power. The strength, though? She didn't have access to the Physical branch.

"He looks like him," Requiem said, again looking at something *beside* Kilal instead of at him. She held out a hand, and the shadow sword reappeared. "He even heals like him." She sniffed the air; her eyes focused on him once more. "But you don't smell like him."

She lunged forward, blade leading the way. Kilal lowered

his gravity and twisted, narrowly avoiding the sword. It passed by his chest. Before she could respond to his quick movement, he wrapped both arms around her. He squeezed her tight, pinning her arms to her side, and lifted her off her feet. The shadow blade dispersed again as it was knocked from her grip. He raised his strength back to a hundred percent, using more of the precious little time he had with that power.

"I've been in the Ashen Lands," he said, readjusting his hold against her squirming. *Plagues, she's strong!* "I was trapped there for ten years." Kilal's mind raced to come up with whatever was necessary to convince her of his identity. "Lilliana, too." Her breathing began stabilizing, and the squirming eased. "Alright? I'm going to let you go. When I do, we need to get out of here. Then we can talk. Okay?"

She nodded.

Kilal took a deep breath—and released her. She landed lightly on her feet and turned. She peered up into his eyes, and again, a flare of rage sparked as he looked upon her ruined face. *Who did that to her? And how?* Arbiters, even without a healing Carving, could recover from any nonmortal wound with time and rest. And Requiem *had* a healing rune. So, had her wounds happened recently? Or was that something else he needed to add to the ever-growing list of things that had changed while he'd been gone?

He reached out to touch her scars, and Requiem tensed. Kilal could only imagine her self-consciousness. Thankfully, she let him.

The tissue was hard, calloused, almost like scales. Her eyes softened as his fingers brushed over the damaged skin. She leaned into his hand, and for a moment, he let himself think it was over.

Her eyes hardened, and her lips again curled into a sneer. *Son of a—*

A sword was in her hand and sweeping up through the arm touching her face, slicing it from his body quicker than he could recoil. He let out a whimper as the pain tore through him, but he sucked in a breath and reined in his will. His cheeks almost burned as much as the severed limb from the sound that escaped him.

Kilal leaped back as white energy crackled around his arm. Bone began growing, and muscles, sinew, and skin with it. He hit a desk and stumbled.

Requiem took advantage of the brief weakness.

She jumped forward and kicked him in the chest. His sternum crumbled, and the wind left him. As well as the ground. He crashed through the wall, colliding with the hallway opposite them. Slumped onto his butt, he gasped for breath as Requiem stalked through the hole, sword in hand.

Kilal raised his gravity. The floor groaned, then gave way, and he fell through. It wasn't much, but each second gained was another second healed.

Requiem didn't give him even one, though.

She jumped on his back, and he grunted. As they fell, she jammed her sword through his spine. Kilal went limp, everything on fire and numb simultaneously. His body slapped against the floor like a wet noodle.

Fear gripped his heart. She wasn't removing the sword, and as long as she left it there, he wouldn't be able to heal. He was as good as dead. If she wanted to, she could keep the blade pinned in his spine for another twenty-four hours, waiting for his Carving of Immortality to wear off.

And when it did, she could kill him.

Why was she doing this? Couldn't she see it was him? Really *him*?

Rage warred against his fear. Picturing the dial of his gravity control, Kilal twisted it to maximum. His body jerked from the abrupt change, and he crashed through the floor again. Level after level, the two broke through. With each floor they smashed through, his body became a little more like paste. Fortunately for him, he couldn't feel anything anymore.

That also meant he couldn't tell what Requiem was doing, but she didn't let go of the sword, nor continue to cut him, so he assumed the fall was keeping her off-balance.

When they broke through the final ceiling and hit the marble floor of the base, his body went *splat*.

Requiem dove off him right before the impact and took the weapon with her.

His spine was the first to heal—he *really* wished it hadn't been.

White energy crackling all about his body, Kilal kept his eyes on Requiem like a bunny watching a prowling fox, despite the anguish engulfing him. For the first time in his...well, existence, he was grateful for the pain he'd endured crossing the Veil only a few days ago. Having one's very existence unraveled and re-knit again and again made everything else slightly more bearable.

Slightly.

Fortunately, Requiem didn't seem in a hurry to finish the job. After skidding to a stop, she stood erect and watched him. Kilal could only imagine the sight she beheld as his body, only moments ago, more goo than anything, pieced itself together and solidified into the form she should recognize.

When control of his arms returned, looking upside down at Requiem, he lifted a hand out to her.

"*Please*," he croaked through still-regenerating vocal chords, "it's me. Kilal."

As if his voice were the catalyst she needed to finish him off, she strode forward, the expression on her face anything but trustworthy.

His mind raced. What could he say to make her believe him? Grasping at straws, he found a memory he thought might work. And if it didn't, maybe it would give her pause long enough for him to finish regenerating.

"I'm sorry, I should have...listened," he said—she hesitated. Good. "When you asked me...not to take...her with me. I should have...listened." Searing agony. His body felt not much different than when Tor'et had turned him into a human torch.

Focus on her. Ignore the pain.

Requiem froze. She dropped the sword. It dissipated into wisps of shadow. She raised a quivering hand to her open mouth, and a tear dropped from her left eye. "Kilal?"

"I'm so sorry," he said again. He wished he could find something else to say, but what else was there? "She's still over there. In the Ashen Lands. Lost." Finally, his body was formed enough to push himself onto all fours. He still didn't have much from the knees down.

"I'm...but....how?" Requiem said, still not coming closer. "It's been *ten* years."

"I know." Kilal winced as his feet grew. "Not a day has gone by...without me knowing it was another day I was separated from you."

Well, it wasn't *every* day, but she didn't need to know that.

With a loud sob, she flung herself into his arms, uncaring about his bloody clothes.

She shook with uncontrollable weeps and gasps. Holding her, engulfed in her warmth, Kilal wondered when the last time she'd cried like that was. From the way her body trembled against his, he imagined it had been a while.

Standing in the center of his enemies' base of operations, having encountered two already and knowing that, at any moment, they could come bursting in on them, he clung to Requiem with a fierceness rivaling hers.

Let them come.

For ten years, he'd fought for their reunion. Two things had kept him going during that period: finding his daughter and holding his wife. Plagues take him if he didn't revel in the moment.

She sobbed until, eventually, she had nothing left, then she snuggled against his chest.

Kilal gently pushed her back and smiled. "We should get

going. We have a lot to talk about."

It was her turn to place a hand on his cheek. "I almost killed you," she murmured. "I'm so, *so* sorry. What would I have done?" He sensed the question wasn't for him but an open-ended one she never wanted the answer to.

"Don't worry about it," Kilal said and winked at her. "You may have felt like you were in control, but really, I had you right where I wanted you. If you hadn't come to your senses, I was ready to make my move."

She took a deep breath and pursed her lips. Peeling herself away from him, she patted him on the chest and gave him a small smile. "Of course. I'm sure you *let* me sever your spine. And falling twenty-three stories to splat into a pile of human mush was just to give me a false sense of victory."

He pointed at her and shrugged, smirking. "Now you're getting it."

Requiem shook her head. She reached out and again placed a hand on his chest with a sigh. "Let's get out of here."

Kilal shook his head. "My apartment is still intact. We can stay there."

She grunted. "Not likely. Wolfe will send Sienna after us, and once she's on your trail, you won't lose her."

"Either way, we need to stop at my place, even if only for a few minutes. I have a...guest...there I can't turn my back on."

Her eyes hardened, and her nostrils flared. "A *guest*?" She took a deep breath. "Fine. We'll get this *guest*. And then we'll be on our way."

Kilal could imagine what she was thinking. He'd only been back for a few days, and he'd managed to acquire a stranger before contacting Requiem. He nodded before looking away, his cheeks warm. Now wasn't the time to clarify the guest wasn't some kind of lover.

As they stumbled through the swinging glass doors, Kilal wondered what had become of Chuck and Bron. Their bodies were gone. Hopefully, they made the smart decision and went home.

Spirits lifted by the potential of the future, he left the Heirs' headquarters with a smile on his face. A few hours ago, he'd entered the building intending to find information about Jayden and possibly enact some much-delayed vengeance. Instead, he'd come away with Requiem.

It was better than anything he could've imagined, and despite the army waiting on the other side of the Veil, despite his daughter still being lost, Kilal would allow himself one simple emotion, if only for a few minutes.

Hope.

~ WOLFE ~

Wolfe gazed down at the pair leaving the building from his third-story office. The wall facing the city was one-way glass with a reflective coating. Even if one of the departing Arbiters decided to look back, they wouldn't spot him.

"So, that's Godsgraive, the Immortal Arbiter?" He absently rubbed his well-kept, oiled salt and pepper beard.

"Yes," Fazin said.

"A welcome foe." Wolfe tapped the green gemstone inlaid on the metal band around his left forefinger. "Where have you been? You released Requiem to him in exchange for his name." It wasn't a question. "And you discovered nothing from her before deciding to let her go?"

"I...did not."

Wolfe turned from the window and leveled a glare at the mad scientist. For a second, the only noise came from the tapping of his nail against the green gemstone. Fazin looked from Wolfe's face to the ring and back again. He paled, and blood trickled from Fazin's nose.

The scientist wiped his upper lip and stared at the red smear on his finger. "If I hadn't traded that information, he would have killed me. I'm much more fragile than one of my mutants. Jackson barely gave me two minutes before Godsgraive dispatched him."

"And if we don't find a way off this infernal rock before it dies, we'll *all* be dead," Wolfe said with as much vehemence as he could manage. "Don't pretend like you wouldn't have traded *my* life for his name. Your bloody addiction for knowledge will get us all killed one day."

Tap. Tap. Tap.

Fazin didn't respond. He only stared at the green ring.

A gust slammed the door open, and Tor'et barged into the room. Crusty blood covered his face, and his shirt was tattered and torn. One suspender hung, ripped in half, to his side.

"You're just letting them leave!" he yelled. "After what he did to me?" Tor'et lifted a hand towards Wolfe and brought two fingers together.

Tap. Tap. Tap.

Blood dripped from Tor'et's eyes, nose, and ears. His face twisted into a visage of pain. Bending over, the insufferable man threw up on the silky-smooth red carpet.

Tap. Tap. Tap.

He dropped onto his hands and knees. Bile continued to spew from his mouth. The scent of Tor'et's stomach contents filled the room, and Wolfe felt no shame when he removed a handkerchief from his vest pocket and brought it to his nose.

Fazin took small steps towards the door, but when Wolfe turned his ire on him, Fazin stopped in his tracks.

Wolfe knelt beside Tor'et. Maintaining the handkerchief over his nose, he grabbed Tor'et's hair and wrenched him back so they were eye to eye. Wolfe may not have had an affinity for amplification, but he was still strong.

"You would use your power against me? Power from the stone *I* gave you?" he asked, keeping his voice innocently mild.

Tor'et blinked a few times before swallowing. "Forgive me. I acted in haste."

"Before losing Ahnk, did you discover anything from him?" Tor'et's gaze darted to Fazin, eyes wide and pleading. "He won't help you," Wolfe said. "Answer my question." He tugged on Tor'et's hair to remind him of his predicament.

Tor'et licked his lips. "He wouldn't budge. If I had more time, I—"

Wolfe smashed his face into the pile of vomit. As Tor'et tried to scrub the bile from his cheeks and keep from retching again, Wolfe stood and eyed Fazin.

"More time? *Five* long years we've had. And now that we're finally this close," Wolfe held his thumb and forefinger an inch apart, "to figuring out *something*, you Plague-born, Ash-eating idiots throw the opportunity away." With each curse, his voice sharpened.

Tor'et and Fazin swallowed and bowed their heads. They wouldn't meet his gaze. Good. Bloody fools needed some humility crammed down their throats.

"Are you two children I need to continually remind of why we're here?"

"No," they echoed.

Wolfe unleashed a wave of crippling nausea. Their legs gave out as swells of sickness slammed into them. Blood flowed from every orifice. Foam seeped from their mouths as they gasped for breath.

Their writhing and gagging brought no joy. Wolfe wasn't one to indulge in inflicting pain. But he didn't shy away from ensuring his men feared him more than anyone else.

Including the infamous Godsgraive.

When he was content they'd learned their lesson, Wolfe released them from their agony. Breath filled their lungs again, and he could only imagine the relief at no longer being under the influence of his Godstone.

While Tor'et and Fazin regained their composure, he returned to the window.

The city was calm. And mostly dark. The forecasters predicted it would be a clear night, so the order had been to turn off ninety percent of the artificial lights. Ophir and Dampir, high above them and unhindered by any clouds, filled the void.

The land was dying, and every ounce of energy preserved was another that could be used later.

"We don't have much longer. I can *feel* it. The decay of the Schism and Veil stretches. The corruption beneath the Dead Zone deepens. The Veil weakens. If our end isn't at the hands of the Ash Fallen, then it'll come from the death of this world. I intend to be off this dying rock before either of those happens. Requiem and Ahnk know something.

"This is how you're going to fix what you've done," Wolfe pressed. He flashed them a cruel smile. "You're both going to leave my presence immediately and apologize to Sienna for ruining her hard work."

The two men paled again, and Fazin shivered as if a freezing wind had just whipped across his skin.

"Then, you'll send her to me. If she isn't in front of me within the hour, I'll kill you both and find new wielders of your stones.

"Afterward, you two will personally lead an expedition into the ruins beneath the Undercity. Requiem and Ahnk may have destroyed the knowledge they discovered, but I'm willing to bet there are many more nests scattered beneath us. If either of you comes back empty-handed, I'll sever your bond and kill you."

All pride fled from the pair as they shoved past each other in their attempts to be the first free from his glare.

When the door shut behind them, Wolfe retreated behind his desk and slumped into his chair.

Hopefully, Sienna won't kill them.

He closed his eyes and rested his chin on his chest. Sienna would track Kilal and Requiem, keep an eye on them, and report back to him. A confrontation with Godsgraive was not yet in his best interest. Soon, though, it would happen. And when it did, Wolfe would have the upper hand.

Reaching into a drawer, he pulled out his last bottle of Brown Sunshine. He uncorked it and sniffed while swishing the contents. The tension eased from his shoulders as the scent of home lifted his spirits.

"How do we get off this bloody rock?"

Silence answered him as he brought the bottle to his lips.

PART TWO

~ CHAPTER 19 ~

Once again, Kilal slinked through his city like an outlaw on the run, which was closer to reality than he cared to consider.

Him, The Immortal Arbiter, the founder of the Keepers, and the protector of Silent Haven; on the run.

He'd considered many outcomes for his life over the last two centuries, but that was not one of them. Nor was being led from rooftop to rooftop, barely keeping up with *Requiem*. How was he, with gravity almost completely removed and his strength boosted, barely able to keep up with a woman who, last he knew, didn't have access to a Physical Carving?

Despite his current predicament and the number of mysteries piling up around him, Kilal couldn't resist a small smile.

Requiem Ror!

They were together! Sure, she'd tried to kill him, just like the scientist had foretold, but...well, she didn't. And considering whatever she'd been through in the last ten years to leave her so scarred, both physically and emotionally, he didn't hold it against her. So, for the moment, just being with her would be good enough.

They entered his apartment building through the front door. If Sienna really was on their trail, he wouldn't be returning to apartment 707 for long; if ever again. So, what was the point of descending from the roof stairwell like a thief in the night? Either way, the lobby attendant cared more for his newspaper than for doing his job. He barely glanced over the pages before returning to whatever lies the Heirs and the Governing Seats had orchestrated.

The elevator was quick, and before Kilal knew it, he was alone with Requiem, and so close he could smell her. Sweat and blood; now that was a perfume a man could get behind.

What do I do here?

After so much time, did she have another man in her life? If not, did she even want him in hers anymore? Could what they had for the previous half-century really be rekindled by a quick prance through the city and an elevator ride? Their legal bond and their emotional ones likely held little to no ties to one another anymore. Or at least, potentially for her.

It's not as though he could have expected her to become celibate in his absence, especially since she'd believed him dead.

A single realization struck him harder than any other: he didn't care. *Ten years* he fought for their reunion. Plagues take him if he'd squander the opportunity. What was he? A young boy with the wisdom of a raindrop and flippant hormones?

Kilal wrapped his arms around her and pulled her tight against him. Her head rested perfectly on his chest. Just as it used to.

"I missed you so much," he said, running a hand up and down her back. "I'm so sorry. I shouldn't have gone. I should have listened to you." He rested his forehead on her hair. The softness was a stark contrast to the scars on her face and the callouses on her hands.

"Yes. You should have." Her words were quiet, yet they carried a condemnation and anger Kilal wasn't prepared for. He froze, hand halfway up her back, and she used his stiffness to remove herself from his embrace.

She didn't look at him as she turned back to face the elevator door.

"Don't act like you can reappear out of nowhere after all this time and think everything can return to the way it was. Because it can't."

He opened his mouth, shut it, opened it again. "Req, of course I don't think that. I can't imagine what you've been through. But you need to know that I'm back, and I won't le-"

She whirled on him and leveled a finger inches from his face. "Don't you dare say it!" Tears glistened in her eyes. "*Don't* you *dare.*"

The elevator dinged, and the door slid open. Without another word, Requiem exited the lift and turned left. Kilal stood there, stunned, until the door began closing. Only then did he shake himself and step into the hallway.

Kilal followed Requiem in silence. He hadn't expected their reunion to go well, but he definitely hadn't expected what happened. Especially not after the affection she'd shown at the Heir's headquarters.

Things were going to be a lot more difficult than he'd anticipated. And that was if there even was a chance to rekindle anything. Maybe their flame truly had been extinguished.

Could he accept that? Of course not! At least, not yet. If he could endure ten years of fighting, two years of torture, and an eternity of agony from crossing the Veil, he could endure Requiem's anger. Otherwise, he might as well go back to the Ashen Lands and continue his search for Lilliana.

He'd returned to warn his land of the looming invasion, but that was the excuse he'd used to convince himself it was the right thing. The real reason was standing at his door, refusing to meet his gaze.

And he'd throw himself off the Edge of the World before he gave up on that fight.

~ CHAPTER 20 ~

"Kilal?"

Allyria barreled down the hallway when he entered the apartment, nearly crashing into him as she rounded the corner. She hopped from foot to foot, peering up at him. "You're alive!"

"Of course I am," he said. Then he cocked his head and narrowed his eyes. "Did you expect me to fail?"

Allyria ignored the question. "So, did you do it? Did you kill them?"

He sighed. "No."

"But you said you would." She drew her lips into a flat line.

Kilal ran a hand through his hair and gave her a sheepish shrug. "I tried. I did give Tor'et a good beat down, but he got away."

Allyria slumped forward until she could run her fingers over the carpet. "Well, I guess that's better than nothing. Maybe they'll get the point and leave us alone now."

On the contrary, little lady. Now that they know I'm alive, I imagine they'll make me their number one target.

A finger tapped his shoulder.

Right.

"Allyria, you know how I have a habit of picking up stray girls?"

She planted her hands on her hips and shook her head. "First of all, I'm not a *stray*. Second, please don't tell me you brought another one back here. It's cramped enough as it is."

"Cramped? Really?"

Lilliana had never claimed such a thing. And he'd always found the place spacious enough.

Requiem's finger dug harder.

"Well, Allyria, meet Requiem Ror." Kilal stepped to the side.

Allyria's eyes widened, and her jaw dropped. "*The* Requiem Ror? As in, the Requiem Ror who's been fighting Wolfe and his goons for five years?"

Kilal scratched the back of his head. "Yes?"

"The same Requiem Ror who killed a Death Plague at the Purification Plant?" *Wait, what? Was that true?* "The same Requiem Ror who survived the battle between the Keepers and the Heirs of the Promise?"

"The same," Requiem said gruffly and brushed past them, nearly shoving the much taller teenager aside. "I need a change of clothes. Then we're out of here." She disappeared into Kilal's room and slammed the door behind her.

Allyria blinked. "I guess I expected this meeting to go... differently."

Kilal placed a hand on her shoulder. Allyria started and jerked away from him.

Bloodshed and Oaths. You can't do that.

"She's been through a lot," Kilal said. "I think we'll just have to be understanding of that."

"What's happened to her? Her face? Was it always like that?"

"No."

"Can't she use the Mind branch and access healing Carvings?" He nodded. Another mystery. "*So* why doesn't she?"

Kilal stared down the hall, wondering the same thing. "Probably because she can't."

"Can't? I thought healing Carvings could mend *anything*."

"They can. Which means there's something powerful enough to inflict wounds impervious to them." He turned a questioning eye on Allyria. "Also, I suggest not mentioning anything about it to her."

Allyria nodded, as if that was something even a baby would know.

A loud bang echoed out from his room, and Kilal winced. What was Requiem doing?

Allyria leaned closer to him and sniffed a few times. "You smell like burning."

He shrugged. "Well, I was set on fire."

"Should I get used to things like that from you? Limbs ripped off. Getting set on fire. Leaving in the middle of the night and coming home with mysterious ladies?"

"The first two, yes. The last...I never *plan* on that sort of thing happening."

Allyria returned her hands to her hips and gave him a disapproving glare. "Good."

He moved past her and into the kitchen. Reaching beneath the sink, Kilal tore away a fake wall and pulled out a heavy black backpack. A second, empty one came after that. He tossed it to Allyria.

"How many things do you have hidden behind walls?" She caught the bag and threw it over her shoulder.

"We're leaving soon. Probably won't return for a while. Put some clothes in there and anything else you've come across you may want with you."

Her whimsical face grew somber. She turned on her heels and disappeared down the hallway leading to Lilliana's room.

Kilal opened his bag and rummaged through it. Plenty of cash. Four small bars of aznium wrapped individually in leather cloth so he could handle it. Aznium knuckles. Kilal smiled as he carefully unwrapped the weapon and slipped his fingers through them. They were cast from bronze, but a thin layer of aznium was inlaid over the knuckles. A very deadly weapon against Arbiters; one he only used on rare occasions, but considering how the last twenty-four hours had gone, he had a feeling those occasions would become much more frequent.

The remaining contents of the bag were typical instruments an Arbiter would need: two more sets of carving knives, two plastic-wrapped blocks of combat rations, a bottle of water, three rags tightly folded into small squares, and last and even rarer than the aznium bars and knuckles, Kilal pulled out two vials of a blood-red liquid.

The vials were small, no bigger than an average human's pinky finger. The glass was enchanted by an Arbiter who could harden material. No amount of physical trauma could break the glass. But what was in it was what made the vials so precious.

Dragon's Blood.

At least, that was what it was called. The secret to making it had long since been lost. Those two vials were the remaining of the four Kilal had purchased for an enormous fee almost three decades prior. It was entirely possible they were the last vials of Dragon's Blood in existence.

Kilal pressed them to his chest and closed his eyes. Dragon's Blood was an enhancement drug that allowed Arbiters to break through the ceilings of Carvings. Ceilings were natural boundaries that limited their usage. Kilal's Carving of Deific Strength allowed him to access strength up to a hundred times the strongest human, but only for a small duration. It was *possible* to access more than a hundred times...but doing so would likely kill the user, and if it didn't, the agony endured by breaking through a ceiling was enough to paralyze. Dragon's Blood changed that.

But using the compound didn't come without a cost.

The two times Kilal consumed the drug, he'd fallen unconscious for three days afterward.

If only he'd brought them with him when he went north with Lilliana. Would it have been enough to stop Gabriel and the ambush he'd planted? And if he'd never been transported to the Ashen Lands, would he have been able to stop the Heirs of the Promise and protect the Keepers?

The red liquid swirled and swished in an unnatural way as if Kilal had shaken the vial. He lost himself in the movement as his mind drifted to the possibilities of a changed past. Every time he pondered such topics, his thoughts inevitably wandered towards one idea: time travel. Arbiters, even after a thousand years of carving, still only understood a fraction of the power they had access to. Couldn't it be possible there was a Carving that would let him go back to that event ten years ago and change what happened? And if there wasn't, what about the lost technology in the ruins to the north?

If there had once been teleportation devices, was it so far off to consider that the Sunlight Domain also had access to time travel? But if they did, wouldn't they have used it to save themselves from the invasion of Avinoth and his Ash Fallen?

Kilal sighed. Reality was, he would probably never know. And until he did, he had to face the facts: the past was the past. His only option was to keep moving forward.

But what if it's real? There are Carvings that can slow down time for the user for short periods. What if I take the four runes used in that design and test different variations?

The combinations and possible revisions of each rune were nearly infinite, but if he stumbled upon them, like so many Arbiters stumbled upon new Carvings...the ramifications could change the world forever.

"One problem," Kilal mumbled. "You don't know the runes used for that Carving."

He sighed. Why did he do that to himself? Get his hopes up when there was never any hope to begin with?

While tucking the vials back into the bag, Kilal's hand brushed against another object stuffed into the bottom. The surface was cracked leather, worn from overuse. His breath caught and his hand shook as it closed around the sketchbook.

Hesitantly, he pulled it out.

How long had it been since he'd touched that book?

"Ten years," he muttered. Just like everything else.

The book nearly squeaked as he opened it. Time hadn't been kind to it, but to be fair, Kilal had used it...a lot.

Reverently, he flipped through the pages, scanning each with a tinge of hate and awe. He held two hundred years of Carving knowledge in his hands. Every design he'd discovered on his own or stolen from others. It was probably the most extensive collection of Carvings in existence. The price the Heirs of the Promise were willing to pay for Allyria's head would be nothing compared to what they'd offer for the treasure trove of insight between his fingers.

Kilal ran a thumb over a thinning page containing a sketch along with dimensions and notes of one particular design.

The Carving of Immortality.

To think he'd actually documented it, especially after knowing what it did to anyone who'd etched it but him. He should rip the page out and burn it. He should burn the whole bloody book. Yes. That's what needed to be done. But his hands wouldn't obey. And he couldn't blame them.

How could he erase so much hard-earned knowledge?

"Because you stole most of it," he growled. "How many lives were destroyed in your pursuit of mastery?"

"What's that?" Allyria asked from the other side of the window into the kitchen.

Kilal snapped the book shut and shoved it into the backpack. "Nothing."

"Doesn't look like nothing."

"*Nothing*," he repeated, harsher than intended.

Allyria winced. She fumbled around in her own backpack and tried to hide her hurt.

He sighed. "Sorry."

"Whatever."

"What did you pack?"

"Some clothes. Soap. Toothbrush. Toothpaste. Toilet paper."

Kilal scrunched his nose. "Toilet paper?"

She shrugged and reddened a little. "I don't know where we're going. And I'm not about to get stuck in the wild without some."

He contained a smile. The things the youth thought of. "Fair enough."

"And don't even bother asking for some." She wagged a finger. "I see that grin trying to break through. You think I'm silly. Just a *girl*. Well, when you're making a mess, you'll wish you had some toilet paper of your own."

Kilal burst into laughter.

Allyria crossed her arms and glared.

"Well, I should go check on our guest," Kilal said. He hoisted his pack onto his shoulder and retreated down the hall to the closed door of his room. He rapped his knuckles on the frame and waited for an answer. When no answer came, he reached for the knob.

It turned without his assistance, and the door swung open.

Requiem stared at him from the dark recesses of his room. She was newly clothed in a fresh pair of jeans, a long-sleeved shirt, and a dark blue hoodie, which she'd pulled up and over her head, her hair tucked in behind it. A black backpack hung from one shoulder.

"Let's go." She brushed by him.

A spark of anger flared in Kilal. He snapped his arm out and blocked her path. "When are we going to talk?" he said, keeping his voice low. "I understand how you're feeling right now, but there's still a lot we need to discuss."

Darkness flashed in her eyes, but it was gone as quickly as it came. "I've got a guy waiting for us. He'll take us to a place we can...talk." She said the last word as if it left a sour taste in her mouth.

Kilal didn't want to let it drop. He'd rather have had it out with her right then and there, and that Sienna person could take herself to the edge of the world, but common sense won out. He wouldn't get anywhere with Requiem that way. He could only hope that by the time they arrived wherever it was they were going, she'd be more willing to communicate.

He dropped his arm and stepped out of her path. "Okay."

As she stepped away, Kilal swooped into his room. He threw on a change of clothes and was behind Requiem again as she opened the front door. Allyria followed without more than a gesture from him, and together they left the apartment.

~ CHAPTER 21 ~

The sun was up and the cool breeze from the night before was gone. Sweat trickled down Kilal's back, sticking his shirt to his skin. The trio took advantage of a break in traffic to jog across a busy street. Back on the sidewalk, Kilal and Allyria followed Requiem in silence.

Vehicles droned by, sputtering and spitting gray smoke from their exhaust pipes. Food vendors were set up on the sidewalks, and a particularly tasty-smelling stand pulled at his nose as they passed. A portly man with a gut as merry as his smile waved around meat on a stick. A long line of people waited to get their hands on the treat. Kilal's mouth watered as the savory scent infiltrated his nostrils.

Maybe the combat rations he and Allyria had dined on weren't all they were cracked up to be, after all.

A man bumped into Kilal. The stranger muttered a curse under his breath and kept walking. Kilal flashed a look of irritation at his back but didn't say anything. That sort of thing happened often. He'd never figured out whether it was because of his large frame or if people just didn't care. Or both.

Requiem stopped abruptly and approached a street vendor hawking jewelry. She'd remained silent during their quick trek across the city, and Kilal hadn't pushed her. Allyria managed to keep up with them well enough, but as they waited for Requiem, she took a moment to lean against a light pole and catch her breath.

The vendor was a greasy fellow with patchy clothes and grime under his nails. When Requiem approached and the man opened his mouth to speak, Kilal recognized the sham for what it was. The vendor's teeth were pearl white. No one with teeth that gleaming was as poor as the guy portrayed himself.

"My lady, may I offer you an aznium-infused ring? A perfect surprise for any Arbiter wishing to put their hands on the fine misses. Or perhaps I may interest you in this necklace made from the bone of a War Plague? Get too cold and give it a crack. It'll warm you right up."

Kilal had half a mind to smack the man and his fake wares right off the street.

Allyria wandered up to the stand and poked around at the junk. "Wow! How did you get your hands on stuff like this?"

The sleazy salesman knuckled a thin mustache and barely contained his own excitement. "My desire to bring only the highest quality of goods to the citizens of Silent Haven knows no bounds, little misses."

Kilal rolled his eyes.

Allyria, completely fooled by the sham, shuffled through the rest of the items as if they were long-lost fabled treasures.

He stepped up beside her and pointed at a white necklace made of interconnecting rings. "This the War Plague one?" he asked.

"Of course, good sir. The story of how I came across such a thing is nearly worth the price of the necklace itself!"

Kilal drew his lips into a flat line. *I'm sure it was.* "War Plague bone is famous for being impervious to physical damage, correct?" he pressed.

The vendor wrung his hands together. "You are absolutely correct."

Kilal picked up the necklace and held it up to the sun, inspecting it as if that were the appropriate thing to do. The material was flimsy, and a small chip in the white paint used to fake the bone caught his attention.

Allyria stopped her own perusing to watch him.

"Impeccable," he said, inflecting the word with as much awe as he could muster. The vendor nearly glowed with the anticipation of a sale. Kilal rolled a section of the necklace between his thumb and finger. "The quality is so subtle. It's light, almost frail. I'm surprised by how brittle it feels. I never would have thought the bone of a War Plague would feel so...cheap. Unless," Kilal broke it with barely a squeeze. The vendor paled. His face shifted from outrage to embarrassment and back. Kilal kept a flat glare on the man. "Unless it's just really old?"

Allyria snickered.

Requiem nudged him aside and shot him a quick glare as if asking him if he was proud of himself. He returned a smug smile; he was.

"I'm looking for something that'll remind me of better times, times when we didn't have to fear the light," Requiem whispered.

The vendor froze and finally tore his gaze from Kilal to look at her. His eyes focused for a touch too long on the scarred side of her face. Kilal tensed, but Requiem either didn't notice or didn't care.

Allyria opened her mouth, but Kilal was quick to catch her eye and give her a slight shake of his head.

The man rubbed grimy hands together in front of him. "Of course, my lady. Come with me. I have more products in the back which may suit your needs." He opened the door into the two-story building behind his table of junk and held it wide for Requiem.

"They're with me," she said.

The vendor flicked his eyes to Allyria, then Kilal. "I'm sorry, my lady, but there will not be enough room in the back for them. I apologize, but these days, I grow short of space."

Allyria leaned closer to Kilal and whispered in his ear. The fact she could do such a thing was a testament to her height. "Not enough room? Is the building not his?"

"He's not talking about the building."

"He's not?"

Kilal shook his head, cutting the conversation short. Even a stray word to the wrong eavesdropper could jeopardize them.

"That's fine," Requiem said. "But you'll be the one to tell your boss why you left The Immortal Arbiter standing with his hands in his pocket at your stand."

The vendor's jaw dropped, and he slowly turned his head to Kilal. He kept his gaze on him for much longer than before as he studied his face and size. "Is it really you?" he whispered.

Kilal nodded.

"But how? Where?"

"Enough," Requiem interrupted. "The product?"

The vendor gestured with his head for the three of them to enter. He never took his eyes from Kilal, who wanted to squirm under the scrutiny. The man was looking at him as if he was some sort of god returned from the dead.

"Praise Sha'tum for your return," the vendor whispered. He reached out and touched his arm. Was he verifying Kilal was truly standing before him?

The hallway inside was sparse and cold. Lights from the ceiling lit their way as Requiem led them through. The hall deposited them into a wide room containing dozens of crates filled with more junk the man was selling, as well as tables covered with fake jewelry.

In one corner, the vendor began moving some of the crates, revealing a manhole. The metal cover slid open with a screech. Allyria gagged when the ripe scent of sewage smacked the group.

"Three," the vendor called down.

"Three?" came the response. "You know I don't have room for that!"

The vendor smiled. "One of them is Kilal."

"Who the bloody ashes is that?"

"The Immortal Arbiter."

"The Immo—Bloodshed and Oaths, is that a joke?"

Requiem started down the ladder but stopped before fully disappearing. "You should close up shop and disappear for a time. There's a good chance Sienna is following us."

The vendor paled, but to his credit, he gave a curt nod. Despite his seedy activities, the man before them was more than just a seller of counterfeit goods, and Kilal felt a little guilty for embarrassing him earlier. Glad he grabbed more money from his apartment before they left for good, Kilal swung his backpack in front of himself and fished out a few silver coins.

"Sorry about breaking the necklace." He handed the vendor the money. "Hopefully this more than makes up for it."

The vendor gaped at him. "I could never!" A smile blossomed on his face. "Besides, now I can sell a necklace touched *and* broken by none other than The Immortal Arbiter!"

Kilal groaned, but slipped the coins back into his bag. At least, the tale told by the vendor would be an honest one. "What is your name?"

The man jumped, then stuttered a response before calming himself and trying again.

This is going to get bloody annoying if this is how everyone is going to react to me.

"Shaimish."

Kilal held a hand out to him. Shaimish stared at it, blinking, before accepting it. "Thank you, Shaimish."

The vendor burned bright red and barely managed a grunt and nod of his head.

Requiem disappeared into the sewer, followed by Allyria and Kilal. The ladder was covered in a layer of rust, and Kilal's hands came away with an orange-red film.

Two lanterns parted the darkness of the sewers. One hung from a pole on the front of a long, narrow wooden boat with three benches across the width of it. The other dangled from a similar pole on the rear end. The boat, tied to a metal ring on the wall they stood on, swayed lightly on the thick sludgy water. Chunks of rotten food, dead animals, and things Kilal would rather not think about, floated by.

Allyria lifted the neck of her shirt over her mouth and nose. Kilal took a deep breath and smiled at her, exhaling as he did so. She scrunched her face in disgust and shook her head.

"Take us out of the city," Requiem said.

The man who would row them stood stone still with an oar in his hand. He didn't acknowledge her. Kilal was the only thing he seemed to see. "Bloodshed and Oaths, it's really you." He bore the same expression as Shaimish had.

"So, you're pretty famous?" Allyria whispered beside him.

"Apparently."

"Can't be that famous," she muttered. "I'd never heard of you."

At least there was one.

"If you would like to keep staring," Requiem stepped onto the boat with barely a shudder from it. "I'll make sure Sienna takes you first when she arrives."

That seemed to do the trick. The rower jumped.

Allyria hopped on with the grace only a teenager could muster. The boat jerked, and she lost her balance. Requiem snatched her arm, catching Allyria before she tumbled into five or so feet of sewage water. When she regained her footing, Allyria was quick to take a seat on the middle bench.

"Thanks," she said.

With only three riders, the boat had sunk nearly halfway. It was clearly not meant for many people. Allyria seemed to register that as she looked at Kilal, looming over her on the wall.

She winced. "I'm not sure this is going to work."

"Have faith, little one. I am, after all, The Immortal Arbiter."

She rolled her eyes.

Kilal lowered his gravity and stepped onto the boat. Allyria cringed and braced herself, but the boat rocked less than even when Requiem had stepped onto it. As he took a seat on the rear bench, Allyria gave him a confused and embarrassed look.

He shrugged. "You probably shouldn't have had that last bite of food."

Flat lips and a shake of her head was her response.

"Take us." Requiem settled beside Allyria, who had returned to covering her nose with her shirt.

"Right," the ferryman said.

With the boat untied and pushed into the center of the dark stream, he slowly and with great care propelled them through the sewer canal.

"What's your name?" Kilal asked.

"Colton, at your service, sir."

Shamish and Colton. I'll need to remember those.

"If we're just leaving the city," Allyria said, "why are we going through the sewer? Couldn't we just take a car? Or run?"

"We have to assume Sienna is on our trail," Requiem answered, her gaze fixed on the shadow-filled path they glided along. "Wolfe isn't going to be happy I escaped. Sienna less so. She's the greatest tracker I've ever encountered. Her sense of smell is uncanny. Which is why we're taking to the sewers to move about the city."

"So the stench masks our smell?"

"Exactly."

"She'll track us to the warehouse and down here, then lose us," Allyria reasoned aloud.

"Who created this network?" Kilal asked. "The ferry, the vendor, I assume there will be someone waiting for us at our next destination. It's very elaborate and well put together. Was this your work?"

"You'll find out soon enough."

Kilal gritted his teeth but said nothing. He would endure her cold shoulder, for now.

The going was slow and smelly. And quiet. Allyria tried her best to engage Requiem in conversation, but Requiem maintained her silence under the persistent barrage of questions. Eventually, Allyria gave up.

Deterred by the stone-like Requiem, she turned to filling the silence with humming.

The woman in front of him was the main focal point for Kilal during the next few hours. Her hoody was up, despite the stagnant, warm air, and her long, silky hair was tucked into it. She was merely two feet in front of him, so why did it feel like she'd never been further away? At least in the Ashen Lands he'd been able to dream of the magnificence of their reunion. She would throw herself into his arms. He would twirl her about. They'd lose themselves in each other's eyes, and happily ever after they would live.

Kilal snorted. Reality was often much crueler than any hopes and dreams he could come up with. And the current reality didn't prove otherwise.

She could have her distance for now. Whenever they reached their destination, he would engage her. Ten years he'd waited; he could wait a little longer. But they *would* speak, even if it meant holding her down.

A little longer couldn't come quicker.

~ CHAPTER 22 ~

"Almost there," Colton said. Sweat riddled his forehead, and he wiped at it continuously with a grungy rag.

"Finally," Allyria muttered.

Colton pushed the boat up against a stone wall. Kilal held them steady while the ferryman tied it up. The three exited, and Kilal returned his gravity to normal. A ladder, slightly less rusty than the one they'd descended, led out from the sewers.

Kilal fished out the coins he'd tried to give Shamish and handed them to Colton. He took the money eagerly and shoved it into his pocket.

"Thank you!"

"What will you do now?" Kilal asked.

"Not return to the warehouse, that's for sure. I'll head to a different pick-up zone, park the boat, and head home. We try not to do more than one procurement a day. Lowers the chances of getting caught.

"It's good to have you back," he added, shaking Kilal's hand. "We're all looking forward to the day you shove the Heirs back to wherever they came from."

Guilt tugged at him. He hadn't returned to do that. They were only on his radar now because they could possibly lead him back to Jayden.

You'll abandon Colton and Shamish the same as you abandoned Lilliana.

Kilal nodded and said nothing. He wasn't sure his voice was prepared to make words in a calm and emotionless way.

Ear-grating scraping of metal against metal echoed through the sewer as Requiem shoved the manhole aside and climbed out of sight. Allyria was right behind her, Kilal soon after. Allyria took a deep breath and spread her arms wide.

"Ah, fresh air, how I never respected you." She smiled at the sky and took another deep breath. "But never again!"

The street they were on could no longer be recognized as such. Grass and foliage had long since taken over the area. The city loomed far in the distance; the skyscrapers were still visible. Between Kilal and Silent Haven, the land was barren of most sentient life. Stones, bricks, and the skeletons of buildings were still recognizable, but they were so old, when he pushed on a portion of a still-standing brick wall, it toppled.

"Whoa," Allyria said. "What happened here? Has it always been like this?"

"Have you never left the city?" Kilal asked, dumbfounded.

She reddened and pursed her lips. After a glance at Requiem, she leaned in close to Kilal and put a hand to the side of her face, blocking off the sight of her mouth from Requiem. She spoke in a whisper. "What about bad parents, living in the Undercity, and being on the run would lead you to think I've spent my time frolicking around the countryside?"

"Good point. But you haven't even heard of the history of Silent Haven?"

She tapped her foot on the grass and planted her hands on her hips. "Yeah. Just like I haven't heard of you."

Kilal bit off a sarcastic remark along the lines of 'How have you survived this long?' It really wasn't her fault. He just couldn't comprehend how a Prime Arbiter knew so little about the world.

"Come on," Requiem said. "Our ride should be that way."

They fell into step behind her.

"So, what did happen here?" Allyria pressed, running her hand along what looked like a segment of a stone wall that had fallen against another.

They crossed beneath an arched segment of rubble. Plant life had long since moved into the territory and everything was overgrown. Allyria picked a yellow flower poking from a crack in the arch above them. Moving her hair back, she placed the green stem behind an ear.

"Five hundred years ago," Kilal said, "the Veil weakened enough to allow a large force of Ash Fallen through. It was the largest this side of the Veil had seen since the invasion of Avinoth. No one was ready for it. The land had grown fat and the people lazy. The Ash Fallen decimated the two cities closest to the Veil, the Red City and Veilside. The final battle was fought here, in these ruins.

"Silent Haven used to stretch all the way out here." Kilal stopped and turned back to the city, pointing. "Where you can see the edge of the structures, that's where the army was stopped. Everything up to that point was decimated, as you can see. Now, this area is referred to as the Dead Zone."

"How many people died?"

He shrugged. "Tens of thousands. A thousand years ago, when Avinoth invaded, nearly eighty percent of the population was wiped out. Five hundred years later, it had barely begun to recover. Another five hundred years later, and we've still barely begun to recover."

Kilal broadened his steps, forcing Allyria to as well. Requiem hadn't stopped for them, and his heart rate was picking up. He wouldn't let her out of his sight again!

"Did they fix the Veil? After the Great Invasion?" Allyria asked. Kilal nodded. "How?"

"The same way they created it."

"And that was?"

"The Carving of Sacrifice."

Allyria hissed. "Arbiters died to make the Veil?"

"And only Prime Arbiters could carve it."

"Wow. Does that have anything to do with why there are so few of us?"

"Partly, yes. The power of Carvings is a gift given to all people affected by the Bloodshed. That gift is passed down through bloodlines and has been referred to as the Prime Gene. After the Bloodshed, all Arbiters were Prime. As more generations were born, each after the original had a lower and lower chance of passing along the Prime Gene. Eventually, High Arbiters were born, and with them, the High Gene was passed down. The restoration of the Veil after the Great Invasion was a huge blow to the survival of the Prime Gene. Not long after, the Enlightened Gene was formed, and now, a thousand years after the Bloodshed, the Prime Gene is so rare only one Prime Arbiter has been born in fifty years."

"And that was me?"

Kilal nodded. "High Arbiters, while not as rare as Prime, are still uncommon. And even the Enlightened Gene is being bred into rarity."

"Doesn't that mean eventually there will be no more Arbiters?"

Kilal shrugged. "Maybe. I don't think Sha'tum intended this gift to be with us forever. It was given so we could defeat Avinoth and the Ash Fallen. We weren't supposed to still be fighting this battle a thousand years later.

"Kind of puts us on a clock." He sighed, thoughts of the force being raised on the other side of the Veil dancing through his head. *And that clock is going to be stopped much sooner than we think.*

"What caused the Veil to weaken?"

"Don't know." He had suspicions but no hard facts.

It was a scary thought. What was stopping the same thing from happening again? Did the Ash Fallen know something they didn't? Was that why they were raising an army?

Allyria giggled and pointed at a small fluffy animal hopping through the ruins. "What's that?"

Kilal raised a brow. "A rabbit."

The bunny pulled a blade of grass from the ground, gobbled it up, and took off.

"Are they rare?"

"Not once you get away from the city and out of the Dead Zone."

"I really don't know much, do I?" Allyria said.

He picked up a pinecone and tossed it at her, bouncing it off her shoulder. "That's a condition called 'being a teenager.'"

She scowled. "Haha. Very funny. I'm trying to be serious here." She hauled up a large boulder nearly half her size. The signature copper taste indicated she was activating a Carving. She grunted and hoisted the boulder over her shoulder. Allyria tossed it, and it crashed onto the street behind them, cracking it.

She smiled.

"Don't do that again." He kept his voice soft, though he wasn't impressed. "That's a waste of your Carving." She flinched, and Kilal had to assume it had nothing to do with his tone. "Look, I understand the fun, the excitement of using Carvings. You just picked up something probably five times your own weight and chucked it ten feet. It feels great. But the reality is," he showed her his bare wrist, "the more you use your gift, frivolously or appropriately, the sooner you will have to carve again.

"It's bad enough we have to do it every forty-eight hours. Do you want to cut your flesh more frequently? And what if you find yourself fighting for your life? Do you want your Carvings to run out because you were goofing off with them earlier?"

Allyria seemed to withdraw into herself. She fell silent and kept her eyes on the ground.

Was he too tough on her? He thought he was making his case in a relatable manner, but the way she shuffled her feet and gripped her backpack straps said otherwise.

Lilliana had been hard to raise, but compared to Allyria, he may have to accept that he had it easier than he realized with Lilliana. At least with her, she hadn't come with the trauma Allyria carried.

That girl tried so hard to create a facade of strength and unbreakability. But Kilal was quickly learning just how fragile that front was.

A horn sounded in the distance, followed by the rev of an engine. Three old, worn-down pickup trucks slowly rolled towards them along the beaten-up road. Kilal and Allyria stepped off the path, giving them a wide berth.

Each of the three vehicles carried a dozen or so crates strapped into the bed of the trucks containing an assortment of fruits and vegetables.

As the small caravan passed, spewing black exhaust smelling like smoke and must, the lead driver looked at Kilal through the windshield and waved. Allyria waved back, but Kilal stood frozen, a stoic statue and tense.

Were others going to burst from the bed of the vehicles and attack? Nothing, there was no sensation of Carving use, but the sight of other humans gave him pause, which made no sense. It was normal for farmers to cart their wares into the cities. That's how the cities got their food, after all.

Only when the farmers passed, and the thrum of the engines and stench of the exhaust had faded to a slight buzz did Kilal snap himself from his paranoia. He shook his head, clearing the expectation of an attack.

Allyria stared at him, concerned. Best to break the tension.

A chunk of a collapsed building, slightly larger than Kilal, caught his eye. He tapped her on the shoulder and pointed to it. "Bet I can throw it further than you."

She straightened and brightened into a mischievous smile. "Of course you can. You can access more than ten times your strength."

Kilal crossed his fingers over his heart. "I promise to not use more than that."

She flashed her teeth at him and hopped, clapping her hands. "Wait." She froze and turned a suspicious look at him. "Is this a test? You just told me not to use my Carvings frivolously."

He sighed. "Sometimes I get so caught up in the future. I forget to live in the present."

Allyria's grin returned. "Me first!" She scooted off to the large chunk of stone and circled it, looking for a handhold. Eventually, she found one. She struggled to lift it over her head, and when she finally did, she stumbled back a step before getting her balance and tightening her core.

With a loud grunt, she threw the boulder as far as she could. It landed about five feet in front of her with a loud crash. She stared at the distance with hands on her hips and a tapping foot. It really wasn't a terrible attempt, but she probably expected to toss it further than that. She hadn't yet learned that strength wasn't the only thing to take into consideration when using the body.

"Well, that stinks," she said as he walked up beside her.

"No, it was really good. For a girl." He smiled at her growl and gestured for her to step back. "Now, watch and learn."

Gripping the stone the same way Allyria had, he thrust it above him and spun in a circle twice, picking up momentum with each pass. After the second, he planted himself, snapped his hips forward, and used the force to toss the chunk of stone a good twenty feet.

Allyria stared wide-eyed. "You...you used more than ten times!" she accused.

"Nope. I used my strength and body. You used just your strength."

She peered up at him, probably debating whether he was telling the truth. Finally, she bowed before him. "Teach me, master," she said in a deep voice.

Kilal smirked. "In time, young one."

He looked around. Requiem wasn't next to them. Anxiety gripped his chest. Where was she? His breathing returned to normal when he found her not too far from them. She'd stopped and was standing in the shade of a half-story building, leaning a shoulder against it. From within the recesses of her hoody, Kilal spotted a smile on her face. When she noticed Kilal looking at her, though, the smile slipped away. She turned on her heels and strode forward.

"She's not like how I thought she'd be," Allyria said.

"Which was?" Kilal started walking, his eyes lingering on Requiem's backpack.

"Nicer."

Kilal grunted. *She used to be.* "I'm sure she's been through a lot," he said. The ruins of Silent Haven passed by them, memories of bygone times.

"Didn't you say you've been on the other side of the Veil?"

"For ten years."

"I imagine you've been through a lot too," Allyria said. "But you don't act like that. Why?"

Kilal took a deep breath. "Requiem was as good a person as one could be. She was kind, soft, loving, and gentle. She empathized, almost to a fault, with people in pain. I never saw her kill or even attack someone. She always used her Carvings to help. Always. For her to be as she is now; I can't imagine what could have happened to her. Generally, whatever causes that intense a shift in people is bad. Real bad."

Allyria nodded along as she kept in step with his long strides. "That makes sense. What about you, though? You didn't answer my question."

"I don't have an answer to it. I don't know."

"I feel like I've changed over the past few years, too." She picked up a fist-sized rock and chucked it at some bushes which had sprung up beside the overgrown road. "What about you? Have you changed?"

Kilal nodded.

"What happened on the other side of the Veil?"

In a blink, the sky turned gray, and ash descended around him. His chest tightened. His heart rate quickened. Breathing became difficult.

It's not real. It's not real. It's not real.

Kilal kept his eyes straight ahead and focused on nothing except those three words. It's not real. Allyria's voice droned in the background, becoming an annoying buzz. Shadows sprung up around the ruins, silhouettes of various Plagues and Mannekins.

It's not real. It's not real.

His breath came quicker and quicker, shallower and shallower. Pain gripped his chest, and his fingernails bit into his palms, drawing blood.

The silhouettes circled around them, and more and more sprung up from the darkness. They moved with Kilal and Allyria, encircling them.

The shadows parted, and another figure emerged. It was huge, at least two feet taller than him. Broad shoulders with spikes. Its heavily muscled frame shook the ground with each step. White eyes burned behind slits in its helmet.

Ashen Kane.

No!

Kilal roared and punched the wall of a half-collapsed building—his wrist snapped like a twig, and a dozen or so bones in his hand shattered.

In his panic, he hadn't accessed his Carving.

The gray sky lightened, and the shadows began dissipating. But it wasn't enough. Kilal reared back and punched the wall again with his healing fist, breaking more bones. He focused on the pain, letting it numb everything else.

White energy crackled around his hand, and as it mended, the searing beneath his skin drove the rest of the shadows away. The large one was the last to vanish, and as it did, it lifted a finger to point at him.

He was coming for Kilal. Ashen Kane beat him once, and he'd do it again. And next time, he wouldn't escape.

Blue sky and orange sun peered down on him. Kilal reigned in control of his pounding heart and panting breaths.

Allyria stared as if she were looking at a ghost. "Sorry," she mumbled and looked away.

Did she think it was her fault? Her face was the color of a tomato, and her eyes glistened. He had yet to see her that vulnerable. How could he explain the truth to her?

Searching for answers, Kilal caught Requiem's gaze again. Was that...concern on her face? Like before, it was gone the moment she realized he was looking at her.

Frustrated with himself, he let Allyria carry on ahead of him. He could defy death, kill Plagues, and even worse, but he couldn't comfort her. She held fast to the backpack across her shoulders and kept her head low and her shoulders hunched. He gave up searching for the right words. That was a battle he never won.

Kilal broke into a jog. Maybe if he ran fast enough, he could outrun his shame.

He passed Allyria without a word and caught up with Requiem. "Where are we going?"

"We're almost there." Requiem didn't look at him. "Another two miles."

"And what should we expect to be waiting for us?"

She exhaled loudly, and Kilal had to stop from curling his lips into a snarl. Why was she treating him like he was an annoying child? Didn't he have the right to know what they were walking into?

"Transportation."

"All of this because of Sienna?"

"Partly. Wolfe has eyes and ears all over the countryside. There's no telling who's watching or listening for him. This is the best way we've found for inconspicuous travel."

"An entire system created to avoid one individual. Is she really that dangerous?"

Requiem stopped and grabbed his wrist. She stared into his eyes with an intensity that almost sent him reeling. "If you ever encounter her, don't fight. Just run."

When she let go and continued walking, Kilal ran his hand through his hair. "Tell me about her. What makes her so dangerous?"

"She's fast. Faster than you. Almost as fast as Zip."

He raised a brow. *Impressive.*

"She may even be stronger than you. If not, then she falls just short. The difference, however, is she's always at max strength. Their power doesn't decay."

Kilal whistled. Even if she wasn't as strong as him, the fact that she should come close and operate at that level constantly wasn't a pleasant thought. If he ever encountered her, he'd have to finish the fight quickly.

"Her sense of smell is uncanny. Supernatural, even. If she gets your scent, there's nowhere on this side of the Veil you can hide. As if that isn't enough, her reflexes are almost divine. Even if you could get close enough to hit her, odds are she's already anticipated the attack and will dodge it."

"She sounds like the ultimate killing machine."

A low growl came from the shadow of her hood. "She's killed many of my...our...friends. More than the other three combined. And one day, I will make her pay."

Kilal's blood boiled. So, that was the one responsible for the majority of his friends' deaths.

Maybe she was as tough as Requiem described, but Sienna hadn't met him yet.

Anticipation rose in his chest like a newly sparked fire. He'd meet her one day, and when he did...

"Ahnk said they aren't Arbiters."

Requiem froze mid-stride and stared, searching his eyes. What was she looking for? "You met Ahnk?"

Kilal almost slapped himself. Why hadn't he said anything about the Silver-tongue?

Maybe because, up to this point, this is the most she's allowed the two of us to talk.

"I found him tied to a chair and tortured by Tor'et. The son of a Plague managed to escape me, but I was able to get Ahnk free. He's the one who told me where you were being held. Not sure what happened to him after that." That last point was a little embarrassing. When Ahnk had mentioned Requiem, Kilal had taken off without a thought for the mentalist's safety. He hoped the Arbiter had escaped.

"You fought Tor'et?"

He nodded. "He turned me into a human bonfire with the snap of a finger. Then he blew a tornado from his mouth. Never seen anything like it."

Requiem nodded. Bloodshed and Oaths, did she have to keep that bloody hood up all the time? It had been concealing her face since leaving his apartment. Was it to hide her scars? Kilal wanted to reach over and pull it down. She didn't need to be ashamed. She was a beautiful woman with or without them, and after so long being separated, he wished he could admire that beauty. But he suspected if he so much as made a gesture to pull the hood down, he would probably end up missing a hand.

"He's powerful," Requiem said. "And sadistic. Of all four, he's the one who truly loves hurting for the sake of inflicting pain. And Ahnk is correct; they aren't Arbiters. We don't know where their power comes from, nor where they came from. I think their power has something to do with their jewelry, but I don't have evidence to back that up."

Jewelry?

"Tor'et had a ring with a yellow gemstone and matching earrings," Kilal said, thinking back to his encounter with two of the Heirs. "Fazin had a blue gemstone. What about the others?"

"Sienna has a band around both biceps, covered with red stones and a matching choker. Wolfe has a green gemstone on his left forefinger and a matching nose ring."

"Interesting. How easy would it be to get one of them alone? If we captured one and took their jewelry, we could examine them and test your theory."

Requiem snorted. "Good luck with that. Fazin always has an entourage of minions to mutate. Tor'et would fly away. Sienna is, well...Sienna. And Wolfe hasn't been seen outside their tower in months."

So, it would be difficult. But not impossible.

"How did you and Ahnk end up as Wolfe's guests?"

She actually looked at him. And smirked. "Guests. That's one way of putting it." She backhanded the husk of a tree, splitting it in two. "I screwed up. Got overconfident and distracted. Sienna's been after me for some time. Her persistence finally paid off, and we were captured, which is why Sienna will be all the more on our trail. She doesn't like it when her prey gets away. Especially if that prey is me."

The more Kilal heard of that Heir, the more it seemed inevitable the two of them would meet. And if she was out for Requiem, he'd make sure the 'killing machine' wouldn't be able to threaten the woman he loved ever again.

A crunch followed by a gag came from behind them. They turned. Allyria held a square combat ration, a small chunk removed. Her face was scrunched as she chewed. A shiver followed the eventual forced swallow of the brown paste.

She waved the block in front of her. "I mean, seriously, we have the power to heal, run faster than cars, and control the elements, and this is the best thing we can come up with?"

A smile crept onto Requiem's face. "Don't worry. The more you eat it, the more you'll be surprised that you never get used to it."

Allyria froze and pointed at Requiem. "Kilal, do you see it?" He frowned. "She's smiling. She's actually smiling!"

Ah.

But the smile vanished.

Requiem turned on her heels and stormed away, though not before muttering, "Teenagers."

Kilal chuckled and shook his head.

Allyria came up beside him. The twitching of her lips exposed her poor attempt at feigning seriousness. "What? I just didn't think she was capable of showing good emotions."

Kilal leaned in as close as he dared and put a hand over his mouth. "Me neither," he whispered.

She giggled, but another bite of the combat ration removed all joy from her, and the smile slid away as quickly as Requiem's had. Allyria returned the block to its plastic container and swapped it in her backpack for a bottle of water. She gulped it so quickly, and for so long, she must have been parched.

"What's past these ruins?" she asked after catching her breath and falling into step at his side again. "How far do they go?"

Kilal recalled the classes he took after his Awakening. One of them was History. As fewer Arbiters were born, the training camps he'd stayed at for his first few years eventually died out. What would have been the point of maintaining schools when there were only a handful of students? That's how the training of new Arbiters became the task of more experienced ones, as mentors instead.

Whether he wanted it or not, he struggled to deny his relationship with Allyria was unavailable.

"The ruins extend for about a ten-mile radius from the outskirts of the city. Beyond that, the farmlands start. Most of the food in Silent Haven is grown and raised out here and brought in.

"You may have noticed, but our city doesn't produce much in the way of food. We rely on these farms for that. And in return, we protect them from Ashen raids that manage to not only pierce the Veil but make it this far in. Or at least, we used to. I doubt, with the way the Heirs are running things, there are many Arbiters out here patrolling and protecting the farmlands anymore."

Allyria considered that for a moment. "Wouldn't it be easier to protect the farmers if they were closer? Why not clear out these ruins and raise food here?"

"That's a good question, and one not easily explained," Kilal said. "Req!"

Up ahead, Requiem turned around. He held up a hand and closed all but one finger. She nodded but still managed to take a stance, saying, "Make this quick."

Kilal guided Allyria off the road to a nice patch of ground clear of debris and covered in green grass. "Looks like a good place to grow a garden, right?" She nodded. "Dig about six inches down."

Allyria raised a questioning brow, but did as he said. Dropping to her knees, she dug with her hands. The first few inches of earth she removed was normal brown soil. Eventually, she reeled back and glared at her hand in disgust. "Eww! What is that?"

"The reason we can't grow plants or raise livestock here."

The most recent chunk of soil came up black and gooey, almost like oil. Allyria shook her hands, and the inky mush splattered onto the ground. "But what is it?" She rubbed her hands frantically on the grass, trying to remove the smelly, corrupted soil.

Kilal knelt beside her and stuck a finger into the hole Allyria had dug. He lifted his hand and rubbed the sludge between his thumb and forefinger before sniffing it. Mold. Decay.

The Ashen Land pulled at him; that was what he'd spent the last ten years smelling.

He stood and rubbed the mud on a pant leg. "The battle which took place here corrupted the land."

Allyria looked around, puzzled. "But there's green grass here. And other plant life. How come they can grow?"

"Now that is a mystery. The only guess we've been able to make is that anything which doesn't need to penetrate too deeply into the earth can thrive. But that idea fails a little when it comes to livestock. With the grass, we figured at least cows, sheep, goats, and the like could manage. But they died within a few days of eating anything that grows here. And from the written accounts, it wasn't a pleasant sight—the animals rotted from the inside out."

"But," Allyria tapped her chin, "the rabbit from earlier?"

"It'll be dead soon."

Kilal used a foot to push the removed soil back into the hole. When it was covered, he nodded at Requiem, who looked as if she'd been waiting for them for an inconceivable amount of time.

"It's been like this for five hundred years? Have we ever tried fixing it?"

"We have. Nothing's worked."

"Do we know what caused this? Besides the battle, I mean."

There were theories, and these theories used to be taught to Arbiters in training. But that was before his time.

"We don't know. The closest thing I've been able to figure is, whatever happened here, happened on a much larger scale in the Schism."

"That's where the final battle with Avinoth was fought?"

Kilal smelled the crater before he saw it. He called for Requiem again and pointed in the direction of the sour, dusky musk. Requiem turned to Allyria and seemed to understand his intentions. She headed back to them.

"Come on," he said. "I want to show you something else."

Allyria groaned. "Please tell me it won't be a rotting corpse."

"Nothing so morbid," he assured.

Kilal led them off the overgrown road, passed a few bushes clumped together, and through the skeletal remains of some lost structure.

Allyria gasped. "What is that?"

Before them was one of six craters scattered throughout the Dead Zone. The hole was at least deep enough to fit a one-story building and wide enough to lay a three-story building in it.

"Is it...alive?"

A waft of decay and mold blew up at them, and she staggered back, covering her nose.

Each of the craters was the same size and structure. But it was what was contained within them that marked them as different from the rest of the land. The insides of the craters were lined with the same black soil Allyria had dug up. No plant life of any kind grew along the walls, though they seemed to breathe, the edges rising and contracting in a steady rhythm as if it were some alien organism. Fist-sized bubbles along the surface grew and popped. A thin layer of bubbling inky ooze covered the bottom of the crater like a blanket.

"It's not," Kilal said. "At least we don't think so. But to be fair, we don't understand anything about this corruption. Neither here nor in the Schism. We don't know what caused it, how to reverse it, or if it's even reversible. And yes, the Schism is where the last battle with Avinoth was fought.

"Hundreds of Prime Arbiters lost their lives in that confrontation. Whatever happened there corrupted the land so completely it's become an impassable terrain full of nightmarish creatures."

Allyria shivered. "Have you ever tried to cross it? Has anyone tried to cross the Schism?"

"A long time ago, expeditions were tasked with crossing it," Requiem said, stepping up beside them. "The goal was to discover just how much of the land was ruined and how far the Schism went. No one returned. Decades passed, and humanity began restoring itself. Someone thought it would be a good time to send a few more expeditions over, but the outcome was the same. We haven't tried since."

Allyria backed away from the festering wound of a crater,

and Kilal followed. "But what about you two? Have either of you ever tried it?"

Requiem shook her head.

Kilal suppressed a shiver. "I tried. Didn't make it very far. And I'll never go back."

Goosebumps prickled his skin as memories of the twisted, nightmarish land and his romp through it returned. What a fool he'd been! After discovering the Carving of Immortality, crossing the Schism was one of his first orders of business. Think of the fame! He, Kilal, discoverer of Immortality and explorer of the Schism. It didn't take him long to learn that in that dark place, fates far worse than death awaited. Creatures he encountered there, grotesque and abominable, still haunted his dreams from time to time.

Allyria must have read the fear in his eyes; she didn't press further.

"Our point of contact isn't much farther ahead," Requiem said.

"So where are we going after this?" Allyria hopped in front of her, walking backwards. "How many more secret locations will we have to stop at? How many people do you have working for you? How did you organize this? Are you the one in charge? Or is someone else?"

Requiem glared at Kilal as if the barrage of questions was his fault. "She's not much worse than you."

He smirked and shrugged. "What can I say? We're curious people."

Requiem maintained the glare but leveled it at Allyria, who remained oblivious. Or at least unfazed. "And you know what they say about curiosity?"

She raised her hand. "I do! Curiosity killed the cat."

"Curiosity killed the teenager."

Allyria stopped in her tracks. Her hand slowly fell to her side as Requiem brushed past her. "She's kidding. Right?" she asked Kilal.

"I wish I could give you a definitive yes."

Before she could respond, Requiem broke into a jog. It seemed she'd finally had enough of their pace and was ready to arrive at their next destination.

The jog turned into a sprint, and Kilal was forced to activate a small portion of his strength Carving to keep up. Allyria matching his strides indicated she was doing the same. But Requiem? She held fast to them without access to the Physical branch. Technically, what she was doing was impossible. But she'd been breaking every rule Kilal understood as universal since he found her unconscious and tied to a chair.

The next two and a half miles flew by. Literally. The ruins blurred by as they reached breakneck speeds. He watched for any signs that Allyria was approaching the end of her stamina. She never gave any.

A feeling punched Kilal's gut, and he skidded to a stop. He grabbed Allyria's arm, halting her as well. Their skidding ripped up the ground beneath their feet. Requiem, too, slid to a stop and gave him an inquiring look.

The sensation grew in his abdomen. A warm, uneasy curling.

"Something's not right."

He studied the horizon, and Requiem followed suit. Despite her treatment of him, it comforted him that she still trusted his instincts.

"What do you mean?" Allyria asked.

"I don't know. Keep your eyes open and stay alert." He turned to Requiem. "Any chance our rendezvous has been compromised?"

She shrugged. "There's always that chance."

"How much farther?"

She pointed to a cluster of half-collapsed structures nearly overgrown with vines and foliage. Kilal estimated the point to be about five hundred yards away.

"Let's keep going," he said.

They didn't break into a run. Instead, they adopted a stealthy approach, keeping to any cover and shadows they could as they zigzagged their way forward. Kilal instructed Allyria to keep a safe distance from them but to continue following. She objected, but it changed nothing.

The closer they drew to their destination, the more twisted his gut became. Anticipation clawed at his insides. Was it Sienna waiting for them? A wicked smile worked onto Kilal's face.

I hope so.

~ CHAPTER 23 ~

"Arbiters!" Requiem hissed from behind the trunk of a fallen tree.

They were a hundred yards from the cluster of overgrown ruins when they spotted the source of Kilal's 'bad feeling.' Three men and two women paced between the wreckage.

"How did they know to come here?" Allyria asked.

"I don't know if they did," Requiem said. "The Heirs have Arbiters patrolling the outskirts of the Dead Zone. This could be one of those groups, and they just happened to stumble across this point. Or they've captured and tortured information from one of ours."

Kilal didn't like how calm she sounded speaking of the possible torture of one of her own companions. Something like that should generate anger or fear. Not...boredom.

He monitored the Arbiters, studying their movements. "'Just so happened' rarely turns out to be the case." He slinked closer. As he did, the picture before him cleared. Maybe 'just so happened' applied after all.

The Arbiters' movements were sloppy, lazy, and annoyed. He couldn't hear what they were saying, but short, snappy dialogue came from the clearing.

"Should one of us carve something that will let us hear them?" Allyria asked.

Kilal and Requiem threw her a withering scowl. "If you want to cut your wrist so you can hear what they're saying, go right ahead," he said. "But I'll pass."

"Oh." She lowered her eyes. "Sorry."

Was she even aware of rubbing her wrists?

The shadows cast by the surrounding ruins in a ten-foot radius flickered and morphed. For a moment, he tensed, convinced he'd slipped into another traumatic vision, but as they stretched and elongated, the darkness reached for Requiem. Was she calling them?

She crouched, stone-still, staring at the group of Arbiters like a statue of a fearsome huntress. The look in her eyes, the reveal of canines through a curled lip, indicated her plan for handling the group.

Kilal rested a hand on her shoulder. "We aren't killing them."

She narrowed her eyes. Her nostrils flared, and the shadows pooling around her broke into a frenzy of movement. "Don't be naïve. They're the enemy. They will kill us if they get the chance."

"The *Heirs of the Promise* are our enemy."

Requiem leveled a finger at the Arbiters. "And who do they work for?"

Kilal searched for the words to help her understand. He *had* to convince her. He wasn't an assassin. He wouldn't kill without even giving them a chance at redemption.

"I understand, but what if they were given a chance to break away? What if they knew there was a place they could go, a people to fight with and for? I have to believe that not all Arbiters turned to those sons of Plagues for their own self-gain. What if they did it because they didn't know they had a choice? Shouldn't we give them that choice?"

Allyria stared as if seeing him for the first time.

A low growl rumbled in Requiem's throat. She pulled back her hood and shook out her hair, displaying the scarred right side of her face. "They *had* their chance. And our friends died because of the choices *they* made."

Kilal ground his teeth until his jaw ached. Did she think he didn't want vengeance? He'd just found out what happened. His pain was *fresh*. He wanted nothing less than to pop the heads of the five Arbiters waiting for them. But he couldn't go back to being that man.

There was a time when killing and Kilal were nearly inseparable.

This time's different, the familiar, blood-hungry voice whispered. *They deserve to die for what they've done. Give them what they deserve. Just like you gave Trench Coat and Crave.*

No! That's not the same! I gave them a chance—five chances. They left me no choice. Besides, he let Blondie go. That counted for something, right?

"We give them a chance," Kilal said, rougher than he intended. "*If* they don't take it, then we end them."

"Why do you care?" Requiem asked. "They're ash-eating oathbreakers who kill for money. Why are you fighting so hard for them?"

"Because we're a dying breed. Unless there's been a sudden jump in the number of Awakened Arbiters in the last ten years, I wager there are even fewer of us now than when I vanished. Because they're our brothers and sisters. Because they swore the oath just like us. Because..." He swallowed the lump in his throat. "Because I have to believe we all deserve a shot at redemption. No matter what."

They shared a look. Requiem broke it first. But not before he saw understanding in those eyes. She knew his past. All of it. And if those Arbiters in the clearing didn't deserve redemption, then...what hope did he have?

She scowled. The shadows flickered and crept up her legs like black ooze. Allyria pushed herself back on all fours.

"*One* chance," was all Requiem said.

Kilal let out a held breath and nodded. "Skirt the perimeter. Stay out of sight." He eyed the shadows around her.

"No. I'll march right in there with you."

"No offense, Req, but you haven't exactly had the most welcoming persona. If I were them, and you stepped into that circle, I'd assume you were there to kill me. Immediately." Her face grew darker with each word. "So, please. Let me talk to them. Maybe if they know The Immortal Arbiter is still alive, they'll see reason."

She placed a hand on a fallen tree beside her. Shadows crept along the white, dead bark, straight for her hand. Her lips moved slightly as if she were speaking, but too quietly for him to hear. Was she...talking to the shadows?

"Please," he said, slumping forward. Why did he even need to explain himself to her? "I *must* do this. I wasn't here for you or anyone else. So many of my friends, so much of what I created, I only just found out is gone. I couldn't save them. I couldn't be here for you, and I can't change the past. But maybe I can save even one of these five. If there's a chance, I *have* to try. *Please.*"

Her mouth opened and shut. She formed words but bit them off before they could come out. "Fine."

Kilal gave her a grateful smile. "I'll approach. If they attack, or if I attack...you know what to do."

"What about me?" Allyria asked.

He raised a brow and took a deep breath. "I have a *very* important task for you." She leaned forward and rubbed her hands together. "I need you to...sit right here and not move from this spot."

The anticipation turned to a pouty glower. "Come on; I'm a Prime Arbiter! I can fight, too."

"That's exactly why you *won't* fight. Being a Prime doesn't make you invulnerable nor inherently more powerful than an Enlightened. Those Arbiters are experienced. Each one of them, regardless of their class, is more than capable of killing you." Allyria reddened and opened her mouth, but Kilal cut her off. "*No.* You're not ready."

"Ready?" he asked Requiem, not giving Allyria a chance to respond. There was nothing she could say to change his mind.

Allyria muttered something he couldn't understand. Requiem nodded.

His Carving of Gravitational Control became a knob in his mind, and he rotated it counterclockwise, lowering it as much as it would go. His body lightened. He wasn't going to just walk in there and announce himself. He was Kilal, *The Immortal Arbiter*. His entrance would be fitting of someone of his reputation. Switching the knob to represent the Carving of Deific Strength, he rotated it clockwise, maximizing his power.

Kilal propelled himself high into the sky, leaving an open-mouthed Allyria and a brooding Requiem far beneath him.

~ CHAPTER 24 ~

Kilal crashed into the clearing, aiming his descent to put him in the center of the five Arbiters. Right before landing, one of them spotted him and let out a cry. Not that it would do them any good.

The ground parted around him, and the earth shuddered. The overgrown mounds of stone and collapsed walls encompassing the area shook and crumbled. All five of the Arbiters fell with various levels of grace and dignity.

The protected circle was visible to all who looked that way.

Kilal stood waist-deep in the center of a five-foot radius crater. His increased strength absorbed much of the impact, but not all of it. His right leg had snapped from the collision. Pain nearly brought tears to his eyes. He lowered his gravity and leapt out of the hole. Slowly, like a feather, he drifted back to the ground.

Normally, he wasn't a fan of extravagant displays of Carvings, but he was hoping it would propel the encounter to an amicable conclusion.

That particular group didn't dress as the previous three he'd encountered. All five presented themselves in a manner befitting an Arbiter: normal clothing.

"I'm not here to fight." Kilal kept his hands out wide.

"Bloodshed and Oaths, who the Plague are you?" a man

to his right said. He had a clump of dirt in his hand, which turned into a solid sphere of rock as he cursed.

Kilal shook his head. "Don't show me your Carving," he rebuked. The man reddened. "Unless you're ready to use it."

The stone-holder sneered. He reared his arm back and launched the rock at Kilal. It zipped toward him at an unnatural speed. Kilal caught it and crushed it into a fine powder.

"Like I said, I'm not here to fight." He patted his hands together, clearing the residue from them.

Of the five Arbiters, Kilal recognized none of them. They all seemed to be in their late twenties to early thirties, except for one. He had dark skin and kept his head down, but when Kilal was able to steal a glance at his hairless face, fearful eyes, and quivering lips, he estimated him to still be in his teens. And way out of his league.

"What's your name, son?"

The, by all rights, boy started, removed his glasses and began cleaning them.

"You aren't the one asking questions here, got it?" That came from a woman to his left. Shoulder-length hair, unremarkable features, arrogant stance, and hungry eyes. "Like Jasper asked, who the Plague are you? Haven't seen you around before. You registered with the Heirs?"

The third man kept in Kilal's peripheral sight. Every time Kilal moved, so did he. A glint of light reflected off something around the man's neck. A necklace with a silver curved sword medallion.

Impressive. Unless he took it from the corpse of another Arbiter.

The medallion was the symbol of a blade master. Whoever that man was, he was part of the Guild of Blades, an organization of weapon experts located in New Cita, and only New Cita. There were never more than a few blade masters alive at a given time.

Whether he'd stolen the medallion didn't matter. Kilal

wouldn't underestimate that Arbiter. If he truly was worthy of the title, then he'd prove to be a fearsome foe.

Kilal had faced only two blade masters in his long life, and the only reason he'd survived both encounters was because of his immortality.

The last member, a woman in a pristine white jacket, studied him with an inquisitive eye.

"I refused to register," Kilal said. "We are Arbiters. We work for the Sunlight Domain, not an organization of power-hungry men and women. We protect, not oppress. That was our oath."

Jasper laughed. "That's rich! In case you haven't noticed, the people don't want us protecting them. They don't want us here at all!"

"They'd rather us all die than continue reminding them of their powerlessness," the woman with hungry eyes said. "Why would we keep fighting and dying for a people like that?"

Those were valid points, ones Kilal had wrestled with for a long time. "Do you think the way we've treated the citizens has had anything to do with how they treat us? Arbiters have a history of not caring about the consequences of their actions. Up until the Right of Recompense became law, how many citizens lost their homes? Possessions? Loved ones? And the only answer they were given was, 'Be thankful you're protected from the Ash Fallen.' Who needs to fear the Ash Fallen when your protectors are the ones destroying your homes?

"The reality is, for a long time, we've not been good stewards of the oath we swore and the gift we've been given."

Jasper snorted. "You call Carvings a gift? Hilarious. I didn't know gifts were supposed to come with the cost of cutting yourself. *Every. Other. Day.*"

Kilal stayed in the center of the small clearing. His only movements were to keep the blade master from leaving his sight. Some may have called it arrogant, letting unknown Arbiters have his back, but he knew they weren't capable of much. Those who stayed in groups and preyed on the weak never were. They used their numbers and willingness to hurt—and even kill—to ambush their targets.

They wouldn't be expecting their victim to be...well...*him*.

He gave Jasper a sad shake of his head. "We can't change the past. We can't change Carvings and how they work. But we can make this world a better place. We can preserve the land and the people Sha'tum died to protect.

"I didn't register with the Heirs because they're the epitome of what's wrong with this world. I will stop Wolfe, and I will do what I can to repair all the things he's broken. You can help me. It's not too late to turn back to the oath you've sworn. It's never too late for that."

Hungry Eyes looked ready to tear his throat out. She paced back and forth in front of a fallen wall. About fifty yards behind her would be where Allyria was concealed. With the protective cover of the old stone gone, Kilal was glad he couldn't see the redhead. Hopefully, that meant she was hiding and not disobeying.

"You think I joined the Heirs for money or some other means of self-gain?" Pressure rose behind his eyes. "You think I *want* to go back to protecting the ants of this world? I joined them because they created an order in Silent Haven I can stand behind.

"Arbiters should be at the top of the food chain, and you can take your oath to the edge of the world! Why should we grovel to the normals? Why should we die so they can live? They want us to protect them? Good. That protection will come at a high cost."

"Don't you think I understand that!" Kilal snapped. "I had my head split open a few days ago by a bottle. *Because of what I am.* You think that made me feel good? Of course not! It made me want to smack the fool who did it. And that's *exactly* why we *shouldn't* be killing each other.

"We share a bloodline, a gift, a calling. An oath. We used to be many, but now we are few. The whole world is against us; rightfully or not, it doesn't matter. Instead of killing each other, for the Heirs, for our own self-gain, or for any other reason, we should be protecting each other, from the Ash Fallen, from those we protect, and from the likes of that oathbreaking organization.

"That's what's supposed to make us different." Kilal pointed at his wrist. "Not what we can do, but *who we are*. The world, the Ash Fallen, they kill each other. If you want to be better than them, then be different!"

Silence.

Finally, Hungry Eyes spoke. "Even if what you're saying is true, what makes you think you can stop the Heirs? You, one man? The Keepers couldn't, so how can you?"

The other female who'd been studying him so astutely took a step forward. "Because this isn't any normal Arbiter. This is the Immortal Arbiter."

The man in his peripheral cursed. Jasper stumbled back. The young one shook and paled.

Hungry Eyes blanched, then scoffed. "Kilal's been dead for ten years. Why else would Wolfe have taken over? You think the Immortal Arbiter would *let* the Keepers get themselves slaughtered? And why reveal himself now?"

"Because I was in the Ashen Lands," Kilal said.

"The Ashen Lands?" Jasper snorted. "Right! You crossed the Veil, which is impossible, hung out for a decade, then re-crossed the Veil? I don't think so."

Kilal gave the man a toothy smile. Jasper's words were strong, but his flickering eyes and twitching hands told another story.

"The white energy," the teenager mumbled. He startled, almost as if surprised by his own voice, and began cleaning his glasses.

"What are you talking about?" Hungry Eyes snapped.

He pointed at the crater. "When he jumped out, there was white energy around his right leg. It didn't last long. He must have broken it in the fall. And he floated back to the ground. The Immortal Arbiter used a Carving of Gravitational Control. And he has to have a powerful strength rune to collide with that kind of force and only break one limb."

"You've got a good eye on you, kid," Kilal said. "And an even better understanding of Carvings."

The young man fidgeted, but Kilal saw the smile wrestling to be let seen. How did he get himself entangled in the Heir's web?

"What the Plague do you know, Garret?" Jasper snapped. "You're barely out of your diapers, and you think you can lecture us? Where'd you even get any of that information, anyway?"

Garret backed away. "I-I've heard about him. He's famous."

"His reputation is based on a load of exaggerated stories!" Hungry Eyes railed. "Immortality? To the edge of the world with him! If he's discovered immortality, then why not share it?"

Kilal winced and forced the memories back into the darkness inside himself. "Your faith in me and my history matters little. Because I'm not here to fight. I'd like to leave this confrontation with all of our lives intact."

Hungry Eyes and Jasper maintained their hostile stance. "Even if it were true," Hungry Eyes said, "and you were *the Immortal Arbiter*, that wouldn't change anything. We were tasked with patrolling this area and either killing rogue Arbiters or making them return to the city with us to register. So, *Kilal*, what will you choose?"

"Besides," Jasper cut in, "even *if* this is the Immortal Arbiter, imagine the reward for his head!" He looked at each of them in turn. "We could retire and never have a want or need ever again."

"Because we'd be dead," Garret mumbled.

"The boy has a point," Kilal said. "So, I'll give *you* two options: leave this confrontation peacefully and promise you'll not return to the Heirs. Or join me. Please, trust me when I say I *cannot,* I *will not,* let any of you leave if you continue traveling the path of an oathbreaker."

The silence was palpable.

"I'm out," White Jacket said. "I don't feel like dying today. Garret, I suggest you do likewise. You're too young and smart to die."

"What?" Jasper hurled a look of disgust and hate at her. "You coward!"

"You'll fight," Hungry Eyes said menacingly. "With us or against us. But either way, you're not walking away."

"You may be a Prime," White Jacket cocked her head, "but he's *immortal.* And a Prime. I'll take my chances with him."

Hungry Eyes growled, and Kilal's senses were overloaded. Copper filled his mouth, his ears buzzed, and a warm tingle caressed his skin. She was activating her Carvings.

Another Prime? How did he not know her? Did his decade in the Ashen Lands really deteriorate his memory that much? Or did he never have the influence on the Sunlight Domain he thought he had? Either way, if she was a Prime, he needed to rethink his course of action. With a Prime among them *and* a blade master, there was no telling what the rest of them were.

Kilal took a step back and, to his right, turned his shoulder to the edge of the crater while keeping the blade master on his left.

"I always knew you'd betray us one day, Nanomia." Hungry Eyes said. "How many times have I told you that, Jasper?"

Jasper snarled. "More than once."

The conflict was slipping in a direction that would lead to a slaughter. Kilal could almost feel Requiem's anticipation for the fight. Where was she? He couldn't spot her, but she had to be sneaking nearby. How much time would she give him once they started fighting? He needed to rein in the situation before it rained blood.

His show of power, the revelation of his identity, and even the mutiny of two of their members wasn't enough to sway them into peace. It was time for him to show the trio what was at stake.

Kilal braced himself. He lowered his gravity and raised his strength. Constricted like a viper moments before striking, he propelled himself across the crater and straight at Jasper.

A cry of shock filled the clearing; by Hungry Eyes, he surmised. Kilal loomed behind Jasper, nearly head and shoulders taller than the man. With one hand on his neck, Kilal lifted him off the ground and held him as high. Jasper squirmed and kicked. Chunks of soil broke free from the ground. They formed into rocks and shot into Jasper's palm. Kilal increased the pressure on the feeble neck in his grasp until Jasper could do nothing but drop the stones and pull at his hand.

"If you want a fight," Kilal said, raising his voice to be heard over Jasper's squeals, "then you can have your fight. But the moment either of you makes a move, his head goes pop."

The blade master froze, but Hungry Eyes didn't seem to notice her partner's hesitation. The only thing she seemed to be able to focus on was Kilal, and by her heavy breathing, curled lips, and flared nostrils, he was willing to wager it wasn't because she thought him handsome.

"Stand. Down," Kilal said.

Jasper kicked a foot back and connected with Kilal's jaw. His mouth snapped shut, and he bit his tongue. The taste of copper filled his mouth, for once, not because of a Carving.

Bloodshed and Oaths!

"That wasn't nice," he growled, giving Jasper's neck another squeeze. The squeals turned into cries of pain, and Jasper's attempt to pull his hand away weakened.

"I'm a *Prime* Arbiter," Hungry Eyes growled. "And I know what Carvings you're using, *Immortal Arbiter*. But you don't know mine." She said the last part with a wide smile, as if she'd seen the future and how the encounter would end.

Kilal lowered Jasper enough for his feet to graze the ground and rolled his eyes with pursed lips. "You are a *child*." His patience was running out. Trench Coat and Crave's blood had not yet washed from his hands, and already he was going to add more alongside theirs? Why did Arbiters have to be so bloody stubborn and prideful? "I've lived for two hundred years. What makes you think you'll last one minute against me?"

Her eyes glowed white, and matching flames sprouted from her skin.

Garret dipped behind a grouping of collapsed stones, and White Jacket scooted for her own overgrown, rocky obstacle.

"Because you're *old*. You're a has-been who's lived off an exaggerated list of accomplishments. You let the Heirs kill your friends and take over your land. How powerful can you be to just stand by and let that happen?"

Kilal's nostrils flared, and the muscles on his neck and arms bulged like steel chords. Jasper squealed louder. "I didn't *let* anything happen!"

The blade master pulled two short rods, a palm's width in length, from his pockets. A silver aura surrounded them, and they elongated and evolved into twin daggers. Carving of Metalwork. So, he was at least a High Arbiter. *All* blade masters, at a minimum, had access to Physical Carvings. The question was, what aspect of his physical attributes was he enhancing? Speed, agility, strength, or some combination of them? Copper—a mix of his own blood and the power around him—already flooded his mouth from Hungry Eyes, which left him somewhat blind to the Carvings he was using.

Kilal was left with trusting his instincts.

"Last chance," he said. "Stand down, or I will kill him."

Hungry Eyes sneered. "If you were going to kill him, you'd have done so already." The sneer flared into a cold smile.

A strange calm settled over Kilal like a cozy blanket. Exhaustion and a whisper to rest crept in. He'd worked so hard, been on the move for so long; rest was the least of the things he deserved. Even if only for a few minutes. He fought back a yawn and strained to keep his eyes open. His arm started lowering.

Sleep.

The rest he'd had in his apartment had been a welcome reprieve, but it wasn't nearly enough to make up for ten years of little to none for days on end. He could lie down right there and probably sleep for a year. So, what was stopping him? Everyone he cared for was dead, anyway. Why keep going?

The calm turned to a mild euphoria. A lazy smile slipped onto his face.

Sleep.

Jasper's feet touched the ground, and Kilal's fingers began opening. His vision narrowed as slumber pulled him toward unconsciousness.

What was he even doing there? Who were these people? Would they mind if he laid down for a bit? Faces flooded his drowsy mind. Did he know them? With them came a familiarity...and sadness?

Something inside him stirred. And that something was displeased.

A face came by, one he recognized more than any other. A name pierced the veil of sleep and exhaustion.

Lilliana.

Lilliana!

Kilal roared. He shook his head violently and focused on the image of his daughter. The soothing spell dropped off him like a wet cloak—and just in time, too. His fingers had nearly opened entirely, and Jasper was working to pull himself free.

He clenched down on Jasper's neck again, and with his other hand, gripped the top of the man's head. "You *dare* violate my mind!" he bellowed. Kilal didn't know which one it was who'd done it, but he had a guess it was Hungry Eyes. "You think I haven't felt the touch of a soothing before? This goes against *everything* Arbiters have built! I warned you. I WARNED YOU!"

Jasper's head went pop.

"You...you killed him," Hungry Eyes stammered.

Kilal growled and wiped the blood off his hands and cheek. His mind was raw, like a freshly opened wound. And he hated it. He gave her a wicked smile. "You still think I'm too *old*?"

"No. No! NO!" The white fire around her erupted into an inferno, and Hungry Eyes became a fiery feminine form and nothing else.

Bloodshed and Oaths!

The blade master was sneaking behind him, and Kilal was more than content to let the man think he was unnoticed. He prepared himself for the attack.

A figure burst from the dark recesses of the ruins behind the blade master. Hair splayed out, eyes blackened, Requiem sliced her sword of dripping shadow at him. He leaped back, narrowly avoiding the blade. He was forced into another bound backward; Requiem didn't give him any time to recover.

What was she thinking? She couldn't handle a blade master!

Kilal shot forward, aiming to intercept the dueling pair. He wouldn't lose her again.

The blade master regained his footing and pressed Requiem into a defensive stance. Kilal couldn't get there quickly enough, especially not after a beam cut right through his legs. He collapsed with a bloody splat.

Through blurry vision and scorching pain, Kilal followed Hungry Eyes as she slowly stalked a tight circle around him. Her gaze glimmered with the anticipation of a kill.

Foolish girl.

She moved with a lazy saunter. Did she really think she'd already won? Did she not see his legs regenerating?

Hungry Eyes threw her hand forward, and another red beam burst from her palm. Kilal was ready; his gravity was already as low as possible. He shot his strength up and shoved himself away with his arms. Arcing through the air, he dodged the laser. He landed on weak, wobbling legs. They weren't worth much yet. They barely had enough strength to propel him behind a chunk of stone, missing another ray, but he managed.

"I told you!" Hungry Eyes said. "You're a has-been living off exaggerated stories. After you're dead, I'll make sure history knows you for the fake you really are!"

Kilal propped his back up against the stone, urging his legs to repair quicker. She cackled as she blasted the rock he hid behind with more heat. It rolled off the stone, burning his hair and covering exposed skin with third-degree burns.

When his legs finished expanding to their original size, in one swift motion, Kilal rolled onto his belly, scooted himself up onto all four, and sunk his fists deep into the stone. Gritting his teeth against the pain, he lifted the massive rock with a great heave and surge of strength—and charged Hungry Eyes, using it as a makeshift shield.

He caught her by surprise. The flames around her went out. It was her turn to leap aside, but Kilal released the stone shield and snatched her ankle in an iron grip. Hungry-Eyes lurched to a stop mid-lunge and slammed to the ground. They locked gazes, and he stomped on her leg.

The bone crunched, and she screamed.

"You should have taken my advice," he said through labored breaths and a cruel grin. She should have. But he was glad she didn't.

She lifted a hand. "Wa—"

Kilal pivoted, whipping Hungry Eyes into the air and over his shoulder. Spiking his strength, he smashed the screaming woman into the ground.

The rocky earth didn't respond the way it did when Kilal plunged into it, or even when Requiem's sword made contact. It barely reacted to the impact. The same could not be said for Hungry Eyes.

When the red mist settled, he held an ankle attached to a foot and shin and not much else.

He dropped it.

Breathing laboriously, Kilal rubbed the back of a hand over his face. It came back crimson. Everything in a five-foot radius was red.

Chest tight, mind still raw, he struggled to rein in his emotions. Now that Hungry Eyes was dead, though, he turned his attention to Requiem, hoping he wasn't too late.

His jaw hung open.

The blade master was prostrate on the ground, lifeless and headless. Requiem didn't have a scratch on her.

Kilal sucked in a deep breath. He hated how everything had unfolded. It wasn't only the killing of the three Arbiters; they made their decisions—but he didn't have to *like* it so much.

He thought he'd contained that part of himself better.

How many times had he tapped into his blood-hungry darkness to survive his ordeals in the Ashen Lands? How could he have believed after crossing the Veil that he'd have somehow left that side of him behind?

The horrible truth was it seemed to be just as immortal as the rest of him, and the joy he found in killing was back. He would have to deal with it.

A simmering chuckle echoed in the recesses of his mind.

~ CHAPTER 25 ~

"You know these three?" Kilal asked Requiem. She released the sword, and it dispersed like the ripple of a pond.

She nodded to the splatters of red that used to be Hungry Eyes. "That's Inferno. She is, *was*, a powerful Prime. She operated in Vitrol before Wolfe showed up, but never made herself known to the Keepers. I imagine she didn't have to be persuaded to join the Heirs. Probably was their first recruit. She's been on my list for a while. Glad I get to cross it off."

Kilal wondered who else was on that list. "The other two?"

Requiem walked to the crater and eyed Jasper's body before nodding. "Probably. But nothing springs to mind." She tossed a pebble at the other headless body. "Also don't know. But if I did, he wouldn't be much of a blade master."

Kilal nodded. Blade masters were a quiet sect of Arbiters; unknown, unseen, and unheard.

"Hey there," White Jacket said, approaching them from the other side of the crater. "Requiem Ror, I presume? It's a pleasure finally meeting you two. Requiem, you have been a role model of mine ever since I was young. And Kilal, I am *so* happy to see that you're not dead."

Kilal and Requiem shared a look and shrugged. Neither of them knew who she was.

White Jacket gave them a sheepish smile and tossed a

shoulder-length lock of hair back. "Right. You probably haven't heard of me. I'm Nanomia, but you can call me Nam. I'm just a boring old Enlightened Arbiter. Elemental branch. I'm thirty-one. I haven't killed anyone yet, so hopefully that goes a long way when you're determining what you should do with me. My parents are dead. Don't have any siblings. I was born and raised in New Cita. Never even left there until I registered with the Heirs in Silent Haven five years ago. Does that answer your questions?"

Kilal frowned. "I didn't ask any."

Nanomia mirrored his expression. "That's right. You didn't." She blushed and smiled. "I've always been told I talked too much. Inferno said she'd fuse my lips together one day. Glad that won't happen! She was pretty cruel. Jasper and Hendrick weren't much better. They really liked hurting people. Right. I'm doing it again. Do you have any questions you wanted to ask?"

"Absolutely not!" Requiem snapped.

Before he could let this woman endear herself to them, Kilal *did* have a question for her. One question which would decide whether she would live or die.

He leaped over the crater and landed beside Nanomia. Holding himself up straight, he adopted a posture of authority. He didn't want to scare or threaten her, but he wanted her to understand the position she was in.

Craning her neck back to look up at him, she paled in his shadow and stepped back.

"You have willfully aligned yourself with an organization that not only recruits murderers like Inferno but rewards the killing of fellow Arbiters and benefits from terrorizing the citizens of the Sunlight Domain. The citizens we swore an oath to defend. So, tell me, Nam, why should I let you live?"

The overly talkative Arbiter suddenly had nothing to say. She looked at Garret, who shifted his weight from one foot to the other and stared at the ground.

When she finally answered, her words no longer carried the frivolity they just had. "What other choice was there? I'm not a fighter. My mentor was a drunk. I gave up on her and life as an Arbiter shortly after becoming a mentee. When the Heirs of the Promise arrived, killing all the Arbiters who *could* fight, what was I supposed to do?"

"Die with them," Requiem said.

Nanomia blanched. When the blood returned to her face, Kilal felt like he was seeing the real woman she hid behind a mask of carefreeness. Her eyes were hard, and her jaw tight. "Sorry, but I'm not going to die for a cause no one's willing to put the time into teaching me. I swore the oath when I was twelve. The Arbiter who Awakened me handed me off to a woman who didn't care. And that was it. So, I'm *sorry* for not dying for a cause and a people who didn't give one bloody ounce of care about me.

"Like I said before. I haven't killed anyone. I haven't collected any bounties. I've just...existed...since the bloody Heirs took my livelihood." She brightened into a glowing smile. "But I *would* like to live, so please don't kill me?"

Kilal rubbed his eyes and turned his back on the group. Blood covered the cracked, overgrown cement. What type of building used to be erected there? A store? An apartment or home? A school? It didn't matter. It was gone, and so was that piece of knowledge. Now, all that remained was a memory, and even that was fading.

Could he really blame Nanomia for joining the Heirs? If she'd lived in Silent Haven, the city of the Keepers of the Oath, then he might have had different words for her. But the truth was, Arbiters had started failing long before Wolfe and his Heirs showed up. The reason the Keepers had never been able to reach the other two cities was because there weren't enough Arbiters left who cared. Nanomia's story was but one of dozens.

"Alright," he said, turning back to her. "I won't kill you, but

I'm not going to let you go. You're coming with us."

Requiem snapped a pronounced, "No!" but he was already prepared for that response.

"You're going to head up, or at least be a part of, a resistance of Arbiters and citizens trying to take down Wolfe."

"Fine," Requiem muttered. "But she better be able to keep up with us."

"What are you talking about? I thought we'd be meeting someone here who would take us to our next destination."

"I never said there'd be someone waiting for us. What *was* waiting for us was a vehicle."

"Okay," Kilal said, not understanding the issue.

"But that car," Requiem walked past him and to the other side of the clearing where a large stone wall wrapped in vines had been resting against a pile of rubble. That stone wall had collapsed when Kilal crashed into the ground. Requiem stopped at the edge of the broken barrier, and with an ease she shouldn't have had, picked up a chunk bigger than her and tossed it aside. She did the same with two more pieces before he realized what she was trying to show him.

Beneath the fallen wall was a rusted and very crushed vehicle.

"Your little display of strength did more to harm us than help us."

His blood boiled as Requiem glared at him from beside the smashed car. Was she really blaming him for that? How long would he have to endure her unkind attitude and demeanor?

Something snapped. Enough was enough.

"Maybe if you had *talked* to me and stopped treating me like an annoying inconvenience, I would have *known* that a *vehicle* was hidden here!" Kilal roared. Garret and Nanomia slowly backed away, and through the anger, he noticed Allyria beside Nanomia. The redhead matched the others' backward strides. "I asked you what was here! You had a chance to include me in the plans, but instead, your response was, 'You'll find out when we get there.'

"I've been *very* patient with you. I've been on the other side of the Veil for ten years. I've been a prisoner for the last two. Two *long* years of torture, and you know what kept me going? The hope that Lilliana is still alive somewhere out there and that one day I would see *you* again. My *wife!*" When had his vision grown so blurry? He shook his head and pinned her with a renewed glare. "I knew our reunion wouldn't be easy. But I didn't think you'd treat me like you wished I'd never returned."

Allyria studied the vines hanging from a cracked structure. When Nanomia noticed Kilal looking at her, she joined Allyria. Garret's focus was on what the two ladies were looking at as well.

No—he wasn't staring at the vines. He was staring at Allyria.

Requiem kicked the vehicle, denting metal and forcing a screech from the steel joints. Her lips moved slightly, but Kilal couldn't hear what she mumbled.

He wiped his cheeks and prepared for a fight.

"I'm...sorry," she said, facing him. "But if you thought we could just go on together like the last ten years hadn't happened, you're mistaken. I don't know what you've been through, but you don't know what I've been through, either. I'm not the woman you left behind. And I don't..." She trailed off. Her eyes glistened, which was a good sign. It showed she was still capable of emotions besides anger and irritation. "We'll talk. I promise. But right now, what's important is me getting back."

"Why? What is more important than *us*?" Kilal's own missions and priorities continued to nag at him, accusing him of abandoning them in the hopes of returning to a life of youthful bliss.

Requiem looked at the other three suspiciously, then approached Kilal. When she spoke, it was in a whisper. "We found a catacomb far beneath Silent Haven. Beneath even the Undercity."

"What?"

Excitement radiated from her. "It contained dozens of ancient texts about the world *before* the Bloodshed."

Kilal's own excitement intensified to match Requiem's.

All knowledge of times before the Bloodshed had been lost hundreds of years ago. The few remaining texts which were salvaged during the centuries following had been maintained in a vault in Veilside, and only the Mothers were allowed to know their contents. But when the Ash Fallen swept through the Sunlight Domain and wiped Veilside from the land during the Great Invasion, the texts were lost with the city, and there were none alive who knew what the texts contained.

If what Requiem was saying was true, that was a discovery of a lifetime. Of *many* lifetimes.

Kilal leaned over and pressed his forehead to hers. His hands shook and goosebumps prickled his skin. "What did you find?" All thought of his mission, of the three Arbiters standing behind them, was gone. The world could have ended, and Kilal wouldn't have noticed.

"We found it, Kilal." Her eyes sparkled. "We found the first hint!"

His mouth was dry, and no amount of swallowing would fix it.

"Hint of what?" Allyria asked, worming up beside them.

Requiem didn't seem to mind that it wasn't Kilal asking. "Travel to other worlds."

~ CHAPTER 26 ~

Travel to other worlds? So it was true? There really were other worlds out there? Jayden's taunt was the first thing to come to mind, and Kilal's thoughts raced with the possibilities.

Another memory poked at him.

"Other worlds," Allyria whispered, staring at the sky as if staring hard enough would let her see those very mysteries.

"That's what Fazin was trying to get from you, wasn't it?" he asked.

Her grin grew mischievous. "We burned everything before they found us." She pressed a finger to her temple. "Now the only way to access that information is up here. And Ahnk."

Kilal's jaw nearly hit the floor. "You...*destroyed*...all of it?"

"Well, that doesn't seem like the best option," Allyria muttered.

Kilal and Requiem glared at her.

"Why don't you go meet our new friends," he told the redhead.

Requiem poked a finger into the girl's chest. "And do *not* say a word about this to the other two."

Allyria didn't meet her eyes.

"Promise me," Kilal said.

She threw her hands into the air. "Fine, fine. I won't say anything. You guys are no fun!" She turned, and if a walk could be considered *grumpy,* that was how Allyria returned to Nanomia and Garret.

"I wasn't going to let Wolfe or Fazin get their hands on it," Requiem continued when she was out of earshot.

Kilal felt as if he were a child who'd just been given the gift of a lifetime, only to have it immediately taken away. "Of course. Of course," he said, trying to rein in his disappointment and irritation. "I just would've loved to read them."

She placed a hand on his elbow. The defensiveness was gone, and for the first time since he'd found her, there was no animosity as she looked at him. "I wish you could have as well. But Ahnk and I thought we'd covered our tracks well enough." She frowned and shook her head. "If only we hadn't let ourselves get distracted, but we never would have guessed in a million years that would be what the catacombs contained. We lost track of time. If we hadn't, if we'd been wiser, you may have had that chance. I'm sorry."

Kilal was so taken aback by Requiem's change of demeanor, his ability for speech left him.

"Sienna showed up," Requiem continued. "It was all we could do to destroy everything before she took us." She wouldn't look at him.

Kilal rested a large hand on her shoulder and lifted her chin with the other. Her right, half-closed eye had a cloudy appearance to it. Was her vision affected by whatever caused the scars? If so, it hadn't hindered her in her battle with the blade master.

"You did the right thing," he said. "I can only imagine how difficult that decision must have been for you. But letting Wolfe get his hands on knowledge like that would be more dangerous than destroying it."

The glow from moments before returned to her cheeks and eyes. "And think about it! If there's one chamber like that, there must be more."

She was probably right. Much of the Undercity was either

collapsed from an unknown disaster or simply abandoned. No one expected the labyrinth to have treasure hidden *beneath* it, let alone of that magnitude.

"We need to return." Kilal was already planning for the expedition. "We'll get you to where you need to go. Then we'll make haste for the Undercity. Only a few of us. We don't want to draw attention to ourselves. Maybe me, you, and Ally—"

His breath caught.

Lilliana.

What was he doing? How quickly he forgot about her in the face of...*knowledge*. And what about the whole of the Sunlight Domain? Wasn't he supposed to find Jayden and his comrades?

But what if that answer isn't found in saving the Sunlight Domain but leaving it? And even if it were, what about his daughter?

All enthusiasm drained from him like a burst bubble.

"What? What is it?" Requiem asked. She'd always been able to read him, though it wasn't like he was great at hiding his emotions.

"Like I've tried to tell you," Kilal started. It was an antagonistic start, and he immediately regretted it. He took a deep breath and began again. "I've been trapped in the Ashen Lands for ten years. Lilliana and I were separated when we were accidentally teleported there. I've spent those ten years looking for her.

"I only came back because there's a figure calling himself Ashen Kane who's raising an army of Ash Fallen. Soon, he'll pierce the Veil and finish what Avinoth started. So, as much as I want to, I can't go with you to the Undercity."

Requiem blinked a few times, and Kilal could only imagine what was going through her head. "Okay," she said. "We need to get going. The quicker we get back, the sooner we can come up with a plan. Lilliana's really in the Ashen Lands?"

He nodded his head solemnly.

"But she's still alive?"

A speck of ash descended onto Requiem's shoulder. The low buzz of voices, his constant background, intensified. The question hurt. He couldn't think like that. Of course she was alive. She *had* to be.

"Yes."

Requiem would never know how grateful he was when she didn't press him. Because the reality was he didn't know. And if he let himself *really* think about it, the answer he gave her would seem childish and naïve.

"We aren't going to be able to move quickly," Kilal said, purposefully changing the subject. "Garret and Nanomia won't be able to keep up with our speed or endurance. How far do we have left to go?"

Requiem looked off to their right. He caught another subtle, almost imperceptible movement of her lips. "Half a day's trip in a car."

Kilal did some quick math. "You and I could do that trip in slightly more than that. Allyria has shown strong potential as an Arbiter, but she's still a fledgling. She won't be able to keep up, either."

"Then we'll leave them."

"Not an option." She opened her mouth to protest, but he cut her off. "We *won't* leave them," he said sternly.

The animosity returned. "Then what do you suggest?"

Kilal ran a hand through his hair. "We're about to hit farmlands," he said more to himself than Requiem. He looked left to right, trying to get his bearings so he could place himself on a mental image of a map, but everything looked the same; the remnants of a city lay in both directions. "I think there should be one not too far from here. But it has been a while. And a lot has changed since I've been gone."

"There is one," she agreed, almost begrudgingly. "If we maintain a *normal* pace, we could make it there in an hour. What do you want from there, though?"

Kilal clapped once in triumph. "A vehicle."

~ CHAPTER 27 ~

"Could we have found a *smaller* car?" Allyria whined from the back seat where she sat, squished between Garret and Nanomia.

Being far outside of the cities, most vehicles consisted of large tractors or trucks capable of carting huge quantities of produce. The farmer Kilal had negotiated with had been unwilling to part with either of those, but the 'city vehicle'— as he called it—he could part with. So, the five Arbiters had crammed themselves into a car made to seat four.

Nanomia didn't seem to mind. Her window was rolled down, and her eyes were half-closed as she basked in the blowing wind. Garret, who was pretending to look out his window but continued to sneak frequent glances at Allyria's pale leg—a direct contrast to his dark one—which was pressed against his, could have been auditioning to be a tomato.

Kilal couldn't help but smile. He could cut a limb off and grow it back in seconds, but understanding the mystery of teenage hormones was something entirely beyond him. Sure, he'd been a teenager once, but that was about a hundred and ninety years ago. Not something he entirely remembered. And most of Lilliana's teenage years had been ripped away from him.

"I'm sure Garret doesn't mind," he said.

Garret started and shoved himself up against his door. "It's alright," he murmured.

Allyria rolled her eyes, oblivious to the boy's taking to her. "He's just being nice." She nudged Garret with an elbow. "Don't be intimidated by him." She leaned closer and loud whispered, "I saw him cry once."

Garret paled, probably at the thought of the great Immortal Arbiter weeping. But two could play that game.

"Allyria, I just wanted to apologize again for purchasing the wrong-sized diapers for you. I know how much you have trouble controlling your bowels when you're excited, or scared, or anxious, or tired—definitely tired."

"KI-*lal*," she looked close to exploding.

Kilal turned in his seat, wrestling with his seat belt. He didn't miss the smile on Requiem's face.

"Calm down, Allyria." He mustered as much concern as he could on his face and in his tone. "You remember what happened last time you got upset?" He turned his attention to Garret, who was staring at him in horror. "It was *not* pretty." Kilal paused briefly and stared out the window before embellishing a shudder. "Never knew teenage girls were capable of such a *mess*."

She squealed and the redness of her face put Garret's to shame. "That's *not* true!" She swiveled her head from Garret to Nanomia. "It's not true. He's lying! Really, he is."

Nanomia patted her knee. "It's okay, hon. Accidents happen. You don't need to be embarrassed or defend yourself."

Allyria scrunched her face into a mass of anger. "But that's just it. An accident *never* happened! I have nothing to defend myself about."

"Of course not," Kilal said. He widened his eyes and addressed their new friends. "Whatever you do, don't ask her about the way we met. Let's just say someone without a nose wouldn't have been safe." He scowled and clamped his nose between a finger and thumb.

Allyria balled her hands into fists and shrieked, "He's lying!"

"If you don't believe me, check her pack. She carries spare toilet paper in there *just in case.*" Her red hair became a perfect match for her cheeks. Kilal raised an eyebrow and gave her a look.

Lesson learned? Don't tell others about what you saw in my apartment.

He faced the front as Allyria vehemently tried to persuade Garret and Nanomia that he was lying.

"I forgot how good you were at getting under their skin," Requiem said from behind the wheel. She'd been adamant about her being the one to drive after Kilal purchased the vehicle for a price twenty times its worth. He didn't mind. It had been ten years since he'd driven. And he didn't know where they were going.

"A gift, some would call it," he said, taking in her smile like the warm rays of afternoon sunshine.

"*Some* would call it that."

The world flew by around them. Requiem kept them on the main road, which hadn't been maintained. While not anywhere close to the decay and overgrown nature of the paths in the Dead Zone, the patchy, uneven street they traveled showed signs of many years of lack of maintenance. The edges were crumbling, cracks webbed their way through the gray pavement, and potholes decorated the surface like acne on a teenager.

Was it because of the Heirs and the leash they had on the Governing Seats? Or was it a much less ominous reason: people were traveling the countryside less and less, so no one saw the reason to maintain the roads?

They'd already been on the path for little more than an hour, and they'd only passed three cars and two tractors, both of which didn't have an Arbiter escort.

Kilal rolled his own window down and let the refreshing

breeze flow around him. The whipping wind drowned out Allyria's and Nanomia's back and forth. The air was cool on his exposed arm as he moved it out of the window and laid his hand flat on the rooftop.

"Remember when these roads were full of life?" he said.

"I think 'full of life' was before my time," Requiem said. "Even still, I do remember when there was more life than this."

"And tractors had Arbiter escorts?"

She snorted. "We're a little preoccupied these days to spare the manpower for farmers."

Even though no one could hear it, it felt good to drum his fingers on the metal roof. "Farmers are what keep us alive," he retorted. "If the Heirs were smart, they'd control the farm- lands. Control them and you control the Sunlight Domain."

An abandoned farm passed on their right. A green tractor, more rust than paint, lay on its side in a deserted field. Once- tilled land was overgrown with grass and weeds. The barn was a skeleton of its former glory, with its double-sliding doors torn from their hinges and its roof caved in. The one-story home was forsaken and in not much better condition than the barn.

It was the second farm they'd passed in such a shape.

"What happened here?" Kilal said.

"Nothing that hasn't been happening for a long time. The world's dying. Always has been. We just never saw it."

"Was it on purpose? Did we not want to see it? Or did we ignore it because we didn't know what to do about it?"

Requiem eased into the lane of oncoming traffic, passing an abandoned truck with silver and bronze peeling paint on the side of the road. "Probably a little bit of both."

Kilal continued the drumming of his fingers. "Maybe being gone for ten years shined a spotlight on the decay, but this side of the Veil looks worse than it ever has."

Requiem didn't respond. What was there to say?

"Traveling to other worlds. You really found evidence of it?"

She hissed, "Not here."

Not here, Kilal thought, almost mockingly. Then it hit him. *Right.* Requiem had been captured, and probably tortured, for that information.

Fazin's first words rang in his mind. *Tell me what you found, and I'll stop your suffering.*

Whatever Requiem had discovered, Wolfe wanted it. She hadn't given up any information, but the same couldn't be said about the three Arbiters in the back seat. They would squeal like pigs. Not that Kilal would blame them. They didn't have a stake in the game yet. Or at least, they didn't *think* they had a stake in the game. Not to mention, he didn't know Garret and Nanomia. For all he knew, they could be spies.

But Nanomia turned against Inferno.

She joined the winning side, his gut responded. His side, to be precise. Exactly what a spy would do.

He didn't know who to agree with, his brain or gut. At least, not yet. So, he'd treat Garret and Nanomia in the most practical way he could: like he didn't know them. And really, he didn't.

That also meant he couldn't mention Jayden, another puzzle piece to the incomplete picture of interdimensional travel.

Later then.

His list of things to discuss with Requiem was rapidly growing. The world would decay around them before they could finish hitting each point.

"The Keepers are gone," she whispered, yet the four words packed a punch most War Plagues couldn't manage.

Kilal closed his eyes. He sighed and pinched the bridge of his nose. "I know. The Heirs."

"Bloody Heirs," Requiem cursed.

"I didn't understand at first," he said. "How could we have been so widely defeated? But after fighting Tor'et and Fazin, I understand a little better. They were both easily on equal footing with a Prime, probably even more powerful. Clearly, they aren't Arbiters; their power doesn't come from Carvings. So, what in the bloody moons are they?"

Nanomia, apparently eavesdropping on the conversation occurring three feet in front of her, leaned forward. "I've met Tor'et and Wolfe. Not exactly *met*, I more saw them. Up close. Twice. They're about as different as can be. Tor'et is a narcissist, and Wolfe is all broody and glum. And their clothing! Tor'et should take a page from Wolfe's book and tone down the style a touch. Everything from his shoes to his hair screams, 'I really love myself!' Bloodshed and Oaths, he even wears eyeliner. Why does a man need to wear eyeliner?"

Kilal raised a brow. "What's wrong with a guy wearing eyeliner?"

Requiem glared at Nanomia. "Did you seriously interrupt our conversation to discuss the wardrobe of Tor'et and Wolfe?"

"What? Of course not! I'm just trying to point out that no matter their differences, there's one thing they always have in common. Their jewelry. Rings, bracelets, earrings. Doesn't matter what the format is because they always have that one thing in common."

"The stones," Kilal and Requiem said.

Nanomia looked from one to the other. "Right," she said slowly. "I don't know what it means, but it's gotta mean something, right?"

Kilal drummed his fingers on his knees. Nanomia had been engaging Allyria in conversation, but obviously the woman had her ears open for their talk. His gut gave itself a congratulatory pat on its back as his brain sulked.

She's as much a spy as Garret is a serial killer, his mind responded.

A quick gesture of his chin and Nanomia leaned back and asked Allyria how she and Kilal had met. Spy or not, he'd have to be careful with what he said around that one.

"Whatever it was I found," Requiem said, speaking slowly and carefully, changing topics yet again, "I haven't had much time to decipher and consider what it means. Sienna saw to that. Let me think about it some, and I promise, when we arrive, it'll all be explained. What I discovered, it's bigger than everything else. What you've been through. What I've been through. Everything."

"And what about Lilliana? Every second I spend here is another second she's on her own in the Ashen Lands. Is this 'discovery' bigger than her?"

The car hit a deep pothole, and the metal rust bucket rattled and shook as if it was going to fall apart.

"I don't think you're supposed to hit those," Allyria said.

And just like that, the moment passed. Requiem didn't answer his question, and Kilal was happier that way. He knew what she would say, and he couldn't bear it.

Because deep down, he'd agree with her.

The possibility, though small, of striking off into another world, a world not operating on dwindling time, *was* bigger than everything else.

A hand rested on his as he stared out the window.

"Trust me. Please."

Requiem showing him affection? He almost couldn't believe it after the way she'd been treating him.

Did he really have any other choice but to trust her? What else could he do? Scream at her? Threaten her? Bribe her? Of course not. His options were to pout like a child or accept his current situation for what it was.

"She probably doesn't want to talk about it right now." Allyria's head loomed between the two of them. "She probably thinks we're spies for the Heirs or something like that."

Requiem slammed on the brakes. If not for her seatbelt, Allyria would most certainly have gone through the windshield.

"Hey! what wa—"

"Enough of the eavesdropping," Requiem said. Her voice was calm, but Kilal could sense the simmering anger. "The front seat is for adults and adult conversations only." She shoved

Allyria back with an elbow.

"It's not my fault. I'm bored," the girl muttered.

"Besides," Requiem continued, "I don't think the Heirs would count on teenagers who can't control their bowels."

He burst into laughter as Allyria let out another shriek.

Settling back into his seat, Kilal scanned the countryside.

A large community of farms passed on the left. The smell of dung and chickens oozed through the car windows. Not the most accommodating of scents.

A dozen or more people moved about the farmstead, some herding sheep, some carrying crates of vegetables and fruit they'd just harvested, and more than a few kids chased each other. It was good to see the folk up and about and children laughing and playing. Their entire world revolved around growing food for Silent Haven. They didn't have to worry about anything else.

Kilal wondered what it would be like to live such a simple life.

~ CHAPTER 28 ~

Requiem didn't seem to want to take advantage of their opportunity together to talk, so Kilal thought of other ways to spend the time.

Something Nanomia said earlier stuck out. She'd received next to no training as an Arbiter. Neither had Allyria, and he didn't even know what Garret was capable of. His expectations weren't high with that one.

"Garret, what classification of Arbiter are you?" he asked.

The boy nearly jumped out of his skin. He stammered for a moment before calming enough to speak clearly. "Enlightened. Sir."

Allyria snickered. "You don't have to be so formal."

"How old are you, and how much training have you been given?"

"I'm seventeen, and...not much." With downcast eyes, he tucked his chin against his chest. "My mentor fired me. Said I...wasn't worth the time."

What a sad state we're in, Kilal thought. Being a mentor was once one of the highest privileges an Arbiter could obtain. "I'm sorry you were told that, but that's a load of ash. Every person born with the Enlightened Gene is worth the time."

Garret lifted his head just enough to see a slight upturn of his lips.

"What branch do you use?" Kilal asked. Somehow, during all the fighting with Inferno and her cronies, he hadn't sensed any Carvings from Garret. That could either be because he hadn't activated any or because all of Kilal's senses had been overwhelmed by Inferno. The major downside to being able to sense Carving use. If there's a Prime nearby, and they are using all three branches at once, they essentially make any other Arbiters 'invisible.'

"Mind, sir. I mean, uh, Kilal."

"We've got two Enlightened, one High, and two Primes," Allyria said.

"Who's the other Prime?" Nanomia asked.

Allyria puffed out her chest and hoisted a thumb at herself. "This girl!"

"Really?" Kilal hadn't thought it was possible, but there was even *more* adoration in Garret's brown eyes.

"I've never met a Prime so young," Nanomia said. She was looking at Allyria as if seeing her as the all-powerful Arbiter the girl was trying desperately to portray herself as.

Allyria beamed. "And I'm the Immortal Arbiter's mentee!"

"Wow. You're so lucky!" Garret said. It was the most emotion he'd shown since Kilal met him: slightly more than neutral.

Requiem readjusted her rearview mirror to gaze at Allyria. "Being a Prime isn't something to brag about. Our classification has nothing to do with us. It's a random chance determined at birth. You were just very blessed."

The girl's bubble burst. Leather creaked as she sat back with arms crossed and stared daggers at the back of Requiem's head. If only she knew how fortunate she was that Requiem couldn't see the look in her eyes.

When Allyria turned her gaze to Kilal, he gave her a slight shake of his head. *Knock it off,* he hoped he was communicating. Whether that was what she understood, he didn't know. Either way, her features softened, and she turned her attention to some torn fabric on her jeans.

"She's right," Kilal said, addressing all three of the back-seat dwellers. "Your classification is nothing to be proud of *or* ashamed of. I've met Enlightened Arbiters who could best any Prime because they were that good at what they could do. You can't control what or how many branches you can use, but you can control how hard you work at mastering your skills."

Nanomia nodded enthusiastically. "So, what do you say?" Kilal raised a brow. She raised both of hers. "About being my mentor, too?" She said it as if it should have been obvious.

He pursed his lips and shook his head. "Sorry. I only ever take one mentee at a time. The more I have, the less of my time and instruction I can give to them."

Nanomia didn't seem hurt by the refusal. Instead, she grabbed onto the back of Requiem's chair and pulled herself forward until they were almost cheek to cheek. "What about you? Two ladies defying the odds, making the world a better place?"

Requiem readjusted the rearview mirror again until she could see Nanomia's beaming face. "No."

The smile vanished, smothered. Or it would have been if Nanomia hadn't caught the release of emotion and righted it. "That's okay," she said, renewing her smile, though it looked more plastic than the earlier one. "I'm more of a lone wolf, anyway." She returned to staring out the window and trying her hardest to keep the hurt and disappointment concealed.

She wasn't doing a very good job.

Allyria must have noticed because she turned pleading eyes on Kilal. "Is there someone else who could mentor them? Anyone?"

He leaned back in his wrinkled and cracked leather seat. "Let me think about it."

A list instantly formulated in his mind of potential candidates. The only problem was he had no idea if they were still alive. Regardless, Nanomia and Garret had been through enough rejection from the world of Arbiters.

Kilal gritted his teeth. Somehow, someway, he would find them a mentor.

~ CHAPTER 29 ~

Fingers drumming on the roof of the car, boredom seeped into Kilal like a disease. And with boredom came time to think. Too much time to think. Along with it came memories. And with memories came...

Need to occupy myself.

The three fledgling Arbiters could become a good distraction.

The chair squeaked in protest as Kilal turned halfway around. The three in the back stopped talking and stared at him. "First question," he said. "And this one goes to Allyria."

They exchanged looks of confusion, but those quickly gave way to excitement. Allyria sat up straight and leaned forward as if her very life revolved around giving the correct answer to his question.

"During our encounter with Blondie, what branch did she use?"

Allyria moved her lips and tapped her chin. "She...threw pink bolts of energy. So...Mind?"

"Wrong."

Allyria wilted.

"Anyone else?" he asked.

Nanomia shrugged. "Remember, until a few years ago, I was removed from the world of Arbiters for about two decades.

And if you think the Heirs gave two ashes about training me, you're wrong."

"Garret?"

"Elemental," he said, looking at Allyria almost apologetically.

"Correct."

"But how?" Allyria whined. "It was energy or something. That isn't an element!"

"That's a good point," Kilal said. "Garret, why do you say Elemental?"

"If you can see it, it's from the branch of Elements."

"Exactly." He gave Garret a proud wink.

"Lucky guess," Allyria muttered.

"Ignore her," Kilal said. "She doesn't like being confronted with the reality that she *doesn't* know everything."

Allyria narrowed her eyes, but she turned her chagrin onto Garret as if daring him to agree with Kilal. The boy squirmed in his seat. His eyes darted from Kilal to Allyria until finally resting on his hands.

Kid really needs to lighten up. But considering the little information the teenager already shared about his past, there was more to his behavior than just a shy personality.

"Blondie was condensing air," Kilal explained. "It wasn't energy."

"Air isn't pink."

"Allyria, if you try talking less," Requiem said, "and listening more, you might become a decent Arbiter. If not, this constant need to defend yourself and lessen the achievements of others will lead you either to a life of solidarity or no life at all."

The girl's shame and embarrassment was palpable.

Garret suddenly discovered something very interesting on his glasses to fiddle with.

"She's right," Kilal said. "A basic tenet of being an Arbiter is elevating others higher than yourself. At least it used to be. This foreign concept is known as humility. Just because today's generation of Arbiters is composed of self-serving, arrogant sons of Plagues doesn't mean you have to be that way."

The three in the back returned their attention to Kilal. Allyria seemed grateful to have the focus off of her.

"What Garret said about the elements is one of many rules of Carvings," he continued. "If you can see it, it's Elemental.

"Moving on, start listing out the different classes of Arbiter based on their combination of Carvings."

"Mage is an Enlightened Arbiter who uses Elemental Carvings," Garret said.

"Mentalists can only use Mind Carvings," Nanomia chimed in.

"A Fighter uses only the Physical branch," Allyria added.

"Good. You got the easy ones. Now, the combinations of High Arbiters."

The whir of the engine blended with the ricketing of the wheels rolling over uneven pavement and the rushing wind through open windows.

"Bruiser. Physical and Mind," Garret said. Kilal nodded. "Oracle. Mind and Elemental."

The boy was right, but he was the only one answering. Kilal leveled a flat stare at Allyria and Nanomia.

"I...don't know these. Any of them," Allyria admitted.

"Same," Nanomia echoed. "And going forward, it would probably be best if you assumed I don't know anything, and the hole representing my knowledge is more like a chasm."

"And going forward, it would be best if you'd stop hiding behind your lack of knowledge and stop using it as an excuse to not try."

Nanomia winced but had the wisdom to say nothing else.

"Do you know the rest, Garret?" Allyria asked.

"Arcanist uses Physical and Elemental."

"And what about Prime Arbiters?" Kilal asked. "What are the titles for those possible combinations? And Garret, no answer from you." It was a trick question that fooled most students.

Allyria's mumbled thoughts could be heard by everyone.

Nanomia rolled up her window. A mischievous smile and

glint appeared in her eyes. "There aren't any. A Prime is a Prime. They use *all* branches."

Allyria smacked her palm against her forehead.

"Nice thinking," Kilal said. "But are you sure you wouldn't rather go back on your answer and remind me of how little you know?"

Nanomia snapped her fingers, then jabbed one at the roof. "That reminds me. Have I told you guys how little I know of the world of Arbiters?"

Garret actually cracked a smile.

Allyria wore a mask of annoyance. "No. Not even once."

"Really?" Nanomia said. "Well, I know *very* little about—"

Requiem swerved the car to the left. Kilal had raised his gravity. He didn't budge an inch. The same couldn't be said about the three in the back. Garret nearly tore his belt open in his haste to get off of Allyria.

"You sure you don't want me to drive?" Allyria asked.

"Sorry," Requiem said. "I thought I was supposed to avoid potholes."

Allyria rolled her eyes and mumbled something.

"Mentalist," Kilal said, referring to Garret. The boy stared out the window.

Nanomia reached across Allyria and poked him in the side, spooking him. "I think he's talking to you?"

Garret turned wide, innocent eyes to Kilal. "Sorry," he said. "I'm not used to being called that."

"Get used to it. All of you. It's what you are, and that will never change. Now, what Carvings do you know?"

Garret and Allyria started. "Kilal, that's supposed to be a *secret*," she said.

"Not from me, it's not."

"Okay, but what about," she replaced words with a finger pointed at Requiem. Kilal blanked his face, to which Allyria changed tactics. She pointed with her chin and raised her eyebrows.

"Do you mean Requiem?" Nanomia asked.

Allyria blushed and stammered an unconvincing, "No!"

Kilal chuckled. "As I was asking, Garret, your Carvings?"

"I don't know many," he admitted. "Basic Healing. Protective Shell. Telekinesis. Mind Reading."

Requiem mumbled a curse under her breath. Kilal shared a look with her as the car quieted. The traction of tires and the hum of the engine filled the silence.

Allyria, who'd turned to biting her nails to hide her red face, gasped and faced Garret. "You aren't using Mind Reading right now, are you?"

He paled and shrunk into his seat. "No! Of course not!"

She narrowed her eyes and pursed her lips. "Good. Not that I have anything to hide," she was quick to add.

Kilal studied the boy. *Mind Reading.* He shared a look with Requiem. Mind readers *never* shared that they knew the Carving. *Ever.* Not just because it was banned centuries ago but because known mind readers were avoided like a Plague.

His thoughts drifted to the molestation of his mind by Inferno. It was one thing to know Carvings associated with mind manipulation; it was much different to actually carve and use them.

That Garret revealed his knowledge of it, of his own volition, proved just how naïve and untrained he was.

Kilal knew the Carving for Mind Reading, too. Very few of his acquaintances knew that about him, though. He'd abused the rune many times over in his early days of immortality. But no longer. He swore an oath to never use Mind Reading again, and he'd made good on that promise for over a century.

It didn't sit well with him that someone had taught that young boy such a dangerous and banned Carving. Especially considering said teacher had then abandoned Garret. It was like giving a baby a weapon capable of mass destruction, teaching the child how to use it, then deserting them but leaving said child still equipped with the weapon. It was...irresponsible, at best.

"Who was your mentor?" Kilal asked.

Garret rubbed sweaty palms against his pant legs. "Morning Dove."

Morning Dove? She was an eccentric, middle-aged lady who kept to herself. Kilal had no idea she was capable of mind reading. As was the norm.

"Bloodshed and Oaths!" Requiem hissed.

Kilal raised a brow. "Hm?"

"Morning Dove was murdered five years ago in New Cita," she said. "It was all over the news. I've never seen anything like it. The brutality of it warranted Arbiter assistance in tracking down the killer. Whoever it was, they were never found."

"That was a couple of weeks after she released me from mentorship," Garret said quietly. "The day after the Heirs of the Promise showed up. Maybe...if I had been there, I could have done something to help her."

If you'd been there, you'd have been the second victim that night.

Kilal scratched a day and a half's worth of stubble on his chin. Murdered the day after the Heirs showed up. Coincidence? Unlikely.

"How old were you when you became an Arbiter?" Allyria asked.

"Twelve."

"Twelve? That's so young!"

"That's actually pretty normal," Requiem said. "You were just abnormally old when you went through the Awakening."

Allyria chewed on her lip, staring out the window.

"Who have you shared knowledge of Mind Reading with?" Kilal asked.

"No one!"

"Good. If you do, I'll kill you."

A deafening silence fell over the car.

All the blood drained from Garret's face, and he looked ready to hurl. Allyria glared at Kilal as if rebuking him for taking a joke too far. Nanomia stared out the window. Requiem nodded her agreement.

"Don't you think that's a bit harsh?" Allyria asked.

"Not as harsh as killing him just for knowing it," Requiem said.

The girl's glare darkened. "You'd kill someone just for *knowing* a Carving?"

"A lot of horrible things have been done by Arbiters with that rune and others like it. Mind Reading is the gateway to Thought Planting, and eventually, Mind Manipulation. There's a reason why in the history of Carvings, only those three have been banned."

"The Mind Hunts," Garret said. "Morning Dove told me about them."

Another dark blot in my life I'll never forgive myself for.

"The what?" Alyria asked.

To Kilal's surprise, it was Nanomia who answered. "Citizens and Arbiters alike turned on any suspected of using thought-related Carvings. If you were found to use one, or if you were even suspected of using one, you were as good as dead."

Allyria gasped. "That's horrible! There wasn't a trial or anything?"

Kilal turned back around in his seat and faced the front.

Your fault. Your fault. Your fault. Your fault.

He closed his eyes and sank into the chair. The voices grew in number and strength.

"From what I've heard," Nanomia said, "the things Arbiters were doing with those Carvings were horrible. Murder. Robbery. Kidnappings. Torture. Maybe some Arbiters were killed unjustly, but if you ask me, ridding ourselves of true evil is worth that price. A few suffer so the majority don't have to."

True evil. She wasn't technically wrong.

How many lives did you ruin in your thirst for power and knowledge?

"Just because a few do horrible things, doesn't give anyone the right to kill people *suspected* of doing something similar," Allyria argued. "And it definitely doesn't give anyone the right to kill someone because of something they *might* do. How can murderous acts be called good because they're being committed against others who perform horrible acts? Evil is evil."

The car shook as Requiem hit another patch of weathered road.

Though a part of Kilal agreed with Nanomia, Allyria was also right. Calling it anything else but evil was self-righteous, but sometimes, a monster was the only thing that could kill a monster.

"You can think that." Nanomia's tone was devoid of the innocence she was trying to portray. "You have every right to. But eventually, you'll have to take a step out of that sheltered world of yours and join the rest of us in reality."

Pressure rose behind Kilal's eyes. He could nearly taste the tension. Things were rapidly spiraling out of control. He should do something. Lead them. Guide them. Teach them.

Dozens died because they were suspected of doing what you started. You're the real monster.

Blood and the taste of copper filled his mouth—he'd bitten his own tongue.

"Sheltered?" Allyria said through gritted teeth. "You think because I'm a teenager, I don't know what real life is?"

"That's the general assumption of teenagers, yes."

"I..." Her voice quivered.

Do something!

Another memory responded, one of him breaking the arm of an older gentleman who wouldn't give Kilal the location of his hidden fortune. He could have used mind reading to extract the information from the elderly man, but Kilal had always enjoyed the application of physical torment over mental.

There was just something...personal about it.

He bit his tongue again, on purpose. He should do something about their bickering, but how? It was keeping everyone's focus off of him.

"I watched my father *murder* my mother," Allyria snapped. "Do you know why? Because he caught her talking to a male Arbiter. Guess who he turned his anger onto after she was dead?"

A loud exhale and sigh followed. "I'm sorry, Allyria," Nanomia said. "I shouldn't have let my mouth get the best of me."

"Whatever."

A thump signaled Allyria had slammed herself back into her seat, probably with her arms crossed. Now was a time to train Allyria to handle her emotions, to provide her an ear to allow her to talk about what she'd been through.

The same went for Nanomia. The older lady knew far more than an Arbiter with no mentorship and a lack of overall experience with their history should. She clearly held animosity toward what happened with the Mind Hunts and possibly all Arbiters in general. And Garret needed to have his moral compass checked and possibly repaired to ensure he didn't abuse the Carvings he knew.

"Wake me when we get there," Kilal said.

The list of things he needed to do and *should* do kept getting longer. But now wasn't the time for that. He needed to empty his mind and focus on something that would anchor him back to the present.

Requiem touched his hand, and it was the most loving thing she could have done.

If anyone alive knew even a little of what he was going through, it was her.

~ CHAPTER 30 ~

Kilal jolted awake and slammed his forehead against the roof of the car. Sweat coated his brow. His heart raced, and unease snuck up on him like an assassin in the night. He looked for the source of whatever it was that woke him.

Requiem half-stared at him and half-watched the road. Her concern was evident.

"Sorry," she said. "You were...mumbling."

By the anxiety pulsing through his veins, Kilal couldn't imagine he'd been mumbling anything he wanted the others to hear.

"Who...did you want to stop?" Allyria asked. Her concern for him was even more deeply rooted on her face than Requiem's. "What were they doing? Does it have anything to do with your time in the Ashen Lands?"

"The Ashen Lands!" Nanomia said, eyes wide.

Garret stared at him like he was some god risen from the dead. Kilal slumped back into his seat. They didn't need to see him rolling his eyes.

"Yeah," Allyria said. "He got teleported there ten years ago with his daughter. He's only been back for about five days."

"Ten years? That's—" Nanomia's horror morphed into expectant curiosity. "What was it like?"

Why was everyone always so desperate for details, as if

they had a craving to satisfy or he'd just come back from a theme park?

"Gray," Kilal said.

"Gray," Nanomia repeated, as though it were the single most important word she'd ever heard.

Allyria leaned forward and tapped him on the shoulder. Kilal almost jumped out of his skin. Physical contact? From her? "The group I used to run with had a young boy in it. I think he was twelve. Everyone called him Scamp. He was so skinny. And scared. When he slept, he sounded...like you did. Always pleading with someone to stop. He would never talk about it. When I pried, he'd shut down even more than normal. He wasn't with us long. He..." Her eyes filled with tears, and she cleared her throat. "He killed himself.

"You're not going to do that, are you?"

Already tried. It didn't have the outcome I expected.

He drew his lips into a flat line and blanked his expression. "If I do, I'll take you with me. I wouldn't want to force any of these fine people to take care of you." He expected some sort of blow up, but for the third time in the past few minutes, Allyria surprised him.

"Deal."

Her warm smile was contagious. He couldn't help but replicate it.

"Is that—" Garret grabbed the sides of Kilal's seat and pulled himself up, inadvertently brushing his shoulder against Allyria's. She jerked away and scooted against Nanomia, "—the Veil?"

Three sets of eyes followed his gaze.

"Whoa," Allyria said.

"Bloodshed and Oaths," blurted Nanomia. "I never thought I'd see it."

"Why are you taking us *toward* the Veil?" Kilal asked, rubbing sweaty palms against his pants. It was too soon. He wasn't supposed to be back there yet. He was supposed to have

Jayden and the others with him.

"No one would ever suspect an abandoned Veil barracks would still be in use," Requiem said.

Great.

Far in the distance, the world seemed to end and drop off into a black abyss. For someone who knew nothing of the Veil and the Sunlight Domain, they may think just that. Kilal, however, was intimately familiar with the darkness.

As far as human history was concerned, he was the only one to have physically crossed it.

The Veil was a wall of black energy piercing the sky and stretching to an unreachable height. Not just above, but also below; it penetrated the earth to an unknown depth. Simply put, it was impossible to navigate the Veil any other way but through it.

They were still too far away to make out anything other than a dark horizon, but as Requiem drove them closer, the characteristics of the Veil became clearer. Lightning, or an energy akin to the elemental force, crackled, cracked, and fluctuated all about the surface.

The three passengers upheld a reverent silence as the Veil drew closer. Allyria now knew the origins of it, but did the other two? He would wager Garret did, and by Nanomia's strange knowledge of the Mind Hunts, he would assume she did too. The silence, however, was too comforting to violate, so he placed it on a mental list of topics to discuss later.

For now, it was all he could do to keep his breathing stable and his mind blank. The Veil was never a joyous landmark to be around, but for Kilal, it held a special type of memory: of existing in a constant state of vaporization and regeneration.

A shiver ran up his spine.

The Veil, if touched, would reduce the object to a state of nothingness, eradicating whatever it touched at an anatomical level. It was impassable. As such, the mystery of Ashen raids on this side was still a mystery. That was until Kilal was imprisoned beside the man who instructed him to find Jayden, the Professor, and Aya.

According to Eldon, the Veil's power weakened over time. Something Kilal, familiar with the Great Invasion due to the degradation of the barrier, already knew. What he didn't know was how the orbit of the Sun, Ophir, Damphir, and the third moon—Cartal, the dead moon—affected the degradation.

Once every fourteen days, the moons and the sun's orbital path would bring all four into perfect unison. The sun, being the furthest from the world, would be completely blocked by the three moons, with Cartal being the foremost of the celestial bodies. During that time, which lasted only four hours, the Veil weakened.

The change wouldn't be noticed by most humans. They'd still be vaporized on contact, just slower. But to someone like Kilal, the weakening was enough for his Carving of Immortality to keep him alive.

It took all four hours for Kilal to pass through the Veil. It was the longest, most eternal few hours he'd ever endured. Barely more than a skeleton and muscle, Kilal traversed the quarter mile of darkness in a constant state of agony as his body was ripped apart and regenerated. He couldn't see. He couldn't hear. He couldn't even scream. All he could do was place one painful step in front of the other and hope.

Hope he wasn't going in circles. Hope he could reach the other side before the moons revealed the sun. Hope his mind wouldn't be destroyed in the process.

Another shiver ran up his spine. The only reason he'd been able to endure the crossing was thanks to the torture he'd endured for the two years he was a prisoner in the Tower of Eyes. Without the constant pain he'd been forced to undergo during his imprisonment, he wouldn't have been able to sustain the trauma.

Next time I'm there, I should thank my torturer. Without him, I'd probably still be stuck over there.

Yes. A proper thanks was in order. One he'd deliver with his fists.

"Wow! Your hideout is in the shadows of the Veil?" Allyria scooted so far forward she was nearly sitting between Kilal and Requiem. "That is so *cool.*"

"That is *not* cool," he said. "The Veil siphons life from everything around it."

"My grandmother told me stories of her father's time as a Veil Warden," Nanomia said. "He worked one week on, two weeks off. Any more than a week of living so close to the Veil was too dangerous."

Veil Warden? Those hadn't been around for a long time. Too long even for Nanomia's great-grandfather to not just know about them but actually have *been* one.

Kilal took a sidelong glance at her. The young woman had her chin resting on a fist and was staring out the window. She looked innocent enough, but already in the short car ride, she'd alluded to a knowledge of events most living Arbiters didn't know about. Especially not one who supposedly had as little training as she did. That, plus hiding her personality behind that bubbly charade begged the question: who was she? Was Nanomia truly a naïve Arbiter who'd been removed from her calling most of her life? Or was she hiding a dark side?

A glance wouldn't answer his questions.

If he ever found himself alone with Requiem, he'd need to talk to her about Nanomia. The more eyes on the mysterious woman, the better.

Kilal caught Requiem studying her in the rearview mirror. Maybe he wouldn't have to warn her after all.

"We don't live there," Requiem said. "We've taken up shelter in the various abandoned farmlands. The barracks, however, is where we meet. Every second and fifth day of the week, we gather and plan for the following days. Because of the dangers associated with living this close to the Veil, no one's ever thought to look for us here."

The fifth day of the week, Dusk, was today.

Kilal couldn't argue with her logic. He wanted to. Any location was better than a Veil barracks. History taught that the

Wardens became obsolete because the number of Arbiters had dwindled too much to allow for the constant manning of the strongholds, but that was only about ten percent of the problem. The real problem was more associated with the information Nanomia had shared. Veil Wardens never stayed longer than one week. But even that was found to be too long—and it was discovered too late.

Kilal, along with a few others throughout history, believed the corruption of the Veil not only siphoned the life from its surroundings but, in the case of Arbiters, also siphoned life from the Prime Genes, the genetic trait which made someone an Arbiter. He believed that phenomenon, along with the sacrifice made to fight back the Great Invasion, had a major influence on the reduction of their kind.

The theory had never been proven. Even the mention of it had been so thoroughly rejected, one only brought it up if they wished to destroy their reputation.

By the time Kilal was born, the Veil had been all but abandoned. A fraction of the Wardens remained, and only a handful patrolled the barrier at a time. Two hundred years later, the barracks' only purpose was to provide a testament of what used to be: a memory of days when Arbiters weren't on the verge of extinction.

Every single one of the three dozen strongholds were abandoned, and Veil Wardens, once a prestigious title, was now no more than a few sentences in a textbook.

Requiem caught him staring at her, and his concern must have been evident. "I know what you're thinking," she said. "And yes, we've considered it. But this really was the only option. As destructive as the Veil is, it has proven a positive benefit."

"Besides keeping the Ash Fallen where they belong?" Nanomia said.

Where they belong is probably in another world.

Requiem ignored the interruption. "Sienna can't track us there."

Kilal crossed his arms and considered the implications. "That makes sense," he said. "The closer you get to the Veil, the more powerful the stench of...wrongness...becomes."

"And what exactly does *wrongness* smell like?" Allyria asked, still nearly sitting between them both.

"Remember the rotten soil? From the crater?" She nodded. "Like that."

"Ewww." Allyria pinched her nose. "And we're going to be staying in that?"

"Yes," Requiem said.

"But not for long," Kilal shot a look at Requiem, daring her to challenge him.

"And how long will that be?" the girl asked.

Kilal's trepidation at being so close to the Veil made irritation flare. "Question time is over." His words came out much harder than intended.

Allyria threw herself back into her seat and crossed her arms. Her foot tapped incessantly on the center console.

Kilal shoved the guilt down and closed his eyes. He'd have time enough to make up with her. Now, he just needed to endure another moment of anxiety. And that was best done in silence.

~ CHAPTER 31 ~

The car came to an abrupt stop; only when the engine cut off did Kilal open his eyes. They'd arrived. The stronghold, a husk of what it used to be, loomed over them. They parked within its great shadow.

The Veil not only sucked the life from living things. It did so even from inanimate objects. The stones of the barracks were pale and brittle. Cracks wove their way through the structure like bolts of lightning through clouds. It was a surprise that as much of the standing building still stood. Of the four towers, one at each corner, two hadn't fared well under the scrutiny of time and had collapsed long ago. Those sections of the barracks had become unlivable. But the remainder of the two-story structure remained intact enough to be hospitable.

A shadow darkened a large opening on the upper floor, and Kilal barely made out a human shape before it receded. Once those openings had been used to fire projectiles, both physical and elemental, upon any invading Ash Fallen.

Requiem had parked them in front of the stable. It was a wooden structure with a great eight-foot-tall, one-foot-thick wall enclosing it. An iron bar door could be unlocked and swung open. The wall contained only a handful of sections still reaching eight feet. The rest barely rose to Kilal's waist, and some parts were even lower.

"What is that for?" Allyria asked, pointing.

"It's a stable," Garret said. "It's where the Veil Wardens kept their horses."

"Whoa! As in, *real* horses?"

"Are there any other kinds?" Nanomia asked.

Allyria blushed. "I don't know! Didn't they go extinct or something?"

"They're not extinct," Requiem said. "But they're protected. You'll only find them on farms now."

Horseback riding. That was a skill Kilal never learned. And he couldn't say he was disappointed. Trusting a beast to carry him from one location to the next *safely* was not something he was keen on. He'd rather put that trust in his own two legs. Or a vehicle. Those at least didn't have minds of their own.

"Come on," Requiem said. She led them up to an enormous wooden door, its width capable of letting three Kilals stand shoulder to shoulder in it. "We're late."

"I'm sure they won't mind," Allyria said, skipping up beside her, "when they see who you've brought with you."

"Why would they care that Requiem brought you?" Kilal asked, exiting the vehicle. It was high noon, and he'd forgotten just how hot the sun could get. Sweat already glistened on his brow. He hastened his steps, desiring the protective shadows of the barracks, eyes shielded against the light.

Allyria flattened her lips. "I was talking about you."

He snapped a finger and pointed it at her. "That *does* make more sense."

She shook her head and dropped back to whisper something to Nanomia. The girls shared a giggle. Kilal imagined it came at his own expense.

He paused at the large door, relishing in the cool cover of the shadows.

Anticipation, excitement, fear, anxiety. Waiting for Requiem to open the door, they all filled him to a point he had difficulty differentiating one feeling from the next.

Who am I going to discover is dead and alive?

Saltik, Violet, Jorgen, Langston, Alistair, Nineve. Those were but a few of his closest friends. He'd assumed they were all dead, but with the revelation that some still lived, he'd have to experience the pain of actually *knowing* some of them were gone all over again.

Besides that, he was about to be reintegrated into the world of Arbiters, something he'd not intended on doing when he planned his return. How should he greet them? A hug? A smile? An apology? An explanation?

Stop worrying, you old fool! This isn't a battle to save lives. It's a bloody social gathering.

Somehow, that made it worse.

"I think you're supposed to walk *through* it," Allyria said from beside him.

He gritted his teeth and crossed the threshold.

Stale air seeped out from the dark recesses of the interior, blasting him with the oppressive stench of decay. It wasn't like that of the Dead Zone. This was more natural, if natural could be a word used to describe the decomposition of materials just by being in the vicinity of the Veil.

Requiem looked back at him. "Everyone will be upstairs."

Their footsteps echoed on the stone floor.

"This place is really creepy," Allyria said.

"It's our proximity to the Veil," Kilal replied. "It's unnatural, and our senses know it."

She grunted. "No wonder the Wardens died out. Who would want this job?"

"That had nothing to do with it!" Nanomia said. a little too touchy.

The interior was much like the outside. And the world in general. Plain, decrepit, lost in the past. The air was old, musty. It reminded him too much of his time in the Ashen Lands. Kilal passed a wobbly table with a layer of dust so thick he mistook it for a tablecloth.

In a corner, an old, rickety, spiraling staircase with holes in the steps awaited them. Requiem ascended without a protest from the steps. After lowering his gravity, Kilal's large form was able to take them in a similar silence. The same couldn't be said for those behind him.

He wasn't sure which was louder—the creak of the staircase beneath Allyria's feet or her squeak each time one groaned.

His trepidation rose the higher they ascended.

The second floor, similar to the first, greeted them with darkness. One window, cut into the wall to their right, was the only source of light. It was also the same opening Kilal had seen the figure standing in.

Requiem led them across the open room to a door with light peeking through the cracks. The hairs on Kilal's neck rose. It was so quiet Garret's nasally breathing turned grating. He should be able to hear conversation coming from the other room. Or movement. Anything. So why didn't he? Kilal stared at the back of Requiem's head.

Was the meeting an elaborate plan to kill him? Was she in league with Gabriel Sunsetter? Did she intend to finish what that oathbreaker started ten years ago?

Kilal started. Thankfully, the darkness hid it from the others.

What are you thinking? Requiem, in league with Sunsetter? And all this? If she wanted me dead, she would have ended me when she severed my bloody spine.

The wooden door creaked as Requiem pulled it open. Kilal gritted his teeth and barreled past her when the opening was wide enough. Whoever was in that room, their first impression of him after his decade hiatus wouldn't be of him cowering in the shadows.

The sudden change from darkness to light as he crossed the threshold blinded him. Kilal squinted. For a second, the people in the room were only blurry shapes. And in that heartbeat, he realized one important, possibly life-altering, fact: he had no idea what to say. Not that it mattered. His vision cleared, and under the scrutiny of dozens of eyes, some belonging to people he knew, he froze, palms sweaty.

Twelve humans surrounded a large wooden table. Jaws dropped, and eyes widened. A few gasps filled the silence, and utterances to Sha'tum followed.

Four blank faces belonged to the Arbiters Kilal didn't recognize. Among the other eight, their names, along with fond memories of each, raced through his mind.

Leyloni. She was an average-height woman with curly, brunette hair and green eyes. Two fingers were missing from her left hand, and her lips were stuck in a perpetual frown. A Mage, and a bloody powerful one.

Lemuel was a dark-skinned man with short-cropped hair. A pink scar stretched from his left cheek, over his nose, down his jaw, and disappeared beneath the collar of his shirt. He was an Arcanist who was deadly with a weapon, doubly so if wielding any type of polearm. Combining his weapons skill with the stone element to enhance his defenses made him all the more formidable.

Enoch, also known as the Whisperer, moved his lips silently, murmuring into the ear of a bald, plain man known as Enoch's Voice. Enoch was a Mentalist and a soft man who looked like he belonged in a kitchen or at home, raising four children. But it was all part of the illusion he created to be underestimated.

Kilal knew of a few who'd made the wrong choice to underestimate Enoch. One died from a brain hemorrhage.

He swallowed the groan bubbling in his throat. Enoch was never caught without his Carving active. The only way he safely spoke was through his Voice, another Mentalist who used a Carving that protected his mind from Enoch. No one knew why the bald man took that role upon himself; most assumed he was coerced. Kilal had even investigated the subject but came up empty-handed. He was never able to prove Enoch was forcing anything upon his Voice.

Of all the Arbiters to survive the last decade, of course Enoch had to be one of them.

Enoch only ever used one Carving. Its exact function was a mystery to all but him. Kilal assumed it gave the ability to enhance *others'* sense of hearing. It wasn't a popular opinion. Most thought Enoch could enhance his own voice, but Kilal had never known a Mind Carving to be able to do that.

When Enoch spoke, he was capable of anything from deafening any human within range to melting their brains. Kilal never understood why an Arbiter would choose to use a power that could only affect *humans.*

As his eyes hovered on Enoch's emotionless face, the familiar unease at his presence returned.

Emotion flooded Kilal. He was back. He was *home,* surrounded by his brothers and sisters. Ten years of exile, torture, pain, and suffering led him to this moment. He felt no shame or embarrassment for his tears. Those were his people, and he was finally reunited with them.

His knees gave out, and he collapsed.

Or would have, if a kick hadn't come out of nowhere, aimed right at his jaw.

~ CHAPTER 32 ~

Kilal pivoted, narrowly avoiding the kick. As the leg swept by, he grabbed it and jammed his other hand into the figure's chest. Locked tightly to the assailant's body, Kilal lifted and slammed them to the ground. His heart pounded. Adrenaline pulsed through his veins. His vision blurred, and all he saw was a threat beneath him.

Something attacked him, *there* of all places, surrounded by friends? Who would be foolish enough to do such a thing?

He scampered on top of them, placing a heavy knee against their sternum, leaning into the full weight of his two-hundred-and-seventy-pound frame. Kilal didn't stop there. He rammed his palm against the side of the opponent's chin and forced their head to the side.

Prepared to crush the person's skull in one brutal blow, he hauled a fist back—a hand grappled his wrist. Kilal whirled on whoever would dare interfere.

It was Requiem.

"He's not your enemy," she said softly. "He's an idiot, but he's not your enemy."

The chest Kilal knelt on spasmed, and a strange noise emitted from the man's mouth. Laughter? Bloodshed and Oaths, what was going on? When he took a second to analyze the situation, his chest brimmed with joy and bubbled out into his own embarrassed amusement.

"Alistair, you bloody, ash-eating son of a Plague!"

Kilal leapt off the man and pulled him into a warm embrace. They clasped each other, taking turns lifting the other up and squeezing until they grunted, giggling like adolescents the whole time.

"I give! I give!" Alistair gasped.

Kilal gave one more satisfying crunch before letting his friend down and pushing him at arm's length.

Alistair. How he'd missed the dark-skinned, bald, bearded man, nearly as tall as him but half as wide.

Like Kilal, Alistair was a Prime and one of the oldest Arbiters around. Not as old as Kilal, but a hundred years was nothing to scoff at. He'd been present for Alistair's Awakening when the man was ten years old. The moment it was revealed Alistair was a Prime, Kilal had taken the boy under his wing and become his mentor. Their friendship had been solidified ever since.

"I almost killed you!" he laughed.

Alistair shrugged. "You been gone ten years." Kilal forgot how much he missed the man's gravelly, country accent. "And even back then, you were far *beyond* yah prime. I was simply testin' the state of your ancientivity."

Kilal raised a brow. "Ancientivity? Is that your attempt at being polite? Well, are you going to tell me how I did?"

Alistair winced. It was a subtle thing, but Kilal did not miss it. His old friend was clearly concerned for him. "Failed. Had yah right where I wanted."

He burst into laughter. The idiot really *did* have him right where he'd wanted. If that had been a real fight, Alistair would have, at the very least, escaped, if not outright killed him.

Allyria stepped up to the two and studied them. "I don't think you had the upper hand. Kilal was about to break every bone in your face. Unless...is that what you mean by having the upper hand?" She looked from Kilal to Alistair and back.

"Is that some sort of game you play? First to bleed wins?"

Alistair stroked his beard. "You tellin' me you never heard of *the* Alistair Mountain-Breaker?"

Allyria placed her hands on her hips. "Nope."

He gasped, stepped back, and placed a hand over his heart.

"Don't be offended," Kilal said. "She also never heard of me."

"Bloodshed and Oaths, girl! This the first time you ever stepped outta wherever that hole is you grew up in?"

Before Allyria could respond, Garret stepped up beside her. "The Mountain-Breaker can manipulate any substance found naturally occurring in the wild." He tapped his foot against the floor. "Like stone."

She shrugged. "I don't see how that put Kilal at a disadvantage."

She's coming to my defense?

Alistair broke into a wide grin. "Who's this little flame?"

Allyria's hands curled into fists, and her cheeks turned a slight shade of red. "I'm *not* little. I'm taller than most of the people in this room."

He leveled a condescending look at her. "I was referrin' to your ego, little flame."

Allyria's face turned crimson. "You better hope that nickname doesn't stick," she growled before storming back to stand at Nanomia's side. Alistair's chuckle followed her the whole way.

"My turn," a soft, velvety voice said.

Alistair's eyes widened as he was lifted off the ground and tossed aside. He landed unceremoniously on his side with a loud grunt. The aggressor was a young woman with tear-stained cheeks.

"Violet," Kilal said with a warm smile. He opened his arms, and she rushed into them, wrapping her own around him.

"Uncle," she said, voice muffled by his shirt.

He'd first met Violet while hunting two notorious serial killers. The Twins, the media had labeled them. Violet's sister had been one of their victims.

Back then, Violet was still known by her birth name, Martha. Their paths crossed on one particularly gloomy night when Kilal had been hot on the Twins' trail. Violet, too, had been hunting them. She'd been young, twenty-two. Kilal had tried to convince her to go home, that he would deal with the Twins, but she wouldn't be turned aside. Against his better judgment, he let her join him, his justification being if she was going to go after the Twins, it would be better if he was with her.

Together, they found the serial killers. Violet demanded revenge and insisted on killing them. When Kilal refused, arguing to bring them to the authorities, she'd attacked *him*.

The brother-sister killer duo managed to escape because of Violet's interference. They killed four more times before Kilal caught up with them again. They were executed a week later. Violet blamed herself for those four deaths and clung to Kilal's side like an extra appendage.

Because of her attachment to him, Violet never held Requiem in high regard, despite his wife taking the young girl under her wing and mentoring her. The beginning of their relationship was rocky, but as Violet matured, she became an admirable lady and Arbiter.

When Lilliana entered the picture, she'd taken to Violet as if the purple-eyed woman were an older sister.

Admirable or not, Kilal would have to be careful with the news of Lilliana's present predicament. More so even than himself, Violet didn't take the loss of a close one well. She never did talk about what happened to her sister, but whatever it was impacted her in a life-altering way.

After the death of the Twins, Violet had taken her sister's name. A remembrance of the similarity she and her sister had shared: their violet eyes. Or so she'd said. Kilal never met her sister, and despite knowing Violet for over forty years, that was the only thing he knew of her sibling.

Kilal gave her a final squeeze before separating. There

were so many Arbiters from his past that were important to him. He counted himself blessed for each that had survived his absence, and Violet was near the top of that list.

"I missed you," she said softly and only for his ears. "I never doubted you'd return. When everyone else gave up on you, I didn't."

"Thank you," he said, brushing a freshly fallen tear from her cheek. "But I'm back now, and I wo..." he trailed off, recalling Requiem's rebuke of making promises.

I promised Requiem I'd return with Lilliana.

Kilal scanned her face. There was something different about her. "Your hair!" Her brunette hair was styled with one side longer than the other. "It looks really good!" In all his time knowing Violet, she'd never once done anything about her appearance. No fancy hairstyles, no makeup, no jewelry. Such things had never interested her.

A grin flashed onto her deceptively youthful face, and for a moment Kilal hoped she could get her mind out of the past and into the present.

"You can thank me," Alistair said, still lying on the floor. "I finally convinced her to take care of herself. We were all gettin' *so* tired of her mopin' around and actin' like the world was endin'."

Kilal winced. Did the man have to be so unaware of the possible impact of his phrasing? Alistair didn't mean them the way they sounded, but he would have thought the century-old Arbiter would've come to some understanding of how to choose words wisely.

Looks like some things really never change.

Fortunately, Violet didn't seem bothered, so Kilal kept silent.

"So," she said, looking back at the entrance Allyria had stormed out of. "Where is she? Where's my little shadow? She's got to be all grown...up...by...." Violet's dark skin paled with each passing word.

Kilal rubbed the budding tears from his eyes. "She's..." How could he explain it? "Not here."

Alistair leaped to his feet. All the mirth and levity were gone. "Then what the bloody ashes are we doin' sittin' around here? Let's go get her!" He seemed to understand the reality of what Kilal *didn't* say.

"One thing at a time, Alistair," Requiem interjected. "We have other matters to deal with right now."

Alistair and Violet recoiled. He beat her to the punch and spoke first. "One thing...other matters...This is my bloody niece you're so cavalierly talkin' about!"

"You don't think I know that!" Requiem said, turning a deadly glare on him.

The two looked like they were about to exchange blows. Kilal didn't want to see who would come out the winner. He forced them to step back by pushing in between them.

"Trust me," he placed a hand on Alistair's shoulder, "I know how you feel. But I came back for a reason."

Alistair exhaled a long breath from flared nostrils before nodding. "Where were you? I almost got myself a little concerned."

Kilal faced the rest of the room and noticed, for the first time, Ahnk leaning in a corner beside an opening in the wall allowing a cool breeze through. He gave Kilal a brief nod, which he reciprocated. Some of the guilt slipped off him. It seemed he'd worried more about Ahnk's safe return than he realized.

"I'm glad to see you made it out safely."

A mischievous smile slid onto the man's narrow face. "And with no broken bones."

Kilal wished he had more time to greet each member, but Alistair's reminder of Lilliana's present fate urged him to keep moving. He'd have time enough for hugs and stories once he had his daughter back.

In the center of the room was a large, wooden, circular table with twelve chairs. Kilal strode over and pressed his palms on the surface.

"For the last ten years, I've been trapped in the Ashen Lands."

~ CHAPTER 33 ~

The room erupted in a cacophony of gasps and questions. Kilal let them babble as he took a seat at the table. He couldn't deny the warmth and familiarity blooming in his chest. To be back, surrounded by Arbiters, fellowshipping, planning, and communing, was something he'd dreamed of for so long. Sitting there, he realized how much he'd taken moments like those for granted.

Never again.

Requiem took the seat to his left, and Alistair the seat to his right. Everyone else seemed to take that as their cue to be silent and sit as well. Everyone except Ahnk, who remained leaning against the corner, Allyria, who stood behind Kilal, resting against his chair, and Enoch, who remained at the one porthole in the room, gazing out at the Veil and the dying land around it. Even Nanomia and Garret joined them.

The table was large, capable of seating twenty comfortably. Each empty seat was a loss Kilal internalized as his fault.

If only I'd been here.

Enoch snapped his finger, and his Voice approached. He allowed the plain man to whisper something into his ear.

When Enoch was done, his Voice straightened. "You disappeared for ten years. We have lost many brothers and sisters during that time." Enoch continued to stare out of the porthole

as if the words he 'spoke' weren't bloody hurtful. "Now you return, claiming you've been in the *Ashen Lands*? Can you think
of nothing better to justify your absence? Or did enough of us
finally die to warrant your grand return?"

Requiem hissed, and Alistair made to rise. Kilal held an
arm up, stopping his friend.

Violet either didn't see Kilal's gesture or didn't care. "Bloodshed and Oaths, man! How dare you!" she snapped. The air
around her shimmered.

Enoch finally faced the group, but only long enough to give
Violet a nasty smile. A taunt.

"I see ten years hasn't improved your charisma," Kilal said.
It was awkward to talk to the back of Enoch's head. He flared
his nostrils and curled his lip. "If you *ever* insinuate, allude to,
or downright say I had anything to do with my brothers and
sisters' deaths, I'll tear your tongue out."

The room froze.

Copper tickled his tongue. The source was unexpecting.

"And if that doesn't teach you your lesson," Allyria growled.
"I'll...I'll...rip something else off of you!"

Kilal turned his hulking body around in the too-small
chair to stare in wonder at her. If he thought he'd given Enoch
a nasty look, Allyria's was putting his to shame. And as clumsy
as she sounded trying to be tough, there wasn't a hint of pink
in her cheeks.

When she caught him staring, he winked. A slight grin was
her response.

Violet smirked and returned to her seat, seeming content.
Kilal, too, was content with the turn of events.

Every hour that went by, he grew fonder of the redhead.
For a moment, he almost hoped Enoch would test their threats.
He was very curious to see what Allyria would 'rip off.'

One of Enoch's Arbiters, an unfamiliar face, shot to her
feet and pointed at Kilal. Or was it at Allyria? "You always let
your *pets* fight your battles for you?"

Kilal smirked. "Only the battles I don't consider worth my time."

"Like you," Allyria growled.

The female Arbiter seemed about to burst a blood vessel. Kilal readied himself for an attack.

That wasn't how his return was supposed to go.

A slap on the table echoed in his ears and took the attention off of him.

"Enough," Requiem said coolly, looking at the still-standing, red-faced woman. "This is *not* what we are here for. Understand?"

The other Arbiter nodded curtly and hurried to retake her seat.

Kilal eyed Requiem with bewilderment. Did she just take control of the situation with barely any effort? And if Kilal didn't know any better, he'd say the other woman had responded with *fear*. Of Requiem.

The grating scratch of his nails raking his scruffy jaw filled the room.

Enoch snapped his finger again. Kilal prepared himself for whatever response would be needed.

The Voice drew in a deep breath. From his time with Enoch, which was more than he wished, his Voice presented not just the words but also the mannerisms in which Enoch spoke. "Ten years." Another intake of breath, this time much sharper than the first. "Have you really been in the Ashen Lands?"

At least any sense of doubt or condescension had been abandoned.

Kilal readjusted his seat, using the motion to mask a wave of anxiety. With everything that had happened over the last few days, it was easy to forget that last week, he was escaping from the Tower of Eyes. He'd never truly recover the sanity he lost in the ash-covered land, but with so little time separating him from his decade-long ordeal, the most he could hope for was resilience.

Where do I start?

Even though he recognized two-thirds of the Arbiters around the table, he only really knew a few of them. Besides Alistair and Requiem, Leyloni, Lemuel, and Violet were the other three he'd spent many years with. And Enoch. Unfortunately, Enoch. The four with the Whisperer, though, he didn't recognize. Ahnk he knew of, but had only just met.

Even though Kilal never understood or agreed with the way Arbiters presented themselves, it was a fact that they dressed or held themselves in a manner causing them to stick out in a crowd. Blondie, Tattoos, and Trench Coat were extreme examples of that, but whether it was their clothes or physical features, Arbiters were always easy to spot.

Violet had bright purple irises. Allyria had her striking red eyes and matching hair. Ahnk's thing was his unnaturally perfect teeth and captivating smile. There was the way Requiem held herself, not to mention the scars. Even Kilal, though he tried his best to look as normal as possible, couldn't hide that he was always the largest human in the room. Even plain-looking Enoch had an aura that made anyone wary of him.

Simply put, it was impossible to hide that an Arbiter was... well...an Arbiter. Or at least, Kilal thought so.

The final Arbiter in the room he knew only as Forest. The green tattoo of a tree on his left cheek gave him away. Like his name implied, Forest's mastery of the Elemental branch, complemented by the use of Mind Carvings, made him the bane of many Ash Fallen when met in the wild. In the city... not so much.

Even considering Garret, Nanomia, and Allyria, for the most part, Kilal was surrounded by men and women he knew and trusted. So why was he so apprehensive about sharing his ordeal? His chest tightened and his pulse quickened. He was short of breath.

Get a hold of yourself!

A flake of ash swirled before him, followed by another. And another.

Not now!

"Why don't we share with Kilal what has happened while he's been gone?" Ahnk said. His voice was silvery and crisp, unnaturally so, but Kilal didn't sense the use of a Carving. Maybe the man was just that smooth. Either way, he couldn't look at Ahnk, no matter how grateful he was for his intervention.

"You're right."

Kilal didn't see who spoke; his eyes were planted firmly on his thighs. But he'd never forget that deep voice capable of vibrating his very bones.

"You probably don't recognize the land you worked so hard to protect," Lemuel said.

"*We* protected," Kilal corrected.

"Wait," Enoch's Voice said after the snap of a finger. "We may know you, Immortal Arbiter, but we don't know the three with you. Before we reveal our information and risk it traveling back to the Heirs, they will be tested."

"Tested? How do you propose to do that?"

One of Enoch's men stood. He was a sloppy fellow with thinning hair, a splotchy beard, and a gut hanging over his belt.

"Truth Seeking," Enoch's Voice said.

Kilal's eyes nearly bulged from his head. He shot to his feet, knocking his chair over. "You will *not* use such a Carving in my presence!"

A light touch on his back gave him pause. Requiem looked disappointed, but not with him. All the air rushed from his lungs. She agreed with it?

"I know it was banned," she said, "but things have changed. A dozen or so of us were killed in a raid after our second official meeting as the resistance. Killed because one of us was working with the Heirs. We didn't decide to utilize Truth Seeking lightly, but we also didn't see any other choice around it."

"It was either that," Enoch's Voice said, "or risk more

deaths because we refused to use a tool that could help preserve our own lives."

Kilal narrowed his eyes and ground his teeth, but he didn't
have any reason to dispute their logic. The time they were in
was more different than any an Arbiter had faced. Unfortunately, it made sense to use a Carving that would have been
considered illegal before. But he didn't have to like it.

"Fine. But you'll test me as well."

Enoch smiled, and his Voice said, "Of course."

Kilal gestured for the three younglings to rise and come to
him. They stood in a line, shoulder to shoulder.

"Answer truthfully," he said as the balding man approached.
"He'll know if you don't. And answer quickly. If you try to fight
the coercion, it'll be...painful, to say the least."

Kilal turned to the man who would question them. "Your
name?"

"Trale."

He nodded. "Proceed."

Trale nodded too and turned to Nanomia. "Do you currently work for, in any fashion, the Heirs of the Promise?"

"No."

"Are your loyalties with the Heirs of the Promise?"

"No."

"Where do your loyalties lie?"

Kilal ground his teeth. Yes and no questions were one
thing, but using the Carving to seek out other information was
immoral at best, dangerous at worst.

Nanomia didn't hesitate. "Myself." She flippantly waved a
hand in front of her. "Myself."

It wasn't a terrible answer, but it wasn't a good one either.

Trale looked to Enoch, who shrugged and gestured for
him to continue. The same first two questions were asked of
Garret, with the same answers as Nanomia.

"Where do your loyalties lie?"

The boy paused. He looked around the room, hesitating

on Kilal before returning to Trale. "The Keepers of the Oath."

Kilal smiled.

Trale nodded before continuing to Allyria. "Do you currently work for, in any fashion, the Heirs of the Promise?"

"You think I'd bloody well be here if I did?"

Kilal hid a smile behind a feigned yawn.

Trale wasn't as impressed. "Answer the question."

"Bloodshed and Oaths, no!"

"Are your loyalties with the Heirs of the Promise?"

"Not bloody likely."

"Answer th—"

"No! No, they're not."

"Where do your loyalties lie?"

Allyria flicked her eyes toward Kilal so quickly he almost missed it. Her face blossomed like a tomato. "I...I...WhoeverisagainsttheHeirsofthePromise." Her answer came out rushed and without a pause between each word.

All eyes turned to Enoch, waiting. Eventually, he nodded, and Trale turned to Kilal. His answer was the same for the first two questions, though his third was slightly different.

"The Keepers and *our* oath."

The tension in the room seemed to dissolve as the questions finished. But the buzzing in his ears, the sensation indicating a Mind Carving was in use, remained.

"Where have you *really* been the last ten years?" Enoch's Voice asked.

Trale rushed the question out, copying Enoch's word for word before anyone could say anything.

The tension returned in a flash.

Kilal's fury grew. It was one thing to use the rune to verify they were all in a safe place; it was another to weed out whatever information you wanted from whoever you wanted.

He leaned forward, resting his knuckles against the stone tabletop, and looked past the interrogator to bare teeth at Enoch. "You're crossing a line you *don't* want to cross," he said through clenched teeth.

Trale visibly swallowed. A bead of sweat trickled down his forehead. "Answer the question."

Another reason the Carving was banned was because of the consequences of not answering a question asked under it.

Kilal's body tensed, his muscles spasming and twitching. His fists clenched so hard his nails dug into his palms, drawing blood.

"Answer the question," Trale said again.

Kilal became a mass of tension and pain as violent shakes took over his body. He kept his teeth clamped shut, fighting his jaw's impulse to open and speak the words demanded of him.

Enoch met his eyes, and the passivity in them, the lack of empathy, infuriated him. Blood trickled from Kilal's ears. Enoch could order the question to be rescinded, but despite the pain he was clearly in, Enoch appeared content to let him suffer until he answered.

Kilal's Carving of Immortality kicked in, covering him in a twisted armor of flashing white energy. It worked to heal the damage the other rune was causing, but even immortality soon wouldn't be enough to save him. Truth Seeking couldn't kill him, but it could keep him in a constant state of agony. Arbiters had once used it to torture information from other people, their own kind and civilians alike. But Kilal's anger at such abuse was enough to help him endure.

Until a hand on his back caused him to fight the stiffness in his neck to turn and look at the source.

Requiem stared at him, eyes hard. "Answer the question."

It was her willingness to let him be hurt in such a way, to verify where he'd been that caused him to give in. His determination to resist fizzled. He would have sagged forward if his body wasn't tight with cramps and mini-seizures.

"The Ashen Lands," he said. At once, the pain ceased.

The room was quiet, all eyes on him, despite none of them meeting his gaze. Even Alistair looked away, embarrassed.

Others ranged from outrage to shock to apathy. No one spoke up to denounce what just happened.

Requiem wouldn't meet his gaze.

"Thank you. Let's continue," Enoch's Voice said as if he hadn't just endorsed the torture of a fellow Arbiter.

Kilal propelled himself over and across the table in one powerful lunge. He had Enoch's face in his hand before anyone could react. He squeezed Enoch's jaw shut and slammed him against the wall, holding him there. The man dangled a foot off the ground. But even at the mercy of Kilal, who could kill him with a quick flick of the wrist, Enoch looked like *he* was the one in control.

Shouts of outrage rang out, but no one rushed to Enoch's defense.

He kept apathetic eyes on Kilal. He knew Kilal wouldn't kill him because Kilal had morals. Bloodshed and Oaths, in that moment he hated that about himself. But even Kilal had lines that shouldn't be crossed, couldn't be crossed.

"I was willing to allow the use of a banned Carving if it meant potentially saving lives. But you just proved why it should stay banned. If I find out you use that again on anyone else, I'll kill you and whoever uses it."

With Enoch still pressed against the wall, he turned to face the rest of the room. "You've all been warned. We find a better way to test the loyalty of newcomers. No exceptions."

He didn't wait for a response. He wouldn't allow any negotiations.

Truth Seeking *would not* be used. Period.

Enoch dropped gracefully to his feet when Kilal opened his hand. Without another word, Kilal returned to his seat.

Allyria smiled brightly at him and gave him a thumbs up. He couldn't help but smile back.

"I was surprised to see the state of Silent Haven when I returned," he said, breaking the tension and silence. "Homeless people on the streets. Abandoned buildings taken over by the homeless, most of which are hopeless drug addicts. The Right of Recompense all but forgotten. The citizens are more openly hostile toward Arbiters than I've ever experienced. Bounties on Arbiters being paid in aznium. Worship of Sha'tum banned. The holy place desolate and run down, its Mother living in squalor. And the obvious one...the Heirs.

"Ashes! What happened here?"

Enoch snapped his finger, and everyone remained silent while he spoke to his translator.

"Because you left a void which needed filling. And Wolfe, Fazin, Tor'et, and Sienna filled it."

"No," Kilal said. "That's not good enough. The Heirs showed up *five years* after Lilliana and I disappeared. If it was a simple matter of a power vacuum, why did they wait so long?"

Violet drummed purple fingernails on the tabletop. When had she started painting them? "The moment you were gone, the bloody vacuum formed. The Keepers weren't enough to maintain order among the less reputable Arbiters in Silent Haven. We were forced to turn our full attention inward. This left New Cita and Vitrol void of the little Keeper influence we had there.

"It started small at first; ash-eating Arbiters began testing the limits. A robbery here, a rumor of a bribe there, Arbiters offering their services for pay. We did what we could to...*incentivize*...them to maintain their bloody oath, as well as the citizens to abstain from dealings with Arbiters like that. But we didn't bloody make much headway." She grimaced and paused.

Lemuel's deep voice filled the quiet. "A year after you disappeared, these small dealings escalated. A few banks were robbed by Arbiters. There were rumors of assassinations. Establishments like small stores and businesses were forced to 'hire' Arbiters for protection."

"Bloodshed and Oaths!" Violet growled. "Bloody Arbiters became nothing more than lowly thugs forcing bloody payments from small bloody businesses to keep them from destroying their bloody livelihoods. And the sons of Plagues had the audacity to call it 'protection.'"

"Blackmailing small businesses turned into large businesses," Lemuel continued, emotion building on his face. Despite his chiseled jaw and stoic persona, Lemuel was one of the softest men Kilal had ever had the privilege of knowing. He was recalling events from over half a decade ago, but for him, and probably most in the room, the wounds hadn't healed. "The Governing Seats were the next to be targeted. A few of the good ones ran into 'mysterious circumstances' and disappeared. The Seats who hadn't disappeared allied themselves with the oathbreakers.

"That's when the Right of Recompense was abolished. Tensions rose in the streets. Arbiters, if found alone, were attacked. Some killed. Didn't matter if they were a good one or a bloody oathbreaker."

"Things got bad. Real bad," Requiem picked up the tale when Lemuel paused for breath. "The whole city was ready to burst, and when it did, no one would rise the victor." She crossed her arms and stared at the stone ceiling. "We were forced to make decisions none of us were prepared to make."

Sitting to her left, Kilal could only see the twisted mass of scars on that side of her face. Since entering the abandoned barracks, she'd removed her hoodie.

A smile, inappropriate for the topic at hand, slipped onto his lips.

She's comfortable here. This is her family, and she doesn't feel the need to hide who she is.

No one in the room stared at Requiem. No one even seemed to notice the scarring.

Of course they don't, you idiot! They weren't just reunited with her a day ago.

"We were trying to handle the situation as peacefully as possible," she said. "We approached the Governing Seats. We pleaded with the populace, and even the oathbreakers."

"There are so few of us left," Violet jumped in, looking at Kilal, "killing our brothers and sisters just couldn't be an option."

Was she seeking his approval? The way everyone looked at him, at least the five he would consider among his closest friends, he couldn't escape the impression they wanted—*craved*—his support for their actions, which was ridiculous. They didn't need his approval. Each of those five, and from what he knew of Ahnk and Forest, were better men and women than he'd ever been. The last thing they needed was validation from *him*.

"Until it was the only option," Requiem said. She uncrossed her arms. Placing her hands beneath her thighs, she shuddered.

So, there's still compassion and kindness beneath that cold, hard exterior.

Kilal placed his own hands beneath the table and, hidden, dug his nails into his palms until he bled. It was an unfair thought, and one he hoped to never share with the woman he had fought so hard to return to. Of course there was still compassion and kindness in her. It was who she was, and that would never change!

A finger snapped.

"Fear was the only thing that kept the oathbreakers lurking in their dank holes," Enoch's Voice said. "When that... fear...was no longer present, they skittered out of whatever pit they'd been hiding in. And only fear would send them back."

Requiem and Enoch shared a look and a nod. Kilal, more inquisitive than most, noticed what others may not have, or what they already knew. The depth of respect Requiem and Enoch shared for one another. It was...surprising. She'd never cared for him and his willingness, almost enjoyment, of dealing brutally with any who forsook their oath. The two of them had never liked the pale, fragile Arbiter. But the way she nodded to him now, almost in agreement, drove Kilal into a deep curiosity.

Lemuel cleared his throat. "Not all of us agreed with that sentiment," he growled.

"And more of us died because of the...disagreement." Enoch smiled as his voice spoke.

Lemuel slammed a fist against the table, but a hand on his shoulder from Violet calmed him. Their shared expression was similar to the one between Requiem and Enoch.

So, there is a rift here. Some wish to kill the oathbreakers, and others disagree.

Kilal kept his mouth shut. He wouldn't give into the inquisitive eyes and open ears waiting to hear which side he was on. He was never for killing Arbiters, despite the dark part of himself still tucked away deep inside. But as he discovered with Trench Coat, Crave, Inferno, the blade master, and Jasper, sometimes it was the only option.

"Some would say the *wrong* Arbiters died," Lemuel said, casting a glare of pure hatred at Enoch.

Enoch's eyes gleamed with a mischievous glimmer. As his Voice repeated his whispered words, Enoch held his arms out wide, an invitation to Lemuel and any who would stand with the bearded Arbiter.

"You may always attempt to make good on the many threats you've leveled my way. I will not stray from my convictions. A rabid dog cannot be saved. It can only be put down."

Kilal hated that he and Enoch shared the same analogy when it came to oathbreakers.

Lemuel and Leyloni shot to their feet. Leyloni? She was as quiet and non-confrontational as they came.

"How dare you refer to our brothers and sisters as *dogs*," she shrieked, eyes shifting from clarity to insanity with each word.

"Maybe it's you who should be put down!" Lemuel said, pointing at Enoch.

Once again, the room erupted into a cacophony of voices, screaming threats of violence and hate. Enoch's four Arbiters against Lemuel and Leyloni. Violet joined the fray, but from the bits and pieces Kilal could pick out, it had nothing to do with the disagreement and more to do with just being violent.

Alistair and Requiem raised their voices, trying to get everyone to calm down.

It wasn't working.

Kilal sat quietly, hands on his lap. The voices—his own voices—rose up, excited to have others to play with.

Your fault! If only you'd been here! If only you'd listened! Die! Die! DIE!

He bolted to his feet and smashed a fist on the table, cracking it into two. It collapsed inward with a loud bang.

Everyone stared in stunned silence.

"How have you all not been killed yet?" he said, lips curling with each word. "No wonder Wolfe and the others were able to walk into our land and take it; you're a bunch of children!"

"That's just not fair, Kilal, we—"

"I've been *trapped* in the Ashen Lands for *ten years*," Kilal pressed on, cutting Alistair off. "I've spent that time fighting for my life. Every. Single. Day." He looked for something else to break, but the split chunks of the large, circular table gave him pause. Instead, he walked to a square opening in the wall and pointed at the looming black curtain of violent energy. "Just beyond the Veil, an army is gathering so big, when it crosses, it *will* kill everyone. We won't be able to stop it. Our existence is on a clock, and our time is almost up.

"I returned, abandoning my search for Lilliana, who may be dead for all I know, to prepare my land! My people—you!" He looked at each Arbiter in turn until they met his eyes. "My brothers and sisters. And for what? To rally a bunch of bickering teenagers? You all should be ashamed of yourselves! We're on the verge of extinction. Not just Arbiters, but *humanity*."

The rage, the passion, his energy, his desire, it all left him, sucked from him in one violent realization.

"I shouldn't have returned." His voice, like his spirit, was devoid of emotion. "I lost Jayden. I lost Lilliana. My sanity. My family. Everything." He focused on the group before him, realizing he was mumbling to himself. But he didn't care. "We're dead."

Ash descended from the stone ceiling.

Kilal held out his hands, revealing the emptiness in them, and shrugged. "We're all dead."

The echo of his footsteps lingered in his wake as he abandoned the room.

Another pair, much softer and lighter than his, followed.

~ CHAPTER 34 ~

The Veil crackled and popped; white and black energy zipped and twisted all about the dark surface like some dance only it was knowledgeable of.

From atop the ramparts of the roof, Kilal could see everything over the half-mile between the barracks and the barrier. All objects capable of hindering sight were torn down when the structure was first erected. No trees, no boulders, no small hills or man-made architecture of any kind. *Nothing* could pierce the Veil without being detected.

Or at least, there was a time when nothing could pierce the Veil without being detected. But that ended a long time ago.

Despite the lack of large objects, both alive and not, Kilal imagined there used to be grass, maybe even various plants of a short height, in the kill zone between barracks and Veil. But the spreading corruption and the Ashen Lands behind the wall had sapped most of the life from the land in the open space.

Stretching from the barracks, there were a few dozen feet of thin greenery, but it quickly faded into rock and dirt.

There were concerns among the populace of the Sunlight Domain, particularly the scientists, that eventually the corruption at the Veil would reach so far inland it would affect the food supply of the citizens. No grass meant no food for cattle, which meant no food for humans. Kilal didn't agree with the fear-inducing conclusion. Yes, eventually the spread of corruption *would* result in the eradication of mankind. But that would happen in thousands of years. The Veil had been up for one thousand already, and there was less than a half-mile of lifeless ground.

Mankind's extinction, either by their own hands or by the army across the Veil, would happen much sooner.

Kilal slumped against the waist-high stone wall, grateful for the solid structure keeping him up.

"Why do you feel so defeated?" he asked himself quietly. "You knew things would be different. And you knew it wouldn't matter. You have a mission. Wolfe, Enoch, the Keepers, none of them matter if I don't stop Ashen Kane. If I don't, we'll all be dead, anyway. So why?"

"You created the Keepers, didn't you?"

He started. Allyria walked up beside him and leaned against the wall too. Her height was still strange to him; she stood nearly to his shoulder.

"I did."

She stared at the Veil, eyes never staying still as they took in the monstrous barrier. What had it been like for him the first time he saw it? Was he impressed? Scared? Awed? He wished he could remember, but that was a time he tried to avoid revisiting.

"The group of orphans who betrayed me, I brought them together," Allyria said, eyes still on the Veil. "If it wasn't for me, who knows what would've happened to them? That's why it hurt so much when they turned on me. Maybe that's why you feel so defeated. You only just found out that what you created was destroyed. And what's left seems to be more interested in bickering about their differences than uniting. I bet it hurts. A lot." She twisted her face into a mixture of disgust and confusion. "And what's with that Enoch guy? He's *so* creepy!"

Kilal wasn't quick to respond. She was right.

Instead, he gave her a little push on the shoulder and a

knowing smile. "You know, you're wiser than most of the adults I know. Or knew. I think I'll keep you."

He hadn't thought his words were going to be that impactful, but the way she blushed and looked everywhere but at him revealed the truth. And the moisture in her eyes. That too.

"Thank you," she said.

It was enough.

"Hope I ain't interuptin' none." Alistair approached. The rampart was becoming a popular place to be.

Allyria quickly rubbed at her eyes, keeping her back to him. "You are!" she said indignantly.

Alistair raised a brow at Kilal. "My grandest apologies, little flame, but I too am here to cheer up the most infamous of infamouses, the Lord of Scowls. What say we team up for this endeavor, shall we? This one is notoriously difficult to cheer up. We're all gamblin' he operates a fourth Carvin', which keeps him in a perpetual mood of the dankest grumpiness. But we must not be deterred by this. Defeat is not an option."

Kilal scowled. Allyria giggled.

"Whose side are you on?"

Alistair and Allyria exchanged smiles before he answered with, "The side of truth!" She nodded along with him as if she'd been saying the same thing for years.

Alistair's mood flipped from levity and joviality to somber in an instant; a swing Kilal was all too familiar with. He squeezed between Allyria and Kilal, forcing her to take a few steps back, and joined them on the wall.

"You're too hard on them," Allistair said quietly.

"Too hard? Did you see the way they fought? Don't we already have enough enemies?"

Alistair wheeled on him, jamming a finger into his broad chest. "And that's your problem. If the little flame weren't here, I'd crack that thick skull of yours right here and now. You spent an hour with us, and you've already determined we've failed? Who's the bad guy, and who isn't?

"Of course I saw! I've been seein' it for five years. And you know what?" He jammed a finger into Kilal's chest again, forcing him to take a step back and away from the wall. His sternum cracked and there was a jolt of pain, both from the mild injury and the following healing. "No matter what, we've always got each other's backs.

"Enoch's a frustratin' son of a Plague, but if there's one thin' I can count on in this world, it's his hatred for the Heirs of the Promise. Just like you, just like the rest of us, he's lost as much as everyone else. It ain't fair to any of us for you to show up after ten years and think you can just take over.

"I believe ya when you say you've been in the bloody Ashen Lands, and I can't imagine what you've been through. But it ain't been all daisies and picnics for us, either. You've just found out your friends and family are all but destroyed. That pain is fresh for you. But ya know what? It's still fresh for me, too.

"Bloodshed and Oaths, I *lived* through it! I watched Cinder *melt*. I saw Juniper get his bloody head ripped off by that she-Plague, Sienna. I was there when they invaded our headquarters and murdered dozens of us. It may have been five years ago, but there ain't a night I don't see them when I close my eyes. And Requiem...well, you should talk to her yourself. I don't think any of us would be here if it weren't for her."

Was Alistair rebuking him? And after a ten-year hiatus? Kilal didn't know if he should be proud of his former mentee or annoyed. Either way, like Allyria, Alistair was right, and each word he threw at him cut deep.

Alistair sighed before continuing. "What I'm tryin' to say is, don't write us off. Not yet. You're back! The bloody-Immortal Arbiter is back! We should be celebratin', not lamentin' our future."

Allyria swung her head from Kilal to Alistair with eyes nearly as large as the moons.

Kilal sighed. "It's been so long since I've been around other Arbiters. I think I forgot what it was like." He rapped his knuckles against the stone wall. A breeze, cooled by the sinking sun, brushed his skin. "I thought when I returned, everything would be as it used to be. And I keep thinking it can be like that again. But it can't, can it?"

Alistair shook his head and exhaled loudly. "Well, I'd be lyin' if I said I ain't sorry."

"I just..." Kilal paused. His eyes on the black curtain so many of their ancestors had died to erect. "I just don't want to accept that. But I need to. I'm not in charge anymore. This isn't my land. Silent Haven is no longer my city. Ashes, these aren't even my people anymore. And I was wrong for thinking they were."

Kilal clapped Alistair on the back far harder than he should have. But after the rebuke he'd just received and the way Alistair ungraciously lurched forward, it was worth it. "Now that I've been thoroughly reprimanded," he said, ignoring the grumbles of 'that wasn't very necessary,' "I think I'm ready to resume our gathering."

He nodded to Allyria. "Come on, lit—"

"Don't even start that!"

Kilal grinned. "Come on, *Allyria*. I think we have a meeting to observe."

~ CHAPTER 35 ~

The first thing Kilal noticed upon re-entering the room, besides Requiem's eyes following him all the way back to his chair, was the fully restored table.

Someone has some rendition of a Regrowth Carving activated.

He couldn't help himself from instinctually analyzing each Arbiter in the room and the threat level they represented with this new knowledge.

Stop it! These are your friends and allies. They don't deserve to be thought of as prospective enemies.

Except he didn't know anything about the four Arbiters with Enoch. And a decade had gone by. A lot could've happened in that time. A lot *had* happened in that time. He'd already recognized Requiem wasn't the same person she'd been before. It would be safe to assume the others were different as well.

So how did he trust, unconditionally, when he didn't know them anymore?

He just had to because he didn't have any other option.

Alistair took the seat beside him, and Allyria clung to the wall, slowly inching her way closer to Ahnk, who still stood in the corner.

The tension in the room had dissipated to the point that Lemuel was actually talking to one of Enoch's men. Lemuel broke into booming laughter.

Maybe Alistair was right. Maybe he had been too hard on them.

Kilal vowed to not open his mouth again until it was his turn to talk. Recently, it seemed the more he spoke, the more apparently his lack of manners and common decency he'd obtained in the Ashen Lands became.

Bloodshed and Oaths. He couldn't be that hard on himself. If there was one thing he'd recognized over his long life, it was that trauma was never easy to overcome. And whether he wanted to admit it or not, the last ten years of his life had been nothing but traumatic.

"I think the Immortal Grumpiness has had his fair fillin' of updates for now," Alistair said. "I'm sure I can catch him up on anything else after this. If I was a gamblin' man, which I most certainly am, I think we're all dying to hear—besides what Kilal's been up to—what happened with our favoritest Arbiters, Ahnk and Requiem, over the last few days. I'm sure everyone has noticed how giddy and excited Ahnk has been since returnin'. The fool's looked like he's 'bout to piss himself."

"I think *annoying* would be a better adjective," Violet said, rolling her eyes.

"Dear Violet," Ahnk said in a whimsical tone. "How could I be anything but giddy and excited when returning to such a beautiful woman as you?"

He was attempting to joke and poke fun at her, but Kilal could glean the truth of the matter from the twinkle in Ahnk's eyes when he looked at her.

Violet scrunched her face and growled, "Say that again, and your jaw won't work for a week."

He laughed. "What is it with you Arbiters and your Physical Carvings? Is violence the only way you know how to solve anything?"

"Yes, it is," Requiem said, turning an eye to Kilal.

Ahnk let out a long, exaggerated sigh. "Fine then. If you'd

prefer me to not make mention of your stunning beauty, then I promise I'll try my hardest to not see what is plainly before our very eyes. However, in the end, to honor your request, I may just have to take extreme action. These eyes of mine have served me well, but our time together may need to come to an end."

"Allow me the honor," Violet said in a threatening voice. She might have the others fooled, but the slight reddening of her cheeks said more to Kilal about her true feelings than any word could.

Good for her. She deserves some happiness.

He let his gaze linger on Ahnk's handsome face. There was an innocence in those eyes most Arbiters no longer had. There could be worse options. But if he ever found out Ahnk was misusing his Carving to influence Violet to do things against her will, he'd kill him.

The only reason Ahnk's power hadn't been banned too was because *no one* but him knew it. And, from all reports, many from trusted sources, Ahnk was a good man, better than most. He would never misuse the Carving.

But if he did...it would be his last time.

"To be fair," Ahnk said, brushing a lock of hair from his eyes, "it's Requiem who found the intel. Once we became aware of Sienna's presence, we didn't exactly have the time to share what we read, between fending off Sienna and destroying the trove of books. So, I'll let her take over from here." He flourished a bow to Requiem. "The floor is yours, m'lady."

"Thank you," she said, voice flat. "But first, I'd like to catch Kilal up on the events leading to our capture." She rearranged her chair so she could face him. "A little over two years ago, Enoch got the bright idea that there was more to our world than we knew. Where Sienna, Tor'et, Wolfe, Fazin came from. Their mysterious powers and the stones they wear. The technology behind the Purification Dam. The ruins beyond the Northern Mountain. The twisted creatures in the Schism."

Enoch's finger snapped, and everyone looked to him as he whispered into his Voice's ear.

"Your disappearance," the bald man said, gesturing to Kilal.

"*My* disappearance?" he said, intrigued. What did his disappearance have to do with Enoch's idea?

"The distress signal you answered came from the north," the Voice said, relaying the message. "Then you simply disappeared. We all knew you wouldn't run, you wouldn't leave us. You are far too loyal for that. And how does one kill someone immortal? So, I began searching."

Kilal almost felt flattered. Enoch? Searching for him? "You...crossed *through* the Northern Mountains and entered the ruins beyond?" He shivered and goosebumps sprouted on his arms.

The ruins beyond the Northern Mountains were as mysterious as the events which created the Schism. The earliest map still in existence was believed to be over five hundred years old. It was one of only a handful of items which predated the Great Invasion.

The map didn't account for the Northern Mountains, nor the ruins beyond them. It was simply...blank. It was a mystery, both perplexing and fascinating. Why did the map exclude those areas? There were many theories, one of which Kilal proposed after his first visit to the ruins a hundred and fifty years ago.

They were intentionally left out to discourage any foolish enough to venture there.

Before Kilal's time, scholars, with the help of Arbiters, tried to study the ruins. Most didn't return. The few who did either wouldn't talk about what they saw or couldn't. Either way, all who returned from those expeditions eventually either killed themselves or died from mysterious circumstances.

It didn't take long for people to stop going.

Kilal believed the ruins predated even the Bloodshed. On his handful of trips through the Northern Mountains and into the ruins, he'd always felt an agelessness to the air. Eerie was a...pleasant way to describe the atmosphere of the ruins. The place did things to the minds of those who traversed it. Kilal had been on four separate trips to the ruins, and on each one, he'd seen things.

Horrible things.

His first trip, he'd barely managed to stay twelve hours before he fled south. When he went the second time, he promised it would be different. He surpassed twelve hours, but not by much. The third trip he'd undertaken nearly a century after his second trip. He managed to stay for three days. On the fourth day, a group of farmers found him wandering aimlessly, babbling to himself. He spent the following two weeks locked up in an insane asylum with no Carvings active. The only reason he knew he'd been to the ruins at all, let alone a three-day stay, was because of the pages and pages of notes he'd taken while stuck in his white-walled and barren 'room.'

He didn't remember any of what he wrote, but after returning home and reading dozens of his written pages, he burned each one and vowed to never return to the remnants of whatever civilization used to reside north of the mountains.

His belief that the ruins predated the Bloodshed was based on one of the events he'd witnessed and scribbled down. He'd seen a vision of the city as it once had been. Beautiful, full of color and life. And Sha'tum. Before he gave his life, Sha'tum had walked those lands, interacted with the people, and blessed them with his presence.

Of course, no one believed Kilal. What he'd recorded was just the ravings of a madman. He didn't even know what to believe. He wanted to have faith that his vision was true, but then he'd also have to believe that the other visions were true, too. And he *really* didn't want that.

His fourth time in the ruins was when he fled north through the mountain pass with Lilliana. He'd not done so lightly.

"I...was not there long. Barely twenty-four hours lapsed

before exiting the south entrance to the tunnel," Enoch said through his Voice. "But when I came to, I discovered a most curious thing. I had a piece of a map with me. It showed a labyrinth of ruins *beneath* the Undercity."

"You returned with something?" Kilal said. "I've never heard of that happening."

A snap of the finger, followed by, "We were all quite surprised."

"I know it was a while ago, but do you remember...*anything?*" Kilal pressed. It was an unsympathetic question to ask. He would never want anyone prying into his visits to the ruins, but he just couldn't help himself.

Enoch blanched and gestured for his Voice to listen. "One thing, to which I will not speak of. Here. Later, we may speak of it." He didn't leave room for discussion, and Kilal let the conversation move on.

Requiem leaned over and whispered, "He told us he didn't remember anything."

Wait, Enoch had lied to everyone for two years? Based on his own time in the ruins, and the events and visions he'd encountered, Kilal had a sneaking suspicion as to why he'd remained silent.

The Whisperer gestured to Requiem, and she continued. "The map was hard to read at first. It was drawn during a time when Silent Haven looked much different from it does now. Between that obstacle and avoiding the Heirs and their oathbreaking mercenaries, our search was slow. They have eyes and ears everywhere in the city, both above and below the sewers. We couldn't exactly search at our leisure. With so few of us covering such a large area with what felt like blindfolds on, it took time before we were able to start matching the current layout of Silent Haven with the one on the map.

"Even after that," Requiem continued, "our search was slow. Much of the map extended under the Dead Zone, which only led to areas either caved in or too corrupted for us to enter."

"What were you hoping to find?" Kilal asked. It was all very fascinating, and he, more than most, craved to know the past. But with the Sunlight Domain in disarray, he would've thought there to be a better use of the Arbiters' time.

Like dealing with the Heirs.

The room went silent and there were a few uncomfortable shifts in chairs. Kilal raised a brow. "Was that the wrong question?"

Violet cleared her throat and flashed a look of irritation at Alistair. "Of course not. It's just that...the answer has been the bloody source of...disagreement among us. For those who believe in the truth of the matter, it's been bloody difficult to swallow. Like a spoonful of ash. The other group thinks we're bloody fools for believing. At least that's what they're telling themselves. Bloodshed and Oaths, they just don't want to believe."

Violet's answer was about as helpful as no response at all. Before Kilal could say as much, though, Allyria raised her hand. When the attention turned to her, she blushed and dropped it.

"I'm probably speaking for myself, but...*what is everyone talking about?*"

"I second that," Nanomia said.

Something passed between Enoch, Requiem, and Alistair. Something Kilal was *very* interested to discover. Neither Alistair nor Requiem had ever been on good terms with Enoch. Yet there they were, working with him, showing him the respect they would normally show someone they considered a leader.

Enoch nodded to Alistair, and that seemed to be what the three were waiting for.

"Tell me, little flame," Alistair said. "What great being created our most wonderful world?"

Allyria narrowed her eyes and looked at Kilal, who shrugged. If she thought he had any idea what was going on, she was terribly mistaken.

"Sha'tum," she said. "And stop calling me that."

"And who created us?"

Again, "Sha'tum."

"Right. Now, the trick question, how many worlds did our beloved Sha'tum create?"

She laughed as if it was the most ridiculous question. "One. Ours." Kilal, and it seemed Allyria, noticed the pained expressions on some of the Arbiters' faces in response. "Right?" she asked with none of the confidence of her previous answer.

So, that's what this is about. Requiem said they'd discovered the reality of interdimensional travel, and now this.

But what exactly was Alistair getting at? Even entertaining the topic was already borderline heresy. Not that it mattered to Kilal, considering he was also on the path to learning about the possibility of other worlds. But he'd kept that theory to himself while trying to track Jayden down and deal with the Heirs, not even daring to mention it to his new mentee. Whereas Alistair was speaking about it in a room full of Arbiters.

"If Sha'tum created us and only our world, where did the Ash Fallen come from? And Avinoth?"

It was a question that had always plagued Kilal. He'd never accepted the answers regurgitated by all he asked. He leaned forward, intrigued.

Allyria frowned and tucked a lock of hair behind her ear. "Well, they were always here. We just...lost any information about them. But of course, Sha'tum created them. If he didn't... well...that's just not possible."

Alistair exhaled loudly. He sat back and crossed his arms. "My deepest apologies, little flame. But it seems that just is no longer so."

Nanomia shot up from her chair, knocking it backwards with a loud bang. "What you're saying is blasphemy!"

Lemuel shifted in his seat. "And what about it is blasphemous?"

She gave him a condescending glare. "Please, we all know.

I don't need to tell you."

Allyria squeaked. Nanomia rolled her eyes. Kilal was glad to see, however, that the condescension was not there when the older woman looked at Allyria.

"You don't know, do you?"

"I...there weren't a lot of opportunities to attend a service at a holy place, nor were there many copies of the scriptures in the Undercity," Allyria said. "The little I know is from what I've heard in passing."

Nanomia sighed, but it was the sigh a mother gives a curious child. "Sha'tum created our world. He created us so he wouldn't be lonely. He walked with us, teaching us all we needed to know to grow and become the civilized nation we are now. Or were before the Bloodshed. He didn't create other worlds. He didn't have a beginning, and he wasn't supposed to have an end. He was and still is the one and only creator. To suggest anything else is blasphemy."

Allyria nodded along.

"Sha'tum created all things, and he is the only creator," Lemuel said. "And yet, Avinoth and the Ash Fallen exist. How?"

Nanomia turned her anger onto Kilal. "How can you sit here and let him talk like this?"

He chose his words carefully. The last thing he wanted to do was force an untrained Arbiter back into Wolfe's waiting arms. "Avinoth and his Ash Fallen appeared out of nowhere. Have the answers we were always taught about all this never seemed strange? That Avinoth and his followers were humans who rebelled against Sha'tum's will, and because of that, he and his followers were turned into the monsters we know as Ash Fallen?"

"Of course I never thought that was strange!" she said, leaning over the table. "That was the price he paid for rebelling!"

The tale of the Ash Fallen's origins passed down from Mother to Mother and spread throughout all of the Sunlight Domain. It didn't matter that there was no evidence supporting the claim. The only thing that had ever seemed to matter was the lack of evidence supporting the contrary.

"The price Avinoth and his followers paid for rebelling against Sha'tum," Kilal said. He almost felt sorry for Nanomia. She'd clearly chosen to turn a blind eye to that belief her whole life, and it was only now being questioned, "was obtaining a power which led to a world war, Sha'tum sacrificing himself, and later, hundreds of Arbiters sacrificing themselves to *split our world in half.* Strange price to pay for rebellion, don't you think?"

A dozen different expressions contorted Nanomia's face. Her mouth worked, but she couldn't seem to find the words to refute what Kilal said. Her teeth clicked when she snapped her mouth shut and slumped into her chair.

Poor girl. I remember when I was challenged with something similar. I'm sure I looked about the same as her.

"*So*...are you saying," Allyria's head swiveling back and forth, "the Ash Fallen came from another world?"

One of Enoch's men burst into laughter. "That's what *they're* saying. And as I've said, you give me some evidence, and I'll listen. But so far, there hasn't been any."

"Then listen," Requiem said. "A week ago, Ahnk and I took the section of the Undercity we calculated was beneath the ruins of the holy place."

"And a lovely time we had," Ahnk said, smiling mischievously at Violet, who rolled her eyes and scowled. "Just the two of us, alone. Romance filled the air, wouldn't you agree, Req?"

"I would not." Requiem clearly wasn't interested in whatever game he was playing.

Ahnk sighed and shrugged. "Can't please them all, I guess."

"Or *anyone*," Violet interjected, to which Ahnk feigned pulling a dagger from his heart.

The slightest uplift of the corner of Violet's lips was so profoundly a testament of affection, she might as well have jumped into Ahnk's arms.

"The Undercity in that region," Requiem continued, "is nearly abandoned. We encountered a few individuals, but they were less interested in us than us in them. Now that we knew what to look for, it took us less than a day to find our first entrance to the cavernous ruins below."

"I've spent more than a few years prowling the Undercity in my youth," Kilal said. "How did I miss that an *entire catacomb* lay beneath it?"

Under the table, Requiem patted his leg. Was she trying to reassure him? Did she think his ego was so fragile he needed confirmation that it wasn't his fault he missed such a colossal detail?

"The runes," Ahnk said.

"The runes?"

"Enoch was the one to figure it out," Alistair mumbled.

"Did you ever encounter a series of runes, each barely larger than your thumb, etched into an obscure location?" Requiem asked. "Sometimes on a stony wall, others in a corner of the floor or even a ceiling?"

"A few times," Kilal said.

She nodded. "We all have. We just never understood their significance. But when carved by an Arbiter, one who can access the Mind branch, it allows them to see a keyhole invisible to all other forms of sight."

Kilal scratched his chin, then crossed his arms. "I've done that," he said. "The runes always appear in a series of four. The first few times I encountered them, I tried carving them. I've tried incorporating them into the Physical, Elemental, *and* Mind, and it's never done anything. I've tried different orders and even spent time adjusting each rune while experimenting. So, what was I missing?"

A snap of a finger answered him. Everyone waited as Enoch whispered into his Voice's ear, still managing to not face the room.

"Understanding. You must first cancel *all* active Carvings. Each rune must be etched individually and activated individually. Once all four runes have been activated, you will see in the manner intended by those who left the runes for us to find."

Kilal pursed his lips and ran a hand through his hair. That would explain it. He never would've thought to carve the runes that way, let alone *cancel* his already active powers. At that time in his life, he would never have considered voluntarily existing for even a minute without three active Carvings.

The solution to the puzzle of the mysterious runes was far simpler than anything Kilal would have thought, which is probably why no one had ever figured it out.

So how did Enoch?

As soon as the question popped into his head, so did the answer.

"You saw it, didn't you? In the ruins? You didn't come out of there with just a map. You came out with...understanding... as well."

Enoch finally turned away from the porthole, slowly and dramatically, and locked eyes with Kilal. He didn't snap his finger and answer through his Voice or even nod. He just stared. And Kilal saw the truth behind those eyes. The haunting confirmation to his question.

What else did you see?

Enoch turned back to his porthole.

"Like most successful excursions into the *under*-Undercity, we found a civilization long abandoned," Requiem said.

"She's saying we encountered a lot of dust," Ahnk interjected.

She continued as if she'd never been interrupted.

As Requiem recounted the tale of their most recent adventure into the city beneath the city, Kilal studied the woman he used to know. It pained him that she wasn't the version of herself he married.

He'd left behind a quiet, passive, caring, and quick-to-follow woman. He'd never known her to hurt another human being, let alone kill. Nor speak assertively in groups of more than him, and he especially never knew a Requiem who led others. And in the last thirty-six hours, each and everyone one of those character traits had been rendered obsolete as efficiently as Kilal carved.

"As little as we found," she said, once again tapping his knee. Had she realized he wasn't paying attention? "what we eventually stumbled upon was..."

"World changing," Ahnk said, for once serious.

~ CHAPTER 36 ~

Kilal leaned forward, and Allyria, who'd made her way back behind him to lean on his chair, pressed forward on it. Garret plucked his glasses from the bridge of his nose and scrubbed at them with a cloth he retrieved from his pocket. Nanomia, still flush with emotion, tried her best to appear uninterested. She caught Kilal looking at her and shrugged when he pursed his lips and raised a brow. Even Enoch finally peeled himself away from his window and took a seat.

When the shuffling butts and the scrape of chair legs against the stone floor settled, Requiem continued.

"We found what looked to have been a library of some sort. Five rows of shelves, six rows high, packed full of books. *History* books. We..." she paused, grimacing. "We spent about twenty-four hours in that room."

The reaction to her confession was...surprising. Groans and uncomfortable squirms. Enoch even blanched. For the first time since being reunited, Requiem showed an emotion other than annoyance through a tinge of red on her cheeks. Ahnk stared at the ground, silent.

Was the time spent there really that bad? From what Kilal gathered, the two Arbiters had stumbled upon a treasure trove of world history unknown to everyone. They were the first humans to lay their eyes on whatever had been written there in over a thousand years. Kilal's mouth watered at the potential to one day himself behold such a sight. His hands ached to hold a decaying, fragile, leather-bound book written in the days *before* the Bloodshed.

"Sienna found you, didn't she?" a quiet, nervous voice asked.

Kilal did a double-take. It might have been the most shocking thing to occur in the meeting.

The question had been asked by *Garret*.

When all eyes turned to him, he startled, as if only then realizing he'd spoken aloud. He pressed himself so tightly against the wall, Kilal wondered if the boy was hoping he'd eventually be mistaken as a part of it.

Requiem cocked her head and gave the young lad an inquisitive look. "And why would you presume that?"

Garret, desperate for relief, looked from Nanomia to Allyria. Both somehow managed to shrink back and act like they didn't notice his pleading looks. Garret pulled his glasses off again and ran his shirt over them. Were they even dirty? Or was it just to keep his hands busy?

"S-she is an apex predator," he said, studying his glasses. "Everything you, the resistance, do is catered to avoiding her. It only makes sense that, while in the city, you wouldn't want to stay in one place for too long."

"Plus," Ahnk said, "our favorite huntress *really* hates Requiem."

"I would have thought," Enoch's Voice said after a finger snap, "you, of all people, would have known this and been a bit more careful. You barely managed to survive your previous two encounters with her. You had to know she'd be all the more eager to get her hands on you."

Requiem pursed her lips. "I *did* know that. And every second we gained studying those tomes was a second I counted getting caught worth it."

"What did you find out?" Kilal asked, hoping his tone wasn't giving away his childlike thirst for knowledge; the same thirst which had gotten him into so much trouble in his long life.

"At first, not much," Requiem said. "The books were over a thousand years old. A sneeze could crumble them to dust, let alone a firm grip attempting to disrupt their position. After we both failed to handle a book without it disintegrating, Ahnk swapped his Mind Carving to a mild telekinetic rune."

Kilal didn't understand her need to preface the Carving with 'mild.' It wasn't like there were different versions of tele-kinesis, like there were strength or healing. There was only one. Unless...

Unless they discovered a new variant!

But that was another piece of the puzzle. With Ahnk's ability to manipulate people with his voice, Kilal would have thought the Silver-Tongue was the *best* Arbiter to face Sienna. That is, if he'd had the Carving active, which it appeared he hadn't. And the telekinetic rune they had access to could only manipulate objects much, *much* smaller than a full-grown human.

"Even still," Ahnk said, glowering, "it was difficult to fig-ure out the right amount of touch to apply to the books. I lost more than a few in the beginning. Who knows what they could have contained."

What a shame.

"That's not fair." Kilal's mumbled rebuke was directed at himself, but when Alistair's eyes fell on him, he quickly addressed the room. "I'm sure no one has the experience to know how to handle paper that old."

"Please, Kilal," Violet said. "Let us enjoy the rare moment of humility Ahnk is sharing with us."

"*Eventually,*" Requiem said with an irritated click of her tongue, "we were able to handle the books. But it was slow. We were each able to handle one at a time, with Ahnk turning the pages when we were ready. But what we managed to read was *rich*. Historical accounts of kings and queens from oth-er worlds. Trade routes, treaties, and even mentions of wars between worlds, which were history lessons during that time period. I found mention of two other worlds, but it seemed like there could be more."

A broad grin stretched across Kilal's cheeks until they nearly hurt.

Nanomia and Enoch's man who'd spoken up about evidence shared a cynical look. "Just because it was written in a book doesn't mean it's true," she said.

"How do we know these aren't tales the people of that time told each other?" Garret said, surprisingly.

Kilal's grin was splitting his face in two. "Because I've met two of these individuals from another world."

~ CHAPTER 37 ~

Though everyone present stared at him with varying levels of intensity, it was the three young Arbiters who'd arrived with him who seemed the most interested in what he had to say. Enoch barely spared him a glance, and one more full of disbelief than interest. Requiem flitted from irritated to grateful.

"For the last two years," Kilal started, "I've been a prisoner of what I've named The Tower of Eyes." Recalling the horrific place and time, he closed his eyes and shuddered. His chest and throat tightened, and for a moment, he was unsure if he'd be able to continue. The moment ended when Requiem placed a hand on his knee and gave it a gentle squeeze. When he opened his eyes, she offered him a small smile of encouragement.

A surge of bravery prompted him. "I was...tortured...for most of it," he said, blinking away moisture building along his lashes. "But that's not what I interrupted you for. There was a man whose cell shared a wall with mine."

He was eternally grateful for the lack of questions. He could only imagine the queries looming on everyone's tongues and the restraint they were exercising. Already he'd revealed more about the Ashen Lands than anyone in the history of man knew. A tower? Entities intelligent enough to capture, torture, and keep him alive for two years? Another man? That alone created its own line of questions.

Where did that man come from? How did he get across the Veil? How did he survive? Were there others?

Those were all things Kilal imagined he'd eventually get around to answering, but for now, he was grateful everyone let him speak.

"He called himself Eldon," he said. "He shared knowledge of three other individuals on this side of the Veil; companions of his. He instructed me to find and give a message to them. A message which, according to Eldon, would ensure they would help me. I was hesitant to believe him, but he knew things about the Veil, things I didn't. Like its weakness, which allowed me to pass through it."

Enoch interrupted with a grunt. "Weakness? And that is?" his Voice said.

"There's a time of night when a 'road' of sorts through the Veil would be weakest, allowing someone with regenerative capabilities on par with mine to pass through it."

He shivered with memories of the torment that had enveloped him. Kilal had known pain in his life. So much so, he'd thought he'd felt it all. The Veil showed him how wrong he'd been.

"If that's the case," Enoch's Voice said. "Why have the Ash Fallen not been slipping through, little by little?"

Kilal met Enoch's gaze. "Because their regenerative capabilities are not on par with mine."

"What were these three to help you with?" Forest asked, his tone quiet, almost wind-like.

Kilal raised a finger. "I will get to that, but first, let me finish. Please." Forest nodded, and Kilal wondered if the man thought he actually had any control over what he divulged or kept hidden.

As if the tree-loving worm could make me do anything I didn't want to.

He started, blinking a few times and running a hand through

his hair. Where had that thought come from? And the pure irritation accompanying it? Kilal didn't know, but he didn't like it. No one at the table deserved to be referred to as a worm.

"That's how I returned. I escaped the Tower of Eyes. I made my way through the Veil, and I began my search for Jayden, Ximthar, and Aya. I tracked Jayden down and confronted him in an alley outside *Forget Everything.*"

Violet hissed. "Bloodshed and Oaths! What was he doing there? The bloody, ash-eaten patrons of that nightclub hate Arbiters. More than one, oathbreakers and oathkeepers alike, has been beaten or killed there."

"I gathered as much." Kilal rubbed the back of his head, the phantom pain of a bottle smashed against his skull flaring. "I gave Jayden the message Eldon instructed me to, but he didn't believe me. Apparently, he thought Eldon to be dead for a thousand years."

"The message?" Enoch's voice relayed.

"'He still lives.'"

"Who?" Requiem murmured.

Kilal exhaled loudly before resting his chin against his chest. When had he gotten so tired? "I've had a lot of time to ponder that. And I think...I think the he who still lives is Avinoth."

~ CHAPTER 38 ~

Nanomia shot to her feet and slammed her fists on the table. "Impossible!" she shouted.

More accusations came from Enoch's henchman. Nanomia broke into a loud prayer, requesting Sha'tum look after them in their dark hour. Forest, Kilal assumed, did something with his Carving as a whoosh of air whistled through the portholes. Lemuel paled, and Violet spewed forth a string of curses that would've had any human with a hint of morality blushing.

Requiem hissed, and Alistair stared grimly. His best friend understood how serious he was. The rest may doubt him, but not Alistair.

Never Alistair.

The only two to not give any sort of response were Enoch and...Garret? Kilal cocked his head, studying the boy as he rubbed at a blemish on his glasses. Maybe he hadn't heard the declaration?

Kilal held up a hand and waited for all to be silent. "I have my reasons to believe Avinoth is back." He paused, crossing his arms and chewing on his lower lip. "The Ash Fallen are gathering. Their forces are unlike anything this side of the Veil has seen since Avinoth's invasion. There are untold Mannekins. A hundred-plus Plagues. A dozen Hateful and even a few Sightless."

Another outburst of emotion.

"This army," Kilal continued once the noise died down, "is led by a figure I knew only as Ashen Kane.

"This is not a guess. I've seen it all. I've spent the last ten years trying to stop them. I've even gone head-to-head with Ashen Kane himself...and lost." A few mutters of disbelief echoed through the room. "But it wasn't until I returned and confronted Jayden that the possibilities began clicking into place and becoming something more. Not only did Jayden not believe me, but he claimed to have already killed this 'he' Eldon said was still alive. When I tried to convince him to help me save our world, he responded with, 'I don't care about your world.' And now, with the confirmation of interdimensional travel—"

"My delicate ears are piqued to know just how this confrontation with Jayden concluded," Alistair cut in. There was a mischievous gleam in his brown eyes. He knew exactly how the confrontation ended. He just wanted to have a little fun at Kilal's expense.

Kilal tapped his fingers, one after the other, on the tabletop. "Not well. Not well at all."

Requiem groaned. "You tried to solve the problem with your fists." It wasn't a question. She gave him that motherly-disappointed-but-not-surprised look. The one Kilal hadn't realized he'd missed so much.

"Well, it's a little more complicated than that...but yes."

"Well, I for one," Violet said, coming to Kilal's defense, "don't see the bloody problem with solving disputes with fists."

It was nice to have someone on his side, but he knew Violet wasn't the one to do much for his side of the situation. Early in their mentorship, she'd taken, quite fiercely, to Kilal's method of handling disputes. A little too well, some would say.

Ahnk guffawed. "Everyone here is well aware of that."

Violet glared at Ahnk, and Kilal wasn't sure if she was going to decide to handle Ahnk with the very method in question.

Kilal rapped a knuckle against the table. "As I was saying," he emphasized, bringing everyone back to the point at hand, "Jayden's comment about our world, combined with the evidence of interdimensional travel, and the rising force of Ash Fallen, I believe Ashen Kane is Avinoth."

A finger snapped.

"That's a neat deduction, but it doesn't answer one question, the most important one." The condescension in Enoch's Voice's words was clearly instructed to be added by Enoch. "How is Avinoth still alive? He died, remember? And what does that have to do with evidence of other worlds?"

Allyria leaned forward with furrowed brows. Had she come to the same conclusion as Enoch?

Kilal leaned back in his chair, tipping it back until his weight rested on the back two flimsy legs. They bent and creaked in protest. Before the legs could snap, he lowered his gravity until the chair nearly sighed in relief.

"That's a good question, Voice," Kilal said. "Please relay to Enoch my amazement at his deductive skills."

The Voice paled, and his eyes widened. He didn't want to relay such a message. Not that he had to. Enoch's ears worked well enough. Kilal just couldn't resist an opportunity to poke at the eccentric Arbiter.

Unfortunately, Enoch didn't seem to care.

"If there are other worlds," Kilal said, returning his gaze to the Arbiters around the table, "then it's safe to assume Avinoth came from one of them. And my guess is Jayden, Eldon, and the others came from whatever world Avinoth came from. Jayden said Eldon has been dead for a thousand years, which leads me to believe they fought alongside the original Arbiters against Avinoth. And the message Eldon relayed is that he is not dead.

"Somehow, Avinoth survived. And only Avinoth could rally the forces of the Ash Fallen as this Ashen Kane has."

"It still feels more like conjecture rather than evidence,"

Nanomia mumbled, to which Allyria elbowed and shushed her with a finger over her mouth.

Kilal shrugged. "You're not wrong. But I think the ramifications of being right and not acting on it are too high for us to gamble with."

"You say you returned to find Jayden and two others." For the second time, Lemuel spoke up. He always was a quiet, introspective individual, and Kilal anticipated whatever it was he felt needed to be said. Lemuel tapped his chin. "But what about us? Did we mean so little to you, you didn't even bother to swing by and say hello? After a ten-year absence, I would have thought we'd earned at least that much."

Ashes, Lemuel! Always saying the things everyone else is thinking but not willing to say.

"I deserve whatever hurt and anger I've caused," Kilal said. Regret flooded his voice. "The truth is...I wasn't planning on revealing myself to anyone. Recruit those three and get back to the Ashen Lands—that was it. No one was supposed to know I was still alive."

Kilal held his arms out wide, careful to not smack Alistair or Requiem. "I'm sorry. I didn't expect to be here long, and this might as well be a suicide mission. I didn't think it would be right to reveal myself only to leave again and probably not return."

Were there any words capable of properly expressing his regret and sorrow? If so, Kilal sure didn't know them. The ones he came up with felt like poor excuses and nothing more.

Requiem's chair squeaked from beside him as she scooted back and stood. Despite standing, nearly hovering over him, she barely looked down at him. Even so, he felt a child beneath her withering glare.

"No one was supposed to know you were still alive? I didn't realize I qualified as no one." She addressed the rest of the room, a glimmer of moisture in her left eye. "I need a brief break." She didn't wait for confirmation or approval. She just turned on her heels and left the room.

Kilal looked to Alistair for advice, but immediately regretted it.

"You shouldn't of made that choice for us, friend."

Kilal sighed. Alistair was right. But he couldn't do anything about it now. All he could do was follow Requiem out and prepare for a different kind of battle than he was used to.

A battle, according to history, he rarely won.

~ CHAPTER 39 ~

Kilal caught up to Requiem in the stone hall outside the meeting room. She stood at a porthole with both hands on the lip, leaning.

"Req, I'm sorry. I know it doesn't erase what I did or said in there, but I am. You know you're not no one to me. You're everything to me."

She jerked towards him. He braced himself, thinking she was going to strike him—and she did, but not with the means he would've preferred. "If I meant anything to you, you would have stopped! You would have found me. But you didn't! It was an accident that you stumbled upon me. If that hadn't happened, you would've gone on your way without letting me know you were still alive!"

Being with Requiem for two days, Kilal believed the ruined side of her face couldn't express emotion. He was wrong. It captured anger and hurt quite well.

"I know," he said. "I...I...never meant to come back, not without Lilliana. I've spent a decade looking for her. Ten years! I..." He paused, running a hand through thick hair. "I don't even know if she's still alive. What sort of father abandons his daughter in the Ashen Lands? What sort of father can't even protect his own daughter?"

He stepped up beside her and leaned a shoulder against

the stone wall. Following her gaze, he stared out the porthole. With the Veil behind them, a field of dying grass lay before them. Decaying trees, crumbling brush, even a few carcasses. Far in the distance, he spotted green and brown areas. A forest. The road they traveled to get there pierced the woods, but from Kilal's perspective, it looked more like the forest had opened up for the road, only to collapse in around it.

"Be honest with me," he said, placing a hand lightly over hers. "Look me in the eyes and tell me you would've done differently. I came back because of my bloody oath. I came back because I knew if I didn't, Ashen Kane—Avinoth, whoever he is—would cross the Veil and kill everyone on this side of it. Including you. Despite Lilliana's life being at stake. I didn't want to waste a second more than I had to because every second is another Lilliana is still over there. Would you have acted differently?"

His heart pounded. His chest tightened, and his throat constricted.

Requiem brushed a tear from her good eye. Then a second one. "I...I don't know."

"I should have come to you," Kilal said. "I understand that now. But I think, on top of everything else, I was scared."

Requiem frowned. "Of what?"

The stone was cool against his temple. It felt good; cold was something he'd forgotten about in the Ashen Lands.

"Finding out you were dead." He shrugged. "Or had moved on. Found someone else. Of reuniting with you, only to leave again. You now know I'm going back to the Ashen Lands. I have to stop Ashen Kane, and I'm not disillusioned with the possible outcome of that mission. More than likely, myself and whoever goes with me won't return. I didn't want to do that to you a second time. That sort of hurt...no one should endure... the loss of a loved one not just once, but twice. I was afraid of not just experiencing that myself, but forcing you to as well."

"I'm going with you." It wasn't a question. It was a realization of what he said. Emotion drained from her face, leaving behind something more reminiscent of a statue than a human.

Kilal ran a hand through his hair. It hadn't been his intention to bring her. Only Jayden, the Professor, and Aya. Maybe he was wrong about that too.

"I don't know," he said. "I never thought that far."

Her face was stone, but her eyes burned with passion. And anger. And betrayal. "I'm going with you. This isn't just your fight. This is my land too. I swore the oath just like you did."

His throat tightened at the possibility. Requiem Ror, his former wife, the woman he loved, in the Ashen Lands? "Req, I don't think you understand what you're saying."

She jammed a finger into his chest. Why was everyone doing that to him? "I'm...going. I thought you were dead. The Immortal Arbiter...dead. My husb—" she cut herself off. "Do you know what that feels like? I won't feel that again. I'm going with you."

Kilal caught her arm as she moved away. A ray of sunlight pierced the porthole. "I thought you were dead! I thought *all* the Keepers were dead. It wasn't until I rescued Ahnk that I had any hope you were still alive. So I know how you felt. Please believe me.

"I just want us to go back to how we were." His voice quivered.

She gently removed his hand from her arms. Her face, devoid of emotion, sank his heart. She didn't say anything. She only turned and walked back to the meeting room.

What did you expect, you ash-eating fool! Did you really think it would be that easy?

He hadn't. But he'd wanted it to be so.

Resigning himself to a fate of patiently waiting for the woman who owned the key to his heart, Kilal followed her back into the room.

~ CHAPTER 40 ~

"Are we going to continue this charade of heresy?" Nanomia asked when Kilal entered the room behind Requiem.

Allyria elbowed her in the side, but Nanomia didn't seem in the mood to be forced into silence.

"It's not heresy if it's bloody true!" Violet said.

"No, it's not!" Nanomia snapped.

"So, what? It's all just a bloody coincidence?"

Violet's knuckles whitened as she pressed her hands onto the table and stood, but Kilal narrowed his eyes at her and shook his head. Thankfully, Violet paused and retook her seat, though, from her scrunched brow, she certainly didn't want to be the first to respond like an adult.

Pulling Requiem's seat out for her, Kilal waited for her to sit before he took his own.

"Before we decide what is and isn't heresy, let's hear the rest of what Requiem has to say," he said.

Nanomia's eyes looked ready to bulge out of their sockets.

Requiem nodded appreciatively. "As I was saying, we found accounts of kings and queens from other worlds. Two, to be precise. And they weren't referred to as worlds but as Disks. Our Disk was known as Providence. And there was also Amity and Munificent."

Alistair scratched his jaw. "Those words are just a bunch of gibberish to me. Anyone else?"

All eyes turned to Requiem and Ahnk. Both shrugged, but it was Requiem who answered. "We didn't find anything else on the subject."

"But, in our defense," Ahnk interjected, "we didn't have much time with the books before Sienna showed up."

"Sign from Sha'tum," Nanomia mumbled, too quietly for most without Kilal's sensitive hearing to pick up. Which he was grateful for. He was going to need to sit down with that one. Sooner rather than later.

"Unfortunately, much of what we managed to read wasn't particularly useful. Most were the things I've already mentioned. Historical accounts, trade routes, treaties, lineages. There were a few accounts of Sha'tum walking among the people. Showing up to bless new kings and queens, births, holidays, and special events."

Sha'tum walking among his people? Just like his visions while visiting the Northern Ruins.

Kilal couldn't even imagine what such a thing would be like. To be in the presence of the creator and engineer of the gift of Carvings. The being who selflessly gave up his life to give his people the fighting chance they needed against Avinoth and the Ash Fallen.

A thought pricked at Kilal's consciousness, one he'd had plenty of times before.

Would he, the Immortal Arbiter, ever give up his immortality to save his people? The answer should've been obvious. But, like all other times the question came up, an unease settled in his stomach. Butterflies, twisting, multiplying.

"We did eventually find an account of how these kings and queens and trade agreements were practiced."

"As in, how they moved between worlds," Ahnk said.

With a grin only half of her face could show, Requiem clarified, "The sentinels."

Kilal cocked his head.

There were twelve pairs of sentinels along the perimeter of the edge of the world, an equidistance of two hundred and fifty miles between each pair. Six of the pairs had been lost to the Ashen Lands, four to the Schism, and one to the northern ruins. Only one pair remained, which could, effectively, be visited, and they were located around fifty miles southwest of the barracks.

The sentinels were enormous structures. Each set contained a carved woman and man in elaborately detailed armor with a great sword attached to their backs. They reached nearly two hundred feet tall and fifty feet wide at the base and contained one hundred feet of land between them.

Kilal had visited all six pairs lost in the Ashen Lands and could confirm they were identical to the remaining pair on their side of the Veil.

No one knew who made them, how, when, or why. As far as Kilal had always been concerned, the sentinels simply always were. So, the fact that they were potentially used for interdimensional travel was amazing, but didn't surprise him.

Though that still didn't explain one thing.

"How?" he asked, no-nonsense and clear-cut.

Requiem took a deep breath through her nose. Kilal already knew the answer. She never breathed like that unless she was preparing to give bad news.

"We weren't able to establish that. What we know is travel happened between a pair of sentinels. Travelers came and went through them. It even sounded like there may have been a bridge of light of some sort which they traveled upon. Unfortunately, it wasn't much more than a few minutes after reading this account when I caught my first whiff of Sienna."

"You must forgive her," Ahnk butted in. "But we can all understand how she would've failed to sense Sienna until it was too late. It's not every day we discover proof that we're not alone in this...existence."

It was meant as a joke. Apparently, it was all Ahnk was capable of. But Requiem's grimace proved how funny she thought it was.

Kilal placed a hand softly on her back. Her muscles relaxed beneath his touch. He couldn't blame her, and anyone who would pretend they wouldn't have done the same thing in her shoes would be made to understand that they were a liar.

"And you were doing what while she was...failing...to sense Sienna?" Allyria asked. "Perhaps, re-carving new runes since all you had, from this account, was telekinesis? And I can't imagine that would do much against someone of Sienna's caliber."

Based on her stony face and narrowed eyes, unlike Ahnk, she was not joking.

She's a loyal one.

A personality trait reminiscent of Lilliana. The two were more alike than Kilal wanted to admit.

She's replacing her.

NO SHE'S NOT!

Kilal stopped himself from digging his fingers into Requiem's back. She gave him a sidelong glance, but he shook his head. Despite the assurance, her concern remained.

While Kilal wrestled internally with himself, Alistair was nearly rolling with laughter and pointing at Ahnk. "What's it about'cha that makes the ladies see you as a verbal whipping post?"

"It certainly isn't his pleasant personality or modesty," Violet said, nudging Allyria with an elbow, who cracked a smile in turn.

Alistair roared with laughter again.

Ahnk rolled his eyes but stayed silent. That was answer enough to Allyria's question. He never re-carved a second rune. He'd been as useless against Sienna as a toddler was to an adult.

"Ahnk's right," Requiem said, not joining in the fun being

had at his expense. "I was so lost in the desire to know more I completely forgot about the real danger we were in. And because of that, we had to set the place on fire, burning all the books, before Sienna caught up to us. If we couldn't have the knowledge in that room, then we sure weren't going to let Wolfe get his hands on it. Either way, I just...I wish I'd... paid more attention. Maybe we could have saved something. Learned something new."

She tossed a strand of thick, black hair over her shoulder before slumping forward to rest on her elbows and hands.

It was a snap of a finger that answered her.

"Don't blame yourself," the Voice started. "We all would've done the same thing."

Requiem and Kilal exchanged looks, and Kilal nodded his agreement.

"We know more now than we did then," Enoch's Voice continued. "Not just about the sentinels, but about the evidence of rooms and locations beneath the Undercity containing a wealth of knowledge. If there is one, then there's bound to be more."

Kilal's mouth nearly watered at the thought of coming across one of those archives.

"If anything, this is a huge victory for us," the Voice finished. *Enoch, encouraging? What's the world coming to?*

"Thank you," Requiem said. "We spent a few days being tortured by Tor'et, experimented on by Fazin, and generally beaten by other Arbiters. I, for one, did not reveal anything."

A few gazes turned to Ahnk, who widened his eyes and held out his hands. "Me neither!" he was quick to say.

"And that's where I came in," Kilal said. "I paid the Heirs a visit and was fortunate enough to find both of them."

"Why did you go there?" One of Enoch's lackeys asked.

Kilal didn't like the implication of his tone. His chair creaked as he leaned forward. "To join them, of course." The lackey paled and another one cursed, but no one else responded.

They knew he was lying.

"It was something Allyria said." The girl perked up. "The way she described the Heirs made them seem...otherworldly. After interacting with Jayden and hearing him claim to be from another world, I wondered if Jayden and the four were somehow connected."

"Are they?" Lemuel's deep voice asked.

Kilal shook his head. "I don't think so. After I lost Jayden, I didn't know what else there was for me to do. I would've gone to have a nice visit with the Heirs, anyway. After what they've done to my city, a meeting with them was inevitable."

"How did you get me away from Fazin?" Requiem asked. "His monsters are quite powerful, and he can mutate almost anyone he touches."

Kilal recounted the tale of his introduction with Fazin and how it ended.

"Your *name*?" Alistair said incredulously from his side. "Maybe I should try using it as currency!"

"Now the ash-eating sons of plagues know you're back," Violet put eloquently. "Wonder what they'll bloody do now."

"For starters," Alistair said, "I think Sienna's got herself a new target. Sorry, Req, but your huntress found herself a dainty new favorite prey."

Kilal's smile was genuine. "I look forward to it."

"So, what do we do now?" Allyria's voice was quiet, young. Inexperienced. A stark contrast to the rest at the table.

For some reason, all eyes returned to Kilal.

Sweat tickled his back, and an uneasiness settled in his gut. He shook his head and pushed his chair back, standing. "Don't look at me. I'm in no position to lead anyone, let alone a group."

"The way I see it," Requiem said. Relief filled the void left by the receding unease as everyone turned to her. All eyes except Allyria, who kept her inquisitive gaze on him, "we've been presented with two scenarios: continue searching for evidence of interdimensional travel or prepare for the invasion of Ashen Kane."

"Ashen Kane, whoever or whatever he is, is the bigger threat," Forest said. "I trust Kilal's instincts. If he came back to warn us, then we should prepare."

That wasn't *exactly* why he came back, but Kilal didn't see any reason to correct them. If they wanted to interpret his return that way, despite his explanation, he wouldn't take that comfort from them.

Nanomia nodded. "I agree. Why waste time chasing a myth when an enemy is at our doorstep?"

"Who the bloody ashes are you again?" Violet growled.

"I'm a *bloody* human being who *bloody* deserves to have a *bloody* opinion," Nanomia growled back, mocking Violet's speech.

She stood, and a heated shiver brushed over Kilal's skin, followed by the taste of copper.

"Nam," he said softly. "Your opinion has been heard. Thank you."

Nanomia winced as if ashamed of her own outburst. She gave Kilal a curt nod and resumed her seat.

To Violet, he shook his head, disappointed. His words were more for Nanomia's safety than anything else. Violet was not shy when it came to concluding conflicts with violence.

A cleared throat echoed through the quiet room. "I have a question," Garret said. Only when Kilal gave him the go-ahead to speak did the young man continue. "Why the need to pursue interdimensional travel? If Avinoth is still alive, and he and his army will soon sweep through our land...then...won't he just follow us wherever we go?"

The question was bold, but the tone and squeamish motions accompanying it weren't, though Garret had a point.

"In case anyone hasn't realized," Enoch's Voice said, "our world is dying. Even *if* we stop this Ashen Kane, what then?

How much longer will this world last? We'll only be prolonging the inevitable. Any future we may have, it's not on this chunk of rock."

Kilal was knocked onto his heels. He'd imagined Enoch, more than anyone else, would have opposed him. But there he was, trusting Kilal and his intel, which he had no evidence for. The man really *had* changed.

"It seems," Leyloni chimed in, voice motherly, "our young Garret has a point. What is our duty here? To save our people, or...to save all peoples? If we don't end this threat and instead run, what happens to all worlds when Ashen Kane—or whoever he is—travels to another world?"

"Our duty is to our people," one of Enoch's men said. "And no one else's."

"No," Lemuel said. "We swore an oath to the people. We thought that only pertained to our people, but it appears we were wrong. We can't flee while our enemy is nipping at our heels. Whether it's the next world we inhabit or a different one entirely, Avinoth will leave this Disk eventually. How many worlds will he destroy before he's stopped? No, we mustn't flee. We must stand and fight. Even if it means we die."

Kilal couldn't agree more. Even before he knew of interdimensional travel, he'd already made up his mind. He would stop Ashen Kane, or he would die trying. For him, it wasn't just about his oath; it was personal.

"It's settled then," Requiem said, cutting off any further conversation.

The urge to interrupt and establish himself, once again as the leader, flared, but Kilal resisted. It was Requiem's time, and from what he could tell, she was doing a bloody good job of it.

"Two groups," Requiem continued. "One group will head back to the ruins beneath the Undercity. The other will confront Ashen Kane."

The dislike of the plan was apparent, but no one openly

opposed the idea because there wasn't another one.

"I'll lead up the group making their way to the Ashen Lands," Kilal said, despite craving to be a part of the other team. "Though before I take volunteers, everyone should know, if you go with me...you're probably not coming back."

No one complained or disagreed. Everyone nodded, faces hard and determined. Kilal's heart wrenched, and his throat tightened. Despite the differences between them all, they were a good group of Arbiters. Loyal. Even to the point of death.

When someone finally did speak, he would have preferred the outburst.

"I'll go with you."

Kilal closed his eyes. He couldn't bear the conviction on Allyria's face.

What have I done?

~ CHAPTER 41 ~

Never publicly shame or rebuke a teenager. Kilal learned that lesson the hard way, but all his instincts screamed, demanding he immediately tear down any possibility that Allyria would accompany him.

You've lost one daughter. Afraid to lose another?

She's NOT my daughter!

He didn't want anyone at the table to join him in the Ashen Lands. It was a horrible place, a land of nightmares. The only place he'd found worse than that east of the Veil was the Schism, and just barely. That wasn't part of the plan.

Kilal was supposed to return with Jayden, the Professor, and Aya. That was it. Now...now he didn't know what to do. He couldn't defeat Ashen Kane on his own. He'd already attempted that. And the odds of him finding Jayden again were slim to none. Wolfe knew he was alive and was throwing every resource into finding him. Just like with Claire, the longer he remained at the barracks, the more time he gave the Heirs to find him. He really wasn't even sure if he'd be able to get back into the Ashen Lands.

His plan had never gotten further than 'find Jayden.' He figured he'd hike back to the northern ruins, find the teleporter Lilliana had inadvertently activated, and see if he could replicate whatever it was she did. Simple. Right? But the reality, the truth Kilal had refused to confront, was that he may not actually be able to return to those forsaken grounds.

To Lilliana.

You've known that, which is why you've prepared Allyria as her replacement.

Shut up! Shut UP! SHUT—

Kilal shot to his feet, knocking his chair back and banging the table with his hips. "I...I need to think," he mumbled.

Walking to the nearest porthole, Kilal stopped next to Enoch, who'd returned there while he was gone. The Veil, so close, crackled and shimmered like some monster from a child's nightmare. What was he to do?

A buzz filled his ear. Kilal winced. The wince turned into a grimace. His neck spasmed, and an eye twitched. Pressure built in his skull. Not the sort of pressure when someone was preparing a Carving, but the sort a piece of fruit would feel between the arms of a vise. Something warm and wet trickled from his ears, and the burn of healing commenced.

At first, he didn't understand what was happening. He didn't understand until he did.

Enoch was speaking. The strange Arbiter hadn't moved. He continued to stare out the porthole, but his mouth shifted ever so slightly.

"There's something special about that girl," Enoch's voice— his real voice, not that of the man he used as his speech puppet—invaded his mind. It didn't just pierce Kilal's ears; it felt like it had wiggled into his brain. *"The...little flame. Any chance we have of getting off this Sha'tum-forsaken rock begins and ends with her. I saw it in the ruins. She can't go with you. No matter what."*

The pain dissipated when he stopped speaking.

He'd never experienced Enoch's voice, and for the first time he was grateful. The man had barely whispered, and Kilal was still struggling to focus on the Veil through blurry eyes. Enoch couldn't kill him, but he sure could make Kilal wish he were dead.

"What'cha plan for us crossin' it?" Alistair asked. "In fact, how did'cha both cross it? You know, Lilliana and yourself?"

"The same way I did the first time," Kilal said, still staring at the Veil. There was something mesmerizing about the black wall of energy. The way the white lightning crackled and zigzagged across the surface. The shimmer and occasional ripples on its surface like a rock dropped into a pond. To think such a creation of pure *power* was erected by the sacrifice of his ancestors.

Sacrifice.

Would the next part of his life be it? The end? His battle against Ashen Kane, would it be his sacrifice?

*If it saves the world...*my *world,* every *world,* then *I'll gladly pay the price.*

A world for Requiem to grow old in. For Violet and Ahnk to be together. For Allyria to find something worth living for, *someone* worth living for. A world to send Lilliana home to.

Yes. It would be worth it.

Kilal returned to his seat with an air of anticipation. "Ten years ago, the Keepers' headquarters of Silent Haven received a distress signal from a small settlement of farmers far north. Something I didn't consider then, which has haunted me since, is why I never questioned why the signal was coming here and not New Cita or Vitrol. Both were much closer. I just...I just wanted Lilliana to get some experience." He snorted. "Guess she's gotten more than I intended."

He slipped a hand beneath the table and gripped his knee and squeezed. Hard. Why hadn't he just *thought*? A hand on his cut through the reverie of self-hatred. Requiem didn't look at him, but her fingers halted the pain he inflicted on himself.

Later.

"The settlement was abandoned, and there weren't any Ash Fallen in sight," Kilal said, both hands moving to rest on top of the table. He shifted in his seat and rolled his shoulders while taking a deep breath. "Instead, we found an ambush waiting for us, led by Gabriel Sunsetter."

The room erupted.

"That ash-eating, bloody—"

"Should'ah executed the son of a Plague when we had the chance!"

"Impossible!"

"To the edge of the world with him!"

But it was Enoch's Voice cutting through all others that pierced him the hardest. "You called me heartless. Said I was just like them. Because I wanted to execute him when you wanted to exile him to the Schism."

Enoch left off the end of what he should've said. He had every right to say it. Kilal hadn't been kind to him back then.

He'd taken so many lives in his early years that, for a time, he tried never to take a life again as if that would make up for his sins. He'd even looked down upon his companions who didn't agree with him.

Gabriel Sunsetter had proved to be a bloodthirsty murderer. But instead of listening to Enoch and executing him, Kilal had merely banned him from ever setting foot in a city again.

You brought this upon yourself, is what Enoch should have said. Because it was the truth. If Kilal had executed Gabriel, the last ten years wouldn't have happened. It was as simple as that.

Only, exile into the Schism should've been as good as an execution.

"I'm sorry," Kilal mumbled. "You were right."

Enoch nodded and said no more on the topic.

Kilal was unsure if he was grateful or not.

An arm wrapped around his shoulder. A dark-skinned, long arm. "You couldn't have known," Alistair said. "You were doing what'cha thought best. That's the best any of us can hope for."

Kilal gave his friend a small smile. Then shrugged Alistair off.

"Gabriel had a dozen or so Arbiters with him," Kilal continued. "Lilliana was ready to take on a few Ash Fallen, but she wasn't ready to take another human's life. So, we ran, but Gabriel had anticipated as much.

"We were closed in on from the south, west, and east. I don't think Gabriel expected us to go north. He seemed...hesitant...to follow us through the Pass. But he did.

"We weren't there long, in the ruins. Maybe fifteen hours. Eventually, I knew we'd have to make a stand. Lilliana wasn't ho...." He cleared his throat, breaking up the lump forming inside. When an arm wrapped halfway around his back, he was grateful it was Requiem. "Lilliana wasn't holding up well to the...atmosphere...of the ruins.

"I found a building that looked sturdy enough to make our stand. It ended up not being as good as it seemed. The floor collapsed during the initial assault by Gabriel's followers, and we all fell through. We found ourselves in what looked like an abandoned science lab. There was so much technology I'd never seen before. And it stretched outward farther than anyone looking at the building above would've thought possible.

"As large as the basement was, it wasn't large enough. We eventually reached a dead end filled with more strange technology. It was one of those machines which Lilliana messed around with. She was determined they could help somehow, despite my disbelief.

"Gabriel led an all-out attack against us. I killed the son of the Plague, but I knew we weren't going to win. There were too many of them.

"We never got to the conclusion of the battle. A white light engulfed us all. I...came apart. It was like I was broken down into minute pieces and scattered into the wind. We were transported to the other side of the Veil, then rebuilt. It wasn't painful, just...strange, like the shock accompanying an unexpected fall.

"When the light dissipated and I felt whole again, I stood

in ash, surrounded by more falling from a gray sky.

"Three of Gabriel's Arbiters were teleported with me. I convinced them to stop fighting while we figured out what was going on. And while I searched for Lilliana. Those three didn't last very long, though. Everything, and I mean *everything,* over there has evolved to kill."

Kilal exhaled a long breath. All eyes were upon him, wide and astonished, as if he'd done something revolutionary.

"So, that's where I'll return to. That building. That basement. That machine."

Allyria shot to her feet. "And I'll go with you!"

Kilal withheld a wince. *This will be tough.* He was going to break her heart.

Allyria reminded him of himself too much. She had a fire in her that would keep her fighting and testing her capabilities until it killed her. But she wasn't immortal.

He didn't need Enoch's warning, but it did strengthen his decision. Besides, he'd made a promise to Claire to keep her safe. And traveling to the Ashen Lands to penetrate an army of Ash Fallen to confront a possible god wasn't safe.

But first, "Everyone consider which group you wish to join. I leave tomorrow night. However, before I go, I wish to visit the sentinels. Maybe we'll get lucky and find something which will help us get off this world." Standing, he placed a hand on Requiem's shoulder and looked into her deep, brown eyes. "Would you care to join me?"

For the first time since rescuing her, she blessed him with a smile. A real smile. "I'd love to."

~ CHAPTER 42 ~

"If she's going to join us, she'd better keep up," Requiem had said when Kilal informed her Allyria would be joining them. Yet, despite her words and harsh mannerism, Requiem kept a much slower pace than she was capable of.

Still, the pace was hard, and by the time the quintuple arrived at the sentinels fifty miles later, Allyria was near to falling out.

Alistair clapped her on the back, beaming like a drunken idiot. "That's some mighty fine runnin' there, little flame!"

"I...said...do—" Allyria gave up rebuking him and focused on breathing. Her face was as red as her hair, and her clothes were soaked with sweat.

Kilal shared a smile and a wink with the young girl. Alistair was right. Allyria had kept up with them, two Primes, a High, and...whatever Requiem was. That alone was an impressive undertaking.

"I think...I think..." Allyria panted, bending over. "I think I'm just gonna...gonna...sit down and die for a little bit."

Alistair's laughter echoed across the plains.

"You did bloody good, kid," Violet said. It was the best compliment she would ever give.

"Ah, thanks?" Allyria said, unfamiliar with the praise heaped on her.

The sentinels loomed before them, but before analyzing them, there was something else Kilal wished to check out. Something he'd seen plenty of in the Ashen Lands, but it was different here. Cooler. Vibrant. Not gray.

The edge of the world.

Unlike around the Veil barracks, the grass there was green and the sparse trees and foliage lush. The breeze was full of life. Birds chirped and insects sang, a direct contradiction to the total silence surrounding the black barrier.

Kilal approached the edge in reverent appreciation. The grass continued to the very lip, where it abruptly ceased. He toed that line, reveling in the rush of air that pulsed forth from below. Kilal looked down into the blue abyss, eyes following the side of the world as it turned from green grass to perfectly brown dirt to some strange gray substance twenty feet down. The gray substance continued as far as his eyes could follow.

Again, like most times he stood at the edge of the world; he wondered why no one built a fence or blockade to keep people from accidentally going over the edge. The Governing Seats had tried once but decided it would be too expensive.

No one knew if there was a bottom to the world, if it was just a flat disk floating in space or if it was a cylinder that reached to the bottom of...whatever there was out there.

Like the Schism, plenty of expeditions had been sent out in all directions to discover if there was something, anything, else out there. Unlike the Schism, however, no lives were lost. Everyone always returned, but always with the same news: no end in sight. As far as the world was concerned, the expanse before Kilal was infinite.

Another gust howled up from below, formed and created by a mystery. It blew through Kilal's hair, his shirt, his clothes, ruffling them all. The breeze was cool and refreshing compared to the hot sun.

In the Ashen Lands, there was no breeze, not even at that forsaken realm's edge.

"Wow!" Allyria said, breath regained. "This is it, huh?"

Kilal eyed the girl with an ounce of jealousy. For her, it was the first time experiencing an enigma of that proportion. Her eyes wandered all around, a big grin plastered on her face.

"I forgot how beautiful it is," he said. Allyria looked at him, and he knew what she was seeing. She gave him a small smile. A long blink. A slow nod.

"It's been over a decade since you've seen the edge?"

"Oh no, I saw it plenty over there."

"So?"

"It's different."

"Gray?"

"Gray. Bland. No air. No blue. Listen. What do you hear?"

Allyria scrunched her face and tilted her head back and forth. "Nothing?"

Kilal's smile broadened. He probably would have said the same thing ten years ago. "The birds. The insects. The whoosh of air."

"And that's special?"

Kilal nodded. "Over there, if you hear anything, it means it's time to run, hide, and pray because you're about to be something's lunch."

"I'm sorry you had to go through that," she said quietly. "You're right. The birds are pretty. You don't hear much in the city besides cars and people yelling at each other. Wasn't much different in the Undercity. Except for the car part. There weren't any cars there."

Kilal chuckled but didn't respond. He didn't want to spoil the moment.

Though it didn't take long for Allyria to break the silence herself. "Has anyone ever jumped off?"

That was what she was curious about? Such a teenager.

Kilal shrugged. "Of their own volition? Maybe. The problem with knowing is," he paused, scratching the back of his head as another gust whooshed by, "if someone has, they haven't returned to tell us about it."

Her curiosity was diminished by an eye roll. "Really? Thanks," she said flatly.

"When a person goes over the edge, it normally isn't by their choice."

"What do you mean?"

"A form of punishment used to be tossing criminals over it."

"That's...that's horrible!"

"Is it? They were convicted of the most heinous crimes. Did they deserve to live?"

Allyria frowned and stared out into the blue expanse. "I don't know. But this seems a bit much. How long does it take them to die?"

"We don't know."

"Do they die of hunger? Dehydration? Suffocation?"

"We don't know."

"If there are other worlds, how do we know they can't be accessed somewhere out there, and we're sending our criminals to them."

"We don—" he paused, considering. The implications of that were...problematic.

"Do we still do it?" Allyria asked.

Kilal shook his head. "No. That practice ended a few decades ago."

"Good."

He smiled. Kilal too had been against that form of punishment. It was unusually cruel.

Like when you exiled Gabriel to the Schism?

"You really think there are other worlds out there?" Alistair said, appearing at his side.

Kilal nodded. "I do."

"You think maybe I gots a brother or somethin' out there? Like a twin?"

"Bloody ashes, you're a carving idiot," Violet muttered, joining them at the edge.

"I'm just sayin', if there are more worlds out there, maybe perhaps there's another man as excellent a fellow as me out there as well. Now that would be a sight for sore eyes!"

Allyria's shoulders shook as she fought to contain a giggle.

"Bloody ashes, you're an id—"

"I know, I know," Alistair interrupted. "I'm just bein' persecuted an' all for using my imaginatoriation."

"It's *imagination!*" Violet snapped.

Alistair looked at her curiously. "Is it now? Are you sure 'bout that? I been sayin' it like this for eighty-some years, and no one's corrected me before. You sure you just ain't some sour lady who likes to spoil others' imagingation?"

"You just pronounced it differently!" Violet threw her arms in the air and stormed off in Requiem's direction.

Kilal cracked a smile. "I don't understand why she goads you like that. If she just drops it, you won't have so much fun with her."

"I think secretly she likes me, but I'm too old for her, the poor lass."

"I'm sure she's heartbroken."

Alistair's eyes grew distant, directed at the blue void before them. An intelligence crept into them, an intelligence he tried so hard to hide from others. "Other worlds, huh? Is anythin' we believed true? What else should I stop believin' in?"

"Better to believe in something than nothing at all," Allyria said.

Alistair grunted. "Where'd you find this one, old man? She's far too wise to be a teenager. What's she hidin'?"

"Nothing!" Allyria snapped.

Alistair raised his brows. "Very convincin', little flame."

Allyria sobered and eyed Kilal and his friend. "What about you guys? What were your teenage years like?"

Alistair clapped Kilal on the back. A little too hard. Kilal had to raise his gravity to keep from going over the edge. Sometimes he wondered how someone of Alistair's age could go through life for so long and still, more often than not, act without thinking. Especially one as wise as him.

"Can't complain," Alistair said. "Had this son of a Plague keeping me honest. Most of the time."

"And you?" Allyria said, poking Kilal's elbow.

He pursed his lips. "My mentor...he didn't believe the same as I do now."

"What does *that* mean?"

Kilal squeezed his eyes shut. Allyria didn't understand the wounds she was opening by asking, wounds that never healed. That was a time of his life he wished he could erase all memory of, but the best he could do was just not think about it. Shove it so far down, sometimes it felt like he really had erased them.

Something chuckled from the deepest recesses of his mind.

"It means we got ourselves better things to be worryin' about than teenage years," Alistair said. He placed a hand on Kilal's shoulder, putting enough pressure on it to turn him around.

Kilal gave his friend a nod. His appreciation. There weren't a lot who knew about his past, but Alistair was one of them. Though not all of it. No one knew all of it. Not even Requiem.

Thankfully, Allyria didn't press the issue.

Violet and Requiem were off in the shadow of the female sentinel; their heads nearly stuck together as they studied something on the big toe. It was larger than both of them combined. The feet of the enormous statues alone were taller than Kilal.

Craning his neck back, he covered his eyes from the bright sun and peered up at the statues. The faces were hidden behind helmets with face guards. Their shoulders were wide and adorned in great pauldrons with runes etched into them. A cape stretched nearly to their ankles and appeared to have been frozen in time, swaying to a gentle breeze. Hands at their sides, their appearance stoic, unmoving. Like a guardian standing watch over the Sunlight Domain.

"Let's join the ladies," Kilal said, leaving the edge of the world and the mysteries it concealed behind him.

"Maybe, like the ruins beneath the Undercity, there are hidden symbols on the sentinels," Violet suggested.

Requiem thought about it for a moment. "It's worth a shot, looking for them. Sha'tum knows I don't have any other ideas."

Violet turned to Kilal when he neared. "You're the bloody one who wanted us to come out here. Got any good ideas?"

"Not sure," he said. "I never paid attention to these in the past. But now that they appear to be the key to world travel, I wanted to see them with fresh eyes." He pointed at the male statue on the left. "Allyria and I will take that one."

Allyria choked on a gulp of water from her canteen. "Now?"

"Yes."

She raised both brows and flicked her eyes from Kilal to the top of the sentinel two hundred feet above them. "How?"

He sighed. Before parting from the barracks, Kilal and Allyria had re-carved. But this time, instead of a Stoneskin Elemental Carving, he'd given her his one of Gravitational Control. For that exact reason. Of which he'd explicitly made her aware of.

After a few seconds of silence, and Kilal's only answer being a flat stare, Allyria said, "Oh. Right. Okay." After which, she mumbled, "Lucky me."

"Ah, cheer up, younglin'," Alistair said, grinning. "It's not that high."

Allyria glowered. "Why can't he go up, instead?"

"Because I'm terrified of them heights," he said it as if proud of himself.

Allyria didn't look like she believed him. "You're a Prime Arbiter...and you're scared of heights?"

"I swear on me mentor's old and crusty life."

"Don't look at me," Kilal said when Allyria turned a questioning eye to him. "If you can convince him to go up in your place, you don't have to go."

Alistair guffawed. "Now that's down right mean! You know I ain't going up there. Why give the girl false hope?"

"I'm her mentor. I'm supposed to give her near impossible tasks, forcing her to adapt to the situation, utilizing the training she has. Don't you remember? I figure, if she can convince you to get up there, my job is done."

Allyria huffed. She stomped a foot and pulled at her shirt. Evidently, she didn't want to play his game. "Fine. I'll go up."

"Vi and I will take the other one," Requiem said.

She didn't wait for a response. She leaped, propelling herself up to the knee, where she pushed off and made it halfway up the statue. She clung to the edge of the belt buckle. From there, she hoisted herself again, and in two quick bounds, she landed gracefully on the right shoulder.

Violet was right behind her, except she went for the left shoulder.

Kilal nudged Alistair. "Is that a recent thing?"

"Been doing it for 'long time."

Really? He thought her powers were, at least in part, due to whatever Fazin had done to her when she'd been their prisoner. But if she'd been doing it for a while, that couldn't be the case.

"How does she do it?"

Alistair sobered, the previous mirth gone. "Don't know. No one does."

"Has anyone asked her?"

Irritation flashed across Alistair's face. "You know, for a man I'd call my brother, you can be a right stick in the mud."

Kilal narrowed his eyes. "Because I'm curious?"

"Because you've been gone for a decade—your fault or not, don't matter—and you come back thinkin' to yourself all's fine and dandy and about how it 'should' be."

He recoiled. "Hold on, Alistair. That's not fair."

"Nothin's fair no more!" Alistair snapped. He pointed at Requiem, who was studying something in an ear the size of her. "'Specially not for that one. You think you're the only one to lose anythin'? What about her? She lost everythin' the day you took Lilliana and disappeared. She grieved for months, then eventually disappeared herself. Gone for half a year, that one. When she returned, her face was ruined, and her demeanor darkened. Don't know where she went, what she went through, and no one was gonna ask. We figured if she wanted us to know, she'd tell us. And you know what? She ain't told us."

"Bloodshed and Oaths!" Kilal cursed. "Did anything *not* change while I was gone?"

Alistair's expression eased, and he clapped him on the back, some of his previous mirth returning. "Guess you just more important to us than you care to admit."

That was the truth; the care to admit part.

"Six months, huh?"

"Yep."

"Came back with the power of the glower?"

Alistair chuckled. "Yep."

"And no one knows where she went?"

"Nope."

"When I get some time, I'll ask her."

"Good luck," Alistair said, followed by a mumbled, "stubborn stick in the mud."

Where could she have gone? Kilal couldn't think of a single area in the Sunlight Domain where an Arbiter could go to somehow gain access to previously inaccessible branches.

A thought nudged him. "Has she gotten stronger? Since she returned?"

"Have you gotten older?"

"Yes?"

"There you have it, then."

Whatever power she'd received, Requiem could grow in it. A longing to know the truth warmed Kilal's chest. Maybe he wasn't that much different from the scientist, Fazin, after all. They both yearned for, thirsted for, knowledge of the unknown. But unlike Fazin, he wouldn't risk everything or anyone to obtain it.

"Come here, Allyria," he called. The girl was poking around at the foot opposite the one Requiem and Violet had studied.

She skipped over to him.

"We're going up there," Kilal said, pointing to the belt. It was thick enough for them to walk side by side on it, so that was where they would start.

"And you're *positive* Alistair can't take my place?"

Kilal ignored the question. "Remember how you operated the Stoneskin Carving?"

She nodded. "Picture it as a button. 'Press' it while thinking of a part of your body."

"Gravitational Control isn't that much different, but instead of a button, it's a knob. You're going to 'rotate' that knob clockwise to increase gravity's effect on you, or counterclockwise to decrease it."

Allyria hopped from one foot to the next, excited. "Can I completely remove it?"

"No."

Her lips turned down in a pout. "Would have been funnier if we could," she muttered.

"Carvings aren't for *fun*. They're for defending our land."

"Don't mind him, little flame," Allistair said. "He's just jealous. He had all the fun sucked right from him at birth."

Kilal tossed an annoyed look at him as his prior and current mentee shared a giggle at his expense. "Picture that knob," he said. Allyria sobered and focused again. "Imagine it as similar to your strength rune. Along the knob are two scales, one reading in positive percentages, the other in negative. Go ahead and rotate it counterclockwise to negative fifty percent."

Allyria furrowed her brows in concentration. It wasn't long before her eyes widened. "It feels so...weird." She walked a circle around them. "I feel so light!"

Kilal smiled; her joy was infectious. "Now, jump."

Allyria didn't hesitate. Ten feet off the ground she made it, whooping at the apex before descending back to the ground. "That...was...awesome!"

"Now, get up there on the belt," he said, giving her no time to revel in her new undertaking.

She looked up at her target location, and her smile melted away. "What if I miss?"

"Don't," Alistair said with a chuckle.

"If you do, lower your gravity to negative one hundred percent. It won't fully remove it, but it'll get bloody close. You'll be able to float back down."

"Okay," Allyria said. "Negative one hundred. Float. Got it."

"Give yourself a small boost of strength," Kilal added. "Twenty-five percent should do it."

Allyria nodded, smiling. And jumped.

She soared through the air, arcing toward the belt. For a moment, Kilal thought she'd actually make it. That was until he realized she wouldn't. She seemed to realize it at about the same time as him. Allyria flailed her arms and kicked her feet, none of which helped her.

Kilal couldn't hear the impact as she hit the broad side of the belt.

For a second, she fought the natural order of physics, scrambling at the side, looking for anything to hold on to. Which of course there wasn't, so she fell. And follow Kilal's instructions, she did not.

She screamed as she picked up speed and plummeted.

Kilal reacted at the same time as Alistair. He lowered his gravity, increased his strength, and shot forward. He just barely caught Allyria in outstretched arms before she could break dozens of bones on impact. She paled, staring up at him from in his arms, then yelped and scrambled out of his hold.

"Thanks," she mumbled, bending over to pluck a few blades of grass. Anything to avoid looking at him.

"Want to try again?" he asked.

When she looked at him and nodded, her face was hardened with concentration and determination.

She squatted a few times, testing the feel of gravity, Kilal assumed, and launched into the air again. Her trajectory was accurate, and she landed perfectly on the top of the sentinel's belt buckle.

Kilal followed, and after landing softly beside her, she rolled her eyes.

"Show off," she muttered.

He laughed. "It took me a lot longer than *twice* to do what you just did. Who's the showoff now?"

She beamed. "Well, I have a great mentor!"

The warmth in his chest blossomed, but it was short-lived. Her comment reminded him of his mentor. "Let's split up and look around."

"And what exactly are we looking for?"

"Anything out of place. Specifically, a series of symbols etched into the stone."

Allyria nodded, and the two set about scouring the waist of the male sentinel. Kilal used his mastery of his Carvings to search in higher places, utilizing them to let him mimic, as close as he could, floating about.

They made quick work of the abdomen. Allyria, watching Kilal, began testing her own limits, and it wasn't long before she was half-climbing, half-floating, covering the left side of the sentinel's abdomen shortly after Kilal finished on the right.

They returned to the belt buckle.

"Anything?" he asked.

"Nothing."

"Let's proceed up. We are gonna tackle the shoulders now, so you must be extra careful with your gravity. Overshooting will put you out into open space with no bottom. Smaller jumps, while utilizing footholds naturally worn into the surface by time and weather, combined with increased strength should help you get to the shoulder without incident. Any questions?"

Allyria studied the abdomen and chest, her eyes constantly moving. She nodded.

Sha'tum guide your feet.

Yes, it would be easier for him to grab her and carry her up himself, but then what would she learn? Kilal would be leaving shortly after their exploration. He wanted to ensure she'd have confidence in herself. Additionally, she caught onto everything he showed her alarmingly fast, and there wasn't much doubt that she wouldn't do exactly as he suggested. But just in case, he called down for Alistair and waited for his dark-skinned friend to reveal himself.

"Look out for falling ladies!" Kilal yelled, to which Alistair gave him a thumbs up. He didn't return to his own studies, but waited beneath them for any sign of Allyria dropping.

It was overkill. Even if Allyria did fall, she wouldn't die, but Kilal didn't think she really needed that sort of pain in her life right now. A fall from two hundred feet was much more detrimental to a body than one from one hundred feet.

Content that everything was as safe as it could be while still providing an atmosphere for her to grow, Kilal nodded to Allyria, then took his first leap about fifteen feet up to a place where there were several chips in the stone he could slot his feet and hands into. He could've launched himself to the shoulder, but this way, he could show Allyria what to look for.

He waited for her to scan her side of the abdomen and make her first jump. It was only about ten feet up, but it was a safe position with good hand and foot holds.

The one thing Kilal hadn't prepared her for were the sudden winds which could erupt from the expanse of open space. And of course, one such gust blew at them at that moment.

Kilal raised his gravity, anchoring himself to the footholds just enough to not get swept aside. His breath caught when Allyria squeaked, but when he whipped his head around, ready to jump if need be, she was pressed tightly against the stone.

Attagirl.

When the wind died down, he raised a brow at her. She nodded her readiness for the next jump, and after he made another fifteen-foot leap, she followed with one of a similar distance.

Blessedly, no more gusts bombarded them, and slowly, the pair made their way up the face of the sentinel. Taking longer than normal, but shorter than it should have based on the experience level of one of the climbers, Kilal and Allyria graced the top of the shoulders. Intact and without accidents.

"Same as before," he called out. "And be careful. The last thing you want is to slip and fall. On either side. And don't worry about the back. We'll send someone here with Carvings better suited for a difficult ascent."

There wasn't much chance for them to slip. The shoulders were practically flat and nearly twenty feet at their widest point. Falling shouldn't be something to fear. But he could never be too careful.

Kilal studied every nook and crevice of the statue that he could find. He even shoved his hand into the ear and rubbed all about inside the deep hole, feeling for any strange markings.

"Anything?" he called over to Allyria.

"Nothing."

"Did you check inside the ear?"

"That's disgusting!"

"It's stone."

"But...what if there are bugs in it?"

"Are you afraid of bugs?"

"No! They're just...gross."

"Check inside the ear," Kilal said, "and I won't have you check inside the nostrils."

"Fine," she called back with more than a little irritation.

Content that there was nothing on the shoulder or side of the head, Kilal leaped onto the bridge of the nose, clinging fast to any handholds available. It was a good thing too, because not one second after finding one, a violent gust tried to rip him free.

When it was gone, he called to Allyria. "You fine over there?"

"I hate it up here."

He was glad she couldn't see his smile.

Shimmying about the face of the statue, Kilal paused to peer into an eye. The iris wasn't the same color as the rest of the stone, but the way it was etched and covered in the shadow of the brow, he could imagine it was blue.

"Where are your secrets?" he asked. "You've seen so much. How many people have you let come into this world?" Kilal waited, half expecting a response. But that was just him being wishful. And silly.

When he'd checked every inch he could, including inside the nose, he propelled himself up onto the helmet. It only took a few moments, but like the previous areas, he didn't find anything of importance.

The next spot he proceeded to was Allyria's shoulder, and together they quickly finished what she'd yet to cover.

"Head on down," Kilal said. "And this time, *lower* gravity. Don't raise it."

She glowered at him, muttering something about how funny he was, but most of what she said was lost to another howl of wind. After letting the gust pass, she landed smoothly, and once again Kilal was impressed by how quickly the girl picked up on Carvings.

With Allyria safely beneath them, Kilal easily crossed the hundred-foot gap between sentinels and landed gracefully beside Violet, who'd just made her way onto the head.

"Anything?" he asked.

"Ashes, no! Almost strangely so."

"What do you mean?"

"Do you recognize this stone? The material?"

Kilal'd thought about it. But now that Violet mentioned it, something did seem a little...off. He knelt, studying the helmet more closely.

"It's not quite the color of regular stone," he said. "Too

pale. But not white enough to be marble, either." He'd seen this color before, but whe—

"It looks just like—"

"The barracks. The stone which has been drained of life by the Veil!" they said together.

Bloodshed and Oaths! Why would the sentinels, fifty miles away from the barracks, be decayed in the same way?

Did the magic of the Veil mimic the magic used to open a sentinel portal?

It was another piece of the puzzle. A piece he didn't really know where to put or how to place it. Yet. But it was a piece, nonetheless.

~ CHAPTER 43 ~

They didn't discover anything out of the ordinary, besides the similarities between the stone used to make the sentinel and the barracks. After they relayed the information to Alistair, the four mature Arbiters and one immature Arbiter stuck their heads together under the warm sun, no longer in the shadowy recess of the colossal statues.

"Are we making something out of nothing?" Requiem asked. A fair question.

"Maybe," Violet said. "Either way, it bloody well doesn't make sense. How could the sentinels have been sucked of their essence? The Veil is all the way over there, and nothing else bloody looks like it's been drained."

"It's not a coincidence," Kilal said. "It's too far-fetched to be one."

"You know I always trust your instincts. Well, sometimes. I'm sure it's happened." Alistair said. "But I think this time we need a little more than that there gut of yours."

"If this was a site of otherworldly travel," Allyria said. She blushed when all eyes turned to her. "What if it was that? The power of world travel which caused this phenomenon?"

The four Arbiters stared at each other.

"Bloodshed and Oaths, she's probably right," Violet muttered.

"Getting' out-thought by a child." Alistair beamed.

"I'm not a child," Allyria said. "I'm a Pr—"

"Don't finish that sentence," Requiem said. "Remember the conversation in the car?"

The girl snapped her mouth shut and cast her eyes to the ground. Kilal was impressed; she actually looked ashamed.

"What does this tell us?" he asked.

"That world travel is bad?" Alistair said.

Violet groaned and shook her head. No one else responded.

Kilal sighed. It felt like they were onto something, but they were only left with more questions than answers. "Let's take this back to the others. While we're gone, the rest can study the sentinels. Maybe they can figure something out."

Allyria whimpered and rubbed at her forehead, and power spiked behind Kilal's eyes. He whirled around, eyes darting, searching, Carvings at the ready.

Everyone went alert, following his lead.

"Do you feel it?" he asked.

"We're not alone," Requiem said.

"There's definitely something here." Kilal could almost feel Violet's desire to sink her fists into something. Maybe he really *should* talk to her about that.

"I feel it," Allyria groaned, pointing at her eyes. "Right here, like it's in my brain trying to push its way out."

"Ah, now that's just your imigation," Alistair said, smiling.

"Sometimes I forget you're one of the oldest of us!" Requiem snapped.

"Thank you!"

Requiem and Violet both rolled their eyes.

Kilal focused on the shadow of the sentinel. Whatever it was, it was hiding there.

"Think it's Ash Fallen?" Violet asked.

"No." He'd been around more Ash Fallen than any human had a right to be. He'd know if it was one of them. But if it wasn't, and it wasn't an Arbiter either, what was it?

Movement. There! He sprang forward just as two eyes revealed themselves in the darkness. But as he reached for the feminine figure, it dissolved in his hand and receded into the blackness.

"What was it?" Requiem called.

"Not sure, but it's moving through the shadows," Kilal said. "I don't think we'll be able to physically hurt it."

Requiem nodded. As she did so, some of the darkness began coalescing around her. Her eyes became onyx orbs and puffs of shadow dripped from her limbs. A blade of twilight wisps appeared in her hands, and she sprung forward, sword leading the way. She came up just short of a spot on the sentinel's pinkie toe.

"Show yourself," Requiem said. "They may not be able to touch you, but this blade will sever your head from your spine before you can blink."

The creature revealed itself. It was slightly taller than Requiem and had a female human body, though it was completely black aside from long, white hair and matching eyes.

Requiem pushed the point of her blade forward until it drew red blood from the creature's darkened neck.

"Sister," it hissed, voice animalistic, ancient, and feminine. "This one is pleased to meet you. But your underestimation of this one is dangerous."

Faster than anyone could respond, the thing's head elongated and split in two, revealing rows and rows of long, sharp teeth. A hand with long claws shot out of the center of its chest. Like the head, the hand elongated and grabbed Requiem. It clamped around her and shoved her back, pulling the blade from its throat.

Kilal shot forward, Alistair at his heels, unsure what to do, but the creature let go of Requiem, and as quick as it had morphed into the grotesque thing, it restored itself to normal.

"This one does not appreciate being thought so little of. You found this one because this one let you find this one. Otherwise, this one would have eaten you all."

Kilal stopped short of the creature, keeping a few feet between them. Requiem returned to his side, visibly shaken.

"It called you sister," Kilal said. "You ever encounter it before?"

Requiem shook her head.

The creature lurched backward as if struck. "Sister, you would deny one of your own? This one is hurt."

"I don't know you," Requiem said. "What are you, and why are you spying on us?"

"This one merely follows orders."

"Who is ordering you to spy on us?"

"Not spy. This one has a message."

Kilal narrowed his eyes. "What message?"

The thing purred, and Kilal got the impression it was chuckling. "Brother doesn't like you very much. He enjoyed hitting you. Wishes to do it more."

"Do *you* know this thing?" Requiem asked him.

Enjoyed hitting me? The comment, the shadow-like creature, the elongating head and hand. The pieces all clicked into place.

"Jayden!"

"He's the one who kicked your behind, ain't he?" Alistair asked.

Kilal sucked in a sharp breath. "You do know I don't win every fight I'm in, right?"

Alistair shrugged. "Not with the way you strut 'bout actin' like you can't be killed and all."

"I *can't* be killed."

Alistair rolled his eyes and gestured to Allyria as she joined them. "There he goes again, all chest puffed out and braggin'."

"I'm not—" Kilal caught himself. Instead of engaging with Alistair's ridiculousness, he addressed Violet. "How have you not killed him?"

She grunted. "Thought about it plenty of times. But it would be like killing a child. I'd feel bad."

"Hey! I'm standin' right here, you know!"

"We know," Violet and Kilal said in unison.

"You all are...strange. Not like the other humans. This one is glad she doesn't have to eat you."

"You told us of Jayden," Requiem said, leveling her sword at the creature, "but I don't remember you telling us about this thing."

"This one is not a thing! This one is a Spirit of Gloom and a Royal. You'd do well to remember that, sister!"

"Why do you call me that?"

"This one simply names you for what you are."

"Yeah, Req. She's a Spirit of Gloom. And you're super gloomy. Sisters of gloom." Alistair beamed with pride. No one else seemed as pleased with his joke.

"Jayden," Kilal said, "was he the one who sent you?"

"This one does not like the name you use for brother. Should use real name. Justicus. Yes. Much better."

"Did Jay—Justicus send you?"

"Justicus did not send this one. Ximthar sent this one."

Ximthar; the Professor!

Kilal's heart nearly leaped into his throat. Was this really happening? Was his purpose for returning really going to be realized? There was still a chance his return, his abandonment of Lilliana, wouldn't be wasted!

Yet guilt curled in his gut. Was reunification with Requiem, his brothers and sisters, meeting Allyria a waste? Of course not! Still, he'd returned to find Jayden, the Professor, and Aya. And he thought he'd ruined his only opportunity to do just that. But it appeared fate had a strange way of writing itself, and he was being given a second chance.

"And what message did Ximthar have for us?" Kilal asked, trying to conceal his excitement.

"Not us. You. Tomorrow night. When moons at their highest. Silent Haven Asylum."

Kilal raised a brow. "That's it?"

"It is enough!" it said in an all too familiar way: human annoyance.

"Fine. We'll meet him there. Tomorrow night."

"Hold on a bloody minute," Violet said. "We're just going to take this...thing...for its word?"

The shadow creature *tsked*, and a white line appeared, cutting its head in two once again. "Not...thing. Spirit of Gloom. Royal. Do...not...make mistake again. Ximthar only requests big one to arrive alive. Not others."

"I'd like to see you bloody try something!" Violet said, shouldering her way between Kilal and Requiem.

Requiem wheeled on her. "Enough! This isn't the time for violence." She stepped in front of the fuming Arbiter. "Forgive us...Royal. We're not accustomed to interacting with spirits."

The tsk turned to a purr. "This one accepts apology."

"So," Kilal said, "The asylum. Silent Haven. We'll be there."

The creature pointed a slender finger at him. "You. Not we."

"If you think we'll let him go alone, you're blo—"

Kilal held up a hand, cutting off Violet's outburst. "Tomorrow then," he said, choosing his words carefully. He didn't want to agree to going alone, but he didn't want an argument with that creature, either.

The thing began slipping down into the shadows, her body becoming less opaque. "Tomorrow then." As it slid beneath the surface of the darkness, disappearing, the words became garbled as if spoken underwater.

A giant grin, almost painful, worked its way onto Kilal's face.

"What are you thinking?" Violet yelled. No amount of makeup could dull the ferocity of her features. "What the bloody ashes was that? Spirit of Gloom? I, for one, have never heard of such a thing, and I bet none of you have, either. Bloodshed and Oaths, the way its head split, and it grew an extra arm. Ashes, we're not just going to trust it! We can't!"

"We can," Kilal said calmly. "And we will. Because we have no other option."

I'm back on the trail, he thought, giddy. *I'll be back soon, Lilliana. I promise.*

"Jayden. Ximthar. They're the ones with the answers. I lost them once. I won't let another opportunity slip through my fingers. Let's head back to the barracks." Kilal spoke in a tone ensuring everyone understood the situation was non-negotiable. "We have a meeting to prepare for."

~ CHAPTER 44 ~

"You're leaving me too." A tear trickled down Allyria's cheek.

Upon returning to the barracks and divulging to the group what had happened at the sentinels, Kilal brought her down to the stables to break the news. He knew it wouldn't be easy. But he did have a contingency of sorts, a way to soften the blow.

"I'm sorry, Allyria, but where we're going, it's too dangerous. If I weren't immortal, I wouldn't have survived my time over there. I can't let you accompany me, knowing you probably won't return."

"You're letting Requiem go," Allyria said, running a hand over the wood of one of the dozen abandoned stalls. "She's not immortal."

"If it were up to me, she wouldn't be coming, but I don't control her."

"You don't control me!"

Poor choice of words, idiot.

Kilal sighed. "I'm sorry. That's not what I meant."

"Well, what did you mean?" she said with an attitude as fiery as her hair.

"I meant Requiem does what she wants. There is no knocking sense into her. But you're still young, and the youth should respect the wisdom of their elders. Plus, you're my mentee. Number one rule, for better or worse, of mentorship is the mentee respects the mentor's wisdom."

"That's a dumb rule," she muttered. "What if," she looked anywhere but at him, "you showed me your Carving of Immortality?"

Nausea hit him harder than an Arbiter with Deific Strength. It transformed into fear and fear into guilt.

"No. *No.*"

The wooden wall of the stall she had her hand on snapped with a loud snap. Her face hardened, flushed. She took a step towards him, and the wood in her grip imploded with a loud crack.

"That's so *selfish*," she growled. "You have the answer to save *everyone*, and you hog it all for yourself. What happened to oath this and oath that, and Arbiters are our brothers and sisters, and we're supposed to care for each other? If that were the case, why wouldn't you give them the means needed to *not die.*"

"Careful," Kilal said, matching growl for growl. "You don't know what you're saying."

She took another step forward, glaring at him. They were nearly chest to chest. Only a head shorter than him, she barely had to crane her neck to look into his eyes. "I think I do. I'm just the only one willing to say it to you."

A crack in the earthen floor beneath them appeared between her feet. She was losing control of her Carvings. If he didn't do something, things would rapidly spiral to a depth he didn't want to experience. Allyria's emotions were a storm of anger and misunderstanding, and Kilal's own emotional intensity matched hers.

He could squash the conversation without much effort. Tell her no was no and leave. Part ways in the worst possible manner, furthering her trauma of abandonment, just to go to the Ashen Lands and die, again furthering her trauma. But there was another way. A way which would add to his own trauma but save her from more.

Kilal squeezed his eyes shut and took a deep breath. He'd take option two.

"I shared immortality with someone once before," he said. Allyria grew blurry. "She...she died after activating it. Of old age."

Allyria frowned. "That doesn't sound so bad."

"Old age took her in two minutes."

"What?"

Kilal didn't know if it was a question of shock or an actual request for him to elaborate. "She wasn't much older than yourself, early twenties, but in two minutes, she aged; wrinkled, her hair grayed, her teeth fell out. She was nothing but a withered corpse in my arms. It happened so fast, I couldn't think of anything to do."

"That's...that's not...possible," Allyria whispered, eyes straight ahead.

"I agree. It's not possible. A Carving shouldn't work for one Arbiter but kill another. But that's what happened. I've never taught it to anyone else for that reason. I can't risk it happening again."

Kilal stepped back and crossed his arms, but not before wiping his cheeks. "Do you know what it's like, being considered by everyone—whether they say it or not—as selfish? Being selfish to the magnitude of being able to save everyone but *choosing* not to? You'd think it would hurt, wouldn't you?"

Allyria nodded.

"Well, you're right. It does hurt. But the worst pain that comes with this burden is the loneliness. I'm sorry, Allyria, but I can't give you this Carving. I would if I could, but all evidence points to it taking your life, not extending it."

She looked everywhere but at him. Was she going to rush out of the stables, screaming her hatred? Would she build a wall between the two of them in their, possibly, final moments together? Would that be how she'd remember him?

"I don't think you're selfish," she whispered.

A sad smile worked its way onto his face. "That's a reli—"

Allyria leaped at him, wrapping her arms around his abdomen and burying her face against his chest. And wept.

Kilal was so surprised, he stood frozen, hands at his side. "It's okay," he said, thawing and wrapping his arms around her. He kissed the top of her head—the tension he anticipated didn't happen. "I'm coming back. I promise. I know what you've been through. That everyone's left you. But I'm *not* everyone. I'm going to the Ashen Lands and will wipe the floor with Ashen Kane. I'll find Lilliana. Then, I'll return."

"And how long will that take?" she said, voice muffled by his shirt.

"I..." That was a lie he couldn't make himself say. "I don't know. But I will come back."

"Promise?"

"Promise."

Please forgive me. Please understand if I don't return.

"You'll be happy to know I have a gift for you," Kilal said.

Allyria unwrapped her arms and stepped back. Smiling a little, she rubbed her hands together. "I do like gifts!"

He couldn't help but match her infectious smile. From his back pocket, he pulled out twelve folded pages and handed them to her. She took them, hesitant, a brow raised. She didn't ask what they were, and Kilal was sure it was because she already knew.

Almost reverently, she unfolded the clump of papers and scanned the first one. Her jaw dropped lower and lower while her brows rose along her forehead. "This...this..." She shoved the pages against his chest. "I can't accept this. These are yours. Your blood was spilled for these."

Gently, Kilal took hold of her hand and pushed it back. She wouldn't know how much her sentiment meant to him, but the truth was, very little of his own blood was involved. Most of it was by the original owners of the Carvings while he ripped the knowledge from them.

"And now, I gift them to you," he said.

The light overhead flickered and the room filled with dozens of corpses. The corpses of the men and women he'd stolen from.

Kilal blinked, and the room returned to normal. He took a deep breath, calming his nerves. "Please, you'll be a better steward of this knowledge than I was."

A broad smile nearly split her face in two. "Well then, I accept! Deific Healing?" She nearly cried out the title. "Ha! That'll be the first one I carve." Allyria grunted as she began running her eyes over the sketches and the notes. "Ashes, that's going to be hard to replicate."

It was one of the more intricate and detailed Carvings, with runes requiring details and spacings as small as one millimeter.

"I can't wait to show Nam and Garret!"

Kilal placed both hands on her shoulders. She didn't jump or jerk at the contact, though she peered up at him questioningly. "There's great power in these Carvings. You *can't*, I repeat, *cannot* show them to anyone. That includes Garret and Nam."

"But—"

"Promise me," Kilal said. "There are Carvings in your hands Arbiters—possibly even some we know—would kill for. *Do not* show *anyone*. Showing them to Nam and Garret could be a death warrant for them, let alone yourself. Guard them with your life. This is a huge responsibility, but I'm trusting you to keep them safe."

Her face hardened. "I promise." She gave a curt nod. "A death warrant? Really?"

"There's nothing more valuable to an Arbiter than knowledge. And what I've given you is two centuries of Carvings lost to the world. *Someone* will be willing to kill you or anyone else for them. Especially in the format you have them: documented attempts, handwritten dimensions, notes. Even regular humans will want those sheets. They could be sold for a fortune to an Arbiter. Or an organization like the Heirs. So, guard them. With your life, if need be."

Her face hardened even more. "I promise."

Kilal smiled and wrapped an arm around her shoulders. "Good. Because you'll need these tomorrow and for however long I'll be gone, so ma—"

"Element Imbuement," she wasn't paying attention, "Bringer of Cold, Storm Thrower?"

As she read off the titles of some of the Carvings, heat trickled into Kilal's cheeks. He wasn't the best at naming things.

She clutched the papers to her chest. "Thank you," she whispered through teary eyes.

"I know we haven't had much time together," he said, "but you have a good heart. And you'll be a powerful Arbiter. While I'm gone, look after everyone. Particularly Garret and Nam. But don't let that go to your head. You're a Prime. It's our responsibility to not only look after the Sunlight Domain but to be an example to the Enlightened and High Arbiters. Don't forget that. And learn from Alistair. I'll be handing over your mentorship to him."

"Alistair? Really?"

Kilal chuckled. "He likes to pretend he's a buffoon, but he's one of the smartest men I know, with one of the purest hearts. And don't forget who mentored *him*. Me."

Allyria rolled her eyes. "Fine. If that's what's needed."

"I could also set you up with a mentorship with Ahnk, if you would prefer that?"

Her cheeks turned crimson. "What? Why would I want that?" she snapped.

He grinned. "No particular reason. Let's head back inside."

Arm still around her, a knot formed in his stomach and blossomed into his chest and throat. There was a good chance they'd never see each other again. He squeezed her shoulder, and she pressed into his side. He nearly wept.

The trust she showed him, allowing him to touch her. It meant everything.

Failure in his mission was no longer an option. Not that it ever had been, but he'd once accepted death to be at the end of his mission. A part of him even longed for it. Freedom from life, from his past, from his mind; would it be so bad? But he'd returned. He'd reunited with Requiem, Alistair, Violet. He'd inserted himself into Allyria's life, taking on a fatherly role. And she'd trusted him with that.

I won't fail. I won't die. Ashen Kane, Avinoth, whoever you are, I'm coming for you.

~ CHAPTER 45 ~

For the last time, the Arbiters reconvened at the round table.

"It's been decided," Enoch's Voice repeated. "We'll break into three teams. Kilal and Requiem will meet with Ximthar and Justicus. Myself and those with me will head into the Undercity. Violet, Alistair, and...Allyria will act as bait."

No one was happy about Kilal and Allyria's decision for her to join the decoy team. There was a very real possibility they'd be in the most danger, at least on this side of the Veil. They were to roam the city, both above and occasionally in the sewers, to draw attention away from the other two teams, or assist either of them if necessary.

No one was worried about Sienna catching their trail. If she was coming for anyone, it would be Kilal and Requiem. Which is why he not only volunteered Allyria to be on a team, but ensured she was with Alistair and Violet. If there were a safe place, it was with those two.

Nanomia and Garret would go with Leyloni and Brea, one of Enoch's. A small farmhouse north of their current location was loyal to the resistance and homed Arbiters from time to time. The two new recruits would begin their training there.

"The three teams leave tomorrow at first light," Enoch's Voice said. "We'll take a bus to the Dead Zone. From there, we'll split up and enter Silent Haven through the sewers. This should buy us enough time, particularly for Kilal and Requiem, to reach our destinations in peace. The rest of you have your orders. Good luck everyone, and may Sha'tum guide our road."

***

The night dragged on in quiet solitude. Requiem disappeared into the night without a word. A strange decision considering they could finally spend some time together and talk. Alistair drank himself into a blissful unconsciousness. Kilal was only a little jealous. He caught Ahnk and Violet together on the ramparts of the barracks and didn't want to interrupt.

At one point, he and Enoch crossed paths, but Kilal wasn't *that* desperate for human interaction.

Eventually, he convinced Allyria to practice a few of the newer Carvings. Deific Healing and Deific Strength were the most intricate of the dozen he'd given her. After spilling a lot of blood over the span of a few attempts at each, Kilal was content with her ability to etch them both.

It had taken him weeks to achieve the same level of competency Allyria had accomplished in the span of a few hours. Her ability to carve continued to amaze him. He'd never seen skill like hers. If she dedicated as much time in the first few months of her mentorship with him as he had with his mentor, she'd probably surpass his *current* capabilities.

She could be the greatest Arbiter there ever was.

Unfortunately, fate had other plans for them, and a time of peace for Allyria to dedicate to her studies wasn't in store for her. But it could be argued that the best way to learn was by doing, and she'd be given a lot of doing soon. Kilal just wished he could be with her.

Eventually, it was time for him and Allyria to part for the night. Her demeanor had shifted to one of gloomy grumpiness, and he knew why. She was mentally preparing for their separation. In her mind, what was convincing her he'd return? He could promise her until he was blue in the face, but until he actually came back, she'd assume he was just another person to fail her. And that made leaving harder. But Lilliana was also waiting for him.

And so was Ashen Kane.

Saying goodnight, Allyria refused to let him hug her. She jerked away from him as he made his attempt. Quietly, he sighed. He didn't blame her. How could he? If anything, he pitied her. Would she regret their last encounter for the rest of her life? But what more could he do?

Nothing. I can't do anything about it.

Resolute, determined, and exhausted, Kilal retired to his cot in a dark corner, grateful for the swift arrival of sleep. It may be the last opportunity he'd have to sleep in a bed for a long time. Possibly ever again. So, he'd better enjoy it.

***

The bus ride was just as somber as the previous night had been. Kilal had gotten up early and woke Allyria, to which she'd responded with many grumbles, complaints, yawns, and eye rubs. Everyone else, except a few of Enoch's people, had already been awake. Getting up early to give oneself ample time to carve was common sense for anyone worth their Carvings.

Allyria was still learning what separated an Arbiter from a good Arbiter. And carving early, despite being a teenager's worst nightmare, was one of those things.

The bus, called in by Enoch through another one of his mysterious contacts, arrived shortly after Kilal and Allyria had finished activating their chosen abilities. While they loaded up, Kilal glanced around, searching for Requiem.

"Alistair," he called, jogging up to his old friend. "We can't leave yet. Req isn't here."

"She's goin' to meet us there," Alistair said. "Got herself somethin' to do."

"Something to do?" Kilal repeated. What could she possibly have to do so close to their mission time?

Strangely, he didn't panic. He wasn't even surprised. As if, on some level, he'd been expecting it. And with the odd ways she'd been acting, the real question was, why *wouldn't* he expect it?

One Arbiter short, the group funneled onto the small, rusty bus, packing themselves into it tighter than tentacles on a Pestilence Plague.

Allyria wouldn't look at him. Kilal wondered if her placement, between a window and Violet, was on purpose. Anything to avoid him. Irritation flared, but he quickly beat it back. He had to remind himself, again, that it wasn't her fault.

The only open seat was next to Alistair, who somehow was already fast asleep, snoring, despite having been awake minutes earlier. Kilal had always been convinced the man could etch a fourth Carving to gain the uncanny ability to sleep anywhere, anytime, as if on call.

Once everyone was seated, the bus's engine revved to life, and they were off. No one spoke, no one so much as sighed. All was silent...except the snoring Alistair. There was a respectful reverence in the air for what they were all heading towards. A mission with the high probability of saving their world. Or dooming it.

Like the trip to the barracks, there wasn't much traffic on the road. A few tractors of varying degrees of rust and age and a handful of cars, most trucks pulling barrels and crates of food towards the city or returning to a farm after dropping off its freight. There was a time, even in Kilal's life, where you couldn't drive a minute without passing another vehicle. All the more reason to successfully complete their mission.

Destroy Ashen Kane and stop his army, figure out a way to utilize the sentinels, and get off their floating, decaying rock.

Kilal had been gone for ten years, and during his absence, it felt like the population had dropped the same amount it had during the previous one hundred and ninety years of his life. Setting Ashen Kane and his army of Ash Fallen aside, he didn't know if the Sunlight Domain had another century of life left in it.

Had Sha'tum and the first generation of Arbiters really sacrificed themselves only to give the world another thousand years? Seemed like a waste. But a waste it wouldn't be if Kilal and Enoch were successful.

Kilal resigned himself to a long trip in silence. Silence except for the thundering voices in his mind, reminding him of all the loved ones he'd lost on much simpler missions.

~ CHAPTER 46 ~

"Ouch!" Alistair cried out, lurching forward after Kilal elbowed him in the side. "What'cha do that for?"

Kilal batted his eyes at him. "Was six hours not enough beauty sleep for you?"

"Sixty hours wouldn't be enough beauty sleep for that ugly mug," Violet said, exiting her row, Allyria in tow.

"Well, that's not what'cha mother said last night."

Violet put on a mask of cool indifference. "My mother is dead."

"Right." Alistair snapped a finger. "It wasn't your mother. It was your grandnanny!"

Allyria snickered. Violet guffawed. "If my mother is dead, what makes you think my grandnanny...oh, just forget it!" She didn't stick around to hear anything. Violet pushed past Enoch.

Alistair winked at Allyria. "That's the key to it. Gotta confuse them. Then they get all baffled like and concede defeat."

Allyria burst into laughter. Until she caught Kilal's gaze. Then she blushed and hurried off the bus, also pushing past Enoch, who looked ready to express his annoyance with his *own* voice. Instead, he snapped his finger and the pale, bald, bland specimen of a man leaned forward to hear Enoch's whisper.

"This is your fault," the Voice said to him.

Kilal didn't need to feign confusion. "My fault? How?"

"This is *your* generation of Arbiters. They all look up to you. And this is what we get."

He emitted a low growl. "Enoch, why don't we part ways in an amicable nature? Not mincing words and throwing around hurtful accusations."

Enoch actually frowned. Was he guilted by Kilal's words? Had he expected Kilal to take the bait and argue like the old days?

"You're right," Enoch's Voice said. "Good luck. Bring her back to us."

Kilal wasn't sure who 'her' was: Requiem or Lilliana. Enoch had never been much of a fan of Lilliana, and vice versa. So, it must be Requiem. Was it out of respect for her? Or something else?

He stumbled forward from a push in the back. "Get a move on, old man," Alistair said.

The last two off the bus, Enoch threw a pouch of coins to the driver, and the three teams stood at the entrance to the Dead Zone.

Requiem revealed herself from the shadows of a collapsed building. She waved and nodded to Enoch as if it was perfectly normal to separate herself from the group and arrive at their destination before them.

She approached Kilal, and at least had a nod *and* a smile for him. "Did you get some sleep?"

"I did," Kilal said. "But something tells me you didn't."

There were no indications of a lack of sleep. No darkening of the eyes. No yawns or slumped shoulders. Appearance-wise, she might as well have had just as much sleep as him. And yet, she probably hadn't slept a minute. She wouldn't separate herself from them just to sleep in a different location. No, she had a reason for disappearing.

She shrugged but didn't dispute his statement.

"You won't tell me where you went and why, huh?"

She gave another shrug, but it was almost apologetic. "I'm sorry, Kilal. If your return were under different circumstances, I'd tell you everything."

Because he didn't come to her, he'd broken her trust and had to face the consequence. "I understand."

She studied his eyes, peering up into them. "No. You don't. There isn't enough time. Ashen Kane, the return of Lilliana, the Heirs of the Promise, getting off this rock—there's too much to do, and I have too much to talk about."

"We just had a six-hour drive," Kilal said flatly.

She reached up and patted his cheek. "I know. But I had to prepare my way."

My way? Ashes! What does that mean?

"If...when we return," Requiem continued, "return with Lilliana, after we defeat Ashen Kane, I'll tell you everything. I promise. I want you to know everything that's happened to me, *and* I want to know everything that's happened to you. But our oath dictates where our loyalties and responsibilities lay first and foremost. And it's not with each other."

Bloodshed and Oaths, she was right.

Kilal took her small hand into his much larger one and squeezed. "After. And with Lilliana. We both share our stories."

He didn't want to wait, but maybe he wouldn't have to. Maybe they'd find time to share with each other. It was unlikely, but he could hold out hope. Either way, she was right.

And that's why so many break the oath, a sly whisper echoes through his mind. *Because the oath and the road it forces us to walk is anything but fair.*

Enoch's Voice called everyone together. "Today may be the single most important day in our history," he began. "Our world is dying. Our enemy is at our gate. And it—"

"Can you put a bit more emotion in your words, friend?" Alistair interrupted. "This is possibly gonna be the end for some of us, after all. Would just be nice to be motivated and such, instead of being put to sleep."

Enoch bored a hole the size of an apple into his head. Or at least he would have if he had such a Carving.

Alistair shrugged. "I'm just sayin' what we all thinkin'. No need to go glarin' at me."

The Voice coughed into a fist. Kilal chuckled. If there was one thing Alistair wasn't, it was proper. The man thrived on annoying people. Kilal would have thought he'd be a little too old for such a thing after so much time, but apparently not.

In Alistair's defense, he *was* maturing. When Kilal took him in as a ten-year-old, the first decade or so of their mentorship had been...difficult, to say the least. On more than one occasion, Kilal had let his anger with the child get the best of him. Not his proudest moments.

"And it's up to us to save our world," the Voice continued. "Good luck to everyone, and may Sha'tum guide our fates."

"Bit of a downer," Alistair mumbled.

"And short," Allyria said at his side. They shared a laugh.

Kilal and Alistair turned and gave each other bone-crunching hugs. "Brin' her back, you hear," Alistair said. "Brin' my niece back to me. And take care of the grumpy one. She'll deny it, but she needs someone to do just that."

Kilal smiled. A tear splashed onto his cheek. "I will. And you watch over the little flame."

"Bah." Alistair waved a hand dismissively. "That one'll be lookin' after me."

He chuckled. "You're probably right. But just in case, keep her safe. For me."

In a rare moment, Alistair grew somber. "I promise."

Kilal made his rounds, saying goodbye to everyone he knew and shaking hands with those he didn't, saving Violet for last.

"I told Alistair to look after Allyria," he whispered into her ear as they embraced, "but we both know it'll be you looking after both of them."

Violet giggled and pulled back. Kilal swept a stray strand

of recently combed hair from her forehead and planted a kiss on it. "I'm so proud of you. You've grown so much, and I look forward to seeing you continue to grow."

A sob escaped Violet's throat, and she buried her face against his chest. He imagined she was glad Ahnk wasn't around to witness it. Even though it would be a good thing for him to see that, despite her tough exterior, she was still human.

"Do you really have to leave again? So soon?"

Kilal rested his chin on the top of her head and stroked her hair. "I do. But I'll do everything in my power to return, and this time, with Lilliana."

"And I'll take care of Allyria," she said. "I promise."

"Thank you."

The last person to say goodbye to was doing everything she could to avoid him. She tied her shoelaces, coughed, sneezed, studied a rock, the sky, her nails. Standing in front of Allyria, his shadow cast upon her, she still didn't look at him. She also didn't move away when he wrapped her in a big hug. She shook as her vulnerability manifested as tears.

"I'm sorry," Kilal whispered so only they could hear. He was grateful everyone seemed to understand their need for privacy and moved away from them. "I don't want to leave. I wish I could stay here with you."

"Then stay," she pleaded, adopting a similar posture as Violet, face in his chest, but no arms around his waist.

"I can't, and you know that. We're Arbiters and, first and foremost, we're here to protect our land. Our people. It's something no one but us can understand. It's hard, sometimes impossible, but we do it anyway. Because it's what we were born to do. So, for a little bit, we have to part. You have your mission, I have mine. And we don't want to do it, but we must. Because if we don't, who will?"

He sighed, content, when Allyria wrapped her arms around him, reciprocating the hug. Together, they wept. It hadn't been long, a few days, though it felt like more since they'd met. But their bond, their shared experiences and similar traumas bound them tighter than any blood relation could.

"I'm sorry," Allyria said after a while. "I'm sorry for ignoring you. I thought ... I thought it'd be easier to part if I b-blamed you for it. It was w-wrong. And I'm sorry. P- please forgive m-me!"

Her sobbing increased. He held her tighter and stroked her long, red hair. "You don't need to apologize. Not to me. Not to anyone. You were acting on instinct created by loss and abandonment. No one, including me, can blame you for that." Regardless, she needed to hear the words, even if he didn't need to say them. "But I forgive you."

Allyria pulled back. She reached up and wiped away a tear dripping down his cheek with her thumb. And smiled. "I'll take care of Violet and Alistair. I want you to be able to give them big hugs *when* you return."

Kilal laughed. "Thank you! Those two will need someone to look after them. That's a difficult job, but I believe in you."

With nothing left to say, he embraced Allyria one more time. He nearly had to peel her off him when it was time. Requiem stepped in between them, hugging the young girl and whispering something in Allyria's ears. It warmed his fragile heart, considering how cold Requiem had been toward her initially.

Farewells finished, everyone nodded, some waved, and went their separate ways. Despite his promises and his wishes, Kilal didn't anticipate seeing any of them ever again.

The tears that dripped from his chin for only Requiem and him to see wouldn't be the last he'd shed for them.

~ WOLFE ~

If only the bloody stones could do something about his sense of smell. Something besides enhancing it.

Wolfe twisted and tapped the green gem in the ring on his left forefinger. It was a practice he'd adopted to help release nervous energy.

No, not nervous energy. Anticipatory energy. Not that there was much difference.

"Did you drag me down here to show me something of importance, Arbiter?" he growled. "Or just to smell the pleasant aromas created by the denizens of your city?"

The visitor blanched. Tor'et snickered behind him, if snickering is what it could be called. It was more like a high-pitched squeal. The man was infuriating. Why did the stones have to choose him, of all people? Wolfe had left behind many good men and women. Couldn't any of them have been chosen? It was a question that frequented him whenever Tor'et was around.

"Yes, sir," the Arbiter paled further. "I mean, no, sir."

Tor'et tsked. "What the ash-for-brains means is, the room with the symbols is just ahead."

Wolfe pinched his nose shut, and picked up his pace, forcing the female Arbiter ahead of them, holding a ball of light in her hand, to also speed up.

I swear, if these fools dragged me down here for nothing...

He wouldn't do anything. Besides growl and glower and groan and put the fear of a Plague into them. But he wouldn't do anything *permanent*. Despite the rumors and implications of his overthrow of the Keepers and takeover of the land, Wolfe didn't relish killing. Humans, especially Arbiters, were resources, and where Wolfe came from, resources equated to life.

Since Requiem escaped with the help of the Immortal Arbiter, Wolfe had tasked Tor'et with finding another access point into the ruins beneath the city. Days later, one was located. How Tor'et found it, Wolfe would never know or ask.

The manhole to a tight stairwell and narrow hall was beneath a thick, two-foot layer of waste and sewage. That waste had drained through the manhole when it opened, and Wolfe now had the privilege of slogging his way through the mess.

A dark object, familiarly shaped, bumped into his waist and the stench assaulted his nose, despite it being pinched shut.

Resource or not, if their venture didn't produce any headway in their goals, he may just kill Tor'et for making him endure it. The stone on his finger seemed to react to the desire. A warm feeling flushed through him, an agreement to his predicament.

Tor'et, walking a few feet in front of him, must have sensed something. He turned and eyed Wolfe, smiling. But Wolfe was all too familiar with what it concealed: hate. Tor'et hated him, and he did a poor job of hiding it. Not that it mattered. They had a mission, and the Elemental Godstone had chosen Tor'et.

Wolfe would have to continue trusting the stone's choice, despite his disagreement and confusion with the pairing.

Eventually, the narrow passageway came to an end, and the group had to climb up to the next portion of the strange underground passage. Wolfe was the last to ascend into the dimly lit, nondescript room with piles of broken junk, dust, a few bones, and what looked like collapsed shelves. It was under those shelves that, when pushed aside, the light from the woman's hand revealed a series of four symbols.

Wolfe's breath caught. He didn't recognize any of the runes. Neither did the Arbiters.

"Do it," he commanded, and the male Arbiter canceled his Carvings and etched the sequence of symbols in their place.

Wolfe hadn't been able to get anything from Requiem. She was like a steel lockbox. One without a keyhole. But, unbeknownst to Ahnk and Tor'et, he had a mind reader employed in the room adjacent to the one where Tor'et had tortured Ahnk, and even through Ahnk's tough mental defenses, the reader had been able to pull a few important pieces of information from the Arbiter. Specifically, how to access the ruins beneath the Undercity.

The only reason Sienna found Ahnk and Requiem was because, in their haste to explore the ruins they'd discovered, they'd left the opening slightly askew. It probably would've gone unnoticed by anyone other than Sienna. But it was enough for her to track them. And now, Wolfe knew exactly how to search out entries into the ruins.

Completed, the Arbiter's eyes glowed white. He proceeded around the room, touching four points. Upon completing the fourth, the room vibrated, and the chunk of stone the symbols had been etched into receded, revealing another dark descent.

At least that one wouldn't be half-filled with the city's waste.

Tor'et pushed past the Arbiters. There was an all too familiar hunger in his eyes.

"Wait," Wolfe said, voice barely above a whisper. Tor'et froze.

It was Wolfe's turn to push past everyone. As far as he and anyone else knew, the shadowy recess just made available hadn't held human breath in over a thousand years, and it would be Wolfe's breath to fill it first.

"Sir, the light," the woman said.

Wolfe ignored her and, hands on ladder rungs, descended into the void.

The stones will guide me.

Disease wasn't the only thing the gems gave him power over. They also enhanced his senses; his smell was not the only one impacted.

At the bottom lay a room of similar size to the one above, and almost an exact replica of the one Sienna had found Ahnk and Requiem in. At least, an exact replica *before* they'd set it on fire. But unlike the one above, the condition was much better.

A series of machines lined the opposite wall, machines he'd never laid eyes upon. He would need to send for Fazin. Shelves of books stacked all the way to the ceiling covered the wall to his right. The wall the ladder was connected to held a few hanging storage cabinets, their contents unknown. The final wall was barren.

Upon taking his first step into the room, three blue lines traced the ceiling and floor and filled the space with fluorescent light.

"Ashes!" the woman cursed when the ball of illumination in her palm was snuffed out.

The blue glow had *canceled* a Carving? Was that even possible? Apparently so.

Tor'et and Wolfe exchanged a look, both grinning.

That was big. Whether they discovered anything to help them get off this bloody rock or not, they'd just stumbled on a new way to render Arbiters powerless.

That was very big, indeed.

PART THREE

~ CHAPTER 47 ~

The sky thundered and dumped gallons of rain on Kilal and Requiem as they exited the abandoned warehouse. Lightning cracked and snaked across the sky. Waiting in the doorway, Kilal rolled his eyes.

"I hate getting wet," he muttered.

Requiem smirked. "Now what would everyone think of the great Immortal Arbiter if they knew that?"

Kilal grunted. "Might realize I'm only a bloody human."

She patted him on the chest and smiled.

The trip through the Dead Zone, as well as the boat ride through the sewers, had been uneventful, and they arrived safely and unmolested in Silent Haven. Kilal could only hope the rest of their trip would be much the same. A car was supposedly waiting for them a few blocks over, which they'd take twenty or so miles north to the Silent Haven Asylum. They could make quicker time if they took to the roofs, but they were trying to be inconspicuous, to blend in, and leaping from the rooftops was anything but inconspicuous.

"Never thought—" Thunder crashed overhead, drowning out Kilal's voice. When it was over, he continued. "Never thought I'd return to the asylum." Even without the thunder, the rain pelted hard enough to force him to half-yell.

Requiem stared off into the night, eyes distant. "Me neither."

Kilal cocked his head. "When were you a patient there? You never told me that."

She remained locked onto something in the distance only she could see. "Because it was after you left."

He waited for more, but nothing came. Was that where she'd been for six months? But how would she have gotten powers from her time in the asylum?

"You ready to brave the elements?" Requiem teased.

Kilal sighed. "The great Immortal Arbiter will not back down in the face of such adversity!"

She smirked and rolled her eyes. "Yes, he's *so* brave. But..." She paused and cocked her head. "You should wait here."

"I'm not leaving you."

She again rolled her eyes. "We've both been black marked by the Heirs. Any Arbiter who sees us will immediately try to kill us. Count on it. I can hide in this weather. You can't."

Requiem left it at that, but Kilal understood. She could pull her dark hood up and remain discreet. He, however, couldn't. Yes, the streets were practically barren, but all it took was one person spotting him, recognizing his size, and making a call.

He hated how bloody right she was.

"Fine," he said. "I'll wait inside. Honk when you get here." As she turned to leave, he grabbed her arm. "Be careful. If you run into trouble, scream. I'll come."

She narrowed her eyes and pulled her arm free. "You afraid I'll disappear for ten years?"

Kilal recoiled. The words slapped him, punched him, kicked him in all the wrong places. Requiem lowered her gaze, and he could see the regret in her eyes, but she didn't apologize. Not that she needed to. He deserved whatever anger she directed at him. So, he waited, alone in the dark, for Requiem's return.

He would be lying if he said the voices in his head didn't taunt him, whisper to him, reinforce her statement of disappearing. He audibly sighed in relief when she pulled up beside the abandoned warehouse and honked.

Kilal hustled out from the protection of the building, and even though the car was only a few paces away, he was soaked by the time he pulled the door shut.

The next few days were going to be a delight.

***

Like the rest of their trek to the city, the ride to the asylum was free of any encounters. As they rolled up, rain, thunder, and lightning rattled the car. The eerie lights and noises were a fitting background for the four stories tall square brick building.

Memories of his time there shoved past the others. Would it, too, be different than he remembered? Everything else had changed over the last decade, so why wouldn't the asylum? But, almost uncannily, for a hundred and ninety years, the building hadn't changed much. It underwent occasional repairs, but what stood before him was much the same as when he'd first laid eyes on it. And he couldn't think of a reason why they would've changed the interior to anything but white. The aged building seemed to be stuck in time, never able to be anything other than what it had been created to be.

The parking lot was half-empty. The night staff made up only half the workers as the day shift.

As a bolt of lightning illuminated the building and a clash of thunder reverberated through his bones, Kilal recalled his last visit after his foray into the Northern Ruins. They'd been nights of drug-induced sleep. Much of what he could remember was more embarrassing than not. He'd been a raving lunatic, unruly and mad. But as the days drifted by, his lunacy faded, and eventually, he was considered fit for release.

Kilal, the bloody Immortal Arbiter, deemed mentally fit to leave the insane asylum.

If only they knew the truth of what goes on in this head.

"I don't like this," Requiem said, slowly guiding the car into the closest available parking spot. Which wasn't very close at all. "Feels...wrong."

Kilal grunted. "It's an asylum. Of course it does. It's where we send people we don't know how to help."

"No. More than that. Why are we meeting Ximthar and Jayden here of all places? And didn't you say there was a third you were looking for?"

He nodded. "Aya."

"None of this makes sense." Requiem turned the engine off.

Kilal didn't feel the unease Requiem seemed to. How could he? He was minutes away from meeting the people he'd returned to the Sunlight Domain for, abandoning his daughter in the process. His jubilation wouldn't be doused by the somber reality of where they were and the oddity of it.

"I agree. But we're here, and we have a mission. One we can't fail. So, let's go make some new friends."

Requiem nodded, and together they exited the car.

~ CHAPTER 48 ~

By the time they made it to the glass door entrance, Kilal had forgotten what it felt like to be dry.

Inside the foyer, he harkened back to the last time he was in an open room, staring at a guard and a receptionist. Hopefully, the day's endeavor would be a little more fruitful. He internally cringed and rebuked himself. Was finding Requiem not fruitful? It was about the most fruitful thing he could've accomplished on the trip. If their return to the asylum could be half as rewarding as reunification with the woman he'd dreamed about almost every time he slept in the last ten years, he'd count it as a successful meeting.

Unfortunately, the lone guard—with thinning hair and a wiry mustache wearing a blue button-up shirt barely remaining tucked into black trousers over a bulbous belly—scowled as Kilal and Requiem approached the white counter. The receptionist was a woman that might as well have been the female copy of the guard. And she, too, scowled.

"Arbiters aren't welcomed here," she snapped. Her name tag said 'Lori.' "Get out."

Kilal sighed, and Requiem growled. "Is Dr. Toboggan available?" he asked.

The one good thing about a meeting so late was Dr. Toboggan. He'd been Kilal's doctor during his last visit. He wasn't like the other doctors who anticipated an Arbiter being placed in their care so they could experiment on them. Dr. Toboggan genuinely wanted to help people, Sha'tum blessed or not. And he only worked the night shift.

Hopefully, he still did.

The guard edged closer to Requiem, a hand on the baton at his side. "Dr. Toboggan died three years ago. He was killed by one of your people. Dr. Toboggan was about the only one around here who was kind to you and yours, and you killed him for it. To the edge of the world with the lot of you."

Kilal unclenched his fists. "I'm sorry for your loss. Dr. Toboggan was a good man. He deserved better."

"He sure did!" Lori snapped.

Ashes. Kilal's trump card had been dropping Dr. Toboggan's name. That plan was now obsolete.

The way Requiem's lips curled and her fists remained tight, he didn't count on her for much help in peacefully navigating the conversation.

"Lori," he looked at the guard's nametag; Rufus. No wonder the man was so ill-tempered. "Rufus, I understand your dislike for me and my kind. I really do. But right now, there's someone here we really need to meet. Is there any way we can move past our differences and together work towards bridging that gap?"

Rufus and Lori shared a look—and burst into laughter.

"Bridge the gap?" Rufus said between mirth-filled breaths.

"Understand our dislike for you?" Lori barely got out before another round of laughter took over.

The guard whipped his baton out and raised it in the air. "Get out of here, the both of you, before I split your heads wide open!"

What? Did that simple, old, pudgy man really think he stood any chance against the two of them?

Either way, Requiem made sure Rufus understood exactly how little he could do. She grabbed his raised arm and twisted it until he cried out and dropped the baton. Stepping behind him, Requiem grabbed the back of his neck and cranked his arm behind him until he was nearly on his knees.

"What I just can't comprehend is how little *you and yours* understand our oath. You hear that we aren't supposed to harm you, so you think that gives you a right to do to us as you please? It continues to amaze me how much you forget the part where we're allowed to *defend* ourselves against threats. And since I'm just a little lady, and you're a big, strong man, I feel very threatened." She contorted the guard's arm until his shoulder popped.

Rufus screamed, tears in his eyes.

"Req," Kilal said, raising a brow. "I think he gets the point."

She let go of Rufus and stepped away.

He slowly stood and rotated his arm. "You're lucky you didn't break it, you ugly son of—"

Kilal slapped him. Rufus spun in a full circle and collapsed, unconscious.

"What was that for?" Lori cried. "He wasn't a threat to you!"

"I know." Kilal faced the receptionist. He narrowed his eyes and clenched his jaw. Back straight, he stood at his peak height, casting a shadow over her. "But sometimes, a man just needs to be slapped." He leaned onto the desk, pushing down on it until it creaked and groaned. "Now, are you going to help us, or are you going to continue letting your prejudice against my kind rule you?"

Lori paled. She audibly swallowed and nodded.

"Good. We're here to see someone, or two someones. Jayden and Ximthar. Can you tell me where I can find them?"

"What do you want with them?"

Kilal tried for his best comforting smile. "Now, Lori, that just isn't your concern."

His expression didn't seem to have the effect he'd hoped for. Lori narrowed her eyes and backed up. "I don't think I can give you information like that."

Kilal internally rolled his eyes. Why did everyone have to be so stubborn? He mentally ran through the options left. Kindness was out. He didn't want to threaten if he didn't have to. Rufus was one thing; he'd deserved it. But intimidation was something he left as the resort after the last resort. Which left a final, tried-and-true method: bribery.

It seemed, however, intimidation was a completely viable option for Requiem.

A black sword slid past Kilal. Lori shrieked and retreated until her back was against the wall. Requiem vaulted over the desk and approached until the blade was at the large woman's neck. "Lori," she said in a sweet voice. "Please, tell us where Jayden and Ximthar are."

Pale and wide-eyed, Lori stuttered, "Room 204."

The sword dispersed into a puff of shadows. Requiem lightly patted the receptionist's round cheek. "Thank you. Now, if any wards intercept us, or if there's any indication that law enforcement or back up has been called, the first thing I'll do is come back down here and cut your head off. Understand?"

Somehow, Lori's eyes widened further. She managed a slight nod. When Requiem turned away, Lori slid to the ground and wept. That was probably not how she imagined her shift would go.

Kilal pitied the sobbing woman. She was just a product of the times. Why should he expect her to be anything but a bigot? Not that it made her hate any easier to swallow; it just made it more understandable.

Requiem stepped on Rufus's still unconscious body, making it clear she didn't share his sentiment. And like Lori, he didn't blame her. One can receive only so much hate before they start to reciprocate it.

Up the stairwell they went. They didn't encounter any more staff or wards on their way through the hall, which Kilal was grateful for. He didn't see how that would have gone any better than their discussion with Rufus and Lori.

The asylum was quiet. The patients were fast asleep, some of their own volition, some not. The floors were made of white, slick tiles that somehow swallowed their footfalls, rendering their movements near-silent.

At the door with big irony numbers reading '204,' Kilal rested a hand on Requiem's shoulder. "If this goes south," he paused, and her eyes narrowed. She probably thought he was going to tell her to run or hide or save herself, "don't hold anything back. Jayden, despite his appearance, can't be underestimated, and something tells me this Ximthar is the same."

Requiem's gaze softened, and she nodded.

Kilal took a deep breath and readied his Carvings. Unlike his first encounter with Jayden, he couldn't mess things up again. If he had to fall on his knees and beg for their help, he would. For the sake of The Sunlight Domain. But just as important for his sanity. He had to believe, had to *know*, he hadn't returned in vain.

Exhaling, Kilal turned the bronze doorknob on the white door and entered room 204.

You're going to fail.

~ CHAPTER 49 ~

Two men and a woman waited for them in a room nearly as pearly and plain as the hallway. The woman looked similar to Claire. Gray hair, old, wrinkled, in her final days. She lay on a bed with a thin mattress, comfortably tucked beneath a white sheet. She was propped up and braced against a man Kilal assumed to be Ximthar.

He wore a white suit with a matching wide-brimmed hat. His facial features were sharp. Pointy nose, a chin which could slice bread, and narrow cheekbones. But his eyes were what caused Kilal to linger. Gray like the woman's hair, they were deep-set, almost sunken. And they'd seen *much*. Before the Professor, Kilal felt like a child, as though his two hundred years of life were drops in the bucket compared to Ximthar.

Is this what it feels like for others to be in my presence?

Jayden—or Justicus—stood by Ximthar, hovering. Was he protecting the Professor? Staying close enough to respond if Kilal or Requiem tried anything?

Gone was the goofy outfit from their first meeting and the carefree attitude and demeanor. The Jayden before him was very different from the man he first met. He was still lithe, with slender eyes and slender lips and a mop of brown hair on his head, but that was where the similarities ended.

He was covered in a form-fitting black leather outfit. Kilal eyed the foreign clothing. It bore more a resemblance to the skin on Jayden's arm when he'd transformed it. Every inch of his body from the chin down was covered in the strange material.

Kilal couldn't get the notion out of his head that the black coating was the man's actual skin. A few black tendrils even reached up onto his slender cheeks—definitely skin.

The resemblance to Jayden's arm wasn't the only oddity. The way the tendrils of black crept onto his face was eerily similar to the way the shadows would crawl up Requiem's body when she was preparing to fight.

Arms crossed, back straight, expression a stone mask, Jayden presented an intimidating presence. And like Ximthar, there was an ageless quality to his brown eyes. Standing before the two men, Kilal couldn't confidently say he'd never felt more...young.

From behind Ximthar, a feminine shape seemed to emerge from the Professor's back. The Spirit of Gloom stretched and hovered above him. At least, he thought it to be the shadow creature. The same white hair, white eyes and teeth. It bore nearly the same figure, too, except from the waist down. The thing was just a black strand stretching to Ximthar's back. No legs. No feet. It was almost like some sort of umbilical cord.

"This one told big one to come alone. Instead, he brought sister."

"Do *not* call her that," Jayden said with more vehemence and emotion than his stony face seemed capable of.

What was their infatuation with Requiem?

Kilal narrowed his eyes and weighed every word before he spoke. "My mission is too important to not bring any warrior willing to risk their life to see it complete."

"Your mission," Ximthar said. His appearance was extraordinary, but his voice was as average as could be. "And what is that?"

"To kill Ashen Kane," Kilal said, treading lightly. Last time he'd delivered the message, he'd ended up unconscious. "I think Eldon believed Ashen Kane to be...Avinoth."

Jayden hissed—and his skin *rippled*. "As I said, impossible."

Ximthar ran a hand through the woman's hair and looked at her with an emotion Kilal understood all too well. "Tell me of Eldon." It was a command, and based on his tone, Kilal imagined the Professor wasn't used to not being obeyed.

"We shared a cell together in the Ashen Lands."

Requiem elbowed his side, urging him to say more. Kilal sighed. Inwardly. He wouldn't let those two see any doubt in him. But Requiem was right. He'd screwed things up once, and he was on track to doing it again.

Kilal scratched the two days' growth on his chin, recalling a time he didn't want to dwell on. "Unfortunately, there isn't much to tell. Eldon was a prisoner in the Tower of Eyes. Just like me. We shared a cell wall for almost two years. They tortured me every day, but Eldon only once in a while. And when they did, he never made a sound. I always envied that. Sometimes, I imagined one day I, too, wouldn't make a sound. But then I'd remember why he didn't: he'd been there many lifetimes. And that was something I didn't plan to let happen to me."

Jayden snarled. "You think he *let* that happen? You think if they could get him and keep him there, you had *any* chance of escape?"

Kilal nodded. "You're probably right. Eldon asked me about myself but revealed little of himself in return. But that didn't matter. We shared a pain, the two of us, and that brought us closer than any revelations of our past could have."

Jayden snickered and rolled his eyes. "How poetic."

"Are you always this disrespectful?" Requiem asked.

Jayden's gaze darkened. "Only to failures."

The shadows flickered around Requiem, and those around Jayden mimicked the movements.

"Enough, Justicus," Ximthar said.

Jayden hesitated, and the shadows around him relaxed.

"Your Immortality. How did you maintain it?" Ximthar asked. "Professional curiosity." There was a gleam in his eyes saying otherwise. Ximthar was evaluating him.

Kilal didn't see any reason to lie. "They let me re-carve my Immortality every two days. I'm sure they never had so much fun with a captive before." Despite his best efforts, he couldn't conceal a shudder. Requiem placed a hand on his back, and that one gesture alone was almost worth reliving the past.

"Interesting," Ximthar said.

Kilal moved his hand from scratching his chin to pulling at an earlobe. A flake of ash descended in the middle of the room. "I got the sense Eldon never had someone to talk to, someone to share his suffering with. He felt so...lonely...and I helped fill that void for a while.

"Eventually, I think he realized I was what I said I was: immortal. He shared with me the secret of crossing the Veil and he told me of you two. He gave me my message, and I escaped when he attacked our torturer."

"And what of Eldon now?" Ximthar asked quietly.

Kilal took a deep breath and sighed. "I imagine he's dead."

"Eldon, dead?" The woman said in a scratchy voice before beginning to sob.

Ximthar rocked her back and forth, cooing for her until she stopped crying.

"The Tower of Eyes," he asked when she calmed. "What is it?"

"It's east, far east, all the way to the edge. It pierces the clouds and is constantly surrounded by hundreds, if not thousands, of Ash Fallen. They may even be bred there. The tower is black like ink. On its surface are dozens of eyes of various sizes, gazes roaming the surface, looking, watching, *seeing*."

The light flickered, and for a moment, the walls were covered in those eyes. Kilal squeezed his own shut, not caring who saw him in that state. He clenched his fists until his palms bled. A gentle hand on his back soothed him in a way his self-harm couldn't.

"He's lying," Jayden said, scowling.

"Eldon, Stein, Brack, Reimse, Flora, Zeya, Reas," the woman said in a scratchy yet clear tone.

Jayden and Ximthar lowered their heads and repeated the names.

"Aya's right," the Professor said, smiling at the woman leaning against him.

Aya? So, I've found all three. But why is Aya so...old...compared to the other two?

"The ten of us made a pact," Ximthar said. "We swore we'd die before we'd let Avinoth destroy another disk. He has no reason to lie to us about this. He shouldn't even know about Eldon. We've kept our names out of every historical account. The only way he could know is if he's telling the truth."

The Professor paused and looked at Jayden. "And Eldon wouldn't lie about this. So, tell me Justicus, are you willing to abandon your pact, your loyalty to the Royals and to your spirit and let Avinoth destroy this disk?"

Jayden's skin rippled again, and he dropped to one knee, bowing before Ximthar. "Until I no longer breathe, I will honor my pact, my king, and my spirit."

King?

"Good," Ximthar said. "Then we trust what this man tells us of Eldon. We may not know Kilal, but we know the reputation of the Immortal Arbiter, and like us, he'll fight to his last breath to defend this disk. He wouldn't lie to us about that."

Jayden cast a withering glare at Kilal. "This disk's warriors are too weak. Even him. I barely slapped him and would have killed him if not for his Carving. Truth or not, the two of us should go. Not these pathetic excuses for heroes."

Kilal eyed Jayden. Though lately, he'd been trying to find other ways to solve differences than using his fists, to avoid feeding the disturbing, blood-thirsty itch deep inside, he hadn't been as successful as he'd hoped since returning—objectively against his will. However, with Jayden, they may be as different from one another as a War Plague from a Pestilence Plague, but like the Plagues, they still shared a fundamental base of who and what they were.

They were fighters, and sometimes, there was only one way to communicate with one another.

Kilal spiked his strength and lowered his gravity to zero. He hoped the other two, not being Arbiters, wouldn't be able to sense his Carvings usage.

Barely more than a blur, he lunged. Jayden reacted, which was impressive considering the surprise attack, but he barely had the time to do more than flinch away. Kilal grabbed him by the neck, his large hand easily wrapping completely around it, and lifted him from the ground. Jayden flailed as he was slammed into the wall hard enough to crack it. Dust fell from the ceiling.

Would the others strike too? Kilal kept alert, waiting for a counterattack. He didn't know these people and their powers, and he wouldn't underestimate them like he'd done during his first encounter with Jayden.

He jammed his shoulder up and into Jayden's jaw, keeping his head locked in a twisted, painful position.

Jayden's hands elongated, forming the talons he'd used against Kilal before. He swiped at Kilal's belly, which would have been sliced to ribbons if he hadn't let go and leaped back.

No sooner had his foot hit the floor than he sprang forward again and delivered a thundering blow to Jayden's chin. The wall behind him shook. Jayden grunted and stumbled, but he had nowhere to go, his back already pressed against the barrier.

Kilal darted back to stand by Requiem's side and crossed his arms. She gave him a nod of approval.

Ximthar ignored the whole exchange, focused only on the woman on the bed.

"Don't underestimate me again," Kilal said, as if he hadn't just viciously attacked.

Fortunately, Jayden didn't counter again. Instead, he wiped blood from his jaw with the back of his hand. "Maybe he won't be entirely useless after all," he grumbled. "We should throw him at Avinoth first. He might just be able to provide us a few seconds of distraction."

"Now that's settled," Requiem said, eyeing Kilal, "can we plan our next move?"

"Our next move is obtaining a weapon capable of killing a Watcher," the Professor said, stroking Aya's long gray hair.

"Ximthar," Jayden murmured, face grim, "you know what that means."

"I do, and it's an eventuality the three of us prepared for."

Jayden grimaced. "But...Aya...how can we do that to her?"

Ximthar smiled as Aya grabbed his hand and brought it to her chest. "I accepted this responsibility the moment I chose to become the Sheath."

Jayden squeezed his eyes shut and ran a hand over them. "If you're lying to us," he said to Kilal, face contorted in pained hatred, "I'll kill you."

"Your anger is an insult to Aya's choice," Ximthar said.

Jayden recoiled as if struck. "I...I apologize." He wasn't speaking to Kilal. "Please forgive me."

Aya managed a small chuckle and a dismissive wave. "Just because you don't feel emotion, Xim, doesn't mean you must rebuke Justicus for his own."

The Professor smiled mischievously and ran a thumb over Aya's leathery cheek. "Oh, I feel emotion. Just not the useless ones."

"Oh, stop it," Aya smirked. "The boy still has much to learn from you in the matters of propriety and relationships. Give him a break."

Jayden groaned and shook his head. He muttered, "boy" and cursed. All the while, Ximthar shook with audible laughter.

Kilal watched on, unsure if he should butt in and remind

the trio that time was of the essence, but something about their banter gave him pause. They reminded him of something. Of himself and his closest friends. Jayden, Ximthar, Aya. They were close, almost familiarly close, and Kilal couldn't help but envy them. No, he wouldn't interrupt. Despite not understanding what was going on, the implication of their words... he wouldn't steal the moment from them.

"My love, are you ready?" Ximthar said, returning his hand to Aya's.

She raised her other shaking palm to his face and cupped it. "Yes, my king."

The Professor bent down and kissed Aya. It was a long kiss, a kiss between partners, a kiss that said goodbye. Kilal's chest tightened.

It really would be the last time the three of them would be together.

Aya lay flat on the bed. She closed her eyes and mumbled words Kilal didn't understand in a language he didn't know. A white aura surrounded her. She lifted from the bed, levitating a foot into the air. Her mumbling turned to chanting. The volume grew. Color returned to her skin and hair, and age shed itself from her in an instant. Before them was a young, beautiful woman, regal and impressive. The glow strengthened, and the chanting increased.

Worried the strange ritual could be interrupted, Kilal put his back to the door and increased his gravity. Anyone wanting to get into the room wouldn't be able to.

A black spot appeared above Aya. It expanded, twisted, and sank into the woman. When it pierced her skin, her back arched, and she let out a howl which shook the small space. A slit appeared in her chest and widened—a slit into another dimension.

A dark dimension.

Ximthar stood and reached into the gap in Aya's chest. When he stepped back, he pulled out a sword so bright, Kilal had to look away.

The room was flooded with an unbearable brilliance. Even with his eyes closed, Kilal feared going blind. Not that he would stay blind, but it still wasn't an injury he cared to endure.

When the light receded and a *thunk* announced Aya had returned to her bed, Kilal pried his lids open. She had indeed settled, but she was no longer the young, regal version of herself. Her body had once again withered into its old, worn-out form.

No. It was a third version of her. A dead version.

Kilal caught Jayden wiping wet cheeks as Ximthar bowed to rest his brow against her pale, gray forehead. Even the creature stretching from the Professor's back shook as white tears trickled down her cheeks.

"May Caritos welcome you with open arms, and may you bless Him and our brothers and sisters as you grace them with your eternal presence," Ximthar murmured. Kilal recognized it as a prayer eerily similar to the one offered to Sha'tum at the passing of a loved one. Was Caritos their God?

Prayer finished, Ximthar stood and slid the newly acquired two-foot-long sword of white metal into a sheath at his side, opposite where Kilal stood.

"I'm...sorry for your loss," he said.

"We'll make sure her sacrifice isn't in vain," Requiem added.

Bloodshed and Oaths! What the bloody ashes just happened, was what Kilal really wanted to say, but something about the hardened faces of the two men told him it wasn't the time. They'd just lost someone they loved because of a message Kilal had delivered. They deserved what little peace they could offer them to grieve, even if only for a short time. Though time wasn't on their side, their destination after leaving the asylum would be a one-day travel at high speed. And that was if they made it unaccosted. He would have ample opportunities to question them then.

"We have one week to kill Ashen Kane, or whoever he is," Ximthar said, thumb running over the hilt of the sword at his waist.

Kilal jolted into a straight-back stance. "One week?" He scratched his jaw. "That puts us on quite the constraint. But it's doable."

"Why?" Requiem asked.

Ximthar unsheathed the blade a few inches. "This is the Eye of Oblivion. If it stays in this realm for more than one week, it'll devour all who wield it. This is the only weapon we have which can permanently kill a Watcher. So, one week."

Kilal's mind spiraled with questions. "And what exactly is a Watcher?"

"And why did Aya refer to herself as 'the Sheath?' Will someone else have to become it in seven days?"

Jayden and Ximthar shared a look Kilal was fairly positive parents exchange when their children ask questions the parents thought they should already know the answers to.

"I'm a fighter," Jayden finally said. "Not a teacher. I'll leave that to you."

Ximthar smiled at Kilal and Requiem. It was a sad smile. "There is much to discuss, and if you make it to the Northern Ruins where you were first teleported to the Ashen Lands, I'll teach you of this Disk—and the others."

Kilal narrowed his eyes and readied his Carvings. "How did you know about that?"

"You don't live as long as I have without creating a network of intelligence," the Professor said, a cryptic and almost useless answer. "Like I said, if you make it to the Northern Ruins, to the abandoned Travel Station, I'll teleport us to the Ashen Lands and teach you all I know of the Disks."

"Why there? Is that the only...Travel Station? Is there nothing closer?" Kilal asked.

"And what do you mean 'if?'" Requiem added.

Jayden and Ximthar shared another look, then Jayden smiled. Kilal didn't like that expression.

"Avinoth is more powerful than any of us. If you're going to come with us, you must prove you have what it takes to... survive."

"And how are we going to prove that?" Requiem said. Based on her tone, she liked the idea about as much as Kilal did.

"Justicus and I will teleport to the Ashen Lands in twenty-four hours. If you can make it there in that time, you may come with us."

"What's the catch?" Kilal asked. Twenty-four hours would be pushing it, but they could do it. That couldn't be the extent of the test.

Ximthar looked at his watch. "A tip went to the Heirs of the Promise when you were seen entering this building. I wager you have five, maybe ten minutes before the first Arbiters show up to collect your heads."

Kilal ground his teeth. "You can't be serious!"

The Professor took his seat and returned to stroking Aya's hair.

"Twenty-four hours," Jayden repeated, lips curled into a nasty smile. "I wouldn't waste anymore time asking stupid questions."

"You think this is a game?" Kilal said. "There are civilians here, and you just made this building a warzone."

Jayden shrugged. "Then you'd better not be here when they show up."

Requiem grabbed Kilal by the arm and spun him about before he could give a retort. "We need to go. Now."

He growled but didn't argue. "See you there," he called behind him as they darted out of the room.

~ CHAPTER 50 ~

Requiem led the way, guiding them to the elevator. They passed two wards who wore scowls so efficiently Kilal was convinced their faces knew no other emotion.

"We should take the stairs," he said. "Avoid as many people as possible."

"No. There's no avoiding these Arbiters. If they don't find us, they'll kill until we show ourselves."

They'll kill innocents to draw us out? How did we fall so far? And could they afford to *not* kill any who opposed them, knowing what they were willing to do with their power?

For a minute, he regretted returning to the Sunlight Domain. How many Arbiters had he killed already, and how many more would there be?

Standing at the elevator door, waiting for the lift to arrive, Kilal resolved himself to take out any Arbiters who tried to kill him. He stared at hands already dripping viscous red blood, ignoring Requiem's worried looks. What were a few more gallons in a sea of crimson? What were a few more haunted wails among the cacophony which visited him in silence and loneliness?

He rubbed his hands together, trying his hardest to wash the blood from them. But he'd never be free of it. Not as long as he still drew breath.

The *ding* of the lift's arrival shook him from his nightmarish reverie. The door slid open. Copper flooded his mouth.

"Ashes," he muttered.

Two men stood in the elevator, twins from their identical outfits of black trench coats, matching boots, plain faces with lips too thin, blond, neatly combed hair, and black sunglasses.

"Ashes," he said again, a little louder.

The shadows on the white wall cast by their bodies began dancing.

Kilal shot forward, raising his strength. The twins didn't react, at least not in a manner which would save themselves. The one he sunk a fist into scrunched his brow behind glasses and frowned. That was the last look his face ever made before Kilal's fist shattered it into a visage of mushed gore. The other Arbiter's head slid from its neck, and the two corpses collapsed as one.

He ran a hand, a hand *not* covered in real blood, through his hair and sighed. "This isn't right. Maybe we should just turn ourselves in. Save as many as we can. I don't want to kill any more Arbiters."

Requiem didn't say much in response, but what she did say was all that was needed. "Twenty-four hours."

"Bloodshed and Oaths, this isn't what I was supposed to return to."

"I know."

Stepping over the corpses, Requiem pressed the button for the ground floor. The door closed, locking them in the small metal box with the smell of freshly deceased bodies. Pleasant wasn't a word Kilal would use to describe the stench.

A gentle vibration announced the descent of the elevator. How many more Arbiters would die before they'd arrive at the Travel Station in the ruins? Already, the answer was too many.

Kilal readied himself as the doors slid open. A janitor dipped his mop into a bucket of soapy water, rung it out, and swished it across the white tile. They exited the elevator and made their way down the hall. His eyes never stopped moving, and his mind never stopped analyzing. The janitor whistled as he whisked the mop back and forth. He even nodded cheerily to Kilal when he looked up.

A door opened to their left, and the man who emerged almost lost his head. The ward scowled at Kilal and Requiem but didn't say anything. Instead, he locked the patient's room behind him, cut across Kilal, who had to jerk to a stop to not bump into him, and entered the room across the hall.

Kilal and Requiem shared a look. Odd. When they'd stepped into the asylum, there'd been no one around aside from the receptionist and front desk security. Where did those people come from?

They turned a corner and nearly collided with a ladder holding a man on the top rungs whose upper half of his body was in the ceiling. The removed ceiling tile lay on the floor, leaning against the wall. That made three humans since leaving room 204.

Four and five exited a room two doors down from them. A female ward dressed all in white and standing a few inches taller than Requiem led an old man with dim eyes and a slack jaw covered in drool down the hall.

"It's time for your medicine," she said.

"Don't want no meds," the patient responded.

"Don't start with me, Jav. You're going to get your medicine, and you're gonna make it easy, understand?"

"Don't want no meds," the patient said again, though quieter and slower.

Kilal slowed his steps and waited for Requiem to come to his side. "Something's off," he whispered.

"I know," was all she said in return, just as quietly.

The female ward and her patient stayed ahead of them. Before they turned the next corner, Kilal cast a casual glance back. The janitor had turned down their corridor, and the man in the ceiling was even farther in now. Only his knees and below were showing. The janitor caught Kilal looking at him, and once again matched his wary look with a smile of perfect teeth.

Never known a janitor to have perfect teeth... The thought carried him around the corner, to the third and final corridor before they reached the front entrance.

Another man disappeared into the ceiling at the other end of the hall. From his waist down, like the first, he stood on the top rung of a ladder. A seventh maintenance technician, female, stood near the ladder, juggling four small balls the size of a baby's fist. She occasionally paused to look up at the man in the ceiling before returning to her juggling.

"Don't want no meds," the patient said again in front of them.

He and the female ward stopped. She pulled a baton from a case at her side. Something about the whole thing felt...wrong.

"Jav," the ward said. "We're not going to have this problem again, are we? You remember what happened last time you refused to take your medicine?" She flicked her eyes to the baton.

Requiem hugged the wall opposite them.

"Don't *want* no MEDS!"

Copper filled Kilal's mouth. Heat shivered down his spine. And a low buzzing whispered in his ears.

"Ashes!"

~ CHAPTER 51 ~

Jav pounced on the ward, growling and hissing, snapping at the woman's neck. She threw him off her, and he crashed into Requiem, smashing them through the door with the numbers 103.

The ward turned on Kilal and swung her baton at his midsection.

That was it; why the baton had made him so uneasy. The ward was wearing a glove to protect herself from the aznium—she was an Arbiter.

Kilal lowered his gravity and leaped back. The rod grazed the skin on his exposed abdomen and pain engulfed him. White covered his vision as he collapsed to the ground, shaking violently. He knew the pain; the seizure wouldn't last long. He'd only barely been touched. But in their current predicament, 'not long' could still mean the end.

Gritting his teeth and taking control of his limbs as best he could, Kilal kicked out, blindly. An "oof" and a clatter of metal against the floor signaled his success. He forced himself to his feet, sliding up the wall to give himself some support. As his knees locked him into a standing position, the spasms stopped, and his eyesight returned.

Just in time to take a ball wreathed in lightning to the face.

His nose crunched, his cheeks shattered, and once again,

he was blinded by pain. Hot blood poured from the mess of skin and bones that used to be his face, and for a moment, he almost welcomed the bliss that would come with unconsciousness. But two words kept him awake.

Twenty-four hours.

Kilal slammed himself against the wall, parting the sheetrock and wooden beams like paper. He fell onto his back as he stumbled into the room. A scream of fear lit up his ears; a patient.

Sha'tum, let this one not get hurt, he prayed as he rose to his feet.

Another scream, more bestial, sounded beside him. Followed by nails tearing at his healing face.

Kilal threw himself backward again until he was up against the rear of the room, but the frenzied attack wouldn't be dissuaded. When his eyesight returned, he was shocked to see that it wasn't an Arbiter attacking—it was a patient. The patient whose room he now stood in.

He lifted her off him, keeping her at arm's length. Foam frothed from her mouth. Her eyes and hair were wild, her nails long and sharp. Kilal tried to toss her aside without using any Carvings, but the frail, foolish woman clung to him like a savage dog. She was going to get herself killed!

Her head exploded into a mist of gore and blood, replaced by a ball wreathed in lightning.

Rage that a civilian had to lose her life so those oathbreaking Arbiters could get to him swallowed the millisecond-long surprise.

He jerked his head to the side, avoiding the energy ball. It crashed through the wall against his back and into the room behind him. Slowly, face still throbbing, Kilal let go of the corpse still clinging to him and stood.

Chest heaving, face and torso covered in his own blood, screams echoing all around him, he knew one thing to be a fact: the ambush had failed, and now it was his turn.

For whatever reason, the female Arbiter chose to use the door instead of entering through the hole in the wall Kilal had created. He let the door swing halfway open before kicking it shut. He followed up by yanking so hard on the knob, he ripped it out of the wood. The oathbreaker reeled backward, holding a smashed nose. Kilal stepped into the hall, hot on her heels, and sunk the doorknob into her eye. She dropped to the floor, her body convulsing.

He felt a ripple of released power and instinctually jerked his head back. The other female Arbiter who'd been pretending to assist the man in the ceiling while juggling threw another ball at him. Kilal barely dodged the white orb wreathed in lightning. The attack wouldn't kill him, but he really didn't want his bones crunched again. A third ball followed, and he stepped aside, narrowly avoiding it. A fourth was chucked his way, nearly separating an arm from his body. It hung by a few strands of skin, erupted with white energy.

Kilal grabbed it, gritting teeth against the searing pain, and held it against his shoulder, speeding up the healing process.

A terrible idea.

Another ball slammed into the arm holding the nearly severed one. His hand and half his forearm fell to the ground and puffed into a cloud of dust.

Kilal roared with anger. And pain. He spun, avoiding another orb, and zeroed in on who was responsible. The janitor. He was catching the thrown balls and hurling them back. Kilal was trapped in a narrow hall turned death trap.

Great. He'd let them think they had the advantage.

Kilal spun on the male Arbiter and purposefully strode down the hall. He didn't avoid the next ball, which tore through his chest and out his back. Instead, he smiled, showing teeth warm and slick with blood. The next ball hit his shoulder again, nearly tearing off the newly healed joint, but Kilal forced a wider smile.

"I'm not trapped here with you. You're trapped in here with *me*."

The fake janitor stumbled back, the grin from earlier nowhere to be found.

He wound up and let loose. When the electric orb struck Kilal on the right cheek, shattering it and the eye socket, popping his eye out, the everlasting smile on what remained of his face had to be a hideous thing to be on the receiving end of. Another ball nearly took a leg off at the knee. Kilal adapted by hopping. It only took two quick bounds to cast his shadow upon the now cowering oathbreaker who had, only moments before, been so confident. He raised a shaking arm, but Kilal grabbed it before he could do anything with the crackling orb in his palm. And snapped it.

The ball fell to the floor and rolled away.

Kilal reveled in the man's pitiful wails and kicked him in the chest with a partly formed leg. His arm tore free, and the man sailed down the length of the hall and slammed into the wall. His head bounced wickedly, finding a wooden stud, and covered the place of impact with blood. He slid to the floor, dead.

His point proven, Kilal actively avoided the next energy ball thrown at him. He'd endured enough pain.

But they hadn't.

The female only had one more orb, the others rolling away to remain unreturned. Kilal winked at her with his newly restored face and smiled. She grimaced.

That was when Kilal noticed the man in the ceiling was nowhere to be seen, and Requiem hadn't emerged from the room she'd been thrown into. And there was still another man behind him, if the first one three-quarters of the way into the ceiling was also an Arbiter.

The woman could wait.

Kilal hobbled to the room Requiem had disappeared into. It was dimly lit. A man in white lay dead on the floor, and a struggling Requiem flailed against the tiles under the Arbiter covered in a clear, oily substance. Like the drool he'd been covering his chin with when he'd pretended to be a patient. The substance was making it hard for Requiem to do anything but slide off him. Her strikes slipped from the man's skin. Even her sword couldn't penetrate the slimy barrier. Somehow, it too, slid across him without puncturing. It was the strangest yet impossibly effective Carving Kilal had ever seen.

Despite the slippery oil, the man was still landing blow after blow of his own. If it weren't Requiem being wailed on, Kilal would have found the whole exchange fascinating.

But it was her.

Kilal roared and surged forward on his freshly regrown leg, the excruciating pain paling in comparison to his rage. He wasn't exactly sure what he'd do against the slime, but if he dropped on top of the guy, his frame might be wide enough to keep the Arbiter from completely slipping away. In another situation, Kilal might have shaken his head in embarrassment. The Immortal Arbiter resorting to *falling* on the enemy. Not his most accomplished moment.

Two Arbiters dropped from the ceiling, knocking out the light and slamming Kilal to the floor before he could reach Requiem. It was the missing men who'd been pretending to work in the ceiling. They were strong, strong enough to keep him pressed to the floor even with his Carving of Deific Strength at fifty percent.

Kilal hiked it up to seventy-five percent and pushed himself up onto his elbows before an enormous force shoved him back down, pinning him. His lungs collapsed from the sheer weight, and he helplessly gasped for air he couldn't capture. His head was flat on his cheek, and even though neither of the men were holding it down, he couldn't move it.

From his vantage point, he couldn't see Requiem, but he did occasionally hear the *thunk* of a fist meeting flesh. He had no idea what sort of healing capabilities she had, so as far as he knew, she was suffering potentially permanent damage. Or at least injuries which would take a while to mend.

He roared again. Kilal shot his strength to one hundred

percent and *pushed*—but went nowhere. The harder he tried, the heavier the force pinning him to the floor became.

Squished, immobile, Requiem being beaten just a few paces away, Kilal realized something. He was holding back. He knew it, but... he couldn't let that blood-thirsty part of himself out. Not again.

That Kilal, the part of him he thought he'd killed long ago, was locked away in the deepest recesses of his mind. But the heated thrill that thrummed through his veins after he'd slaughtered the Arbiters that attacked outside the holy place and took out Jasper, Inferno, and Blade revealed the horrifying truth—that the deepest recesses of his mind were becoming shallower and shallower.

Godsgraive brushed his mind, and its touch was so...calming, soothing...reassuring.

I can help, it whispered.

NO!

It laughed. *You didn't mind releasing me when you needed to escape the Tower.*

That was different. There weren't innocents there for you to kill.

Kilal could feel the feigned hurt. *I would never.*

You always do!

It rumbled with satisfaction. *Watch her die then. You know I don't care.*

I'll beat them without you! To the edge of the world with you!

The presence chuckled and receded back into the corner of Kilal's mind he'd trapped it in.

For now.

Kilal howled. He shoved, pushed, squirmed, lowered gravity, raised gravity, decreased strength to zero percent only to jump it straight to one hundred and writhe against the pressure holding him down. But nothing worked. No matter how hard he fought, his force remained matched.

An idea struck him. It was crazy and completely contrary to everything Kilal wanted to do.

Stop fighting.

If the force pushing down matched his efforts pushing *up*, what if he didn't struggle at all?

Kilal went limp. And the force keeping him down disappeared.

The men above seemed just as confused as he was, as if they too hadn't expected the Immortal Arbiter to voluntarily stop. That split-second lapse of judgment was all Kilal needed to roll onto his back, grab them both by the ankle, and squeeze.

Their screams were perfectly in sync. Kilal tightened his grip, crushing their bones until jagged shards broke through the skin. Their screaming intensified. With the men writhing from their shattered shins, Kilal shoved himself to his feet and quickly dispatched them.

Fortunately, the slimeball still wailing on Requiem, who continued fighting back despite a bloody face and no headway made, didn't notice Kilal hovering over him.

Falling on the man wasn't an option anymore. He'd just pin Requiem beneath both of them. So what?

Kilal's mind jolted with the answer. He ripped the sheet from the bed in the corner, twisted it until it was taut between both hands, and looped it around the Arbiter's head. He crossed his hands over each other, locking the tight sheet against his slimy neck. The man grabbed at the sheet, and Kilal wished he could see the wide-eyed shock on his face.

He pulled the man off Requiem, and stood still, further tightening the sheet until the man's face turned blue. When the oathbreaker went limp, Kilal let go.

I told you I didn't need you, he thought, directing it at the dark recess in his mind.

He felt it *shrug* in response.

Requiem, gasping, let him pull her to her feet. "Thank you."

Kilal's worry for her didn't last long. The shadows grasped

at her from the corners of the room. They swarmed up her body, casting shivers of cold down his arm as they covered her face. It was only a few seconds, but the shock made it feel like hours. Still holding her when the shadows receded, slithering back to where they'd come, he blinked at the restored face before him, as beautiful as the day he'd reunited with her. The scars were still there, but Kilal had long since escaped the idea that beauty was only in appearance.

"What are you?" he whispered.

She wasn't using Carvings. He'd even thought maybe she used stones similar to the ones Tor'et and Fazin had, but he'd never seen any on her. The closest replication of her powers was Jayden and his black skin. But that wasn't possible. He wasn't even from their world, and he had to be a thousand years old, at least. So how could Requiem use the same kind of power?

The question was rhetorical and only for himself, but Requiem heard it anyway.

"I'm me," she said in the most pitiful, pleading way possible, as if begging him to see her for who she was, not for *what* she was.

And Kilal, more than anyone else in the world, could understand that desire.

He ran a hand through her hair. "Of course you're you," he said, smiling.

The cold lifeless eyes of the patient barely more than an arm's reach away ruined the rare moment. Kilal reached over and closed the dead man's lids, but a gleam off to the side caught his gaze.

Letting go of Requiem, he kneeled. There was a ring on the guy's hand. An idea drove him to desperation, and he pulled the ring from the Arbiter's stiff finger.

"Kilal! What are you doing?" Requiem said. She placed a hand over his fist. She clearly thought he was looting the body, an act so lowly and depraved, Kilal was almost hurt at the assumption.

He pursed his lips. Even in the dark, he could see her face—at least the left side of it—redden. "I'm collecting a reminder." He put the ring in one of his pants pockets.

"A reminder of what?"

"A reminder to Ximthar of how many innocents had to die for his 'test.'"

Her face hardened, and she nodded her consent.

"Every death will be on his conscience, not ours," Kilal added.

"What makes you think he has one?"

Kilal sighed. She was probably right. "Doesn't matter, I guess." He pointed to the corpse he'd taken the ring from. "He deserves to be remembered. By us. *And* by the man who caused his death."

They left the room together.

Requiem drew stiff as they entered the hall. "There's one missing," she said, counting the corpses on her fingers. "The other woman."

"She fled," Kilal said. "As soon as I killed her catch partner."

Requiem nodded. "You ever seen some of these Carvings before?"

"Some. Not the slimy skin, though. That was...different."

She grunted. "And effective."

"And whatever the two men on me were using, I've never felt that before, either. They used a force that countered whatever effort I used against it. It was also very effective."

"We need to be more careful next time," Requiem said.

"What makes you think there'll be a next time?"

She rolled her eyes. "There will be."

Once again, she was right—he was being dumb.

The hall was in a pitiful state. Blood, probably most of it his, was splashed all over walls, the floor, and even the ceiling in places. One light had been broken, probably from a bouncing lightning ball, casting a shadow over the whole scene. The two corpses were grotesque. It was gruesome, and exactly what a battlefield between Arbiters looked like.

A door opened. Kilal tensed. Had the other woman not run away?

An older looking male with a gruff beard and missing teeth peaked his head out into the hall. He took in the scene... and laughed. Shuffling into the hallway, the old man began throwing his arms and legs about, dancing and giggling.

Kilal sighed. At least he wasn't an Arbiter. Or was he? Kilal, warily, stepped around the man, Requiem on his heels.

The front desk was abandoned; Lori was nowhere to be seen. She was a nasty lady, but Kilal still hoped she'd escaped with her life.

Stopping at the desk, he wondered if Ximthar and Jayden were still there. Maybe he should turn around and go show them the first 'reminder' he'd collected because of them. The only thing that stopped him was the ever-present reminder of the cost of each passing second.

The buzz of someone swinging open the front door echoed through the quiet foyer.

Please no.

"Oi, there! We miss the party?"

Kilal faced the voice, growling. Another group of Arbiters stood behind the leader, the one who'd spoken, he presumed. They were about as outlandish as they came, giving the likes of Blondie, Trench Coat, and Crave a run for their money.

There were four of them—two men, two women—with outfits as bright as the yellow pants Kilal first spotted Jayden wearing. The leader took off gold sunglasses and hung them in the V of a deep green shirt. He slicked back greased hair and blew a kiss at Requiem.

"Shame I've got to kill you, lovely, but the bounty is for your head only. I promise I'll ma—"

Turns out, it's incredibly difficult to speak with a sword thrust through the mouth.

Regardless, the leader still managed to reach up and grab

at the blade, but his valiant effort fell just short. He slid from the end of Requiem's shadow sword, dead.

There was a time when a display of efficient skill like what she just showed would've ended a fight. But that was back when Arbiters were made from a smarter stock. Now, they appeared to only think with the side of their brain that governed greed and self-delusion.

The others gnashed their teeth and growled. Pressure spiked behind Kilal's eyes, and he groaned.

Three more bodies were about to be added to the kill count for the night.

~ CHAPTER 52 ~

By the time they reached their car in the parking lot, the rain had subsided, and a thick mist filled the air. Another vehicle was pulling into the lot, a strange thing for the time of night. When the car lights turned onto Kilal, he gave a friendly wave and smile. Thankfully, the vehicle continued to a parking spot and an elderly man and woman exited. Not more Arbiters.

Kilal had done his best to rinse the blood and gore off, but he was a mess. His shirt was more tatters than material, and the parts that were intact had a distinct red hue to them. Requiem's attire was better off than his, but her dark hoodie was slightly darker around the chin area.

During less pressing times, Kilal would've done all he could to find a new shirt, but time was ticking, so he had to keep the soggy, bloody, holey shirt on; for now.

"What's the quickest way out of the city?" Kilal asked, sitting in the car. The remaining drizzle pittered and pattered on the roof. Once, that had been a soothing sound. Now? It meant nothing.

"Through the city."

"We can't do that. The whole place will be looking for us. What about the west or east exits? We're closest to the west."

Silent Haven had been built with four entrances and exits, aligning with the cardinal directions. There was no other way to enter the city. A large steel wall as tall as two men and as thick as Kilal laying down, stretched around the perimeter.

The wall was never meant to keep Arbiters in or out. It was meant to funnel Ash Fallen who'd survived the Veil Wardens and pierced that far inland. But the Wardens were long gone, and the Sunlight Domain hadn't seen a serious invasion in over a century and a half. And the one Kilal fought in a hundred and fifty years earlier was nothing compared to the Great Invasion five hundred years prior.

"The Heirs had the west and east gates built over. They're nothing but wall now."

"Why would they do that?"

Requiem shrugged. "To better control who enters and exits the city."

"To better control which *Arbiters* enter and exit the city, I bet."

She nodded. "That's the assumption."

"Great. So, we have just enough time to reach the bloody ruins *if* we aren't accosted every step of the way. Which we will be!" Kilal punched the dashboard. Softly. It was still dented by the blow.

Requiem laid a hand on his shoulder as she pulled out of the parking lot and onto the main road, leading them back to the center of the city where they'd be able to hit North Gate Street.

"Lilliana is waiting for me, and I'm stuck catering to the whims of a thousand-year-old man who may or may not be able to help me!" Kilal punched the dashboard again. A little harder than he should have. It caved in, shaking the car. Requiem wrestled with the steering wheel and brought the vehicle back under control.

She cast an annoyed look his way. "You know what will make it even harder to reach Lilliana?"

He winced. "Making our way there on foot."

"Yep."

"No more punching the car."

"That would probably be for the best."

"Well, can we at least keep to as many side roads as possible?"

"No. We're going to keep to every major road, and I figured I'd honk the horn the whole way." She gave him a flat look.

Kilal raised his hands in defense. "Sorry. I'm just...afraid. That's all."

"Afraid of what?"

The pitter-patter intensified. Kilal considered asking Requiem to pull over so he could wash his shirt in the rain. But fear stopped him.

"That she isn't alive. That I'll arrive too late to save her."

"She's alive," Requiem said with an impressive amount of confidence. "I always wanted to believe the both of you were alive. And you were, so I want to believe she is too. But, Kilal, there's something I have to ask, something that's been bothering me. And you may not like it."

He grunted but nodded for her to continue.

"You said the last time you saw Lilliana was in the ruins right before you were teleported. Correct?"

"Yes."

"And when you arrived in the Ashen Lands, Lilliana wasn't with you. Right?"

"Yes. Just three other Arbiters we'd been fighting."

"So, what are the chances Lilliana never was teleported to the Ashen Lands? What if she's been here this whole time? Or was teleported somewhere else?"

Kilal sighed, digesting the implications of the questions. "I've never really considered the possibility that she wasn't teleported with me and the others in that room. And as much as I'd love to believe she'd stayed where she was, I can't. She would have returned to you. But she never did, so she had to have been teleported."

"But could she have been teleported somewhere else? The

Schism? Another world? Even over the edge, maybe?"

He scratched his chin and stared out the window. The continued rhythmic pitter-patter of the rain against the roof was almost relaxing. Almost.

"I...don't know," he said. "I guess...I have to believe she went to the Ashen Lands. At least that way I have hope of rescuing her. If that isn't the case, then there's nothing I can do for her. And I can't believe that."

Requiem sighed. When she didn't say anything, to argue with or comfort him, Kilal took the opportunity to ask a difficult question of his own.

"Soon after Lilliana and I went missing, you disappeared. No one knows where you went. Where did you go?"

"The Northern Ruins."

Kilal started. "Why?"

She didn't answer.

The left turn blinker indicated their upcoming direction at the four-way stop they rolled up to. A car was stopped at each position of the intersection. No one moved. The steering wheel creaked again, and Requiem looked from one car to the next. They couldn't see what the drivers looked like. Between the mist and the bright headlights, Kilal couldn't determine much besides the makes and models of the vehicles.

Requiem eased off the brakes and began rolling forward.

"Stop," Kilal said. Thankfully, Requiem did. "If this is a trap, they'd love nothing more than to catch us in between them. Flash your brights. Let them know you aren't going to be the first one to move."

Was it a trap? He didn't know. And he wasn't going to chance it.

Requiem pulled the switch toward her twice, flashing her lights into the four-way stop. They waited. Just as Kilal was beginning to feel the need to act first, the car to their left—a big truck which easily could have totaled their vehicle—let off the brakes and rolled through the intersection. The other two followed after, leaving them alone.

"Guess it wasn't a trap," Kilal said.

When all was clear, Requiem took a left. The truck in front of them took the next right. Kilal followed the vehicle with his eyes for as long as he could to make sure the driver wasn't going to double back. Paranoia was a blessing when an entire city's worth of Arbiters were after him.

"Power," Requiem said.

"Hm?"

"Why I went to the ruins. I went looking for power."

Kilal turned in his seat to get a good look behind them. Nothing. "Why? You're a High Arbiter. You *have* power."

Requiem let go of the steering wheel with one hand, guiding it with the other. Cars parked along the empty streets passed them by. Half the vehicles looked abandoned. More than a few had wheels or other parts of the body missing.

An abandoned skyscraper loomed in the distance, a constant reminder of the economic status of the city. Barely more than the skeleton of the infrastructure had been finished before it had been abandoned. Why? Why spend the resources to build so much just to let it decay away under the forces of the elements? What led to that eventuality? Was it the Heirs? Maybe it had always been that way, and Kilal had been blind to it.

As they passed the block where the partially-built skyscraper stood, Kilal spotted movement in the shadows. People, probably homeless, moving about. Bonfires in metal drums drew them like moths to a flame. He couldn't make out any faces, but what he could tell from the postures of those sitting, walking, gathering, huddling, they all felt the same. Defeated. Hopeless.

He shook his head, his throat tightening. It wasn't right. Who cared if he protected his city from the forces of Ashen Kane if it would just funnel the city into a much slower death?

"Is there even anything worth saving?" Kilal muttered.

"There always is. There may not be much, but there's always something."

He let her answer settle in his mind. Of course there was plenty worth saving. It would just be much harder when the solution didn't involve punching. He'd fought battles like that before. He incorporated the Right of Recompense, which saw many citizens of the Sunlight Domain re-homed and compensated for their physical or emotional losses. He'd *encouraged* wealthier Arbiters and civilians alike to donate to causes benefiting the poor and homeless. He, himself, had donated not just monetarily, but his time to worthy causes.

When he finished his mission and there were plans for getting off their Sha'tum-forsaken rock, he'd dive headfirst into making things better for his people, not just protect them.

Kilal burst into laughter, and Requiem startled.

"Ashes! What's so funny?" she asked.

He shook his head. "Nothing."

"Didn't sound like nothing."

There he was, making plans for his return like an optimistic fool. He lost to Ashen Kane once, soundly. He had no reason to believe it would be different now. It would be up to Jayden and Ximthar to finish what he couldn't.

But what about Requiem?

Kilal didn't want to think about that. So, he didn't.

"Power," he said, returning them to the conversation, which hadn't been appropriately concluded. "Were you looking for some way to become a Prime?"

Requiem snorted. "No."

"Then what?"

"Real power. Different power."

Kilal sat back and scratched his chin. Her ruined face. Her strength. Her speed. Her control of shadows and the ability to form a blade from them. Even the way she sometimes looked off as if she saw something only she could. How many times had he caught her mumbling to herself, never making a sound but appearing to be speaking to someone?

"Did you find what you were searching for?" Clearly, she had, but he still had to ask.

She turned and looked at him. The left side of her mouth curved upward; the right remained flat.

She's so beautiful.

Requiem's eyes widened, and for a moment, he worried he was staring too intensely. Then she jerked the steering wheel to the left.

A force smashed into Kilal's side of the car. The door crunched. The vehicle lifted off the street and tumbled side over side. Metal screeched as it bent. Windows shattered, and the car frame caved. Kilal's large body bore the brunt of the impacts. His head hit the pavement on one of the multiple nasty tumbles. White lights erupted in his vision. Another tumble ripped his arm off as it flopped out of the broken window.

The car slid to a screaming stop, upside down. Kilal hung from his side, wrapped in his seatbelt. Why did he even wear the bloody thing? His vision was narrow, and everything burned, but he was able to just barely cling to consciousness.

Requiem, also dangling upside down, was unconscious.

Something ripped the door off with a loud screech and tossed it aside. A figure, dark and imposing and backlit by a bent streetlamp, grabbed Kilal and tore him from his chair, seatbelt and all. The large figure twisted him in the air, stood him upright, and slammed him into the car, holding him there. His arm regrew and his blurred vision cleared, and Kilal stared into the eyes of his attacker.

A woman with shoulder-length brunette hair held up in a ponytail. A scar stretched from her left eye and across the bridge of her nose, before cutting a sharp angle down past the right corner of her lip, hardening an already hard face. A choker of red gemstones clung tightly to her neck, and each arm had a matching armband wrapped around bulging biceps. Veins popped from her neck, arms, and the top of her chest, exposed by a brown tank top.

Sienna.

Kilal smiled, showing the huntress a mouth full of blood. "Finally."

He shot his strength to max, wary of how long his Carving had left at that level. He'd used a good bit of his enhanced strength during the two battles back in the asylum. He probably had fifteen, maybe twenty minutes of operating at one hundred percent before he'd run out of juice, but he didn't intend to use it for that long. The fight would be over much sooner than that.

He'd show the world why Sienna wasn't the one to be feared.

Kilal lifted his arms high and brought them down on Sienna's. Hers gave way beneath the magnified force of his twisting body and increased gravity. Free of her grip, he hit her with an uppercut. The instant before his fist met her chin, Kilal raised his gravity to fifty percent, grounding him in place. Anything more, and he'd crash into the sewer beneath them.

The crack of knuckles against her jaw thundered through the misty square, ricocheting off parked cars and scattering into the surroundings. The impact created a concussive blast of wind ripping at their clothes and hair. Kilal almost couldn't believe it had been that easy. Granted, it'd been a while since he'd hit something that hard, but to think Sienna could be defeated with one blow.

Except...something wasn't right.

Sienna hadn't moved. Blood spilled from her mouth and split chin.

Requiem had warned she might be as strong as he was. But she was wrong. Dead wrong. He'd vastly underestimated her and her stones.

"Disappointing," she hissed.

~ CHAPTER 53 ~

When Sienna struck him, Kilal experienced several acute pains as if they were each happening separately from the others. His right cheek shattered, and the force of the blow erupted the cartilage of his nose and blew a hole out his left cheek bone.

At some point during the process, he left the ground. Requiem and Sienna were shrinking. Or was he moving away from them?

Sight abandoned him as his eyes exploded next and another portion of his skull burst. His neck twisted and snapped. If he'd been able to see, he would've been looking at his backside. A thick metallic *thunk* echoed from the impact of his body against a structure.

The skyscraper a half-mile away from where they were attacked.

Thoughts, instincts, feelings. All of them escaped him. He should have passed out. He should have died. But he clung to consciousness, the thin thread of it still there, and squeezed it like his life depended on it. Like Requiem's life depended on it.

When sight finally returned, and his head twisted itself back around, Kilal was lying on his back, staring up at the faces of a few of the homeless citizens he'd passed earlier. When feeling returned, his skin prickling as though punctured by a thousand needles, he felt hands pressing into his pockets, searching. But that wasn't the abnormality.

It was the infrastructure of the skyscraper; it was wobbling.

Apparently, others noticed too, because screams lit up the night. The faces leaning over him and the desperate fingers in his pockets disappeared as quickly as his sight had when his eyes ruptured.

Kilal leaped to his feet, his legs momentarily as unstable as the building he stood beneath. He looked around for the source of the weakening structure—and his heart sank. Before his body had bounced and rolled to a stop, he'd broken through two corner beams of the metal skeleton. It was going to fall, and there was nothing he could do about it.

How many were going to die? Hundreds? Thousands?

Another thought struck him, one somehow even worse.

Alistair and Violet were out there somewhere. If they'd heard the crash of his vehicle, they would be coming in his direction, just in time to either be killed by Sienna or crushed by the falling building. And they had Allyria with them.

NO!

The echoes of his pain scratched out the possibility of beating Sienna in a fistfight. He couldn't. It was that simple. At least not with his current Carvings. And he didn't have time to etch new ones. Not with the skyscraper about to collapse. So what options were left?

Kilal twisted about, looking for any solution which would present itself.

One finally did. And just in time.

The skyscraper lurched to one side, the side he'd crashed through, and began falling, but it was the best scenario. The first building the collapsing skyscraper would fall on was a three-story bank, and all Silent Haven banks had their exterior lined in steel. It could potentially support the weight of the falling structure, at least long enough for Kilal to heave the skyscraper into the street.

It was a terrible idea, but he didn't have many options.

If only he hadn't left his backpack in the car. A vial of Dragon's Blood could be the difference between hundreds of lost lives.

Gravity lowered, Kilal bounded toward the bank. He reached it in two long leaps and hit the top in one powerful jump. Standing on the building, facing the falling structure, doubt curled in his gut. Heaps of it. What was he thinking? It wasn't going to work! Now *he* would be crushed amidst all the others.

But he would survive and carry with him the burden of more guilt.

The building smashed into him. Kilal roared. He increased his strength to one hundred percent and caught the corner of the skyscraper. One tiny man holding the weight of the world. He bellowed his defiance at the colossal structure; it was but another battle. A battle with the lives of thousands at the stake.

"I won't LOSE!"

His veins popped like steel chords. The pressure on his joints pulled them from their sockets. White energy surrounded his entire body as bones snapped, punctured skin, and healed. Agony enveloped him.

Metal bent, screeched, moaned, and matched his scream with its own. Kilal's knees buckled as the bank's supports began bowing outward. Cracks spread on the cement roof, starting beneath his feet and spiraling outward. He sank into the chunks up to his ankles. It wouldn't be long before the whole building gave way. Or the skyscraper split in half. And when it did, all of Kilal's effort and pain would be for nothing. The steel against his hands bent—it was time.

He'd been so concerned about the structure of the bank holding the weight of the skyscraper, he failed to consider whether his own body could withstand it. And withstand it, it could not. Even his near-instantaneous healing couldn't keep up with the damage to his joints, muscles, and bones. It was now or never.

He filled his lungs with as much air as he could. His back felt close to snapping in half, and it was a struggle to breathe, but he sucked in air with all his might and let it out in a deafening roar.

Kilal hoped Alistair, Violet, and Allyria hadn't heard the commotion. Or were preoccupied with a less lethal threat than a collapsing skyscraper and Sienna. But as he stood there, the weight of the world upon his body, breaking it, he prayed with all his might that they would show up. And if not them, anyone else who could help him save hundreds of lives. But as he twisted his body to direct the falling building into the street, a crippling sight caught his attention.

The road was filled with gawking bystanders. Dozens of them. If he tossed the skyscraper, they would all die.

He tried to yell at them, scream at them to flee, but barely more than a whispered command to 'go' escaped him. The pressure pushing down on him kept him from being able to make more than a few gasped words.

Defeat crippled him. There was no way to come out of the situation without an untold number of deaths. Not without a miracle.

A blur caught his attention, a human moving to his side.

That someone was Sienna.

She took a step forward and stopped, cocking her head and staring at him inquisitively. "Why do you care so much for them?" Her voice was about as hard as her muscles were taut. "They're ants. Do you care about ants when you step on them?"

"Please," Kilal rasped, voice barely more than a whisper, feet sinking deeper into the cracking roof. "Your fight...is with me...and Requiem."

Her eyes traveled to his bowed and shaking legs. She stepped closer.

"Please...don't...do...this."

Sienna kicked his left leg, snapping it at the femur. He

screeched, and his body and the bank collapsed.

Kilal and a few blocks worth of buildings, a mix of homes, businesses, and citizens of Silent Haven, were buried beneath tons of metal and debris.

~ CHAPTER 54 ~

Kilal dug himself out of the wreckage and debris of the bank and skyscraper. Standing on top of the massive mound of ruin, he witnessed the devastation that had been wrought by the collapse. Pure and undefiled devastation. Only a handful of buildings, one of which looked like an apartment complex, had been crushed beneath the skyscraper, but the force expelled throughout the surrounding blocks toppled more buildings than were crushed. Car alarms blared and the sirens of emergency vehicles echoed through the city. But it was the cries, screams, and moans of thousands of the dying and mourning, many trapped beneath the debris and destruction, which were the hardest to drown out.

So...much...death.

He hadn't been witness to such a catastrophic event, of so many lost at one time, in...well...ever. Even the invasion of Ash Fallen he'd fought in a hundred and fifty years ago hadn't resulted in that many deaths in such short a time.

Kilal dropped to his knees. Over and over, he pounded the mound of rubble, howling with each strike.

Panting, he snapped his head up, blinking away tears, when Sienna's overpowering presence returned.

She stalked toward him, a specter in the mist and cloud of dust and dirt. Her choker and armbands burned crimson, but most intimidating of all were her eyes. Bright red, they shone just like the gemstones.

Hatred consumed him. If it had a color, he'd burn as vividly as the stones she wore. That woman, that *monster*, was pure evil. She didn't care about anything. Only the hunt. That was the scariest part about an enemy like Sienna. Kilal had seen it in her eyes, just before she nearly tore his head from his shoulders.

In those soulless orbs was...nothing. No shame, guilt, joy, happiness, reverie, anticipation, fear. She existed to kill her target. That was it. And it didn't even bring her joy. It was just what she did. And ashes, she did it well.

In the Tower of Eyes, Kilal had hated his torturers. He'd hated Ashen Kane. He'd hated the very tower itself. He'd hated Gabriel Sunsetter. But most of all, he'd hated himself. Now, he'd found a new target for his animosity.

With each step closer to him she took, his hatred rose until there wasn't anything else to feel. It was only Sienna and what he would do to her.

Kilal screamed like he'd never screamed before. It was as if every single soul who'd ever been hurt by that woman was funneling their rage through him. He grasped onto that, let it pour through him, enliven him, strengthen him. And struck forward.

"I'LL KILL YOU!"

Her form revealed itself behind the curtain of mist and smokey debris. She smiled, but it didn't reach her eyes. They were just as dead as the hundreds of lives buried beneath the rubble. And she would soon join them. No. She wasn't happy, not truly. She only thrived on knowing the hunt wasn't yet over.

Kilal raised his strength back to a hundred percent, and powered by it and his hatred, lunged.

Mid-surge his Carving fizzled out, and Kilal deflated like a popped balloon.

Sienna backhanded him, sending him careening head over heels into more wreckage in much the same state as the first time she'd hit him. But he didn't give up. He'd never give up! Skull, neck, and face healing, Kilal's mind raced. What could he do? How could he stop her? He couldn't out-punch her, especially without his strength Carving. So what, then?

If he couldn't out-*punch* her, he'd have to outsmart her. And he'd need new Carvings for that. But that required time, and he didn't think Sienna would be gracious enough to grant him that, even if he asked politely.

His much-needed time appeared as a dark form in the settling debris. It twirled, coming in fast at Sienna—Requiem, wielding two dark blades, one in each hand.

Somehow, Sienna seemed to sense her approach and deftly maneuvered out of reach of the slashing swords.

Kilal yearned to jump back into the fray and fight at Requiem's side, but he'd be of no use as he was. So, he rolled onto his side and crawled under a fallen steel beam. Emerging on the other side, he scooted himself back until he was resting against the metal support.

Just a few minutes. Requiem, stay safe.

It felt wrong, leaving her to fight Sienna alone, but from his understanding, it was the third time the two had faced each other, and something told him Requiem was potentially harder to kill than he was.

Grabbing the knife kit still clinging snug to his belt, Kilal whipped out his carving blade and went to work.

***

Requiem attacked high, then low, her blades a flurry of movement, keeping Sienna at bay. When Kilal ducked behind the steel beam, she almost cursed him, calling him a coward, but reality struck her.

He was re-carving. Good.

She'd tried to explain to the sometimes-infuriating man that Sienna wasn't an enemy he could out-punch. It only took him experiencing it for himself to believe her.

Hurry, Kilal.

She'd encountered Sienna on two other occasions, been caught on one and narrowly avoided being caught on the other, but never had she outright fought the Heir.

Sienna came at her hard, slapping Requiem's blades aside with every slash and thrust. The woman was bloody fast.

Requiem ducked beneath a punch and landed a deep gash on Sienna's thigh before leaping backward. Her hair parted as she narrowly avoided Sienna's downward strike. Her fist crashed into the ground, sending up a spray of rocks and dirt. Red energy enveloped Sienna's injured leg, healing it.

She may mend fast, but she didn't heal as fast as Kilal.

Only having a few seconds with the upper hand, Requiem rushed forward, slashing. She scored a few more hits, though nothing crippling. But she had Sienna on the defensive, and that in itself was a victory.

Requiem lunged again. Sienna leaped back. She sank her fist into a chunk of rock nearly the size of Requiem and swung it at her. Requiem skidded to a stop but was too late. The boulder smacked into her with a crushing force. She was thrown off her feet and sent tumbling through the air. She managed to land roughly on all fours, but two Siennas marched toward her as her head spun. Requiem sloppily pushed herself to her feet, wobbled, and took a dazed step back.

Was it the end? Would she die there?

A roar answered her.

Kilal emerged from the wreckage.

Bloody ashes, that was quick! No more than two minutes. In the ten-year absence, Requiem had forgotten why Kilal was truly an Arbiter to be envied. It wasn't his strength, his impressive physique, or even his immortality. It was his ability to carve. *No one* carved faster, more precisely, or more efficiently than him.

"SIENNA!" Kilal screamed.

The runes he'd chosen would determine the outcome of the battle. Requiem hoped he'd chosen wisely.

***

For months upon becoming a fresh Arbiter and surviving the Awakening, Kilal had isolated himself, spending all that time practicing his carving skills. He'd etched every Carving he knew and discovered *thousands* of times. He didn't quit until he could replicate them blindfolded.

Deific Strength. Gravitational Control. All the ones he'd given to Allyria and more. And it wasn't just the first couple of months that he practiced that way. Every time he received, found, or stole a new design, he didn't rest until it was mastered. Something he'd even carried into the training of his mentees, back when time had allowed it.

That, above everything else, made him *the* most powerful Arbiter living.

So, when Kilal pulled out his knife and canceled his strength and gravitational control, he wasn't in the least bit concerned that he wouldn't be able to finish the new ones in time. He was concerned over whether he'd picked the correct combination to use next.

A hundred Carvings, at least, he had access to, but most of them weren't worth his time. Not now.

The combination he chose was a strange one. Despite preferring to punch things and manipulate gravity to punch things even harder, he could fight with whatever styles a battle demanded. It would just be...different. So, he chose a combination he'd rarely used before.

Deific Agility and Master of Ice.

Normally, Kilal favored overwhelming offense instead of a semblance of defense, but he wouldn't beat Sienna in a contest of strength.

He just needed to last long enough to wear her down and let Requiem cut her head off.

Here's to hoping that will kill her.

Deific Agility was everything Deific Strength wasn't, and vice versa. Deific Strength let him take most punches and do things like hold up a building. Deific Agility would instead let him bend, avoid, flip, run, and maneuver in a way normally impossible.

If he couldn't out-punch Sienna, then he'd out-maneuver her.

Master of Ice was...exactly what it sounded like. He could freeze the moisture in the air or even in a human's body. In theory, the agility would allow him to avoid Sienna's attacks long enough to turn her into a popsicle, which should give Requiem the leeway needed to cut her head off. But the ice Carving had other benefits, though ones he hoped he wouldn't have to use.

It was nearly impossible to incur burnout from overuse of the Elemental branch, but the one and only time he'd used the full potential of Master of Ice, he'd experienced the brain-melting torment. He'd rather not do that again if it could be helped.

Thirty seconds it took him to carve Deific Agility. A full three seconds longer than it should have. The seizure wasn't pleasant, but after being punched by Sienna and having a building dropped on him, of which he wasn't sure which was worse, he'd welcome the seizure any day. Master of Ice took him thirty-three seconds.

Getting rusty, old man, he chided.

He blamed it on not having a cloth to clean away the fresh blood. He had to slow the carving to make sure he was doing it...perfectly. Yes, that was it. Definitely not him getting rusty.

Finished, Kilal wiped puke from his chin and shirt, even though it didn't matter. He didn't have much of a shirt left, so he tore the tatters off and used the ruined fabric to finish cleaning his face.

Lean, hard, glistening muscle was coated in dirt, debris, and dried blood. It felt awful. Normally he'd have taken a moment to test his Carvings before leaping into battle, but there wasn't time for that. Even the few seconds it would take could be the difference between life and death for a comrade.

Kilal vaulted over the beam like a graceful doe and landed on the other side. Requiem stumbled back, clearly dazed.

"SIENNA!" he roared.

Requiem seemed to shed the dizziness and, with a newfound strength, struck at the Heir. In one vicious blow, Requiem nearly severed an arm from her shoulder, but red energy similar to Kilal's surrounded the wound and healed it.

Impossible! Not even the Carving of Deific Healing could mend so efficiently. The only thing he knew that could was...

His Carving of Immortality.

If she truly was immortal, the battle would be something else entirely.

Sienna managed to slap the flat of the blade away and landed a kick to Requiem's arm. It twisted, and she dropped the sword, which puffed away into shadowy smoke. She followed her kick with a fist rammed against Requiem's chest, but she'd anticipated the second blow. Requiem leaped back enough to, although not dodge the punch entirely, lessen the impact, but it still sent her tumbling backward and smacking hard into a collapsed wall.

Sienna kept her eyes on Kilal as she moved in for the killing blow.

He smiled, the grin only broadening when doubt slipped into the Heir's eyes.

When Kilal darted forward, he was *fast*. He zipped toward her, and Sienna was forced to turn and face her new attacker.

Kilal ducked beneath her punch and bent low. Sensing the water in her body, he slapped her left knee as he passed. The moisture called to him, and he manipulated it, slowing their atoms until they froze. Ice bloomed around Sienna's knee, starting inward and blossoming out, crystalizing the water molecules in the air directly around it.

She stumbled and shifted her weight to her other leg, but Kilal didn't give her a chance to recuperate. He spun on one knee and struck Sienna's frozen leg with a fist. A crack appeared on the surface. That was it.

And his hand broke from the impact.

That's right. He lurched back, his shattered fingers on fire. *No strength Carving.* He'd become too dependent on it.

Sienna growled and lunged. Kilal twisted out of her reach, and she fell on her face. Finishing his spin, he moved in swiftly, leaping over her and slapping her other ankle. It froze over just like the knee.

She grabbed a long iron rod at her side and swung it at him as he rolled to a stand, but he tumbled with the direction of the blow, diminishing the impact. Forcing herself to her feet, both legs moving stiffly and awkwardly, Sienna swung the pole at him again. Kilal let it breeze past him harmlessly and reached out at the last moment to touch it.

Nothing happened.

Sienna grinned, victorious, and used Kilal's confusion as a chance to thrust the pipe through his chest.

Steel doesn't contain water, you bloody idiot!

Kilal grabbed the pipe with both hands. He dug his feet into the ground as they both tugged in opposite directions, trying to dislodge it. His body worked to heal, but with the pipe still in his chest, there was only so much the Carving could mend. He coughed, spewing blood, and stumbled.

He was certain he wouldn't have won the contest even if he'd had the Deific Strength active, but he definitely wasn't going to win without it.

Kilal reversed his intent, trying to backtrack and slip off the pipe.

Sienna hobbled toward him, matching his slowing pace, keeping the pipe in his chest.

He was losing a lot of blood. White energy crackled uselessly around the gaping hole. A wave of nausea hit him, and his eyes threatened to roll into the back of his head. He was losing ground. Sienna was getting closer and closer, though gradually, her movement was drastically hindered, but a few frozen joints were nothing compared to massive blood loss.

A scream shook him to his core, hair-raising and vengeful.

Requiem bounded toward them, slashing both blades at Sienna's neck. The huntress recoiled. She let go of the pipe with one hand and used it to swipe at the swords, but it was all a feint. Requiem kicked off Sienna's outstretched arm, using it to redirect her leap at Kilal.

The black blades sliced clean through the pipe.

Force no longer opposing him, he fell backward, landing on what remained of the pipe and sliding down it.

Requiem pulled the forsaken thing from his chest while he was still on his butt. He grunted, but nodded his thanks and accepted her outstretched hand.

Sienna snarled and threw away the piece still clasped in her hand.

"I'll slow her," Kilal said, chest covered in white energy. "You kill her. Dismember her. Whatever it takes."

Requiem nodded, and the two parted, circling the Heir, forcing her to continually shift her position to keep them both in her peripheral.

Sienna didn't wait long and lunged at Kilal. In another time, when he wasn't standing amidst a mass graveyard, he may have felt honored. Sienna, who—by all accounts—hated Requiem, had chosen him to attack first. Or maybe she was going after the weaker link?

Kilal ducked beneath her blow, weaved in and out of a furious flurry, and sidestepped a front kick. Was it just him or was she getting faster? A punch nearly struck his face. The very force of it passing by cut his cheek. The chunk of debris he'd been standing in front of exploded from the impact.

Bloodshed and Oaths, she was powerful!

But so was he.

Kilal slapped a fist by his face, freezing it at the touch. Slipping his other hand past her defensives, he struck her cheek, immobilizing it as well, and leaped back onto a steel beam. From there, he bounded onto the top of a chunk of building. Sienna awkwardly followed, with Requiem keeping her distance but trailing her.

At the top of the boulder, Sienna smiled, believing him cornered. Kilal let her see his false confusion. She seemed so confident, as if she had him on the edge of a mountain's height fall. Not a ten-foot one. Either way, her confidence was short-lived. He spread his hands wide, an invitation, and took a step off the ledge.

Onto a block of ice.

Water molecules surrounded him; he targeted the ones beneath his foot as he walked back into open air, making a platform. Kilal took a second and third step, until he was a good few feet from Sienna.

Requiem, standing an equidistance behind her, gave him a look he knew all too well: *what's your plan here?*

He didn't exactly have an answer. Part of him was hoping if he stalled long enough, Alistair and his team would show up. As powerful as Sienna was, he didn't think even she could stand up to a group of two Primes, a Violet, and whatever Requiem was. But Requiem mouthed *twenty-four hours*, a reminder of their time ticking away, minute by minute.

Kilal rushed toward her, forcing the Heir to confront him, and only him. Blocks of ice appeared under each step he took, and even once he was back on solid ground. Sienna leaped away, falling ten feet, and used the newly gained open space to keep Kilal and Requiem in her sight. He circled and circled, forming a ring of ice around her. It wasn't the best idea, but any misstep they could force Sienna to make could be the difference between victory and loss.

When much of the clearing they stood in was covered in ice, Kilal attacked. He slid across the frozen rubble as if he'd been doing it since the day he was born—another benefit of his Carving—and attacked. Sienna couldn't keep up with his strange movements, and before long, her legs and much of her abdomen were crystallized.

Requiem chose that moment to attack. She came in fast and strong. Sienna couldn't react quickly enough, and before Kilal knew it, Requiem had taken the Heir's arm off at the elbow—then went straight for the head.

Sienna could barely do more than stumble back and keep her footing. Her right arm was dull and rendered useless by the ice, and what remained of her left was covered in red, crackling energy beneath the elbow. But when Requiem's blade swiped a hair's breadth from her neck, Sienna let loose a blood-curdling scream and *erupted* in red lightning, forcing Requiem to retreat.

Sienna became a pillar of crimson light so bright Kilal was forced to look away. The brilliant glow stretched all the way to the sky, piercing the dark clouds above. Wave after wave of power pulsed from her. It was all Kilal could do to hold on to a lamppost poking from the rubble to keep himself from being blown back.

The power she was emanating was *incredible*. Kilal had never felt anything like it before. His confidence in their victory over the monstrous woman was quickly degrading.

When the red light receded and the pulses of power stopped, Sienna stared at them. All the ice Kilal had embedded into different body parts had melted. Her left arm was restored. But there was an abnormality.

More than half of the crimson stones on the bands around her biceps were dim, lifeless.

Kilal's mind raced with the possibilities. Did the stones grant her a finite amount of power, and she'd just used up a good chunk of what she had? Could Kilal and Requiem stall long enough to force her to use more of her stones until she had no more power left? And if so, did they have enough time for that?

Twenty-four hours. Less than that, with how much time had passed between the asylum and now. A hard enough deadline without a drawn-out battle.

Requiem was the first to respond, leaping at her with a blade in each hand. Sienna moved with a speed and grace she hadn't before, dodging each swipe and stab before landing a crunching kick onto the outside of Requiem's right knee. As she silently crumbled, Sienna kicked her in the chest, planting Requiem onto her butt. The ground gave way into a small crater from the impact, spraying dirt and debris everywhere. Blood spewed from Requiem as she bounced into the air.

Sienna wound up for another kick, but Kilal was already acting. Requiem was fast. Sienna was fast, too. But *he* had a Carving of Deific Agility and wasn't concerned with draining it.

He spiked it to one hundred percent and shot forward, eating up the distance between them in one powerful leap. Grabbing Sienna's kicking leg, he spun her over his shoulder and let go at the peak, hurling her through the air and into a car which had been blown upside down from the collapsing skyscraper. Sienna slammed into the vehicle, and they slid, screeching across the street to smash into a fallen building.

It barely slowed her down.

Sienna exploded from the top of the building. Screaming, she arced overhead, flipped, and descended, leg outstretched to split Kilal in half.

It was time to unleash the full potential of Master of Ice, ashes to the consequences.

Kilal froze the water molecules in the air surrounding his body, enclosing himself in a thick armor of blue ice. The toll of such use was immediate; his internal temperature spiked, but he held firm.

Nothing more than a giant covered in frozen 'armor,' Kilal blocked the descending kick with two arms raised above his head. The impact was thunderous, the cracking of the ice deafening. He sunk into the debris, further and further until he stood in a large crater. The ice around his knees blew out from absorbing most of the impact, but his legs didn't break, though the armor around his arm shattered into a hundred pieces as the limbs snapped.

Just as quickly as his Carving of Immortality worked to heal him, Kilal worked to reforge the broken sections of his armor, refreezing the air around him, enclosing himself once again in a fully-intact suit of ice. But the toll continued to strain his body and mind. Sweat blurred his vision, and from within the confines of his armor, it began to melt from the inside. His body temperature continued to shoot up . Without his immortality, he'd already be out of commission, but as long as his Carving could keep up with the damage done to his body and brain, he could keep fighting.

Kilal grabbed Sienna's foot. He twisted his body around and slammed her into the crater with him. Cracks spiraled out from the impact. Quicker than she could react, he kicked her into the air and punched her in the chest. He'd strained further, growing a six-inch spike at the center of his knuckles, which pierced her ribcage. The force of the blow crushed her sternum and tore a hole in her chest before she tumbled away.

He took a step to follow but stumbled, dizzy. Breathing became labored, and for a second, he saw two of the Heir rise from the ground. Both had red energy crackling around her torso and more dull red gemstones on her biceps.

Sienna shot toward him, blasting chunks of debris behind her. Kilal leapt back, but the momentary dizziness stunted his reaction time, and she crashed into him. She punched his face and followed up with another fist to the sternum. It sounded like thunder had struck twice.

Kilal tore away, crashing through two buildings, before coming to a stop in the dining room of an apartment. A man and a woman huddled beneath their table, staring at him wide-eyed.

He had to get out of there. If Sienna caught him inside the family's home, they'd die.

Leaping to unsteady feet, Kilal roared and raced back to the streets.

Sienna met him in the middle of the open road where the two titans clashed like gods. Blow after blow they rained upon each other, neither giving an inch, neither succumbing to their multitudes of wounds. Their screams could be heard across the city, and those far enough away would wonder what the deafening crashes were caused by.

Even with his Carving of Deific Agility at max, he was barely able to avoid her strikes. But when he couldn't, his ice armor absorbed the impact. Between dodging her attacks, landing his own, and restoring any cracks or chunks taken out of his protection, the world narrowed around him. There was nothing else, only the fight to survive.

Sweat flowed like a stream from his face, from every pore of his body, as his temperature increased and mixed with the melting armor, but he couldn't think of anything else to do.

It wasn't long before Kilal's vicious onslaught slowed, and he was on the defensive. The effects of burnout, despite being unable to kill him, became too great to ignore, but Sienna didn't give him a second to breathe. The moment he avoided one blow or restored a chunk of armor, she'd already attacked two more times.

And he was seeing double again. More often than not, he struggled to block or avoid punches and kicks that weren't there, only to be crushed by the real Sienna strikes. But he wouldn't stop. He couldn't stop. On nothing more than pure instinct and rage, Kilal continued to fight, to block, to dodge, to restore, and land an attack of his own when he could.

They battled so fast, an onlooker would see nothing more than two blurs moving in one direction with a blast of blue, one after the other, breaking up the backward momentum.

Gasping for breath, Kilal's brain would be toast in a few

more seconds. Already his Carving of Immortality had kicked into gear, working to bring his body's temperature back under control, but with every blow he took, it became that much harder for his healing to keep up. Soon, it wouldn't be able to.

His vision blurred again. When he threw a hand up to block a punch, steam rose from the gauntlet. That wasn't good. Sweat stung his eyes. Salt scoured his tongue. And finally, Kilal tripped.

It was over.

Sienna brought an arm back, seeming to hover over him as he fell. Time slowed to a near stop. Still, she didn't smile. Didn't gloat over her victory. It wasn't something she relished in. It was just something she did.

Shadows flickered around them. Sienna hesitated before trying to redirect her attack to defense, but it was too late. She'd forgotten her other foe. Or underestimated her.

Requiem appeared from nowhere, face savage, leg healed, blood coating her chin and shirt, swinging a large blade in a two-handed grip at Sienna's neck.

The Heir swung her head about, absorbing the blow with the gemstones on her choker.

An explosion rocked their vicinity, lifting Kilal into the air and throwing him back. The whole square erupted in black and red flames. He only just caught a glimpse of Requiem twisting unnaturally in the air before she too was engulfed in fire.

He hit something hard. His ice armor took the brunt of the damage, but even so, Kilal laid on his back, breaths coming quickly and raggedly. He couldn't move, couldn't think. He could only lie there, gasping as his immortality repaired the brain damage the overuse of his Elemental Carving had caused. Even the air he inhaled scorched his throat. All he could do was hope the fight was over. Because if not, he was dead.

When he could move again, Kilal slowly, painfully, pushed himself to his feet. His armor was all but gone. A few chunks of ice still clung to his legs and arms, but most of it had melted from either the explosion or his overheated body.

No additional attacks came.

Through still blurred vision, he found Sienna on her back, also gasping. Her face and upper abdomen were blackened. Her eyes were gone, her lips and the cartilage of her nose melted. Kilal could only imagine the searing agony of each breath she took.

Requiem walked up from the other side. The edges of her clothes were singed, but she otherwise didn't look like she'd just been in close proximity to an explosion.

Red energy crackled around Sienna's torso and face. Already she was healing.

"Cut her head off," Kilal croaked. "Let's see how much she can heal from."

Requiem nodded and flicked a wrist. The Heir's charred head slid away from her neck, and the energy disappeared.

"Is it over?" Requiem asked.

He shrugged.

Kilal bent and ran a thumb over the dull and cracked gemstones in Sienna's choker. Each stone was split in varying degrees of severity. Their light was gone. There were no more burning lights, though the ones around Sienna's arms still glowed a bright red.

Let's see about those.

He grabbed an armband, intending to slide it down her lifeless limb and remove it, but his hand locked on it, and Kilal was whisked away to a land of darkness.

***

He floated amidst a ruinous landscape. The sky was blood red. Dark clouds stretched across the crimson horizon. The occasional streaks of orange lightning lit up the night sky. Was it night? There were three dark, ominous spheres in the sky.

None of them gave off light. One, the closest of the three, had a large crack down the center.

The land was scorched, as if a fire had erupted over the surface of wherever he was. The smell reinforced that theory; burning wood mixed with the offensive scent of charred flesh. There were no trees, no shrubbery of any kind. There weren't even mountains or hills. He was on a flat landscape of wasteland proportions. No animals, no life of any kind.

Bloodshed and Oaths, where was he?

He twisted his body about in the air, but everywhere he looked, all was the same. Desolation.

The horizon darkened. It formed the shape of a bulbous head; a head with dozens of dark tentacles reached from one end of the horizon to the other. One eye stretched across his field of vision, centered in the bulbous head. It opened and settled upon him.

Within its gaze, Kilal feared he'd lose himself in the ancientness. He was nothing before the great eye. A babe held more power compared to an adult than he did to the thing engulfing the sky before him.

That thing...that being...was infinite.

A mouth opened. A mouth with no teeth but a tongue which slithered out and slapped against the ground like another tentacle.

"You are not her," it said. Its voice was the crash of thunder, the collapse of the skyscraper, the pain of a concussion, the grind of gravel against gravel.

A feeling enveloped Kilal. One he hadn't experienced since his first voyage into the Schism. Pure, unadulterated fear.

He screamed.

The tentacles growing from the thing's head responded to his terror and reached for him.

Kilal waved his arms around, kicked his feet. He even pumped his limbs as if he were running. Anything to get away from the great being's gaze, but the tentacles continued, slowly but surely reaching, reaching, reaching for him. He was stuck. And even if he could move, where would he go where he wouldn't be found?

"*I do not know you,*" it said. *"But I will."*

Kilal slammed back into his body.

***

Disoriented, it took him a moment to realize Requiem was shaking him, screaming his name.

How long had he been...wherever he'd been?

He released the armband, jerking away from it so hard, he threw both himself and Requiem back. She landed on top of him.

"What happened?" she asked, searching his eyes.

Kilal pulled her tighter against him, clutching her. His only answer was a tearful sob.

~ CHAPTER 55 ~

"Kilal," Requiem cried, shaking him. Tears were in her eyes. "What's wrong? What happened?"

He wiped snot from his nose with the back of a hand. "How long was I gone?"

"Gone? Gone where? You grabbed her armband, then started screaming."

So, not long. Definitely not long enough to visit another realm and that...thing.

Kilal reined in his emotions and recounted to Requiem what he'd witnessed.

When he finished, she was silent. It was his turn to shake her, but much more gently than she'd done to him. If not for his immortality, he would probably have a wicked crick in his neck.

"What does it mean?" Requiem asked, staring at the armband on Sienna's bicep as if it were poisonous.

He shrugged and stood up, helping Requiem to her feet as well. "No idea. But probably not anything good. What I do know is it has something to do with those stones. Have you ever touched one before?"

Requiem shook her head. "Not yet. But—" She reached for the band.

"Are you crazy?" Kilal cried, grabbing her arm. "You're

going to touch it *now,* after what just happened to me? What if you can't come back? What if that...thing...does more than look at you?"

Requiem ripped her arm away and snarled. "She made it back. You made it back. Why would you think I wouldn't too?"

Kilal sighed. Right. Requiem was particularly fragile when it came to him even accidentally insinuating her being weaker than him. "That's not what I meant, and you know it."

She lowered her gaze, frowning. A tinge of red covered her cheeks.

Good! She should be embarrassed.

"What should we do with her?" he asked.

"Is there anything else we can do with her? We've cut her head off. The only thing left is taking the stones, but something tells me you won't let me do that."

Kilal grunted.

Standing in the middle of the wreckage of the fallen sky-scraper—sirens drawing closer and battling against the wails of humans, both of the dying and of the mourning—and the crackling fires popping up around the devastation, Kilal gritted his teeth and balled his hands into fists.

"He's going to pay for making this happen," he growled.

Requiem's countenance darkened until he imagined it matched his. "Ximthar," she said.

Kilal thumbed the ring still in his pants pocket. One reminder. "We need to help."

"Kilal, we can't."

"Of course we can! We have to!"

She laid a hand softly on his and squeezed it. She didn't let go. "This isn't just about the time limit. This is about the fact that every Arbiter in the city is probably after us. And we just lit a beacon announcing exactly where we are. If we stay, more will die. Many more. We have to move."

Kilal's lip curled and he let out a guttural snarl. She was right. Ashes, but she was.

"He *will* pay."

A gleam to his right, under a steel beam, caught his attention, and he walked to it. A hand, broken and mangled, stuck up from the wreckage. A ring was on one of the fingers. Kilal wiggled it off and brushed debris from it. Silver. A name was etched along the inside. Maggie. He placed it in his pocket, beside the other.

Well, Maggie, you'll have your revenge.

"He will," Requiem agreed at his side. "After he helps us."

Kilal wanted to argue, but again, she was right. What he needed was Ximthar and Jayden's help. After that, he didn't care how much they may have done for his world. The death toll was only increasing due to their foolish 'test' and it was enough reason to grant them a swift execution.

"We need to find another car," Kilal said, leaving the devastation behind him. He refused to look back. There was only regret and pain in that direction, and there would be plenty more of that for him to grieve about soon.

***

After returning to the ruined vehicle to grab his backpack, they were able to purchase a beat-up car from an old man with some of the cash Kilal kept with him.

The contents were far too important to leave behind. He took a careful tally of all the items in the backpack, and after concluding everything was still there, they found the old man loitering nearby and purchased his vehicle for at least twice the asking price, but Kilal was in a generous mood. The man looked like he could use something good in his life. Hopefully, he'd given him some of that.

They continued north in silence. After so much death, Kilal wasn't much in the mood for a conversation. The whole encounter plagued him. If only he'd been more astute before Sienna ambushed them. If he hadn't been so preoccupied with talking to Requiem, maybe he would have seen the huntress coming. Maybe he would have been able to prevent a *bloody skyscraper* from falling on the city.

"Stop that," Requiem said.

"What?"

"You know."

Kilal sighed. She really did know him. Even after so much time apart.

Ashes, but he loved her.

"Stop wondering about every 'maybe' situation that could've occurred. They didn't. We did the best we could. *You* did the best you could. Bloody ashes, Kilal, you held up a *skyscraper*! There's nothing you could have done differently. Stop mentally flaying yourself."

"But—"

"No." Requiem wasn't going to let him have his way. "*You did the best you could.* And that's all Sha'tum can ask of us. That's all *anyone* can ask of us!"

"Why do you always have to be right?"

"It's not about being right. It's about someone protecting you from yourself."

Kilal smirked, but the smile faltered. "And that someone... is still you?"

She snorted. "Can you think of anyone else who can do it better than me?"

He smiled. Warmth filled his chest. It wasn't a definitive answer. But it wasn't a no, either. "I can't."

"Then I guess it's settled."

Kilal put a hand on hers and nearly sighed with relief when she gripped his back.

"Req," he said, "I'm sorry. For everything."

Her face hardened and lips flattened. Not the response he expected. "Don't. Not now." As angry as she sounded, as angry as she was...she didn't let go of his hand.

"Okay. Not now."

And for the first time since reuniting, that was just fine.

~ CHAPTER 56 ~

The sun rose over the open farmland surrounding them. Unlike his voyage south of the city and to the Veil, the roads north of Silent Haven were populated. Something Kilal was relieved about. It brought a sense of peace, seeing at least something that used to be familiar. A train of five large, six-wheeled trucks passed them, heading toward the city. A dozen or so crates were packed into the bed of each. If Kilal had to guess, he'd wager they were bringing goods from New Cita.

"We're going to have to get off this road soon," he said.

"I know. We can't risk driving through another city."

"Yeah, no one else needs to die today."

It wasn't ideal, going around, but they were making good time, despite their slowdowns in Silent Haven. Going around the city would add a few hours to their drive, but at the rate they were going, that would still put them in the Northern Ruins with a couple of hours to spare.

A car sped up, nearly hitting their rear.

"Ashes!" Kilal cursed. "Just can't catch a break."

The vehicle backed off of them, honked, and sped up again.

"Just a bloody idiot." Requiem stuck a hand out her window and waved for the driver to pass. He did, horn blaring, announcing his disgust at their slower pace.

A thought popped into Kilal's head, forcing a chuckle out of him.

"What?" Requiem asked.

"Imagine how soiled his pants would be if he knew who was in this car."

She smirked. "Very."

They shared a brief chuckle, a nice reprieve from the real situation they were in, though it was short-lived.

"I'm worried about Allyria," Kilal said.

"She's in good hands. Allistair and Violet will protect her."

"I was so conflicted. I didn't want Alistair to come when Sienna arrived. That would only put Allyria in danger. But as the weight of a skyscraper rested in my hands, I wanted nothing more than for him to help. Then, after the collapse, I could only wonder why they never showed up." Kilal shivered, remembering the death and destruction caused by his battle with the Heir. "The whole city had to hear, if not feel, what happened."

Requiem pursed her lips, squinted her eyes, and shrugged. "Something happened to Enoch's group."

Exactly what Kilal was thinking. It was the only explanation.

"What threat could they have encountered that would be powerful enough to warrant Enoch, of all people, requesting help?"

She was silent. Concern was evident on her face. "A *very* powerful threat."

"I shouldn't have sent Allyria with them. I should've made her go with Nam and Garret. I was a fool...again."

Requiem took her eyes off the road to glance at Kilal and offer a reassuring smile. "Not this time. She's a Prime Arbiter. She needs to be with another Prime. And there's no place, besides with you, where she could be safer than with Alistair. Even if they did encounter a powerful enemy, that enemy still had Violet, Alistair, Enoch, and a handful of other Arbiters to get through to reach Allyria. She's safe, Kilal. Trust me."

He sighed and looked out the window.

The world was different north of Silent Haven. The farm life was active in that portion of the land. He sat back in his seat, rolled down the window, and let a small, contented smile slip onto his face as he watched the simple homesteads go by.

One particular pasture caught his attention; rows and rows of bushes waist-high with yellow fruit growing sporadically throughout. Lemons.

Ashes, he'd kill to sink his teeth into one.

Families walked up and down the rows, picking ripe lemons, reaping what they'd sown in the previous season. Kilal's mouth watered as he tried to remember their citrusy tang. Children too young to help with the reaping ran in yards, laughing and playing. Brothers and sisters teased each other.

Brothers and sisters...

He'd had a brother once upon a time. Once upon a *dark* time.

That was almost two hundred years ago. You've changed. You were manipulated. It wasn't your choice.

A low chuckle sounded in the back of his mind; the deep recesses he tried his bloody hardest to keep locked away. But the last ten years had weakened the mental prison he'd built, confining those desires and memories that were...best forgotten. He'd tapped into those portions of himself to survive on more than one occasion in the Ashen Lands, which didn't bode well for the world.

That monster had wreaked havoc on the Sunlight Domain once. Kilal couldn't let that happen again.

Godsgraive *had* to remain sealed away. If he ever got out again...Kilal would kill himself.

The chuckle grew into full-blown laughter.

Give me time. I'll be back.

Kilal's first instinct was to break something of his, a bone preferably. Anything to punish himself for that time, but also to draw his mind away from the chuckling. After Requiem's little pep talk, though, he couldn't do that to her. Not so soon.

He really needed to develop better coping mechanisms.

There's no coping mechanism for me.

Desperation filled him. Kilal began tapping a leg and biting his tongue until the taste of copper flooded his mouth. What could he do? What could he think about, talk about, anything to draw his mind to a safer spot?

A face flashed before his mind, and the previous taunting turned to grumbling.

"Remember when you first met Lilliana?" Kilal asked.

Requiem chuckled. "I thought you'd stolen someone's child."

He burst into laughter. "You were so mad!"

She glowed with the memory. "I tried to make you return her. And Alistair? He had no idea what to make of her."

Kilal's mirth nearly shook the car. "He was mortified. I don't think he'd ever interacted with a child before that!"

"He probably didn't like the idea of having someone around with the same mental capacity."

Kilal snorted and started choking on his own tears. "He... he poked her. Actually poked her...and...and asked what i-it was."

Requiem chuckled, too. "She bit his finger. Wouldn't let go. He shook her and cried for help. Thought he was going to get rabies or something."

It felt good to laugh, especially with her.

"And Violet? She was finally over her jealousy of me when you showed up with another 'distraction,' as she called it."

He rolled his eyes. "She *hated* Lilliana. More than you, I think."

"Absolutely more than me! She *craved* your attention and approval. And suddenly she had to share it with that little human who was biting Alistair's finger? But it didn't take her long to accept Lilliana."

"Violet always did impress me with the way she could roll with the punches," Kilal said.

"Why do you think so many of us have had hard fates? We've all been through terrible things. Have you ever thought about that?"

Their mirth faded.

"I have. A lot. I think it's because we all start out the same: ripped away from our parents, our brothers and sisters. Then we're handed off to a group of Arbiters who are as skilled at parenting as an Ash Fallen. We didn't spend enough time with our families to know how to guide the young that came to us. So, we taught them all we knew: how to fight. It's no wonder so many of us go astray. We're a product of ourselves."

"That product leaves much to be desired," Requiem said. "We can kill Ash Fallen and each other with the skill of a master, but care for each other, for the young among us? Might as well toss a child to a pack of wolves and wonder why they turn out so...bloody messed up."

Kilal lightly smacked her shoulder in gest. "What was it you were just telling me?" He snapped his fingers as if discovering the secret of a lifetime. "That's right: we did the best we could. Just because it wasn't that good, it doesn't take away from that. We *all* did the best we could. And we'll continue doing the best we can."

"That's assuming we succeed at our mission. There may not be a future for us to be the best us we can be."

He smirked. "Now who's being negative?"

Requiem snorted. "Guess you're just rubbing off on me."

"Ashes! Thanks!" Kilal feigned hurt.

Requiem gripped his hand and squeezed it. Warmth blossomed in his heart. Like it did every time she showed him affection.

Bloodshed and Oaths! I've turned into an adolescent with raging hormones.

The blinker repeated itself, letting everyone on the road know Requiem was taking the upcoming left, right before entering the city.

Like Silent Haven, a large wall encircled New Cita, but behind the wall, it wasn't as advanced as Silent Haven, which was the most advanced of the three remaining cities. There were no skyscrapers, no buildings over three stories.

A long trail of vehicles waited in line to enter New Cita. Trucks of varying sizes containing wares from Silent Haven, or were empty and returning for another load, and a few passenger vehicles. Compared to the traffic Kilal had witnessed entering Silent Haven from the south, New Cita could have been close to bursting.

"How's the Heir's presence here in comparison?" Kilal asked.

"Worse."

"What?" Kilal asked, incredulously. "I find that hard to believe."

"That doesn't make it any less true. New Cita is now governed by some of the worst Arbiters you can imagine. Men and women who truly believe themselves to be greater than those we're to protect. They view the difference between Arbiter and man as great as a god to his creation."

"Inferno was from New Cita, wasn't she?" he asked.

"Inferno was pleasant compared to some of the people you'd encounter here."

Kilal rapped a knuckle against the door. "Were Arbiters always this bad? Was I really that delusional to think the bad apples were few and far between?"

"We all were. The truth is, they're cowards. They wouldn't dare rear their ugly heads when they knew there would be harsh consequences for their actions. Once the threat of those consequences was gone, so too was their deterrent."

"Still, I should have figured it out. I could have been a more common presence in New Cita and Vitrol. That may have changed...something, anything when I left."

"Maybe. And it may not have." Requiem tapped the plexiglass over the gauges in front of the steering wheel. "We'll be out of gas soon, but all gas stations outside of the three cities have been closed."

"Bloodshed and Oaths, why?"

She shrugged. "So the Heirs and their lackeys can artificially control as much as possible. It makes everyone that wants transport that isn't a century old go through them. They even added a tax to all gas sales."

"And no one has a choice otherwise. How much farther do you think we've got before we run out?"

"Maybe two hundred miles."

Kilal cursed through clenched teeth. "That barely gets us a third of the way there. We'll have another four hundred miles we'll have to do on foot. We'll barely make it in time, and that's assuming we don't have any more interruptions."

"You afraid of a little running, great Immortal One?" she said with a sly smile.

He groaned. "I've been doing nothing but running for the last decade." Kilal pursed his lips, then curled them until his face was squished like a wrinkled old ball. "Except for the last two. It's difficult to run when you're chained to a wall."

Requiem patted his hand. "Maybe a little silence would be nice. We're going to need all the rest we can get before we start our four-hundred-mile dash. A four-hundred-mile dash *before* we take on the forces of the Ash Fallen."

"I'd rather stay awake and talk."

"I can't sleep. Not while driving, so a good recharge for myself would be a little quiet. I'm sorry."

Kilal knew better than to argue. He wouldn't force a dialogue onto her. And if memory served, the Ashen Lands weren't a great place to be caught sleeping, anyway. He really should take advantage of the next three and a half hours and get some rest.

Yes, that would be nice. A quiet nap. Peaceful.

Good luck, Godsgrave whispered.

~ CHAPTER 57 ~

True to her guess, the car ran out of gas a few miles from two hundred.

Rest had not come easily for Kilal. It was a battle to obtain what felt like only a few minutes of shut eye. Fortunately, his body didn't need much rest. It was one of the basic benefits of the Awakening. Arbiters had increased stamina and decreased needs for food, water, and sleep. Kilal benefited even more from this with his Carving of Immortality. If he needed to—and in the Ashen Lands he had needed to—he could go indefinitely without any of the three. It wouldn't feel good. Especially the hunger. Constant pain gnawing at his insides. Not pleasant at all.

Kilal pushed them to their limits. He couldn't afford not to. If they couldn't find another car, which he was willing to steal if necessary, they'd be running for *four hundred miles*. The limit was the only option to push themselves at.

What Requiem didn't know, and another reason to push them so hard, was Kilal wasn't sure if he could guide them to the exact location of the teleportation device where they were meeting Ximthar and Jayden. His memory of that time was vague, due more to the mind-bending nature of the ruins. Their search for the location would only add more time, and time wasn't something they had much of.

Kilal had kept his Carving of Deific Agility activated instead of canceling it and returning to his tried and true. Right now, he needed to run, and agility would help him with that more than strength. His Master of Ice, he left too. He told himself it was because it paired better with agility, which wasn't necessarily true. The real reason was he just didn't feel like cutting himself right then. He'd had enough pain for one day.

The run was long and hard. Requiem stayed with him the whole way, and again Kilal was confronted with the possibility of the impossible. Whatever power she'd discovered or obtained, it was *terrifying*. Shadow manipulation. Strength. Healing. Speed. Agility. Mastership of sword fighting. What could she *not* do?

As much as he didn't want her coming with him, the more he thought about it, the more it became painfully clear that she should. He came back for warriors, and he'd be a fool to not admit what was plainly before him: Requiem was a warrior.

A hundred miles in, they stumbled upon a compound of farms. Like the first gentleman, Kilal convinced one of the homeowners to part with a beat-up, old two-seater truck. It wouldn't be much faster than running, but a little faster was still better than nothing.

One of the working men was *large*, and Kilal also convinced him to part with a shirt. He wasn't one who enjoyed showing off his impressive physique.

The truck made it another two hundred miles, forcing Kilal and Requiem to finish the last hundred on foot.

The sun was beginning its long descent, and even though it was still up, Ophir and Damphir began showing themselves, though vaguely. They would be cutting it close, but as long as they didn't run into any more obstacles, Kilal measured they should be fine.

The closer they got to their destination, the larger the specks in the horizon became. By the time they arrived at the tunnel, the specks had become snow-capped mountains looming over the land, casting it into shadows as the sun dipped behind them. Surrounded on both sides by trees, the tunnel entrance, a large, dark mouth on the side of the mountain waited for them. And in front of the tunnel was a group of men and women.

Beside him, skidding to a halt, Requiem growled. Exactly how he felt.

Of course there's going to be Arbiters here. Why wouldn't there be? Except...how did they know to come here?

Of the six Arbiters, one in particular stood out. He was a respectful looking fellow, with a trim beard, bushy eyebrows, a top hat, cane, and a pleasant brown suit. He looked like he belonged in a library studying manuscripts, not at the mouth of a mountain range, ready for a fight. But why did he look so familiar?

They approached the group, hesitant. How long would the encounter take, and how many of them would have to die?

The familiar man bowed and tipped his top hat. "I apologize for selling you the dud that I did," he said with a thick, almost fatherly voice. "But you must understand, I needed to make sure I arrived at your destination before you did."

What? Realization shook Kilal. "You sold me that piece of ash I paid generously for!" He pointed a finger at him.

"Yes, it was a most generous offer, and I thank you kindly for it."

Requiem cocked a brow. "Why? If you just wanted to kill us, why sell us a vehicle? Why not ambush us then instead of now? Don't tell me you needed the money. If you were able to take our heads, the Heirs would have paid you a king's ransom."

The man looked aghast. "Kill you? No. No, my dear. I needed to confirm where you were headed. I admit, it was a leap to assume you'd come here. Fortunately, I was right."

Kilal felt a special kindred spirit towards the stranger. And he didn't know why. Despite the wrinkles under the stranger's eyes, the graying hair, the hunched stoop, and the apparent need to lean on his cane, Kilal sensed the man was much older than he looked, and he already looked like he was in his sixties. He may not be as old as Kilal, but there was an ageless quality in the man's eyes that so many had pointed out to him in his.

"What do you want?" Kilal asked.

The man twirled his cane before pointing it east. "Isn't it obvious? To accompany you on your journey over there!" he said animatedly, like a child surprised with ice cream.

Kilal and Requiem shared a look of both surprise and apprehension.

"What are you talking about, Abram?" one of the other Arbiters said. "We hired you to take us to the Immortal Arbiter and his wench. And you did. Now, we'll kill them."

Requiem hissed. The others may not have noticed, but Kilal spotted the shadows wiggling their way toward her. Soon, she would have a sword the color of darkest night in her hand.

"I must apologize for this," Abram said and pulled a pouch clinking with coins from a pocket inside his vest. "I won't be needing this anymore. Or you." He tossed the bag of coins on the ground in the middle of the semicircular ring of Arbiters.

"Won't be needing us? You think you're gonna kill them both on your own and take the reward for yourself? You're a fool. As if an old fart like yourself has a chance against them."

"You are correct." Abram juggled his cane from one hand to the next. "I don't stand a chance against them. Against you five, however, I won't even break a sweat."

"Against *us*?" a woman said to Abram's left. "You're turning against *us*?"

Abram shook his head, tsking. "I can't turn against those I never sided with."

Requiem pulled on Kilal's arm until he leaned over far enough for her to put lips to his ears. "Should we intervene?"

Kilal shrugged, curious. "Let's see how this plays out."

She nodded and released him.

"Never sided with—what game are you playing at?"

"No game, son. I merely wished to show the good Kilal and the beautiful Requiem Ror that I'm on their side, which is why I chose you five as my offering. You're despicable, cruel, and worthy of your reputation as vagabonds and monsters. You lot are worthy of death and not much else."

Kilal pursed his lips. What was about to happen? And should he stand by and let it? Was Abram going to murder those Arbiters? But if what Abram said was true, and those five were abusers of their powers and truly did have the reputation of monsters? Wouldn't he eradicate them as well?

You're a hypocrite, Godsgraive rumbled. *You kill Arbiters all the time.*

Kilal let out a low growl. *Only those who won't turn from their ways.*

And only you get to decide that?

He didn't respond.

"You're going to kill us?" the second woman said. The group broke into laughter. "Well boys, guess we'll be collecting three heads today. You think we'll get anything for the old one's?"

For a moment, Kilal thought they were referring to him.

"Youth these days," Abram said.

He raised his cane and pointed it at the Arbiter on his far left. She pretended to be scared, shaking her knees and holding her hands up in front of her. Abram slashed the cane from left to right, ensuring his arch swept across all the Arbiters, but it was still a good six feet from each of them.

What was he do—

A red line appeared on each of the five Arbiter's necks. They looked as confused as Kilal felt, but their confusion vanished as their heads fell from their necks.

The five Arbiters collapsed, dead.

Now that was a powerful Carving. And one Kilal would have quickly killed Abram for in his earlier days.

We would've had so much fun with it, Godsgraive taunted.

Shut up!

Why was he being more vocal? It never boded well for... anyone when Godsgrave began waking. Another fortunate reason Kilal was going back to the Ashen Lands. There were far fewer people to kill there, and the ones he'd be with would give Godsgrave a run for his money.

Abram approached Kilal, hand out for a shake. He accepted it, warily.

"In the words of a freshly deceased Arbiter," Kilal said, shaking Abram's hand, "what's your game? You're old. Not as old as me, I suspect, but possibly close. And that begs the question: how have we not crossed paths? And what do you want from us?"

"So many questions, so little time."

Requiem clamped a hand onto his shoulder and spun Abram about. She grappled his neck, lifting him from his feet. "I don't like how you seem to know things you shouldn't. Who are you?"

Abram pleasantly pointed to the hand on his throat. Requiem curled a lip but released him. He coughed once, straightened his vest, and tipped his hat.

"My gratitude for not killing me."

"Your life is still in question."

"Of course, of course. I can answer your questions, but I do believe you're under a time constraint." He raised his sleeve, revealing a silver watch. "Yes. Only a few more hours, perhaps?"

Kilal drew up to his full height, easily towering over the frail man. "We don't know you. What we do know is you planned an event to stop us, here, and led a group of Arbiters to us, a group you knew wanted to kill us. You know things you shouldn't, that no one else knows, and even have expressed a desire to join us. As you said, we still have a few hours, more than enough time to answer a few questions. And more than enough time for me to kill you if I deem your answers...unsatisfactory."

The last part, the part about the time, was a bluff, but Abram didn't know that.

Or did he?

Abram smiled. He tapped his cane against the ground and flourished a hand before him. "Very acceptable compromise. And I, too, hope my answers are satisfactory. I'm quite taken with being alive."

Kilal crossed his arms, waiting. Requiem searched around in her backpack. She found a block of rations and took it out. She snapped a piece off and shoved it in her mouth. A second piece she snapped off and handed to Kilal, who popped it into his mouth and chewed. Like normal, it was terrible. But as he swallowed the pasty, bland substance, his energy steadily returned.

Being an Arbiter and using Carvings may let him operate for an extended length, but that didn't mean it felt good. The rations gave him back a little bit of the lost energy after the two hundred miles run.

"You see, it's quite simple. I dreamed it."

Requiem snorted, nearly coughing up her food. "I guess you're not *that* taken with being alive."

Abram furrowed his brows and looked at Requiem, as if seeing her for the first time.

"On no, my dear. I am, I am."

"Then you're going to have to do a lot better than that," Kilal said, not amused.

Abram shifted. Not his posture, but...something else. His brow darkened and his demeanor turned...threatening. Kilal didn't feel anything, no activated Carvings—and he hadn't felt anything when Abram cut the five Arbiter's heads off, either.

Dreams. Old, very old. Just who is this man?

Knowledge or not, Kilal readied to spring, coiling his muscles tight, waiting for any hint of an attack.

Abram drew himself up straight, and for a moment, Kilal had the same sensation he had when he floated before the tentacled being in the sky in that other dimension. But it was gone as soon as it came.

"I wish I could offer more, but what I've told you is the truth. I dreamed that you'd come here, that you'd be in need of assistance—which is why I sold you my car—that you'd be meeting with two other powerful men, and together the four of you would use ancient technology to teleport yourself to the Ashen Lands. And I wish to go with you."

"Bloodshed and Oaths, man!" Requiem said. "Why would you *ever* want to go there?"

He smiled sheepishly. "Well, that, my lady, is something I wish to keep to myself."

Kilal stepped up to him. Abram stepped back, and Kilal followed. Heels against the pooling blood, Abram stopped. He glanced at the crimson under their boots, and blanched.

"Intimidation is never a good bargaining tool," he said, tapping his cane against Kilal's chest.

"I've found that sometimes it's good to remind people who exactly they're talking to." Kilal put a hand on the cane and pressed it tighter against his chest. "A little reminder of my immortality can go a long way." He smiled a wholly unpleasant smile.

Abram responded with a sheepish grin. "You're absolutely right. I should've known you'd have expected more from me. If you would let me take a step away from this awful mess, I would explain my plan more fully to you."

Kilal stepped away, letting Abram step gingerly from the semi-circle of blood. Content with his current placement, he tipped his hat to Kilal again.

"My sincerest gratitude. You see, I knew you'd question my sincerity if I just arrived here. In fact, I assumed you'd kill me, as you've had to fight your way out of Silent Haven. You'd assume I was another Arbiter seeking to obtain a hefty reward."

Abram paused and gestured at the corpses around him. "Which is why I brought these sorry excuses for Arbiters. So you could see the reality of my sincerity, which has been handed to you on a platter made of the heads of five corrupt and wicked oathbreakers. Additionally, if my dream was correct, and you're going to pierce into the Ashen Lands, you'll need as many warriors on your side as you can get. And I believe I have amply proven my power."

Kilal looked to Requiem. She stared at the man inquisitively.

"What Carving allows you to dream of the future?" she asked. A good question.

Abram tapped his cane to the brim of his hat. The impact was a deep thud. "A good Arbiter never shares his secrets, my dear."

Kilal sighed. The bloody rules of being an Arbiter never seemed to benefit anyone *but* the Arbiter. He wrapped his arm around Requiem and led her away. "What do you think?" he whispered.

"I...don't know. He's clearly powerful, and we could use all the help we could get."

Kilal nodded. "And if he wanted to attack us, he wouldn't need to go through this whole charade to do so."

"But he knows so much. Are you buying his dream story?"

He peered back at Abram, who beamed. "Not at all. But...I don't have an answer for how he knows what he knows."

"Maybe he was sent by someone to help us. Enoch?"

Kilal mulled the thought over. "No. If Enoch really needed help from Alistair's group, there's no way he'd have the means to send Abram to us."

Requiem frowned but didn't argue. "So, what do we do?"

"The only thing we can do in situations like this: trust our instincts."

Her frown remained. "My instincts are telling me to kill him."

"My gut is telling me to let him come with us."

"Then we go with yours."

"Why?"

"My instinct never changes. It always tells me to kill."

Kilal pursed his lips. Just another piece of the puzzle about the woman he loved that didn't make sense yet, and that they didn't have the time to discuss. "We'll go with mine."

He released Requiem and approached Abram. "You're welcome to join us."

Abram beamed. "Excellent choice, my dear fellow. Excellent choice!"

"To be clear," Requiem said, joining them, "we don't trust you, and we don't believe your story. But if you were intent on killing us, all of this would be unnecessary."

"Wise deduction! Wise, indeed."

"Just...don't do anything that'll make me have to respond in a way we'll both regret," Kilal added.

Abram removed his hat and flourished a bow. "I'll follow your lead. You shall not regret your decision."

"Have you ever been into the Northern Ruins?"

"I have not."

Kilal took a moment to explain the mind-bending environment they'd soon find themselves in. No one should enter that mountain without being prepared for what they'd encounter. "Stick close to us," he finished. "And keep communication open. If one of us sees something the others don't, it's not real. Everyone got it?"

Requiem nodded. Abram tapped his cane against the brim of his hat.

"Good. Let's get going. We're running out of time."

Walking around the semi-circle of corpses and blood, Kilal led the group into the dark opening of the tunnel. The tip of Abram's cane lit up with white light, a commodity, but not a necessity for either Kilal or Requiem.

Through the mouth of madness, they traversed.

~ CHAPTER 58 ~

"Interesting," Abram said, studying a section of a mural carved into the tunnel wall.

The path they descended through was perfectly cylindrical. The walls were smooth to the touch, an abnormality considering weather didn't penetrate that deep. It was wide enough for Abram, Kilal, and Requiem to stand at arm-lengths from one another and tall enough for Kilal to stand entirely upright and still have a comfortable amount of room above him.

What sort of Carving was used to cut the tunnel through the mountains? It wasn't completed by tools and hands. The impossibly perfect diameter of the circular pathways and the smooth walls proved that.

Much of the walls were covered in paintings and etchings.

During prior crossings, the murals had meant nothing to him. They were the creative drawings of whoever etched them. But now, they meant so much more.

The section Abram studied showed a meeting of men and women. On one side, the men and women had Carvings on their arms. On the other, the people had glowing, purple eyes. Next to that was a depiction of a man shaking hands with another. The second man had a black shadow stretching from his back. The shadow had two taloned hands, white eyes, and a mouth full of teeth.

Kilal couldn't deny the similarities between Ximthar and the female creature attached to his back.

"They're not random drawings of a creative mind," he whispered to Requiem. "They look like historical accounts of our world meeting others."

Kilal trailed a thumb over the dusty image of a female humanoid with a long, animalistic arm. Further down the tunnel, a section of the drawing forced his heart to skip a beat.

The mural was darker than the rest and depicted a being in the sky. Studying it further, Kilal realized he was wrong. It wasn't in the sky, it *was* the sky. Eight enormous tentacles stretched over the land, tearing bits of earth from the ground. Four tentacles each held a different human, one with a Carving on his wrist, one with glowing purple eyes, one with a shadow being attached to her back, and another with a long, furry, taloned arm and mangy hair.

The creature was the thing he'd seen when he'd been pulled to the desolate dimension.

Kilal tapped the smooth, dusty mural right over its eye. "It's what I saw after I touched Sienna's stone."

Requiem ran a finger over the two-arm's-length long drawings. "What does it mean?"

"War," Abram said, stepping up behind them. "At least, that's my take."

Kilal grunted. War. It did have that feeling. The creature versus four worlds, or Disks, as Ximthar called them. The question was, did it depict the future or the past? Could it have already happened, long ago, and that's why the being was trapped in a wasteland of a realm? Or was it showing what would happen if it ever got out?

He thought back to the collapsing skyscraper. His heart sank, and his knees weakened. If a cross-world war came, the death and devastation caused during the battle with Sienna would be nothing.

Kilal formed a fist and tapped it against the creature's bulbous forehead.

I know you now. I'll find out what and who you are. I'll make sure this painting never comes to fruition.

No sooner had he thought the words than he realized how empty they were. How could he achieve any of those things if he failed his mission to kill Ashen Kane? Or died in the attempt?

One mission at a time. Ashen Kane first. Interworld travel next. Then, this creature.

They didn't pass any more murals as ominous as the one with the tentacled creature. Kilal tried to study them, but his mind kept drifting to that eye in the sky and its wriggling limbs. The feeling of his powerlessness and its ancientness.

Not even Ashen Kane felt anything like the creature he'd confronted in the other dimension. Ashen Kane almost felt... beatable. Comparatively speaking.

That was good at least. Right?

Light nearly blinded him when he exited the tunnel. It was already more difficult to think, the fogginess setting in, and he'd only just crossed the threshold.

"Welcome back," he muttered.

Abram didn't look affected in the least. Requiem rubbed her forehead and winced.

"Is it just me, or does the...wrongness of this place feel stronger?"

The landscape before them seemed to be frozen in time. No matter how often Kilal returned, the ruins always looked the same. The city resembled something stuck between the Dead Zone and Silent Haven. Half-crumbled stone, steel, and brick buildings never decayed. Vines, foliage, grass, weeds; they all appeared to have grown for a few years, then stopped.

Laughter pricked Kilal's ears. A shimmering boy and girl ran by kicking a ball down the cracked and ruined paved road leading out of the tunnel. Requiem and Abram didn't seem to notice the illusion, so Kilal ignored it.

One thing he'd learned about the ruins: if you paid too

much attention to an illusion, the illusion would pay attention to you. Kilal shuddered. Sometimes, the things he saw weren't things he wanted to attract attention from, illusion or not.

Requiem followed something he couldn't see.

"What is it?" he asked.

She responded with a shake of her head and nothing else.

"Well, well, well," Abram said. "I've heard this place toys with your mind, but I never expected it to be true, nor to happen so fast. Does it worsen?"

"Yes," Kilal and Requiem said in unison.

"You came here not understanding what you'd be encountering?" Requiem asked.

Abram smiled sheepishly. "I never intended to pierce the Northern Mountains by myself, madam. I knew I'd have excellent guides."

She frowned. "Foolish."

"Just don't focus on anything you see," Kilal added, "or it'll notice you."

"Notice me?" Abram repeated. "You speak as if the illusions are capable of sentient thought."

"I speak as someone who's encountered these ruins multiple times and still doesn't understand them."

"Ah, yes," Abram said, as if he'd just uncovered a lifelong mystery. "Wise words. Requiem Ror, my dear, you'd be smart to keep this one close to you. Don't let him slip away."

Kilal chuckled and slapped him on the back. The man was old and frail looking, but he was solid as a rock. "It's good to finally have someone around who understands my worth."

Abram tipped his hat. "I'd have to be blind to not see it."

Kilal could practically *hear* Requiem's eye roll.

"Where to?" Abram asked.

"Yes, most worthy one. Where to?" Requiem said with only a touch of mockery.

Kilal studied the landscape. Ahead of them, the road forked into three different branches, each of those, in turn, branching twice more. It was a confusing setup, almost like it was purposefully supposed to be difficult for anyone to navigate the ruins when it had still been a city.

Why would anyone want to build a place so difficult to navigate?

He wracked his brain, trying to remember ten years prior. The sun was practically gone; only a sliver of it peeked above the horizon.

Only a few more hours left.

"It's been a while," Kilal mused. "And I was running from a dozen Arbiters intent on killing Lilliana and me. I didn't exactly stop at each intersection to make a map."

"Sorry," Requiem mumbled.

Eventually, the memory, or at least a feeling from the memory, came to him. "Left," he said, hoping he sounded more confident than he felt.

"Left it is!" Abram announced. He marched off in front of them as if it was him who was guiding them.

The ruins were a creepy place to be with sunlight, but as the day faded away, Ophir and Damphir rose, and Abram lit the tip of his cane again; the ruins took on a more eerie façade. Shadows twisted and morphed into things best left unseen. The wind whistled, and if Kilal weren't careful, he could make out words carried through the air. A slight fog rose from the ground. It was so dense in some areas, it felt and looked like they were wading through knee-deep water.

Arriving at the next intersection, a fountain easily eight feet across waited for them. A woman carved in stone and holding a jar stood in the center of it. Black, brackish water seeped from her eyes, down her front, and into the pool of matching liquid.

"There might have been a time when that would've been a beautiful work of art, but black ooze or not, why the eyes?" Requiem asked. "Why not the mouth? Or the pot?"

Kilal grunted his agreement.

Movement caught his attention, and before he recalled where he was, he followed it.

To their right, between the two collapsed buildings and toppled light poles, a large eye the size of the fountain slipped down the road. It blinked once and focused on Kilal. He snapped his eyes to the left, careful not to let it know he'd seen it.

"Left," he said, passing the fountain and heading down the branching road. He didn't care which direction was correct; he *wouldn't* go right.

"I've never seen architecture like this," Abram said. "The orange bricks, entire walls made of one stone slab instead of a series of rocks meshed together by a sealing substance. The light poles. Do you see what is strange about them?"

Requiem stopped at one of the light poles lying on the ground. She focused on the head of it, a glass box with a pointy top. One of the sides swung open, and she felt around on the inside.

"There's nothing," she said. "So, what held the light?"

Kilal scratched his chin. "Or did they hold the light? Like his cane, maybe the light was contained inside the box."

"But what could have created the light? There aren't any wires, no outlets, no electrical contraptions. It's just an empty glass box. And don't even get me started on how glass has survived this long in this good a condition."

Abram pulled at the brim of his hat. "Yes, very strange. Very strange indeed."

Kilal led them to the next intersection, which broke into three streets, each identical to the other. There, most of the buildings were still intact. They appeared to be of the residential type.

That was confirmed when a curtain moved in a window in the building in front of him, and a woman, skeletal and old, peered at him from behind it. He looked away and noticed Abram, too, staring at something. He was pale, and his lips quivered.

Kilal smacked his chest lightly and was relieved when Abram turned still lucent eyes on him.

"What did you see?" he asked. Something about the man told Kilal he didn't scare easily.

"Something this place shouldn't know about," he responded, his normal joviality gone.

"I don't think this place knows anything," Requiem said. "I think it projects memories, twists them, uses them to hurt us."

"It's not just our memories," Kilal corrected. "I saw Sha'tum walking these streets, greeting folks, handing out gifts, healing people. I'm old, but I'm not that old."

"This place is an abomination," Abram said quietly. "Let's hurry. I don't like it here."

Kilal chose the center road in the fork. Guided by the light of Ophir, Damphir, and Abram's cane, they descended.

Movement continued to pull at him from the corner of his eyes, demanding his attention, but Kilal knew better. The less he looked, the quicker he was out of the ruins, the better off he and everyone else would be. He could already feel the pervasive environment trying its best to wriggle its way into his mind. Memories were distorting, and the desire to look at every motion became harder to resist.

As long as he could remember their path, they'd still arrive before anything truly awful revealed itself.

The next intersection was more of a dead end. Left or right were the two options presented. A rotted wooden signpost hung from the stone wall in front of them, cutting off any forward movement. Something about it rang familiar to Kilal. It didn't fit the ruins. There wasn't much wood in the city. Most structures were constructed of steel, stone, or brick.

He approached the sign, and a waft of rot and mold assaulted his nose.

"Kilal?" Requiem's voice was barely more than background noise.

He ripped the wood sign from the wall, nearly tearing it in

two. "Ashes, it can't be!"

The sign had two names on it. The top name read 'Farmer's Post' and had an arrow pointing left. The bottom read…

"No," Kilal breathed. "Please, no." He didn't want to go back there. Anywhere but there.

A hand on his shoulder tried to turn him around, but he wasn't having it.

An arrow to the right pointed to 'Guard's Hollow.' The small village where he was born.

He shouldn't do it. Of course he shouldn't! But he did anyway.

He looked right.

Down the road, a young man held a much older man up by the neck with one hand. The youth, almost out of his teen years, smiled wickedly at the older man. The resemblance between the two was obvious. As it should be. They were father and son. The youth's lips moved, and Kilal knew exactly what he was saying.

"*Power requires sacrifice, father.*" Kilal dropped to his knees, chest tight, throat constricted. "*And what greater sacrifice is there than spilling the blood of family?*"

Nineteen-year-old Kilal snapped his father's neck. The corpse slapped to the ground with a thud. His father's eyes pierced him, accusing him, hating him. Could Kilal blame him? Of course not. Not just for his father's death, but for the deaths of the others.

His heart slammed against his ribcage. Tears spilled. "No," Kilal gasped. "That's not how it happened."

Something grabbed his arm. Someone spoke to him. But he only had eyes for the scene unfolding before him.

Kilal watched as he proceeded through his home and killed his brother and, finally, his mother, too. His mentor watched from the shadows, encouraging him. All in the false pursuit of power. How easily he'd been manipulated. Just a dumb teenager, easily convinced by his mentor that power could be gained through cruelty and bloodshed. It didn't help that Kilal had already, at that age, shown a propensity for hurting others. He ended up fitting in perfectly with the group of Arbiters naming themselves Deathwalkers. Because he, like his mentor, was a monster.

Even still, that wasn't how it happened!

"No!" Kilal screamed. "No! I didn't..." And much, much quieter, "I...didn't." He dropped onto all fours.

Requiem pulled him tightly to her as he wept.

~ CHAPTER 59 ~

Kilal scrubbed tears from wet cheeks. Requiem guided him to his feet, and he gladly accepted the help. His legs weren't ready to carry his full weight.

"What did you see?" she asked.

Abram, too, peered at him curiously. When he noticed Kilal staring at him, he walked over to a rust-covered bucket and kicked at it playfully.

"That night...my...family...was..." he gasped and broke into tears again.

Requiem stroked his back and cheek. "I'm sorry," she said, knowing exactly what night he referred to. "But that's not you anymore. That boy is gone, dead, a cocoon that blossomed into a loving and caring man who'd rather rip his own arm off than hurt someone undeserving."

That boy didn't kill his family! That wasn't how it happened. But...

"That boy hurt *so many people,*" Kilal said, barely able to get out each word between sobs.

Requiem pulled his head to her shoulder and ran a hand through his hair. "I know. And you'll keep fighting to right the wrongs you've done. Just like myself. Just like Alistair and Violet. And Enoch. And Lemuel and Layloni. And all the others who died fighting the Heirs, died unable to fully repay the debt they incurred in their life. You can still repay that debt. So can I."

"There's no repaying my debt, Req. What's the going rate for a life these days?"

She tipped his head back and smiled. A special smile just for him. "You're right. So, save everyone. Stop Ashen Kane. Stop the Heirs of the Promise. Lead us to another world. You can't account for what you've done, but you can account for what you'll do."

Kilal matched her special smile with a sad one. His tears were gone, the memories repressed. Again. He gave her a kiss on her forehead, purposefully over the scarred, leathery half of her face. It was the most affection he'd shown her in ten years, and the most she'd allowed him to express toward her since their reunion.

She received it with a smile.

"I've lived long enough to know," Abram said, no longer occupied with his rusty bucket, "that we all live lives filled with regret. The true test is to match our regrets with achievements. Your mission is greater than us all, past, present, and future versions. Succeed and bring some peace to the past you, or you'll die trying to escape it."

Kilal nodded. Success was the only option. Not just for his past self, but for everyone.

Wait...

He frowned. "How do you know about my mission?"

Abram beamed. "To kill Avinoth? Well, I dreamed it, of course! How else could I know?"

Requiem pursed her lips and narrowed her eyes. "Dreamed it. Of course," she said, voice as flat as her mouth.

Kilal wasn't buying it, either. The dreaming was fine. He didn't have a good enough reason to doubt the man, but—"And that doesn't bother you? Avinoth still being alive? Our history being a lie?"

Abram tapped his cane against the cracked pavement. It echoed through the night air. A cloud seemed to hover over him, subtle proof that Abram was something far more than he wanted them to believe.

"History is always a lie," he said, voice unusually cold and angry. "The only thing about history that matters is who writes it." He tapped his cane again and grabbed his top hat, spun it on his head, and smiled. The air of anger was completely gone.

Kilal took a deep breath. *Don't forget, Abram's on our side.*

"Well, we should be off, shouldn't we?" Abram said. "Ophir and Damphir shine brightly on us; we should take advantage of their light while the pair is still content to bless us."

Kilal chose the leftmost fork for no particular reason. He'd forgotten the way, so he chose by instinct. The first option which *felt* right, he took, and Bloodshed and Oaths, they'd better be the correct paths.

The next intersection they arrived at was the most disheveled of all. No part of a building stood more than waist high. Another large fountain lay broken and scattered in the center of the four-way. A woman, whole and stone, lay in the center of the broken fountain. Her jar was nowhere to be seen. Or it was everywhere, a powder, broken and ground by whatever destructive force had laid the city to ruins.

The devastation only affected the immediate area. A block further on, and the buildings were half-built. It was as if a giant with a square foot stepped on that section of the city, flattening it, and disappeared.

"It's so quiet," Requiem said.

"I've never seen any life here before," Kilal murmured. "No animals. No humans. Not even insects." He pointed at the middle-right road. "That way."

"Are you saying...?" Abram interjected, accidentally stepping on the back of one of Kilal's boots. "My apologies. Are you saying you've *never* encountered anything real here?"

He pondered the question. The alley was dark; the two buildings on both sides tall enough to block out most of the light from the twin moons.

"Yes, and no. Everything I've encountered is as real as my mind makes it. I've been touched, punched, kicked, and thrown by things I've seen. Things which weren't really here. But my mind thought they were real, so it might as well have been."

"Extraordinary," Abram said, as if it wasn't terrifying. "This place is unlike anything I've ever encountered."

"You knew about me." Kilal changed the subject. Rocks clattered as their footsteps displaced them. "But I've never heard of you. You're clearly older than most Arbiters alive. You use a power I've never seen the likes of and can't sense. And there's just...something about you, something I can't put my finger on. Something that gnaws at my insides, warning me of you. So, how have we never crossed paths?"

He'd realized, since returning to the Sunlight Domain, that he'd greatly overestimated his influence in his land. There were more Arbiters he didn't know than the ones he did. Inferno was a good example. A Prime Arbiter he hadn't known existed. Was it really that far-fetched that he wouldn't know of another Arbiter when he'd already encountered a dozen or so he'd never met or heard of?

Unfortunately, the sad reality was his influence was nonexistent outside of Silent Haven. How much of what the Heirs did could've been avoided if he'd just spent more time policing the whole of the Sunlight Domain and not just a single city?

"I don't have a good answer for you," Abram said.

"Not good enough," Requiem said.

Kilal barely heard the exchange. His mind was somewhere else.

Don't think like that. I'm only one person. I can't be everywhere. And not everyone who swears the oath can be saved.

Godsgraive rumbled in the background. *You could've killed them. Imagine if the likes of Inferno hadn't been left to live. Imagine if Wolfe and his ash-eating companions had shown up to a land united and...good. Not blinded by power, greed, and naïvety.* He laughed, taking the form of a massive headache. *Kilal, the Immortal Arbiter. You should be called the Naïve Arbiter!*

Kilal bit his tongue, drawing blood.

The next block of intersections was nothing like the others. Instead of a large square with a fountain, it was circular, with five roads leading further into the city, each forty-five degrees away from the other. Kilal drew a blank. He couldn't recall the location, and there was nothing to set it apart. He could see a good hundred feet down each road. Only rubble remained of the city block they were in.

"I...I don't remember this area," he admitted.

"Perhaps we took a wrong turn earlier?" Abram suggested.

Kilal scratched his jaw. "No, I don't think so." He racked his brain, trying to recall his last time running through the ruins. "The fighting escalated here," he said, a vague memory surfacing. "A few of the Arbiters caught up to us here. I wouldn't let Al—Lilliana fight."

Bloodshed and Oaths! Had he really slipped up like that?

Godsgraive chuckled in the background.

Kilal *felt* more than remembered the memory. He followed that feeling, picking his way through the ruins as if lured by a gentle tug on a string. A large square stone leaned against a round boulder. He tried to peel the rock away but couldn't.

Right. No strength.

"I made her hide here," he said, pointing at the small opening between the two large stones. A ghost of a smile slipped onto his face. "She wasn't happy about that. Told me she was ready to fight. I told her there was a difference between fighting Ash Fallen and fellow humans, and that she'd understand one day."

"Quite correct," Abram commented from behind. "There's a certain soul-shattering response that comes from killing a human. Something no one, especially not a child, should have to endure."

Kilal eyed the man suspiciously. "I never told you she was a child."

Abram flattened his lips and tapped his cane against the ground. "And what other option was there for the way you speak of this Lilliana?"

Kilal's suspicions remained, despite Abram's attempts to sway him. He returned his gaze to the hole Lilliana had hidden in, only to find a phantom version of his daughter staring back. He stumbled, eyes wide and budding with tears until Requiem pressed a hand against his spine.

"You," he swallowed a lump in his throat. "You don't see that?"

"And what, precisely, are we supposed to be seeing?" Abram asked.

Kilal wiped at his cheeks. "Lilliana." She was young, fifteen still, with shoulder-length black hair done up in a ponytail, smooth cheeks, round brown eyes, and thin lips. She was afraid yet determined to help as needed.

I miss her so much. His chest burned with the anticipation of returning to his daughter.

The phantom crawled out from the hole and headed deeper into the city by one of the cobbled streets. The thread tugged harder at his gut, demanding he follow. Was it the ruins manipulating him, or was it his brain manifesting the answer he was looking for? Or neither, and he was being led into a circle of false paths.

"I think she's leading us," he said, his finger following her path.

"To what, exactly?" Abram asked.

Kilal shrugged and smiled. "Hopefully, where we need to go."

Abram groaned.

"Kilal," Requiem jumped in. "You can't be serious. You know the dangers of this place better than anyone. We can't follow an illusion. We have no idea where it's going to lead us. I'd rather pick a street at random than let the ruins guide us.

The only thing they'll lead us to is insanity."

He grabbed both of her hands and enveloped them in his. "I hear you. I really do. But I believe this is different. I think, subconsciously, my mind is melding with the strange properties of the ruins, and in the form of Lilliana, is guiding me to where we need to go."

Requiem stared into his eyes. Her own, one brown, one cloudy, piercing. "And if you're wrong?"

"You've trusted me up to this point. All of this, everything I've told you, you've trusted. I'm asking you to continue trusting in me. Please." Kilal squeezed her hands for good measure. "Because the alternative is me choosing randomly, a stab in the darkness, and then what? Keep guessing until we're so lost, we'll lose ourselves here or land in the asylum we just came from? Lilliana will be lost. Our shot at Ashen Kane will be gone. I don't see any other way.

"I don't remember how to get to where we need to go. My gut says to follow the phantom. I trust my gut. And I'm asking you to trust it too."

Requiem's eyes hardened and her lips flattened. "I've trusted your gut before. It resulted in the last decade."

Kilal recoiled, stunned at the callousness in her voice. Even Abram looked embarrassed, choosing to loiter off a few feet away from them. Yet, despite the hurt and not a little anger, Kilal couldn't deny the validity of her words.

But he also couldn't change what he needed to do.

"I know. But right now, I don't know what else to do, and we don't have much time left. It's either this or hope in chance. But I'd rather not let chance decide our fate."

Requiem stared at him for a long moment before finally nodding and gesturing for him to lead on.

Kilal let out a small sigh of relief and led them down the street the phantom Lilliana ran along.

"Do I not get a say in this matter?" Abram called from behind.

"No." Kilal and Requiem echoed each other.

Abram muttered a response. Kilal couldn't pick up most of it, but he did catch the words "quite rude" from the strange man.

~ CHAPTER 60 ~

The phantom led them down streets Kilal gave up trying to remember. Was it the debilitating effect the ruins had on his mind which made it so difficult? Or was it simply time?

He spoke his question aloud.

"Both," Requiem replied.

Kilal nodded his agreement.

Much of the path he didn't remember. Fallen buildings. Trees and shrubbery frozen in time, half-decayed, half-flourishing. At one point, they came across a large stone slab suspended in the air. The building it came from lay all about, littering the ground, but it alone hovered above. Kilal tried pressing on it, but it wouldn't budge. He didn't think his lack of strength had anything to do with it.

The trio was quiet. Kilal didn't know Abram, but from the few hours he'd spent with the man, quiet was not an adjective which described him. Requiem, well, he'd grown accustomed to silence from her. She rarely spoke unless spoken to. A stark contrast to the lady he used to know.

Abram had taken to whistling a low tune, one Kilal wasn't familiar with.

As time continued to creep by and thoughts became more and more muddled, Kilal began to worry. Was he wrong in following the phantom? Had he doomed Requiem and himself?

And Abram? He'd asked Requiem to trust him. Again. What if he was wrong? How many times could someone's trust be broken before they lost hope in the individual?

Kilal prayed he'd never find out the answer.

"A question has plagued my mind since the moment we entered this infernal city," Abram said.

Kilal groaned inwardly. *Great.*

"What happened here?"

"No one knows," Requiem said.

"No one? Surely someone knows. Some account written somewhere, some secret historical text. 'No one' simply can't be the case."

"Well, it is," Kilal said. It wasn't the full truth. They did know *something* about the city, but he wasn't about to divulge that to a stranger. "We think whatever happened here predates the Bloodshed. We have a map of the Sunlight Domain from before then. This place isn't on it. That can either mean it popped into existence after the Bloodshed or pre-Bloodshed. The world knew not to come here and didn't even bother including it on maps."

Bloodshed and Oaths! Why did I just say all that?

Requiem's pursed lips and raised brows suggested she was thinking the same thing.

"It's this bloody place," he whispered to her. "It's messing with me."

"Predates the Bloodshed," Abram mused. "Fascinating. I'd love to see this map of yours. I'd wager a bet you don't have it on you?"

Kilal *and* Requiem leveled a look of pure annoyance at him.

He reddened and smiled, chuckling awkwardly. "Right. Of course not. Silly me. What do you think it means?" he added. "This city predating the Bloodshed?"

Kilal rubbed his forehead, kneading the ache building behind it. "Abram, I'm not in the mood for question hour. I can barely remember my time here. Do you really think I'm in a good place to have a philosophical and historical discussion?"

"Would I be correct if I said no?"

Kilal growled.

The entrance to the next intersection was blocked by a large pile of debris. The buildings on both sides of the street had collapsed inward, cutting off not only their path but their sight beyond the mound.

Something about the pile kindled a memory. More phantoms raced past Kilal, their touch on his skin cold and shocking. He watched himself and Lilliana climb the rubble. A pair of phantom Arbiters leaped high above the illusion and landed on top of the pile. They began throwing bolts of condensed air at them. Phantom Kilal and Lilliana parted, one going to each side.

Kilal didn't need to see what happened next. He remembered.

He'd raised his gravity, stopping his sprint, lowered it, raised his strength, and lunged at the pair. He hadn't been about to let Lilliana get hurt. And he wouldn't let her kill.

The pair of Arbiters turned on him. Condensed air ripped into him, but he couldn't be stopped. Wrapped in white electricity, Kilal slammed into the pair, obliterating their weak bodies into a cloud of gore.

"We're almost there," he said. "Right over that pile." There was no need to explain how he knew. They couldn't see the new phantoms anyway.

Thankfully, neither Abram nor Requiem questioned him. The way Requiem winced, rolled her shoulders, and rubbed at her forehead, she was just as ready as him to be out of the ruins.

Cresting the top of the debris, Kilal looked down on a large square his instincts told him was where he needed to be. There wasn't anything out of the ordinary about the location; he just knew. It also didn't hurt that the phantom Lilliana ran into a partially standing nondescript building.

That building held a life-changing secret beneath it.

Kilal pointed to it. It was across from them, neatly tucked between two other structures of matching height. "That's the one. We made it." Did he sound as relieved as he felt? Not just to have made it in time, but to have not misled Requiem?

The descent of the mound was easy. Kilal fiddled with the rings in his pocket on the way down, a reminder of what he owed Ximthar.

"The fool will pay for the pain he's caused," Kilal said, sneering.

Let me OUT!

Godsgraive's demand was tempting in the face of the Professor. If the man was as powerful as Jayden, which Kilal suspected he was, Ximthar just may be the one reminding Kilal of the place he was in. But if he let that part of him out, the ruthless killer who reveled in force and causing pain...

Kilal exhaled loudly. No. He wasn't going to let Godsgraive surface. He'd *never* do that again. For all he knew, the moment that other part of him had control, he'd turn on Requiem. He enjoyed hurting Kilal.

I won't hurt Requiem. I promise. A vibration of a sly smile accompanied the words.

"I know how you feel," Requiem said, eyeing the ring he'd pulled from his pocket. "I want the son of a Plague to pay as well. But don't forget why we're here. Did you return, pause your search for Lilliana, track down Ximthar and Jayden, only to attack them and break our pact? He should pay for what he's done. And he will. But at the right time, and now isn't that."

The moonlight reflected off the gold ring he'd taken from the patient in the asylum, illuminating the inscription along the inside. *Love, Amber.*

Kilal offered a smile for Amber who would never see her husband again. Had she been told yet? Were there any children out there now fatherless?

"I'll control myself," he said.

And he would. But there were varying degrees of control. He'd aim for somewhere in the middle.

The building, what was standing of it, wasn't large, yet when Kilal stood in its shadow, he felt tiny. Beneath the structure was technology no one understood, technology that up to ten years ago, no one knew existed. Teleportation. And with the recent discovery of other worlds, interdimensional travel, Avinoth still being alive, and the being he'd encountered in that desolate realm, Kilal stood in the shadows of Ophir and Damphir and felt...insignificant.

Lilliana's face loomed in front of him, shaking him from his moment of doubt. Now wasn't the time. He needed to be strong, now more than ever. For Lilliana. For Requiem. For the whole of the Sunlight Domain. For Allyria.

Kilal clenched his fists, ground his jaw, and strode forward. He was the bloody Immortal Arbiter. He didn't back down. He didn't cower. He fought for those he loved. He died for them. And he was ready to do it again.

A chill crept up his spine as a blue shimmer passed through him. Another phantom. He'd written about them in his journal from the visit to the ruins prior to his time there with Lilliana. From that account, he'd encountered them, but not nearly to the extent that he was now. Not that he would complain. It was because of the phantoms that they weren't lost. When the shimmer materialized in front of him as a man entering the building before them, Kilal changed his mind; it wasn't too late to complain.

His labored breathing, the beads of sweat, his shaking, clenched fists, the look of pure hate wrinkling his face into a visage fearsome to behold—all of it must have given something away to the others.

Requiem pulled on his arm, concerned. "What is it?" she asked.

He followed the phantom, breaking his own rule, staring

at it, giving it power. It stopped in its tracks. With much discipline, Kilal tore his gaze away, focusing on anything but the illusion. Finally, it began moving again, disappearing into the building.

He'd killed that man once, but he'd give almost anything to do it again. The last ten years had unfolded the way they had because of him. No, killing that man again wouldn't be enough. A lifetime of agony was more suited for—

"Gabriel," Kilal said.

Requiem hissed.

"And this Gabriel garners some measure of significance in your life?" Abram asked.

He didn't answer; instead, he stepped into the building.

Following behind him, Requiem answered in a low tone, "Yes."

~ CHAPTER 61 ~

"And which pile of rubble is this teleportation device hiding under?" Abram asked, looking around the room. The moons shone through the destroyed second-story ceiling, illuminating what must have once been furniture.

Kilal glared and pointed at a collection of sticks, fabric, and torn cushions. "That one."

Abram hopped to and rummaged through the pile, eyes hungry and lips determined. Requiem stifled a chuckle, but he must have heard it, anyway. He abruptly stopped searching and looked at Kilal.

"I see you're having fun at my expense." He dropped a handful of cushion material and placed a hand over his heart, bowing his head. "I hope my trusting nature can continue to be a source of comedic relief for the both of you."

Kilal rolled his eyes, but Requiem actually looked embarrassed; her cheek had a soft red glow to them.

"Really?" he mouthed to her.

She shrugged and pointed to her chest. *I have a heart,* she was trying to tell him.

Kilal narrowed his eyes and flattened his lips. "Right," he mumbled.

She smiled, a slight upturn of the left side of her lips.

The phantom Lilliana and Gabriel were nowhere to be seen.

The couch, in what must have been at one point the living room, was a large L shape. One section was ripped to shreds, but still standing. The other part was covered in dust, but mostly intact.

Kilal had thrown that couch at a charging Arbiter. That was when he'd noticed the door beneath it.

"It shouldn't be there," he said. "The sofa. I threw it."

"Well, I doubt anyone's stopped by to return it to its rightful place," Requiem said.

"Perhaps you're mistaken?" Abram offered. "Maybe it was another couch?"

Kilal ignored them both. He approached the sofa and lifted it, his increased natural strength from being not just an Arbiter but a Prime made it near effortless even without the specific Carving.

Despite their doubts, beneath the couch was a metal sliding door in the wooden floorboards.

They descended the ladder leading into the darkness below— only it wasn't dark. The lights were on, the buzz of machinery was in the air, and the smell of musty *oldness* filled Kilal's nostrils.

The room was just as his muddled brain recalled. It was similar to the one he'd encountered Requiem and Fazin in back in the Heir's tower. Computers lined two of the four walls. Some of the screens were smashed, some of the machines were junked, while others looked relatively new. A layer of dust coated everything, and two bulbs in the ceiling gave off a soft fluorescent glow, illuminating the room.

There should have been three bodies on the floor near the ladder, Arbiters killed by Kilal, one of which had been Gabriel, but they were nowhere to be seen. Not even the remains of decomposed corpses.

Panic struck his chest, tightening it. Had he been mistaken? Was his memory wrong?

"No, I killed them," he whispered. He *knew* it to be true.

He didn't know where the bodies were, and he didn't care. There was no logic to the ruins and how they operated. For all he knew, the mysterious place had returned the room to its state of existence prior to Kilal killing the Arbiters. Regardless, it didn't matter.

He *killed* Gabriel.

"You made it," an irritatingly emotionless voice sounded from the opposite side of the room. "I'd be lying if I said I wasn't disappointed."

Jayden leaned against a tall machine with blinking lights and buttons, arms crossed, face blank. He looked much the same as before, black leathery skin reaching up to his neck, his head the only source of a normal skin tone. Ximthar sat beside him, clicking away at a keyboard, still sporting his white suit and hat.

Now that Kilal knew what to look for, he spotted the shadow creature in the corner of the room closest to Ximthar. The white hair was barely distinguishable from the screen. The creature knew how to hide, but Kilal could make out its vague feminine outline and the pinpricks of white eyes. He didn't make any motion towards the creature; it was best if it and Ximthar thought he didn't know where it was.

The two rings burned a hole in Kilal's pocket until he pulled them out. He thumbed them and chucked them at Jayden. His anger was simmering beneath the surface, ready to be released at a moment's notice. He didn't intend to start an all-out battle to the death, but he did intend to draw blood.

"Pretty," Jayden said after catching the two rings. He dropped them onto the floor and kicked them back to Kilal. "I'm flattered, really, but we barely know each other."

It was almost impressive how Jayden could deliver a statement with zero emotion or inflection yet look like he wanted to rip Kilal's head off. To think that was the same man he'd seen a week ago, flamboyantly dressed and dancing like a lunatic amid women who wanted nothing to do with him.

Ximthar had yet to acknowledge their arrival. He ran a finger over the screen, tracing a line of incomprehensible text.

Kilal curled his lips into a sneer, letting the lid of his anger off slightly, like the top of a pot to let the steam out. "Those belonged to innocent people who died because of the call you made!" With each word, the lid slid off a little more and the volume of his voice raised. "Why did you do that? What was the purpose?"

"I've already answered that." The Professor didn't turn or stop typing. "Justicus and I may not be enough to stop Avinoth. I needed to ensure you wouldn't get in our way. It was a test to measure your strength. You've passed."

Jayden clapped once. "Congratulations. You'll be allowed to join us. How fun."

Requiem took a step forward, and the shadows flickered around her. Jayden's eyes darted over her and narrowed.

"Your *test* killed a lot of people! *You* killed a lot of people. Innocent people. Hundreds of people."

"How did they die?" Ximthar asked.

"An abandoned skyscraper collapsed in the city," Kilal said.

Jayden held his hands out wide. "There you have it. We didn't kill anyone. The skyscraper killed them." For once, he did let emotion slip onto his face. Humor. As if he'd said the funniest thing he'd heard.

Kilal's anger burst open with a roar.

He charged forward, utilizing his agility to quicken his steps. Jayden slashed at him, but Kilal ducked beneath the attack and rammed his fist into the man's chin. Head knocked against the machine, Kilal grabbed Jayden's throat, spun the lithe man about, and slammed him to the floor.

With Jayden pinned, he hauled his knee into the guy's sternum. Kilal pictured the moisture in the air solidifying around them. Ice materialized, freezing Jayden to the ground as the temperature around them dropped.

Kilal pulled a fist back and plunged it into Jayden's face.

It didn't have the impact a punch enhanced by his Deific Strength would have had, but it still felt good. A second punch sent blood splattering from Jayden's nose. A third never came.

The tip of a sword pressed against his throat.

"This is the Eye of Oblivion," Ximthar said. "One cut from it, and not even your Carving of Immortality will save you."

Kilal froze, refusing to even swallow lest he accidentally nick himself.

"Take your blade from his throat," Requiem said, shadows flickering about her.

The shadow creature from before revealed itself, emerging from the dark corner she'd hidden in. "Sister, this one is pleased to see you again."

Requiem spared her a glance, but quickly returned her gaze to Ximthar. "I'm *not* your sister. And I told you to take your blade from his throat."

A blade materialized in each of Requiem's hands. She placed a leading leg forward and held both swords to her side. The two blades merged, becoming one much larger weapon.

Kilal had never seen her fight like that, a sword almost the size of her. It was almost comical, and in the confined space of the room, what was she planning to do with it? But if there was one thing he'd learned in the last week, it was not to underestimate Requiem. If she thought she stood a better chance with the large sword instead of two much smaller ones, he wouldn't doubt her.

Jayden growled and pressed against the ice coffin enclosing him. Thin cracks splintered all over it. Kilal focused on the water molecules in the air, manipulating them around Jayden once more, slowing them until they froze, strengthening the cocoon.

"This will not keep me here," Jayden said, calm and collected, as if he were the one kneeling on Kilal's body instead.

Without argument or fuss, Ximthar removed the blade from Kilal's neck and sheathed it at his side. "Did you come all this way just to fight us? Let Justicus go before he breaks through and rips your head off. Yes, I know—and he knows—you'll heal from it. Which is exactly why he'll do it."

Requiem slid her feet forward. Her face was a mask of swirling emotions. "And something tells me, if I stab you, you'll heal just fine as well."

The shadow creature hissed and presented taloned hands before her. "Sister shouldn't threaten master."

"Onyx, behave."

"*Master* shouldn't threaten Kilal," Requiem growled.

A loud crack resonated through the room. One of Jayden's arms had burst through the ice prison. Kilal had to abandon his post on top of him and roll back.

Jayden took advantage of the reprieve. He broke his other arm free and slammed them both down on the frigid cocoon. It exploded in a cloud of ice shards. A few nicked Kilal's skin. Red drops welled from the cuts.

Free, Jayden turned to Ximthar, yet kept his eyes on Kilal. "Let me kill him," he said. "That's twice I've endured an attack from him. He needs to be shown his place."

"No," Ximthar said.

Jayden growled, then smiled. "Another time then."

Requiem stepped between them, giant sword at the ready. "Aren't you two supposed to be the good guys?"

Jayden rolled his eyes and huffed. The Professor removed his hat and shook his head. "Good. Bad. Those words don't define the likes of us. We transcend the cultural expectations for what 'good' or 'bad' is. Each of us has at one point played the role of a 'bad guy,' is that not correct, Godsgraive?"

Kilal flinched. How did Ximthar know that?

"You look at us with disappointment. Why? Because you painted us with the broad brush of naïvety? You wish to save your world. I wish to kill Avinoth. Both goals are the same, but what we're each willing to do to obtain those goals is what makes us different.

"Avinoth destroyed my world. Justicus and I are all that remain."

Ximthar's gaze lingered on Requiem. "Knowing your reputations, I thought you'd understand us. Our willingness to obtain our end, a good end, at all costs. We were mistaken. Perhaps when your world dies, you'll no longer view your life in black and white. Perhaps when you live as long as we have, the end *does* justify the means.

"If you have a problem with how we operate, that's *your* problem. Do not make it ours." Ximthar's chiseled jaw, pointed cheeks, and stony expression could have made a War Plague flinch. He brushed a strand of black hair from his eyes with a graceful movement. "Do you wish to back out of our...camaraderie?"

Jayden smirked. "If you've decided you can't stand being tied to a bunch of morally gray men, please go home."

"Maybe you should turn on your machine," Requiem said. "And let us go through. *You* go home."

What do I do, Sha'tum? Kilal thought.

Those men, they didn't care about his world at all. They'd caused the deaths of hundreds of *his* people. And for what? To test Kilal? To see if he was worthy, by their own definition, to join them? He'd rather crack their skulls. Smack that fake sneer off Jayden's face. Wipe the arrogance right off Ximthar's.

Maybe Requiem was right. Even if they beat Ashen Kane, was it worth it if they teamed up with monsters to kill another monster?

You're a monster. You'd fit right in.

"Perhaps a truce is in order."

Kilal started. He'd forgotten Abram was with them. "*Now* you intervene?"

Abram smiled sheepishly and thumbed the brim of his hat. "My deepest apologies, but I concluded your dispute with these men was a personal one. I didn't wish to get in the way."

Kilal growled but didn't bother arguing.

"A truce, you say?" Ximthar prompted.

Despite earlier thoughts, Kilal wasn't confident in his, Requiem's, and Abram's ability to defeat Ashen Kane. He wasn't even confident Abram would join them in that battle. The man was a wild card, and Kilal didn't want to place any bets with him. Was a truce acceptable, then? Could he pair up with those men, knowing once their goal was achieved, and if he still lived, they'd part ways at best? And try to tear each other apart at worst?

Once our goal is achieved, all those dead will receive their pound of flesh from these two.

Then it was settled. A truce followed by revenge.

"I can accept a truce," Kilal said.

Requiem slammed her sword into the ground. "*After* you acknowledge what you did. You killed all those people!" She visibly shook and the hate on her face mimicked the loathing Kilal concealed.

He'd never loved her more. He continued to underestimate her, assuming her to be a passionless, emotionless shell of the woman he once knew. But there she was, proving him wrong yet again.

Jayden snorted. "As I said, the building killed all those people. Not us."

Ximthar held up a hand, silencing them both. "Responsibilities for our decisions, Justicus. We must accept them. Yes, Requiem, we take accountability for the outcome of the test we forced you to conduct."

"Sir!" Jayden said. "We don't have to—"

"Quiet, Justicus."

He flinched and snapped his mouth shut, but his eyes told another story.

Requiem nodded. "Thank you. That will do."

For now.

"Then, if there is nothing else to discuss," Ximthar said, "I'll prepare the teleporter. It won't be much longer."

Abram whistled. "Teleportation. To think this civilization was that advanced at one point. Did Sha'tum know it? Did he allow it? Was it him who cursed this city and turned it into what it is now?"

"Why would Sha'tum do that?" Kilal asked, annoyed at the mere accusation.

The Professor returned to drumming away on his keyboard. "When we came across, this place was already like this. But it shared similar technology to our world, which is why we were able to utilize it in the battle against Avinoth and the Ash Fallen. That doesn't answer your question, I know, but I'm sure it does answer another."

One mystery solved. The ruins did predate the Bloodshed. Though what exactly that meant was a different mystery to unveil.

Requiem pulled Kilal aside. She looked over her shoulder at Ximthar. Onyx had returned to being a floating torso connected by a strand of shadow to the Professor's back. She was wrapped around his shoulders and ran a hand, no longer taloned, up and down his spine, though her head was turned and she stared intently at Requiem.

"I don't understand how Lilliana activated this thing," Requiem said, returning her attention to Abram and Kilal. "Look at how long it's taking Ximthar. And he knows what he's doing. How could Lilliana have possibly done all this while you were fighting in this room, without any knowledge of the machine?"

Kilal took a deep breath. "I've wondered the same thing. And...I don't know."

Requiem's face became determined. "Then we'll just have to ask her when we find her."

"Well, maybe not *right* when we find her," Kilal said, to which Requiem responded with a backhand to his shoulder.

"A few more minutes," Ximthar said, "and we'll be on our way."

A few more minutes was all he needed. "I'm going to go

upstairs and re-carve," Kilal said. He thought about suggesting Requiem do the same, but he was no longer convinced she was an Arbiter anymore.

Back under the light of Ophir and Damphir, and with a little space all to himself to just breathe, Kilal slumped onto the section of the couch still with a cushion.

He was going back. He was *going back.* He expected to feel trepidation, anxiety, fear, loss, but he didn't. He felt...excitement.

Godsgraive giggled.

The Sunlight Domain was filled with politics, oaths, pain, suffering, corruption. It was difficult to exist around it all for someone like Kilal who'd been born to fight. In the Ashen Lands, he could do just that. And only that. There were no gray areas, there was no confusion or regret, only the thrill of survival and the knowledge that, at any moment, he could be killed.

Sitting under the moons, alone, Kilal realized how much he missed that. Being back in his world reminded him of how hard it was to be...him.

Everyone expected him to lead, to make the right decisions. That had once been his purpose, after all. But after a decade in the Ashen Lands, that life wasn't for him anymore. He was born to fight, and Bloodshed and Oaths, he did it well.

With Sienna dead, Kilal had confidence Alistair and the rest could handle the other three. The Sunlight Domain no longer needed someone like him. It needed true leaders who could guide the land to the safety of another Disk. The world would soon be moving on, and it would no longer need him. They'd need men and women who could navigate them through whatever political scene they found themselves in. They'd need engineers, scientists, doctors. They wouldn't need fighters.

Maybe it was for the best how things were turning out. He'd do this one last thing for the Sunlight Domain. For his oath. For Requiem, Alistair, Violet, and the rest. For Allyria.

For Lilliana. He'd kill Ashen Kane, and then maybe...maybe he'd finally be able to rest.

That would be nice. Rest.

"I know that look," Requiem said, standing in front of him.

He startled, then smiled a little. He'd hoped she'd follow. "Oh, yeah? What does it say?"

"Nothing good."

Kilal chuckled. "Did you ever think you'd be heading into the Ashen Lands to kill what may be Avinoth?"

She frowned. "A lot of things have happened these last ten years I never thought would."

He grunted his agreement. "I'm...scared."

"You? The Immortal Arbiter, scared? So, you are human after all!"

Kilal smiled. "Seriously, Req. I'm scared."

She sat next to him on the couch. It barely moved from the added weight, though a light puff of dust billowed up. "Of what?"

"The Ashen Lands do things to me, things I was fine with when I was alone. But...I don't want you to see the person I may become over there."

Godsgraive was almost gnashing at his leash in expectation of being set loose.

"I've done things, too, Kilal. Things I'm not proud of either. Things I may resort to over there as well. You don't have a monopoly on inner demons."

It was time. Now or never.

Kilal slowly reached an arm out. He wrapped it around Requiem's shoulder and pulled her to him. And she let him. He almost leaped out of his skin with internal excitement. "I wish you'd share them with me," he said, nuzzling the top of her head with a cheek.

"Will you share yours with me?"

Kilal thought for a moment. Why did he even bother? He knew the answer. And he hated it. "I...I can't."

Requiem leaned her weight against his, resting her head on his chest. Tears almost blossomed in his eyes. "Then..." Her voice choked. "Then you understand why I can't share mine, either."

Cheek pressed tighter against her head, he nodded. "Maybe someday."

"Maybe someday," she repeated.

He squeezed her, never wanting to let go, but Abram poked his head above the metal sliding door.

"Forgive my interruptions," he said after coughing into a fist. "Ximthar is ready."

"Thank you," Requiem said. "We'll be right there."

He disappeared below the floor-line.

"As much as I'd love to stay here," she said, "we have a god to kill."

Kilal let her go, forcing his arm open, fighting to do so almost as hard as he'd had to fight Sienna. Unfortunately, he won the battle. He released her, and Requiem stood.

"I'll be right there," he said. "I still have to re-carve."

She didn't say anything. She only nodded and followed after Abram.

That was that. He was leaving the Sunlight Domain.

Finally.

Despite the chaotic journey, everything had somehow fallen into place. He'd returned to find Jayden, Ximthar, and Aya, which he had, but along the way, he'd gained so much more. Allyria. A rekindled relationship with Requiem. Even reunification with Alistair and Violet had been more than expected. Yes, there were setbacks. The Heirs of the Promise. The obvious decay of the world he'd once called home. But even those had possible achievable outcomes. Sienna, one of the Heirs, was dead, and they had a path to finding a way off their Disk before it died too.

There was no telling what the future held, and there was

still reason to cling to suspicion toward their newest companions. They couldn't afford to let their guards down too soon. Even still, he had to conclude his mission in the Sunlight Domain was a success.

Now, the real battle began.

~ CHAPTER 62 ~

"How did you say you made it across the first time?" Ximthar asked Kilal.

The five members of the assassination squad meant to pierce the Ashen Lands and kill Avinoth congregated around the computer screen the Professor worked on.

"My daughter activated it. I was fighting. I'm not sure how she did it."

Ximthar frowned. "And you were separated during the process of teleportation?"

"We were."

"That would explain how she activated the device. It's actually quite simple. The difficulty is in applying a destination, the number of individuals being teleported, and ensuring they arrive together. That's what I've been working on this whole time."

Did that mean Lilliana really hadn't arrived in the Ashen Lands? Just as before in the car with Requiem, he didn't want to linger on the thought. Because if she hadn't been teleported after all, if Lilliana had remained in the Sunlight Domain and hadn't returned to the people she loved—no.

Kilal cocked his head and ran his hand through his hair, grounding himself. It'd been over a week since he trimmed it, but he still hadn't gotten used to the shortness. "And where do you plan on sending us?"

"That's the last point I need to add. And that will be determined by you."

"Is there a map on the computer?" Kilal asked.

"There is, but it's very old. The chances of this world looking the same now as it did back then is...highly unlikely."

"Better than nothing."

"Agreed."

Ximthar swiveled on his chair and clicked a few buttons. A map appeared on the screen. A very *barren* map. There wasn't much except what one would expect to find on any map, like elevations, mountain ranges, and city names. It *was* old. There was no Veil, and there were even cities where the Ashen Land now was. Names such as Old Towne, Higher Heights, and Shadow Plateau were all new to him.

"Fascinating," Abram breathed, leaning forward next to him. Kilal couldn't disagree.

Studying the layout of what was now the Ashen Lands, he picked a point close to where he believed the terrible structure was. "There. That'll put us about fifteen miles from the Tower of Eyes, and about ten miles from the first sign of gathering Ash Fallen."

"Are you sure?" Jayden asked. "I wouldn't want to pop into existence amid a camp of Plagues."

"What's your problem? For someone so old, you act less mature than a girl I just met. And she's a teenager."

Jayden's face remained flat, but the black skin shimmered, and the veins on his neck and cheek squirmed. Thankfully, he didn't respond, physically or verbally.

"That's where we need to go," Kilal reiterated, pointing again at the spot on the screen.

Ximthar nodded and clicked away at the keyboard. "It's as I thought." He pointed to the map where Kilal had indicated. "This Tower of Eyes is the same place in which Sha'tum used to preside. Back then it was known as the Sun Tower."

"How do you know that?" Requiem asked.

But it was Kilal who answered. "Because you were here back then."

"Indeed," Ximthar said. "It appears Avinoth—or this Ashen Kane—took what was a symbol of Sha'tum's presence and turned it into his own."

Thinking back to what the Tower of Eyes now was, the transformation from Sun Tower was complete. All presence of Sha'tum had been eradicated long ago.

"Before we head into the enemy's hands," the Professor continued, "I wish to know your plan."

Kilal nodded. It was a fair request. "There's a secret passage in the dungeon of the tower leading about a mile out. Eldon told me of it, and it was how I escaped. We'll use that same passage to make our way back inside. From there, we'll proceed as stealthily as we can to the top floor where Avinoth sits."

"What a plan," Jayden said dryly. "Fight our way through a tower of the enemy's most powerful minions before opposing *the* most powerful of them all."

"I never said it was going to be easy, but if you're afraid, now's the time to bow out."

"I gave up fear a long time ago."

"Good."

"Why would the enemy have a secret passage out of their base of operation?" Abram asked.

"Because it was created when it was still the Sun Tower," Ximthar said. "I'm sure Ashen Kane either didn't know about it or didn't think it was necessary to block. The worst thing that could happen is a prisoner escapes. Then what? They're still trapped in the Ashen Lands. It would only be a matter of time before they'd be recaptured or die from the environment."

Kilal nodded along. "Which is why I'm sure the passage hasn't been blocked since I escaped. It hasn't been long enough since I've left for them to take any preemptive action to remove it. And *no one* escapes the Ashen Lands. From their perspective, there just isn't a reason to care. If anything, I was a fluke."

"Have you considered the possibility that they want you to return?" Abram asked.

Kilal concealed a shudder. "Yes. And if so, we can take advantage of their mistake."

Requiem stepped toward the map. She pointed at the location of the Tower of Eyes, then at the location where Kilal wanted them teleported to. "If the passage is only a mile out, why take us fifteen miles away? Why not teleport us to the passage?"

Kilal smiled. "I have my reason. You'll just have to trust me for now. I'll explain everything when we're there."

"Not good enough," Jayden snapped.

Kilal shrugged. "I'm not done recruiting. Humans live in the Ashen Lands. Well, 'humans' is a slight stretch. But there's an Arbiter there who would love to join us when we're ready to invade."

Requiem raised a brow. "Humans? In the Ashen Lands? Are you serious? How is that possible?"

Abram raised a hand. "I second all those questions."

Kilal smiled. "Like I said, I'll explain everything once we're there."

Thankfully, no one pushed the topic further, despite their clear dislike of the secrecy. There would be plenty of time on their travels to answer any questions they had.

Silence reigned as Ximthar stared at the map. The reality was he was the only one who knew how to teleport them, and if he didn't want to do as Kilal planned, the rest of them really had no choice. Kilal wasn't entirely sure what his backup plan was if Ximthar didn't trust him.

Everyone waited. Kilal couldn't imagine what was going through Requiem's mind. When he'd been sent to the Ashen Lands, he hadn't known what was happening. He hadn't had the opportunity to worry, fret, or second guess himself about all the things she could potentially be experiencing.

Regardless, she didn't have much time to do so; Ximthar announced the machine was ready.

"We'll do as you plan," he said, much to Kilal's relief. "Gather together, make a circle, hold hands. If something wasn't entered appropriately, physical contact between us should still ensure we arrive at the same spot."

"One quick inquiry, if I may?" Abram said. He didn't wait for permission. "How do you know how to operate this machine?"

Kilal let a small smile slip onto his face. A good question.

"Master is wise beyond anything simple minds can comprehend," Onyx said.

"Before Avinoth invaded my disk, we had similar...technology to what you see in this room."

"You've had the technology to teleport, and who knows what else, and you still lost to him?" Requiem said. It wasn't meant to be accusatory. To Kilal, she was just making an observation.

Jayden snarled, but Ximthar spoke up before he could respond. "Avinoth corrupted his entire Disk's population. When he invaded, a war of that level had never occurred in my realm before. We weren't prepared."

"Disk?" Abram asked.

"It's what he calls our worlds."

Abram nodded. "Because it's flat and disk-like. Very appropriate."

"We'll have enough time to discuss my history if we survive," Ximthar said. "Suffice it to say, Avinoth has already destroyed two worlds, his and mine. He can't be allowed to destroy this one as well. If he does, he'll move on to the next. He was created for peace but was corrupted for war."

"We'll stop him," Kilal said. "There's no other option." A thought occurred to him, a life-changing thought he kicked himself for not having prior. "And then you can help us get off this Disk using the sentinels."

Ximthar smiled. A knowing, telling smile.

"Finally, something we can agree on," Jayden said. He held his hand out for Requiem to take, but Kilal stepped between the two. He took Jayden's hand and grinned. Jayden grimaced but didn't let go.

"This will not be...pleasant," the Professor warned.

He hit a red button on a pole in the corner. The pole was connected to a large lightbulb-looking object. It turned on with a buzz, showering the circle in bright light. Ximthar took his place between Abram and Jayden, and Requiem took her place between Kilal and Abram. The circle formed, and the group waited.

Kilal took a deep breath, steeling himself for the unpleasant sensation he was already familiar with.

When it hit, he screamed. Or would have if he wasn't being ripped apart at a molecular level. His arms, and across from him, Ximthar and Abram's, began disintegrating. They too looked like they wanted to scream, mouths open wide but no sound escaping them.

Everything went black.

Despite being broken into individual atoms, he still felt Jayden's and Requiem's hands clamped around his. The climate shifted around him, changing from the clammy, dank atmosphere of the ruined building's basement to the warm dryness of the Ashen Lands. Kilal wasn't sure how long the whole process lasted, but he was only able to create a few scrambled thoughts before his sight returned.

An uncomfortable tingle through every organ and slight nausea lingered.

Ximthar and Abram were put back together in millions of little pieces. A second before finishing the construction, they looked like their entire body had been cut into tiny little blocks.

Gray, lifeless, heated, dusty, depressing. The environment of the Ashen Lands.

Kilal released Requiem's hand. Before letting go of Jayden's, he gave it a slight squeeze, just enough to break a few fingers. The two smiled at each other, but there was obviously no love lost between them.

The air was stale and the sky was filled with clouds. Just as he remembered it. It was nighttime, and yet, there was no night. The same would be said of daytime, though; no light. It was always just...gray.

Ash fell, slowly, lethargically, as if it too was affected by the somber environment and wasn't in a hurry to go anywhere.

Behind them, a mountain range stretched all the way east to the edge of the world. He'd capped those mountains and hoped to never have to do so again. The creatures living in those peaks were so wretched and nightmarish they made Plagues look normal.

Kilal couldn't conceal his shiver.

To the north were the mountains. To the south was a plain covered in a foot of ash. Giant sprouts of gray and brown stems jutted from the plains, standing anywhere from five to ten feet and spread out. To the average person, the stems or stalks would look like lifeless trees with no branches. To Kilal, they were tentacles with toothy suckers. They ate the ash and any being unfortunate enough to cross their paths. He never found out, but he was fairly certain a giant creature lived beneath the surface, and the tentacles fed it.

Either way, if they were to cross the plain—and they would have to—they'd need to step very lightly. Those things sensed movement through vibrations on the surface. The ash could absorb some of the vibrations from a footfall, but if they weren't careful, they'd be fighting their entire way across the field. And the sprouts moved quickly.

To the east and west, dead trees covered in dusty soot stood lifeless, clumped together in circles as if protecting each other.

A screech, followed by a roar, and then another scream filled the air.

"Quite lovely," Abram said.

It was a hideous nightmare, but to Kilal...it was the closest thing to home he'd had for the last decade. He hated how comfortable he felt there.

"Well, big man, you're the expert," Jayden said. His black leathery skin had lost some color and looked closer to the falling ash than the night sky it had resembled back in the Sunlight Domain. "Don't get us killed before we can face Avinoth."

"That's the plan," Kilal said.

"First," Ximthar said, "now that there's nowhere to run, a question must be answered."

Kilal didn't appreciate the way the Professor phrased his sentence. Nowhere to run? What was he getting at? "What is it?"

Ximthar pulled the Eye of Oblivion from the sheath at his side and pointed it at Requiem. Abram tiptoed away from her, his cane leaving little holes in the ash with each step.

"It's for her."

Kilal narrowed his eyes. "Put the blade away, and this doesn't have to get ugly." No one was going to threaten Requiem.

"I will. Once she answers my question."

She stepped up beside Kilal, nodding her appreciation. Her eyes glimmered with a question of her own, asking him to trust her. Reluctantly, Kilal nodded back.

"Go on," she said.

Ximthar's face hardened, and his eyes darkened. Onyx appeared from his back and snaked her way around his torso to rest her head on his shoulder.

"How did you bind a Spirit of Gloom?"

Kilal frowned. "Wait, what? What's he talking about?"

Requiem shrugged. "I have no idea."

The Professor shot forward, too fast for Kilal to react. He thrust a hand forward toward her, but instead of grabbing Requiem, he...*pierced*...her shadow, his palm disappearing into it. When he peeled back, Ximthar ripped a creature very much like Onyx from her shadow. Black skin, short, white hair, and white eyes, only with a masculine shape.

The creature kicked and screamed, and Requiem collapsed into a seizure.

Kilal dropped to her side. He scooped her into his arms. "What are you doing to her?" he roared, at risk of inhaling a lungful of ash.

Ximthar's mouth curled into something akin to a half-smile, half-sneer. "Sinestra," he said, ignoring Kilal. "Did you really think you could hide from your king?"

~ EPILOGUE ~

Wolfe observed the devastation with a cool eye. Sirens blared, humans wailed, calls went back and forth between would-be rescuers, and all of it was so...sad. A skyscraper fell. A few hundred lives were lost. A few hundred fewer mouths to feed. A few hundred fewer bodies sucking up the dwindling resources.

It had been three hours since the building collapsed. And still, people wept. What was the point? Did they think if they shed enough tears, the dead would walk again? Wolfe never understood crying. He'd endured hard situations in his life, terrible situations, and he'd never once felt the need to leak from his eyes. Wolfe was a man of logic and results. What result, what *good* result, came from tears? None.

A hand grabbed his and pulled. A dirty hand. An older woman, probably his age yet not wearing it half as well, peered up at him with cheeks covered in dust and tears.

"Please, my lord. My son is in there," she sobbed between each word. "Please, save him."

Wolfe yanked his hand from her grip and wiped it against a pant leg. When the woman reached for him again, pleading once more for him to save her son, Wolfe tapped on a green stone in one of his rings.

The woman ceased grappling for him. Instead, she clutched her own throat.

He strolled away. Once far enough, he dispersed the allergic reaction he'd assaulted her with. Her gasp for oxygen echoed through the debris.

Tor'et stood some dozen feet in front of him, flourishing his hand, producing small tornadoes to pick up large chunks of rubble. The fool didn't need to be performative; Tor'et just thought it looked *cool*. Bloody idiot would get himself killed one day.

Hopefully, that day would be sooner rather than later.

"Any sight of her?" Wolfe asked.

Tor'et lowered his hands, and the two tornadoes, no bigger than a human, disappeared. "Nothing yet," he said. "I don't understand why you insist on finding her? She's dead. Just find another wielder of the stone."

"You wouldn't understand," Wolfe said, eyes scanning the rubble. He didn't feel the need to explain anything to the insufferable man. Sienna had been the perfect candidate for Amplification. She practically embodied it. Raw power and nothing but the desire to serve and hunt. He'd never find another as suited to the red stone as she'd been.

Tor'et thought his power was better used to attract ladies or get rich.

"Keep looking," Wolfe said before walking away. The resulting grumbles and whines from Tor'et weren't something he cared to endure.

Wolfe climbed his way to the top of a large stone pillar, half sunk in the rubble at an angle. He surveyed the wreckage from a higher vantage point.

To think Kilal and Requiem had beaten Sienna. He never would've thought that possible. Wolfe wasn't wrong often, but when he was, he had no problem admitting it. And he'd been wrong about the Immortal Arbiter.

He wouldn't underestimate Kilal again.

A refreshing gust whipped around him. It also cleared out a layer of mist, dust, and smoke further down, revealing a headless body, the upper torso charred.

Leaping from the angled pillar, Wolfe slid down the rubble and dirt, coming to a stop at the side of the corpse. He'd be lying if he said excitement didn't spark in his chest. Of the three of them, Sienna had been his favorite. Fazin was too smart for his own good. Tor'et was an idiot. But Sienna had been *loyal*.

He examined the body and found her scorched head not too far away, hidden amongst a pile of rocks, confirming the remains did indeed belong to Sienna. It was a hard fact to swallow. She'd wielded more than a dozen stones of Amplification.

"I see I wasn't the only one who underestimated those two," Wolfe said. Not that he could be upset with her. He, too, had dismissed their capabilities.

The stone in his pocket seemed to lurch toward the corpse, as if it knew what was coming. Wolfe pulled the black, perfectly spherical gem from the folds of the fabric and stared at it. Tor'et had bonded with the Elemental stone, Fazin with Growth, and he, himself, with the stone of Disease. In his hand was the Death stone.

It was unlike the others. It wasn't worn or tapped into for power. It held a single purpose and could be used only once.

Crouching at Sienna's side, he prepared himself for what he needed to do.

Wolfe stuffed the stone into her gaping neck, shoving it in until his full finger had disappeared into her throat. He shuddered at the slimy innards. He *would not* have done that for Tor'et. Maybe not even for Fazin.

Removing his finger, Wolfe wiped it on the front of Sienna's shirt and stepped back.

One breath went by. Two. Three. On the fourth, her body twitched. On the fifth, it almost jerked into a sitting position before collapsing again. Black energy emerged from her neck, growing and spreading until her whole body was covered.

The Amplification stone had miraculous healing capabilities, but it couldn't resurrect the dead.

A full minute elapsed before the energy dissipated. When it did, a fully intact Sienna, regrown head and all, lay before him.

He hovered above her, waiting. Eventually, she took a deep breath and opened her eyes.

Wolfe smiled. "Welcome back, Heir. Chronos still has work for you."

ABOUT ATMOSPHERE PRESS

Founded in 2015, Atmosphere Press was built on the principles of Honesty, Transparency, Professionalism, Kindness, and Making Your Book Awesome. As an ethical and author-friendly hybrid press, we stay true to that founding mission today.

If you're a reader, enter our giveaway for a free book here:

SCAN TO ENTER
BOOK GIVEAWAY

If you're a writer, submit your manuscript for consideration here:

SCAN TO SUBMIT
MANUSCRIPT

And always feel free to visit Atmosphere Press and our authors online at atmospherepress.com. See you there soon!

ABOUT THE AUTHOR

LANGDON FRANZ lives in Raleigh, North Carolina, with his wife, two teenage daughters, two dogs and two cats. In 2022, he finished his Masters in Creative Writing and has been hard at work creating his own book series ever since. When he isn't writing, he is designing board games with his wife or playing one. Langdon has a passion for all things fantasy as well as creating fantastical worlds others can enjoy.